S0-BNC-901

Dear Mom,

Thank you for all of your love and support! Wish we could see you more often! I LOVE you.

Love,
Michele

HAPPY HOUR

Michele Scott

ZOVA BOOKS

LOS ANGELES

$ZOVA$ BOOKS

This book is a work of fiction. References to real people, events, establishments, organizations, or locales are intended only to provide a sense of authenticity and are used fictitiously. All other characters, and all incidents and dialogue are drawn from the author's imagination and are not to be construed as real.

First ZOVA Books edition 2011.

HAPPY HOUR. Copyright © 2011 by Michele Scott.

All rights reserved.

Printed in the United States of America.

No part of this book may be used or reproduced in any manner whatsoever without written permission except in the case of brief quotations embodied in critical articles and reviews.

For information or permission contact:
ZOVA Books
P.O. Box 21833, Long Beach, California 90801
www.zovabooks.com

ISBN 97800982788080

Cover Design © Daniel Pearson
Cover Photography © Tara Smith

To My Best Friend,
My Mom.

Acknowledgements

I must thank Jessica Park who is a great friend, a wonderful writer and always there when I need a little support, shoulder to cry on or someone to laugh with. I am grateful for you taking your big red pen to this book. I want to thank Lori over at Lori's Reading Corner, who is another huge supporter and who has a keen eye. I am super grateful for your help. And thanks to my friends— Terri, Gilly, Nikki, Sherri, Quelene, Kristy, Siobhan, and Lisa. It's nice to have friends who love me as much as I love them and who I can always count on sharing a glass of wine or two with (or a lemon drop, or a margarita)—oh and not to mention some good eats. Here's to friendship!

Three and a half years ago . . .

CHAPTER ONE

Kat

Kat McClintock was late. This was not good. This would not be good. Damn. Damn. Damn. "Okay, boys, listen."

Neither one of her pre-pubescent sons looked at her. They were far too absorbed in whatever new Playstation, Wii (whatever it was these days) game their father had recently purchased for them. She turned the TV off.

"Hey!" Jeremy yelled. "What are you doing, Mom? Not cool. Turn it back on." Jeremy had evidently bypassed pre-pubescence altogether and jumped right into raging adolescence and his day-to-day tone with her ranged from apathetic to surly.

"Mommy, we were about to kill the boss," Brian, her ten year old, said. "The like, the big boss, you know? The guy to win!"

Thank God. He was definitely still not even close to adolescence. He was still sweet. No one going through puberty would dream of calling their mother *Mommy*. "I'm sorry, boys. I have to go. Your Aunt Tammy was supposed to be here by now. Typical." She shook her head. "Anyway, Jeremy, I need you to take out two frozen burritos and put them in the microwave. There're some bananas and I have some broccoli already cut up in there."

"I hate broccoli," Brian said.

"You like it with ranch dressing."

"No, I don't."

"How come we can't go out to eat? Dad always takes us out to eat," Jeremy said.

Because Dad is an asshole. No, no, she couldn't say that. *Dad screwed me over in our settlement and while he's out wining and dining, I'm trying to get a job to support us.* No, no, not that either. Let go and let God. Wasn't that what Mom was always saying to her? Breathe! Now there you go. This is all one growing experience that will get you to another side of things. The silver lining, or pot of gold, or whatever the hell it was at the end of the rainbow. Better be a pot of gold.

Kat placed her hands on her hips and tried to look official. "I'm having you eat a healthy meal." That sort of sounded okay. "Good food makes you grow big and strong and have a smart brain." She winked at them.

"Frozen burritos?" Jeremy replied.

Too smart for his own good. "Jer, no more lip. Eat the burritos. You know you like them. I'll be back by bedtime and your homework needs to be done. Don't answer the phone unless you see that it's coming from me and call me on my cell if you have a problem. Obviously, do not go outside or open the door for anyone. Leave Squeak in the house. She's on my bed right now. She makes a good watchdog."

"She's a chihuahua," Jeremy said. "Not exactly a watchdog, Mom." He gave her a half smile and the twinkle in his blue eyes left nothing for the imagination. Her oldest boy defined mischief. The kind she knew later in life would break many a woman's heart. She sighed and shook her head. At twelve, Jeremy was getting by on his charm and good looks with his teachers—all blue eyed, olive skinned, and thick dark hair. Brian was, of course, beautiful, too, but he took after her with lighter brown hair. No one knew exactly how to describe his eye color--hazel, brown, green? Kat settled on avocado. It was what her mother called them. Mom never described anything as green, blue, or brown. With Mom it was always *lime, cornflower, hazelnut*, etc.

"But she barks. Can you handle all that? I'm sorry, guys. I'll take you out for pizza on Friday."

"We're going with Dad on Friday and, duh, I can handle it. I'm twelve, not a baby anymore." Jeremy turned back to the TV. "Can we turn it back on now?"

"No. I don't like your attitude, buddy. You're acting like a monkey. Ooh ah ooh." Kat tucked her arms underneath her, and jumped up and down in her best imitation of a monkey. Jeremy stared at her, but Brian giggled. The monkey imitation used to work so well, and now--a stare and one little giggle. "Alrighty then, I am officially a goober. That much is obvious, right? But as your officially gooberish mom, your attitude, Mr. Jeremy—ooh wait." She held up a finger. "If I am goober mom then you must be my goober sons! Ha. So, I need your goober bad attitude straightened out by the time I get home."

Jeremy frowned. "Mom, goober is so old school. You're a nube." Now both boys broke up in hilarity. "But we still love you." He grinned.

"Right. Me nube, you nube." Not only was Jeremy charming, but also downright manipulative when he needed to be, and too damn smart for his own good. "Love you." She went around the cheapie sofa she'd bought at a hole-in-the-wall furniture store. After only a few months, the color changed from light beige to dreary mud. She made a mental note to get one of those shabby chic covers she'd seen at Target once she deposited her first paycheck—which--fingers crossed--would be soon. She kissed each boy on the cheek, with Jeremy responding by wiping it away and grimacing as if he'd been touched by an alien.

At least Brian hugged her back and smiled. "Bye, Mom. Good luck. You'll get the job. I know it."

"Bye, babe, and thank you. You can turn the TV back on after your homework is finished. Leave it out on the kitchen table so I can check it when I get home." Who was she kidding? As soon as those boys heard the car pull out of the driveway of their three-bedroom townhouse in the outskirts of Oakland, she knew the TV and game would be back on.

Guilt dropped in on her again. Guilt that she wouldn't be home to make sure they ate a healthy meal. Guilt that she wouldn't be there to help Brian with his math problems that he'd been having difficulty with. Guilt that she wasn't there when Jeremy wanted to actually talk to her or watch TV with her. Too much goddamned guilt went with divorce, and Kat hated it. But what was she supposed to do? Turn a blind eye? Allow the boys to grow up in a home where disrespecting women was accepted? No. She'd take this guilt. Peace. Breathe in peace and relaxation. Were all those tapes her mom had been sending her starting to rub off on her? The ones with titles like "*Flowdreaming for Peace,*" and "*Balance Through Breath?*"

She got behind the wheel of her jeep and pulled out of the one-car garage the townhome afforded. The place where she and boys now lived was definitely a step down from upper middle class suburbia, but as she pressed the garage door remote, she knew that this place was far more a home than the Victorian they'd lived in, on the edge of Pacific Heights. So what if Perry still lived there with his flavor of the week? Kat sort of believed in karma and where her ex was concerned, she was thrilled with this theory. She knew the man would get his just due. Yep. Perry had kept the classic painted lady and she'd downsized to the three-bedroom with mold under the sinks and peeling wallpaper in her room. But, it had given her back her sanity and a sense of self that she'd lost during those eight years of marriage (technically ten by the time the divorce was finalized). Why she hadn't gotten smart and taken that wake up pill when Perry had told her that he thought that marriage was an antiquated idea, she'd never know. One child out of wedlock had been one thing, but when she'd gotten pregnant with Brian, she had insisted that Perry marry her, or else. *She* should have taken the "or else" part.

Enough of that though, because this was her new life--her new start--and she broke pretty much every speed limit trying to get to it, running a yellow light that was much closer to red than green. Stopping at the next one, she took a good look in the mirror. Yikes. The boys' soccer practice had run late. The coach who thought he was Pele himself preached this whole team effort philosophy: when you sign your kid up for a sport, there is a commitment factor you have to consider and blah, blah, blah. True—Kat believed in commitment. So much so that she had spent years overlooking her ex's over-spending habits and the lies that surrounded them, the flirting here and there with other women ... But when it came right down to bedding one of the women in her book club? That had pretty much made the notion of commitment null and void.

The commitment to the boys' soccer now made her late for her job interview.

With one hand on the wheel and the other in her purse, Kat rummaged around feeling for a lipstick and, hopefully, a hair clip. She needed to get a smaller purse. This was like diving into a black hole. So far she had found one bag of chips, a ton of receipts, a tampon, and a handful of candy wrappers. Aha, there was a clippie. Not the most attractive look, but it would have to do. Now for the lipstick.

Next to the lipstick she knew what she felt. The cigarette wrapper. She winced. To smoke or not to smoke? Serious question. No. She wouldn't do it. She thought about the discussion she'd had with her mother, Venus. Yes, Venus. Kat sighed. It had been Veronica all her life until ten years ago when she hit fifty-five and left Kat's dad to find herself. She moved to an ashram in Oregon, and changed her name. Anyhow, the conversation she'd had last month when her mother visited ran through her mind.

"Kitty, love, you have too many lines around your mouth for a woman your age. You're only thirty-five."

"I'm thirty-seven, Mom." Her mother was totally on her nerves at that point. They'd spent five solid days together and between learning how to make tofu dishes, attending the yoga classes her mother insisted on, and having henna tattoos painted on her feet, Kat thought she would lose it at any moment.

"Age is only a number." She waved a hand through the air. They were seated at Kat's kitchen table drinking green tea. "Look at me. No lines. I have no stress. I take the day as it comes and because of that I have found not only perfection in my outward appearance, but also in my inner spirit as well. Namaste." With her hands in prayer position she bowed to Kat.

Gag.

Mom ran a hand over her face. It was true that she had no lines. But, Kat hadn't forgotten (and apparently Mom had) that before her mother had gone all Hare Krishna on them and left Dad, she'd had one helluva face lift. Veronica or Venus—whatever—her mother looked like a New Age Raquel Welch. That is, if Welch had had the poor fashion sense to don Birkenstocks and a muumuu.

"Kitty Love, I think that you must have too much stress in your life. You look bitter. Or like a smoker might. Have you seen what women who smoke look like? It's not pretty."

Last straw. Right then and there Kat determined she was fixing burgers that evening. "Mom, I am a little bitter, but I'll get through that." Her mother started to interrupt her. She shook her head and held up a hand. "Oh, no, no, I am not going to discuss my reasons why with you. I'm working through it on my own and in my own time, so *you let it go.* And I *am* a smoker."

Her mother's face paled.

"I've been a closet smoker since I was fifteen."

"What?"

Kat took a sip from her tea feeling decidedly good about herself. She smiled and nodded. "Yes. I smoke three to four cigarettes a day. When the boys leave for school I have a smoke. After lunch, I have a smoke, and *then* after dinner, when I take a walk, I have a smoke. And guess what, *Venus?* Sometimes I have a smoke before bed if I'm really stressed out. Been doing it for years."

Shortly after Mom got back home, Kat started receiving self-help CDs in the mail along with yoga DVD's. She figured she had the entire Rodney Yee and Baron Baptiste library.

One day she would do one of those DVD's. She had felt so bad about that conversation that she'd gone ahead and started listening to the CD's. The result being that she'd pretty much stopped smoking. Pretty much. But right now a cigarette would surely take the edge off.

Getting the pack out of her purse, Kat glanced down for a second. When she looked back up, there was another red light, and thankfully she caught it in time or she would have slammed into the back of a semi. Her purse flew to the floor, its contents going every which way. "Shit!" That had to be a sign, right? Stop smoking or die. Duh, as Jeremy would say. It would either be through lung cancer, according to Mom, or on the highway while in such desperate need of a smoke she was willing to risk having the back end of a double wide shoved up her nose.

She crossed the Oakland Bridge and, for the rest of her drive into the city, she listened to her mother's latest gift, Wayne Dyer's *Being in Balance*. By the time she made it into the City, she understood the third chapter fairly well: Your Addictions Tell You, "You'll Never Get Enough of What You Want." Now there was one she'd have to listen to again on the drive home. About the time that the lull of Dr. Dyer's voice settled her into a calm state, she realized she needed to find parking and she was already five minutes late. Great way to go in for a job interview.

Four blocks away, Kat located a space, parked, and then practically jogged to the restaurant, praying she wouldn't look a total disaster when she made it there. After taking a deep breath and smoothing down her clothes, she opened the door to *Sphinx*.

A stylish, brown-eyed, long dark-haired hostess stood at the front. What was she? Twenty-three tops? How did anyone at twenty-three look so put together? She hadn't even managed it by thirty-seven, conscious of the wrinkling in her light blue cotton blouse and the small stain from one of the boys' juice boxes that had squirted out in the car earlier when Brian had poked his straw into it. The boys thought it hilarious that the juice had sprayed everywhere. Kat hadn't noticed the spot until now, face to face with little Miss Shine-and-Sparkle, when she spotted the small red stain on the left thigh of her khakis. *Boys!*

Kat closed her hands around the handle on her purse and smiled. "Hi, I'm Kat McClintock. I'm here for an interview with Mr. Reilly." What she lacked in fashion sense she could at least make up for with maturity.

"One moment. I'll get him for you."

Kat took a good long look around. Modern flair painted in warm shades of green made the restaurant look as chic as Kat had read about in the foodie magazines. The floors were done in cherry wood squares, with a lighter wood of some sort cut out in a diamond pattern filling the center. Gold suede-covered booths lined the walls. The tables and chairs arranged in the middle spoke of elegance in dark woods and gold colored linens. Paintings of the *Sphinx* arranged around the restaurant added mystique to the elegance. She could see herself working here. The décor was nothing compared to the smells coming from the kitchen. Sphinx was the new hot restaurant in San Francisco. She breathed in the decadent smells of garlic, tomato, basil, onion, a bit of curry—totally intoxicating and intimidating all at once.

Then out walked Christian Reilly, the owner and head chef. If there was any truth to the idea that you could actually go weak in the knees at the sight of splendor, well, Kat experienced it right then and there. An actual physical reaction made her reach out and grab the hostess stand with one hand. Christian Reilly wasn't gorgeous in the Brad Pitt kind of way. In fact, to some women he might not even be considered all that great looking. But to Kat, he fit right into her *beautiful* category: hazel eyes, not too tall for her, as she was a petite five-foot-three. Christian had dark hair,—the kind she could run her fingers through—a barely there scruff of a beard, and wrinkles that deepened when he said her name with a slight Irish accent. When he repeated her name and smiled, the lines around his eyes deepened. A man who had lived a little. Nice. Butterfly, stomach-swirling nice. For a second, she had to make sure she wasn't licking her lips.

"Kat McClintock?"

"Yes. I'm sorry. I, uh, yes."

He reached his hand out and she shook it. Strong, tough. Again, nice.

"Why don't we take a seat in the back booth? The lunch crowd is cleared out, so we'll be prepping for dinner shortly. But I think we have about thirty minutes."

"Great. I'm so sorry for being late." Blame it on the parking.

As if reading her mind he turned and smiled. "You had problems finding parking, did you?"

"I did."

They sat down and Christian asked a server to bring them out several bite sized appetizers and two flights of wine—one white, the other red. Kat tried not to give him a questioning look, but she knew she'd failed when he said, "Maybe a bit unorthodox, but you are applying for the sommelier position. I thought I'd see what you know. Tell me what tastes good with what."

She cleared her throat and crossed her legs. "Don't you want to ask me about my education? Where I went to school?"

He waved a hand. "Nah. I want to know if you can pair wines."

She shifted in the booth.

"What do you say, shall we get a start on this?" he asked, and held up a glass of Sauvignon Blanc. "Tell me about this wine and suggest what to order with it."

This was it. *Impress the man with what you know, Kat.* Mhhm, those eyes were looking at her, their color a cross between jade and tiger-eye. Brother, she was thinking like Venus. They were hazel! She lifted up a glass of wine, smiled, and started by holding it up to the light.

Thirty minutes turned into two hours while the sous chef was apparently covering in the kitchen. After the first hour, she was hired. She'd paired every wine he had brought out, could tell him the notes on the wine, and her overall impressions.

"You do know your stuff."

She twirled the glass with a sip of Bordeaux left in it. "Surprised?"

"I looked at your resume." He sat back and crossed his arms. "First job at this, huh?"

Why was it that he seemed to look at her like he could see right through her? She'd heard that in a song before, or maybe read it in a book, and thought it sounded so ridiculous and trite, but Christian Reilly had this look: a look that said, *I'm going to get under your skin, turn you inside out.* "It is. I thought you didn't care what my resume said," she replied, trying so hard to sound cool.

"I don't. I care that you know your wines. What made you decide to become a sommelier?"

"I got a divorce."

Christian raised a brow. "I'm divorced too. Six months now."

"Oh."

"Would you like to have dinner with me?" he asked.

She paused, looking at her wine glass. "Wouldn't that be weird? You're my boss now, right?"

"I could fire you for the night and then re-hire you tomorrow. But if it goes well tonight, I'd have to fire you again." He laughed. "Come on. It's only dinner."

She crossed and uncrossed her legs. "No. I want the job and, I, yes, I would love to have dinner. When?"

"I think I mentioned tonight. Now works for me." His hand brushed over the top of hers as he reached across to refill her glass.

"I, well, I . . ." She'd never been good at this. She had met Perry in high school and married him fresh out of college. "My boys. I have sons and they're at home and they have school. And, I need to get home for them."

He studied her for a few seconds before replying. "Of course. I have a daughter. She's three. I understand. Some other time then. Why don't you plan to start training next Monday, right? I'll have Rachel e-mail you over copies of our menus, wine lists, and some specials I typically serve."

Kat nodded. "Can you give me a minute?"

"Sure."

She got up and headed to the bathroom, not believing what she was about to do. Before she could think twice, she dug through her purse, found her cell phone, and dialed Perry's number, her hands shaking.

"Kat?"

"Hi. I need a favor."

"What is it, sweetheart?"

She hated that. They were divorced! He'd screwed her former friend and after he was done with her, he went for pretty much anything wearing stilettos and short skirts. They didn't even have to be drinking age. No matter what, though, Perry had to play all Rico Sauve and call her *sweetheart* as though she was itching to crawl back to him. Ick. "I'm in the city and can't get home until late and the boys are home. My sister was supposed to come over and watch them, but she didn't make it." She knew she sounded desperate, but for God's sake, when was the last time a man looked at her the way Christian Reilly had? When was the last time butterflies did that dance in her stomach? It was now or never, baby. No more groveling. Perry owed her anyway. Big time.

"Of course your sister didn't make it. She's not exactly responsible. She's an addict."

"She's been sober for seven years, Perry. You know that, and your *responsibility* comment? Isn't the pot calling the kettle black?" Oops, that sorta slipped out.

"Kat, have you been drinking?"

Another thing she hated about him. He always knew if she'd had even one glass of wine. Perry got off telling people he didn't drink, as if it set him above the lushes of the world. Perry's addiction was sex.

"You know what, Perry, I *have* had a glass of wine and I really need you to step up and go over to my place, pick up the boys, make sure their homework is finished, put them to bed, and take them to school in the morning. I'll even drop off their lunches so you don't have to worry about that."

He laughed. "Listen to you. I got bad news, Kit-Kat." She cringed. "I'm in a meeting. So, no can do. Guess you better end your little party and get home like a good girl."

She took a deep breath. She hadn't been great at setting boundaries or defending her needs, but this moron had some gall. How had she ever married him? It was long overdue to call his bluff. "No, you listen here, Paris." He hated to be called by his real name. "I can practically hear the eighteen-year-old platinum blonde gyrating on you. Since when did you start listening to Britney Spears? God, what is that? *Baby One More Time*? Wow." He was so predictable. "That said, get the girl off you, go pick up the boys, and leave me a check in my mailbox. As of now, you're officially three weeks late on your child support." No more groveling.

"When did you turn into such a bitch?"

"The night I found you in our bed on top of another woman. When will you be at my house?"

He sighed. "I guess I can be there in about thirty minutes."

"Thank you." She clicked the phone shut and then reopened it to call the boys. Much to her dismay, they were excited about the new plan. Time with Dad. Yippee-cay fucking-ay. She really did need to get over it. She obviously should listen to more Wayne Dyer.

When she walked back to the table, Christian looked up at her. "Still up for dinner?" she asked.

"I am." He picked up his glass of wine and twirled it between his fingers, smiling.

She about turned to butter right there.

It was in that second hour over dinner that Kat knew, looking across the table at her new boss, that her life was never going to be the same. The man was *adorable*. And the thoughts running through her mind, seated across from him? Bad girl! She'd figured out that just because you have sex with a man didn't mean you had to walk down the aisle with him. She'd made that mistake once and, besides the births of her sons, regretted every minute of it. But she hadn't wanted to sleep with a man in a very long time. She couldn't even believe she was thinking about sex with Christian. God! Hopefully he was thinking the same thing. But what if he wasn't? Then again, what if he was?

Then he took her hand across the table and held it as if he'd always taken her hands and held them. "You're beautiful," he said, and she believed him.

Totally in deep trouble now. It was as if she were a runaway freight train and the engines driving the locomotive forward were her emotions on overdrive. She wasn't about to listen to the common sense angel sitting on her shoulder, the one she often sought advice from since the divorce. She frequently pictured an ivory skin, blonde haired fairy with lapis-colored eyes seated on her right shoulder telling her exactly how to behave in any given circumstance. Kat had named her Logic. She now caressed her shoulder, brushing Logic clean away.

Kat wanted to get Christian naked—boss or not. In non-Kat fashion, she took his hand in return, smiled and said, "What do you like to do for fun?"

That night, while Perry had his once in a blue moon share of the boys, Kat decided she liked Christian's idea of fun.

Back at his two story town home overlooking the city lights, Christian took out a bowl and sliced up some strawberries, drizzled them in Grand Marnier and topped them with whipped cream. He then walked over to his built-in wine cabinet and took out a bottle of Chateau Chasse-Spleen 1959. Holding it up, he said, "Did you ever play spin the bottle when you were a kid?"

Kat giggled. "The kissing game?" He nodded and with a mischievous grin on his face, his cuteness factor sailed through the roof. "Believe it or not I was kind of a shy kid, so I knew kids who played but I never had the *privilege*. Plus I wasn't real cute. Buck teeth."

He laughed. "You're gorgeous now, and I think we should play. I want to play with you." He took her hands and sat down with her on his living room floor. They sunk into the plush white carpeting. "We get to make up our own rules though."

"Okay." Kat had never in her life been so forward with a man and never had she ever slept with a man after only a few hours of meeting him. She was pretty sure that was where this was headed, and it was pretty wonderful.

"You spin," he said.

"But there's only the two of us."

"Yep. That's where our own rules come into play. Here. I'll go first and show you." He spun and the bottle faced the sofa. "Look it's close to you. So now I get to kiss you." He reached out and touched her hair, then moved his finger to her lips, tracing the outline of them with his thumb. "I've been wanting to kiss your lips since I saw you this afternoon."

A warm glow traveled through Kat. "Me too. I wanted to kiss you too."

He inched closer and slid his lips across hers. She pulled away slightly. "You okay?" he asked. She nodded and then leaned forward, running her hands through his dark thick hair. "Your turn." He pointed to the bottle.

She smiled and spun. "Huh. Landed on you." Kat grazed his neck with her lips and she nibbled on his ear. She kissed him on his lips, biting him on the bottom lip.

"You vixen."

She laughed. Christian grabbed the bottle of the seven-hundred-fifty dollar Bordeaux and uncorked it. He stood up and held out his hand. Kat took it and followed him into his bedroom. Don't we need glasses?" she asked, pointing to the wine.

He shook his head and pushed her back onto the bed, he lifted up her shirt, exposing her belly where he drizzled a small amount of wine onto her stomach and licked it off. Kat unbuttoned the rest of the blouse. She sat up. "We should, ah, do you have ah…" It was so awkward to interrupt the moment but all the same she wasn't taking any chances.

He held up a finger. "I'll be back." A couple of minutes later, Christian came back from the restroom, condom in hand. He lit candles by the side of the bed that smelled of vanilla, and turned on his stereo and played Bebel Gilberto. Her seductive voice lingered in the air.

Christian laid down next to Kat, took her in his arms and again kissed her, long hard, passionately. He turned her onto her stomach and drizzled more wine down her back, licking it off of her, as he undid her bra. She rolled back over and fumbled with the buttons on his jeans. He helped her and shook them off, then slid his shirt over his head. Naked together, they took each other in, their eyes lingering. He pulled her onto him. He smelled of cinnamon and rosemary. He cupped her breasts, pulling her closer. He reached up and held her face in his hands.

Kat straddled him, not breaking their stride as he entered her, her hands between his chest and shoulders. As they began to move together, electric pulses ran up and down their bodies. Kat had never been in sync with any man this way before. He flipped her over onto her back, kissing her face, her neck, her ears, his hands caressing her body, her fingers sliding down his back. Kat sighed with pleasure, moving her hips with Christian's, the intensity increasing. She yelled out as small waves of sweet ecstasy rolled through her into one crashing wave, her body trembling as they both reached ecstasy together. "Oh Lord, oh Kat."

He held her in his arms afterwards, stroking her hair, caressing her body and every so often whispering, "You are so beautiful. My God, you are beautiful."

Kat decided right then and there that not only did she love Christian Reilly's version of spin the bottle, she might have just fallen in love with the man himself.

CHAPTER TWO

Alyssa

lyssa Johnson walked out of the funky flat where she taught art classes, a sly smile on her face and a little weak in the knees. This was a great day.

She flagged down a cab and left Soho, heading uptown for the big dinner. Alyssa looked at her left hand spreading out her fingers. The four carat emerald-cut diamond with a band filled with three rows of smaller diamonds sparkled in the sun. The sparkle from the sunrays bounced off the wet pavement and into the late afternoon air, or maybe it was the diamond itself against her dark skin that made everything glow and shimmer. Alyssa couldn't believe it. She was really doing it. Getting married! And to the most delicious man in the world. Terrell Henley.

There was one problem though, a secret she'd shoved so far back into the closet that she prayed the skeleton had turned to dust. She closed her eyes and sunk back into the musty smelling cab, the beauty of the day tarnishing. The memories always invaded her right at those moments when she felt the happiest. It was like a dark angel followed her knowing the exact moments when she might need a reminder of what had happened. This dark angel was sure to keep her from ever having total contentment for the rest of her life. That night rushed back to her in a vividness she couldn't deny. The skeleton had not turned to dust.

She opened her eyes, forcing the images away, but knowing what resulted from that night could somehow, someday, show up in her life. Ironically, almost as if she was being given a message, the sun disappeared behind the clouds again and drops of rain splattered against the windshield. The rhythmic swoosh and glide of the windshield wipers across the glass combined with the driver's choice in country music helped bring her back to the here and now.

But the memory screamed at her, swirling with a rush of

adrenaline. It wasn't a matter of *if* her secret would be revealed. But a matter of when. How would she explain herself to the man she planned to exchange vows with in less than three months?

Terrell would understand. He embodied kindness and compassion. He had political aspirations and was planning to run for congress in the next few years. From there, Alyssa knew his plans were even bigger. His dreams and goals only made it that much more pertinent that she tell him her secret.

Tomorrow. Over lunch she would tell Terrell. He deserved to know, but how would he react? She knew he would wonder why she hadn't told him sooner. Not tonight, though. Tonight was all about the two of them and their engagement. His law partners were throwing a party for them at their favorite restaurant, *Jazzman*. And when Terrell heard his best friend from childhood, James, and his wife, Olivia, were coming, Alyssa thought she'd never seen him so excited. Terrell planned to ask James to be his best man.

James had spoken with Alyssa on the phone to tell her that he and Olivia would be flying in from New Orleans to join them at the party. She'd never met James, but had heard story after story about him and the bond he and Terrell shared growing up. They hadn't seen each other in a few years because James and his wife had an ever expanding family, now with five children. Plus they'd moved from the Big Apple to the Big Easy several years ago, where James owned some nightclubs. This was going to be some wedding—old friends, new friends, family. They would have it all.

The cab pulled up in front of the restaurant. Alyssa paid the driver and got out. Terrell wanted to send a car for her, but she wasn't sure about the timing and insisted on getting a cab. She knew she might be late and, sweet man that he was, he didn't mind at all. He understood what her art meant to her. And today of all days, the art studio owner had scheduled an appointment with Raul Perez, the owner of The Perez Gallery, wanting to show him some of Alyssa's oils. He'd been impressed. Now he wanted to host a show at his gallery! She couldn't wait to tell Terrell. He'd be so happy and proud of her. Everything was perfect. Almost. It would be though. Everything would be fine once she told Terrell her shameful secret.

She opened the door to the restaurant and pushed back the hood on her mink-lined coat, leaving the rain behind. The door shut and the outside world was replaced with a vacuum of loud chatter and jazz over the speakers. The smell of food cooking and the blur of people at the full bar made her smile. Terrell had chosen this place because this was where they'd met. Lots of dark woods, glass and mirrors, and dim lights made the place elegant and warm. It was *them*. So very them from the day they met.

She clearly remembered that day sitting at the bar when Terrell came up next to her. "Anyone sitting here?"

"No." She didn't look up from the white wine she'd been nursing.

"Rough day?" he asked.

She nodded. Her grandmother in Italy had passed away. It was expected but, all the same, Alyssa had hoped she'd see her one last time.

"Want to tell me about it?" he asked.

She didn't answer.

Usually a man asking her about her day offended her. Men in general often offended her and she'd done her best over the years to stay away from them. She forced herself to date off and on and occasionally met a decent guy. But fear always took over and she wouldn't allow herself to get close to a man.

"I had a rotten day too. Lost a case." His voice was strong but sincere. "Looks like you could use a refill. Can I buy you a glass of wine?"

She started to glance up, with the word no at the ready, until she saw who she was about to say no to. She stopped glancing and was now looking. Her heart raced. In that second when her eyes met his, she was speechless for a few moments until she finally replied, "That would be nice."

Terrell introduced himself and pretty much from that moment on the two became inseparable except when at work. He'd done something for her that no other man had been able to. He released demons pent up in her for fifteen years that she didn't think would ever escape her soul. The demons may have been set free, but the fact of that night and what happened afterwards remained buried. The dark angel didn't live inside her any longer but it remained watchful.

"Hey baby. There you are." Terrell made his way toward her through a throng of people and pulled her into him. His lips warm on hers, his body comfortable, his scent familiar; musk and citrus. And those eyes of his were so divine. "How did it go? The meeting with Perez?" He helped her out of her coat.

She grinned.

"I knew it!" He pointed at her. "He's going to do a show isn't he?"

"He is."

"Oh man, oh baby. That is great. Come on in. The usual suspects are here from the office. I've been having a nice visit with James and his wife, Olivia."

"Good. They made it then?"

He nodded. "They did. She is as pregnant as can be again and James looks to be matching her pound for pound. This'll be number six. Six kids! Can you believe that? I told him he better get fixed and then he'll have to go on the post pregnancy diet with his wife. Back in the day there wasn't an ounce of fat on that guy. Guess that's what marriage will do to you." He winked.

"It better not." She wrapped an arm around his waist and snuggled in close. "I like you exactly the way you are."

"That's a good thing, because that's what you're getting."

They walked into the back room reserved for large parties where many of their friends and Terrell's colleagues were having their fill of food and drink. Olivia was easy to spot. Pregnancy became the woman, who tried to stand as Alyssa and Terrell walked in.

"Please don't," Alyssa said. "You don't need to get up."

Olivia glowed like all pregnant women did, but this one had an extra glow. She had the same color skin as Alyssa did—caramel. That's what Alyssa's Italian mother called her—her 'carmella la vida.'

When kids at school teased her and called her an Oreo, her mother said to her. "No, you're not. You're much sweeter than an Oreo. You are a caramel. And caramel is the sweetest of all." She loved her mom for trying to understand and help her. Her father told her to ignore ignorance. That's what he'd done all of his life.

Olivia's black hair cascaded down her back and her smile said it all; she looked to be as sweet as the caramel Alyssa's mama spoke of and a woman who Alyssa liked instantly.

Olivia quickly introduced herself. "My husband will be back in a minute. He's so darling. I'm feeling cold and usually I run hot. Obvious by my condition, I guess." She laughed. "He insisted on running out and grabbing a shawl for me. He took Terrell's car to Bergdorf's to buy one."

"Does sound like a good man," Alyssa said, and slid in next to her.

"You got one, too," Olivia replied.

Terrell beamed. "*I'm* the lucky one." He reached across the table and took Alyssa's hand.

"Terrell tells me that you're an amazing artist," Olivia said.

Before Alyssa could say anything, Terrell jumped in and told her, along with anyone else at the table who'd listen, all about Alyssa's artwork. "It's amazing stuff. Brilliant. My baby is *brilliant*. You'll all have to come to the show. She does these oil pieces of vineyards and wine related themes."

"Vineyards?" Olivia asked. "What made you choose that motif?"

"My mother grew up in Tuscany. My grandparents had a small vineyard there. My parents live there now and take care of the property. And my grandfather is pretty frail these days. I haven't been back for a while. About three years, or so, but Terrell and I are going to visit for the holidays next year."

Terrell smiled at her.

"That's wonderful. I'd love to see your work," Olivia replied.

"I have some pieces in my apartment," Terrell said.

"Great. Can't wait to see them," Olivia remarked.

The waiter arrived with more wine and drinks for the table. As he finished pouring Alyssa's glass, he moved back and she caught sight of a man out of the corner of her eye. She did a double take. A fog filled the room and Alyssa's stomach sank. There was laughter, chatter, glasses clinking, people happy, but all she could hear was her blood racing through her ears trying to drown out anything and everything around her. The room seemed to spin and a wave of dizziness wrapped around her. She blinked. Twice. The fog dissipated and clarity set in.

The man headed straight for the table. Terrell smiled. Alyssa's throat closed. She tried to swallow. He had a Bergdorf Goodman bag. James. He'd called himself Jimmy back then. Twenty pounds heavier, but it was still him. Alyssa's hands started to sweat. Her vision blurred again. Her mouth totally dry. He faced her and reached his hand out to shake hers. Did he not recognize her? He really didn't seem to. She looked at his wife, glittery and amazingly beautiful. James handed Olivia the bag. He removed his hand from Alyssa's. A deep burn ran from her palm all the way up her shoulder and she tried to find words.

"This must be your beautiful fiancée," James/Jimmy said. "She's even more beautiful than you said, brother."

"She is amazing." Terrell looked at her oddly.

He was wondering what was wrong with her. He knew her too well. He was reading her. She had to say something.

She forced a smile. "Thank you." It was all she could say, knowing that the skeleton was out of the closet.

CHAPTER THREE

Danielle

*T*hese things were always so phony. The smiles, the chit-chat, the bullshit. Women in their designer outfits discussing the latest craze in cosmetic surgery and gossiping about which desperate housewife had taken the leap and gone under the miracle worker's knife. Good God, could it be any more dull than that? Get a life, right? But Danielle Bastillia caved every time someone called and asked her if she would participate in whatever charity event their organization represented. Al thought it was wonderful, explaining how necessary it was to keep good community relations. Sure, that was a part of it. However, for Danielle, it always came down to the charity itself. She was a sucker for kids, animals, anything and anyone stricken. Maybe it was the Catholic upbringing and the inevitable guilt that came with it, but come on? How could she turn down the Leukemia Fund for Children's Hospital, or the rescue center for greyhounds? Everyone knew that if you invited Danielle Bastillia to your charity event, she would show up to donate her wines and her time.

Today's event was yet another Danielle could add to her list. She braved a smile at Marilyn Dixon, the co-chair for Homeless, Teenage Mothers. Ah, Marilyn, all cheeky and blonde. Indeed she'd seen the inside of Dr. Get-rich-off-of-women's-insecurities office. Her face was taut to the point where Danielle found herself wanting to touch it to see if it felt like Saran Wrap.

"Danielle, you look absolutely stunning. Vintage Diane, right? It's amazing on you. Love the purse, too. Prada, right? Saw it at Bloomie's in the Big Apple and should have grabbed it, but the hubby was rushing me. He had some meeting or something. I don't know. Anyway, you're seated at my table, and . . . oh, you . . ." she snapped and pointed at one of the servers. "What's your name?"

"John," the young man replied.

"Right. John, can you please move the chairs over there that are blocking that doorway and put them in a back room or something? It's not tidy looking."

The server nodded and scurried off.

One thing, well, two things that Marilyn was actually good at: charm and delegating. She had those down to a tee. Even with her apparent A.D.D.

Marilyn haphazardly flung her hands in the air, cocked her head to the side, and smiled back at Danielle. "Thank you so much for your time today. Your wines are *lovely*. Everyone is singing praises."

Anyone who used the word *lovely* or expressions like 'singing praises,' was someone Danielle could never trust. Especially anyone who looked like Marilyn Dixon—hair dyed a golden blonde that was only natural on three-year-old children, eyes a shocking ocean blue that were surely colored contacts, and skin that was . . . well, that was the clincher. No way the woman could be trusted.

Danielle stared at Marilyn with a mix of envy and loathing. "You're welcome. It was Al's and my pleasure to supply the wines." She smiled again feeling the crinkling of the crow's feet that had recently shown up on her face. She hoped she didn't look as exhausted as she felt. Two days earlier, Danielle had conducted a food drive through the Organic Growers Association. She'd packed and loaded food onto vans with a handful of other folks, then had driven one of the vans into San Francisco to the food bank. Her mind and emotions handled it fine, but her body in full PMS mode hadn't fared so well. Now she found herself wiped out and wanting chamomile tea and her bed.

Marilyn cocked her head to the other side. "By the way, how is Al?"

"He's good. Busy as always. We're both working constantly. And you know how it is with kids. It's go, go, go." What time was it? When could she get out of here, kick off the high heels, and slip out of the Diane Von Furstenberg dress? Not that she wasn't in love with the dress. Diane had a knack for making a dress that showed off a woman's best assets, yet camouflaged less than attractive areas—like that belly bulge that inevitably followed childbirth and hung on into middle age. Middle age! It couldn't have been called *a wiser age, the mature age, the grown-up age?* But *middle age* was a term that meant she gained five extra pounds annually since turning forty a few years ago. Middle age was not nearly as fun as everyone claimed.

For Danielle, the wraparound navy blue dress made the most of her breasts—totally natural and not yet sagging. With good boobs you could usually get away with an extra pound or two, and good boobs fit great in a Furstenberg dress. All the same, Danielle preferred her jeans and T-shirts. For these events, though, she did what she had to, even having her long dark red hair styled and putting on some makeup. No matter what she felt about the charitable brouhahas around town, she did have an image to maintain. Al reminded her of that regularly. They were important people in the community. God forbid anyone think that the owners of Bastillia's Wines had any *issues.* Yes, God forbid she taint their *image.*

Marilyn nodded emphatically as if she completely understood Danielle's life. What a joke, because although Marilyn stood as the president of the woman's club chairing the event, the fact was that Marilyn Dixon never picked up her own children from school—and it was doubtful that she ever really did anything with her kids unless nannies were along for the ride. Her staff consisted of a personal trainer, private chef, nannies galore, and a housekeeper. If the woman ever lifted a finger, Danielle guessed it would be to get a glass of wine for herself. At least, those were the rumors in Napa's gossip-logged vineyard land.

"And the girls? They're good?" Marilyn asked as if she was really interested.

Danielle applauded inwardly. The moment she'd been hoping for. Danielle wanted to palm her hands together and wave them high over her head and do the victory dance. Instead she smiled warmly. There were times to be grateful for that gossip vine. Danielle had learned that Marilyn's daughter had been rejected by Yale. "The girls are great. Shannon earned a full scholarship to Yale. We received her acceptance letter over the weekend. And, of course, Cassie will be starting at Trinity Prep."

Marilyn was rendered speechless. "Why, that's wonderful," she finally said, and rose from her seat. "I guess I better get things started." She walked up to the stage at the front of the room and tossed back the golden waves.

Marilyn smiled brightly at the crowd and Danielle studied her. Yes, it was petty not to like the woman for being fake—sort of— but, dammit, get real. Please, would someone get real around here! She was acting as badly as Marilyn, posing at the luncheon in her designer dress, with her newly colored hair, boasting about her kids for her own ego while carrying a fake Prada purse. Yes, fake. What was the point in spending two grand on a purse when you could get a perfectly decent knockoff for thirty bucks? Maybe *she* was the true fake here. Danielle, at least, knew better than to believe this shit was what made up the real world.

Her mouth went dry. No time for a panic attack or a reality check. She'd stopped popping Xanax a few months ago and had gone on a health kick, even joining the local gym, secretly hoping that Al would notice her again. She'd shed ten pounds and felt better than she had in years, but Al still didn't seem to pay much attention to her, except when there was a problem with the payroll, or the accounts, or an employee. Their life together after twenty years had boiled down to a business relationship, not a marriage, and she missed that connection that they used to enjoy. She missed the jokes they shared about the craziness that went on in the world around them.

That was where she should start being honest—with her own husband.

Marilyn turned to Danielle and asked her to stand. "I'd like to thank the *lovely* Danielle Bastillia and her husband, Al, for donating the wine for today, since, as you know, the alcohol is generally the major expense for one of our events." Low laughter rippled throughout the banquet room.

Danielle tried not to cringe through the smile. She glanced around at the room filled with women from all over Sonoma County—some she recognized and waved to. Two women at another table whispered to each other while one stared right at her. Kind of disconcerting. Was one of Danielle's best assets hanging out of the Furstenberg? The woman in a slinky white dress looked vaguely familiar. She was a redhead like Danielle, but at least fifteen years younger. The woman continued looking at her. Danielle offered a slight smile, but this pretty young thing kept the ice glare on and Danielle had to look away.

Why the hell had she flushed the Xanax down the toilet?

Not able to help herself, she looked back again at the redhead who whispered something in her friend's ear, and they both laughed. Bizarre. What was that about? She checked the twins. Nope, they were in their place with only the acceptable amount of cleavage showing. At forty-two years old, being paranoid over women's cattiness was plain stupid. They probably weren't even talking about her.

Perspiration bubbled at the base of her neck. She really did have to get out of this place. Danielle waited patiently, trying not to look at the woman and her friend again.

Right after the president of the teenage homeless mothers' charity gave her talk and the servers started pouring coffee, Danielle excused herself. She told Marilyn that she needed to pick up one of the girls for a dentist appointment. More bullshit, but it didn't matter because she'd lose it quickly if she had to continue sitting there.

For the sake of her *image*, Danielle did her best to masquerade her run for the door as a fashionable quick strut. She handed the valet her ticket and a few minutes later he was pulling her gray 750 BMW around to the front. When the young man got out of the car to let her in, he handed her a large manila envelope. "Mrs. Bastillia, right?" He cocked a dark brow and eyed her with what Danielle thought to be a rather suspicious glare. Jesus, she was truly losing it. Come on! As though everyone was actually staring at her as she smoothed down the Furstenberg over the Spanx flattened tummy; she decided she'd never wear the damn dress again.

"Yes." Hot asphalt beat through her Stuart Weitzman's and she could feel a blister forming in the back of her heel. How karmically appropriate—blisters from the real Weitzman's and compliments for the fake Prada. *Note to self; time for good knock-off shoes.*

"A gentleman in the parking lot said that you needed this."

"What? What gentleman?" She scanned the area and didn't spot anyone that she knew. All she saw was luxury car after sports model after luxury car, their gleaming paint jobs reflecting spotlights of the sun's rays.

"I don't know. He gave it to me and said that it was important and that you needed it."

She sighed, handed him five bucks, and got behind the wheel. Could the day get any stranger? Other cars were pulling in behind her so she had to drive instead of looking inside the mystery envelope.

A glance in her rearview mirror reflected the young redhead and her friend standing under the awning in front of the hotel. Danielle shook her head, knowing that tonight she was going to the cellar to pull out a bottle of the good stuff, even though Al insisted it was only for special occasions. This was a special occasion—she was losing her sanity.

Maybe the panic had something to do with Shannon's impending departure for college, thousands of miles from home. Could this be the beginning of that empty nest syndrome she'd heard so much about?

At a stoplight, Danielle finally had a chance to open the envelope. She took a handful of papers out and read the first few words.

Her heart raced.

She reread the words, blinking her eyes in disbelief. Her hands shook. Cramps seized her stomach so tightly that she almost vomited as she audibly gasped. It was like getting sucker punched.

Who would do this?

The person in the car behind her laid on the horn. Danielle jerked, glancing in her rearview mirror, and yanked the wheel.

This could not be happening. This was a joke, a cruel joke. But as Danielle read over the papers again, she realized this was no joke.

Her husband wanted a divorce.

CHAPTER FOUR

Jamie

*T*he traffic was a mess today. Probably an accident. Someone who'd had too much wine visiting the local wineries. Thank God, Jamie Evan's exit came before she reached what might possibly be a grizzly scene. Sighing as she turned her Volvo SUV onto her street, her stomach coiled. It had been one of those days that started out kind of depressing, then with an ironic twist had turned into massive excitement. Now hope filled her, causing her to wonder if the day would end on a high or low note. It all depended on the little bird.

That morning, her six-year-old daughter, Maddie, while eating her silver dollar pancakes and watching *Charlie & Lola,* said, "Mommy what is that noise?"

Jamie came from behind the kitchen counter where she'd quickly tried wiping up the coffee grounds that Nathan had spilled in his early morning rush. Already dressed for work, Jamie needed to get Maddie to kick it into high gear. "What noise, pumpkin?"

"At the door. Don't you hear it?"

Jamie walked to the French doors where she heard a faint repetitive thud against the pane. She opened up the door and gasped. "Oh. Oh, no." Jamie knelt down.

"What is it, Mommy?" Maddie swung around in her chair and bent over her mother. "What is it?" she demanded again.

"It's a baby bird! It must've fallen out of its nest." Jamie looked up into the eaves of the patio overhang and spotted the remnants of a bird's nest. The baby sparrow flopped pitifully against the window. Jamie gently scooped it up. "You poor thing. Maddie go out to the garage and get that cage we had for Bunny. It's in the corner by Daddy's camping stuff. Can you carry it?"

Maddie nodded, her dark curls falling into her blue eyes.

Maddie went to get their old rabbit's cage while Jamie examined the baby bird. It didn't seem badly injured, but it was certainly a bit frightened. She was an animal lover, but no expert, and she knew nothing about birds.

"Here you go, Mommy." Maddie bounded in and set the cage down on the kitchen table.

Unsure of what to do and racing against the clock, Jamie told Maddie to sit down and handed the bird to her. "Don't squeeze. Hold it there like that." She grabbed the morning's newspaper, shredded some of it, put it in the cage, and took the bird from Maddie and placed it inside. She then hooked up Bunny's old water bottle, and after washing her hands, took out some crackers and smashed them into small bits and placed them on a paper plate for the bird.

"That's all we can do for now," Jamie said. "We have to get you to school and me to work." She sat down in the chair next to Maddie. "Listen sweetie, we're going to hope that our little friend here lives so it can get better and we can turn it loose, but I don't know for sure if it will get better. I can't promise you. I want you to know that."

"I want to keep it."

"I know. Let's see how it does. Okay? Now run on upstairs, wash your hands, and brush your teeth. We have to haul booty."

Jamie thought about the baby bird off and on all day, her fingers crossed that it would survive. She'd put the cage out on the back patio where it would have some sunlight, but also a little shade from a couple of hanging ferns. As she pulled into the garage, Jamie's fingers were still crossed.

Please let it be alive. Jamie had such good news to share with Nathan, she didn't want the day spoiled. After working at *The Wine Lover's Magazine* for seven years, she had been promoted to editor-in chief! It was a position she'd coveted for quite some time, and through diligence and hard work, she'd made it. She'd finally arrived.

She glanced to the back seat where Maddie lay half asleep. Jamie got out of the car, grabbed her briefcase, and started to lift her little girl from her seat.

"Hi, Mommy." She rubbed her eyes and looked up at her

mom, her baby blues innocent and sparkly. "The birdie!" she said, remembering. She was wide awake now and out of the car, heading for the back door.

"Wait, Maddie. Wait, wait, let Mommy go first." Too late. The back door off the garage wasn't locked, and Maddie was through it before Jamie could reach it. She made it to the patio as quickly as possible, and sighed when she caught the smile on her daughter's face.

"Look, Mommy! It lived. Can I touch it?"

"No, babe. Leave her be." Jamie peered into the cage. She could see the bird looked much better and had eaten most of the crackers. What a great way to end the day. Now Jamie could go ahead with her celebration plans for the evening with Nate. If the bird hadn't made it, Jamie knew that they would've had one unhappy child on their hands in need of a night of comforting—comforting that typically meant sleeping in Mommy and Daddy's bed and taking *all* of the bed while Mommy and Daddy scrunched up into their corners.

"Let's leave the bird alone and go in and fix some dinner. Daddy will be home soon."

"I want to watch it."

"Maddie."

Her daughter frowned. "Five minutes."

Jamie held up her hand. "Five, and don't touch her."

"I wanna name it. I wanna name it Lola, like on *Charlie & Lola.*"

"Lola it is."

Jamie walked back into the house, leaving the door open. The lemon scent of cleaning products hit her now that she knew Lola seemed to be on the mend. The housecleaners! God bless them. Today had been their day. Friday was Jamie's favorite day because she knew she'd return home to find the morning mess gone upon their return. Bliss!

"When is Daddy going to be home? I want to show him Lola," Maddie hollered from the patio.

"Any minute!" Usually Nate made it home first. He must have gotten caught in traffic. Maybe he stayed late? No, he would've let her know that by now. He had to be in traffic. He'd show any minute. Time to pour two celebratory glasses of wine and let it breathe. Then get Maddie's dinner started so she could get her daughter to bed early, new bird or not. Jamie had plans for her husband.

A little celebration. And what went with celebrations? *Veuve Clicquot*. What a good idea. It was their favorite champagne. After the wine and *after* Maddie was tucked in her bed, the *Vueve* would be exactly what tonight called for. And the little black, silk number from *La Perla* that Jamie purchased the week before would be icing on the cake.

"I'm hungry," Maddie whined, walking back into the house. "Lola is just sitting there."

"It's probably best to leave her alone. I'll put her in the laundry room soon. The sun is going down. We don't want her to get cold."

"But I'm hungry."

"You're hungry? You're hungry? Wait a minute. I thought your name was Madeleine or Maddie, but Hungry? No. I don't think so. Unless. Wait! Wait, wait, wait, wait." Jamie shook her head in exaggeration. "Did you change your name?" She picked up her dark curly headed daughter whose eyes were exactly like her father's— eyes that could melt a heart like chocolate on a hot day.

Maddie giggled. "No, Mommy. I *am* Maddie. I want to *eat*."

Jamie set her down and bent to her level, finger on her cheek. "I think that can be arranged. What do you say about some Mac and cheeeeeeezzze?" Jamie wiggled her eyebrows in Groucho Marx fashion, a maneuver that always elicited the same reaction from her daughter—laughter and an eye roll. "Don't you go rolling your eyes at me, Madeleine Elise Evans."

"You're so silly, Mommy." She bobbed her curls. "Plain old silly!"

"I can take silly. But don't you dare call me old. Okay, remember I said that Daddy will be home soon. So hop, skip, and jump out of your school clothes, and I'll run a bath for you. Then get your jammies on and your dinner will be ready. And tonight I'll even let you watch a movie in your room on my laptop."

Maddie frowned. "Why do I have to put my pajamas on so early? And can Lola sleep in my room?"

"It's already after six-thirty. And did you not hear what I said? A movie in bed? How about some popcorn too?"

"What about Lola?"

Jamie closed one eye and looked like she was really thinking about it. "I'll see what Daddy thinks about that." She went to the clutter drawer (the one everyone has in their kitchen, save for Martha Stewart) and dug through it until she found some matches. A little wine, a little candlelight. Ooh, and wait a minute. A takeout menu from Arrivederci's. Perfect.

"I wanna' watch *Zach and Cody*."

"Deal."

"Mommy?"

"What, sweetie?"

"Why do I always have to stay at daycare? I hate staying so late. I'm the last one. *Always*."

Ugh. Shot through the heart. The kid would make one heck of a mother someday. She had the guilting thing already down pat. But how could Jamie blame her? It was true that most evenings Maddie was the last one to get picked up—usually one minute before six o'clock. Mrs. Sheffield, the after-care provider, would regularly place her hands on her hips, furrow her already furrowed brow, and remind Jamie that for every late minute she would be charged five dollars.

"I'm sorry, sweetie. Next week, I promise, I will come early every day." The editor-in-chief position should provide some kind of privileges, like working from home, or leaving early on occasion.

"Good, because Mrs. Sheffield smells like farts!"

Jamie tried hard not to laugh. "Maddie, the term is gas or flatulence."

"Mrs. Sheffield has horrible flatulence." Maddie wrinkled up her nose, and rolled her eyes again.

"Upstairs now. Bath! I'll be up to run it."

"I can do it. I'm a big girl."

"Apparently. You and your potty language. Go then!" Laughing, Jamie kicked off her shoes by the couch and glanced around her tastefully decorated family room. The entire house was tastefully decorated, thank you very much to those brilliant designers who do model homes. Jamie may have lived in a tract home, but not just any tract home. This was Napa Valley, and a million dollars for a tract home was not unreasonable. The home came with that old California architecture—arches and sconces and all that chic stuff, plus a wine cellar. In Napa, even tract homes have wine cellars. They do if they cost a bundle, anyway.

Jamie went into the bathroom and looked at herself in the mirror. She ran her fingers through her blonde pixie haircut, giving it a little mussed up look, then opened the drawer full of makeup and rifled through for the red lipstick that Nate liked on her. After that, she lined her hazel eyes with black liner—viola, the vamp.

Walking back into the kitchen, she looked at the clock again. She called the restaurant and placed an order for shrimp scampi and chicken parmigiana. She started the pot for Maddie's mac n' cheese and then went to the wine cellar, pulled the *Vueve*, and set it on ice.

The water stopped running upstairs. Maddie was splashing around and singing a made up song about Lola the birdie. Jamie smiled, shaking her head and went around her family room lighting candles—all perfectly placed and in various sconces and candlesticks. She would have never picked any of this stuff out on her own. Decorating was not her forte, but she sure loved looking at it.

When Jamie heard the garage door go up and the engine of Nate's Range Rover pulling in, she sighed. Her husband. Her soul mate. Her best friend in the world. She couldn't help smiling thinking of the night to come.

She picked up the wine glasses and tried to strike her most seductive pose, which probably looked more like she'd already had a few drinks rather than the sex kitten persona she was going for.

The back door closed and the tapping of Nate's hard-soled shoes echoed off the tile floor. Then they stopped. He must have been putting his briefcase down. A few seconds later he rounded the corner and she smiled widely, holding out a glass for him. "Hey, hot stuff."

He didn't say anything. His normally clear blue eyes were red and his dark hair was disheveled, as though he'd been running a hand through it. He did that when he was upset.

"You okay? Looks like you've had quite a day. Lose a big case?"

He shook his head. "No, babe. I didn't lose a case." He took the wine from her and sucked it down like water.

Her stomach sank. "You're scaring me. What is it? You didn't lose your job, did you?" She laughed nervously.

He shook his head again and looked at her as if he was about to cry. Nate didn't say anything. He just looked at her.

"Honey? What? What is it? Talk to me. Please."

Tears now slid down his face. "I didn't want to do this. I swore I'd be strong and wasn't going to lose it and frighten you, but, God dammit. God dammit!"

Impatience turned to fear. "Nate, what the hell is going on?"

He took her hand. "Where's Maddie?"

"In the bath. What is going on?"

"I saw Robert Kurtz today."

"Yeah, so?" Her stomach sank. "You have lunch with him sometimes, right?" Jamie asked, knowing that Nate was referring to an old college buddy of his. "You see him sometimes. What? Why is that a big deal?"

"No, Jamie. I *saw* him. I saw him as a patient. I didn't go back to Dr. Riggs. He's retired now."

She closed her eyes and tried wrapping her mind around what Nate was telling her, but it didn't make sense. No. It couldn't. Robert was an oncologist.

"Why? Why did you see him as a patient? What are you saying?"

She tried hard to keep the panic from her voice. Jamie choked back the suffocation grasping her around the throat, making it difficult to breathe. She knew *exactly* what he was trying to tell her, but not until he said the words would she believe him and even then . . . she shook her head. "No. No, no, no. No."

"It's not good. It's back, J."

"No. I . . . I . . . what? It's not back! You beat it. We beat it. We *beat* it. The doctors told us. They said that it was gone. Your chances were really good! Five years and it's been gone." She flung her hands making the safe sign like in baseball. Tears stung the back of her eyes.

"I know what they said, honey. They were wrong. I had a biopsy. It's in my liver."

"You had a biopsy? When? No!" A vice gripped her heart as she watched her husband's face wrinkle up, the tears now streaming down. He rubbed his hands through his hair and nodded. "I didn't want to tell you and worry you. I really thought it would all be okay."

Jamie couldn't speak. Nate set his glass down and pulled her into him, smelling woodsy and warm. He stroked her hair and she wrapped her fingers around the tiny curls at the nape of his neck. Comfort. He was her zone—the soft place she came home to every night. He held her tightly, as if he was as afraid as she was to ever let go.

Today...

CHAPTER FIVE

Jamie

WINE LOVER'S MAGAZINE
FRIENDSHIPS & WINE
By
Jamie Evans

 Friendships can begin in many ways, but for women, at least, they usually begin with a common denominator: Your kids play together at preschool and although the children's friendship doesn't last, the one you made with the other mom does. Or you meet at Weight Watchers and after only losing a pound after a month of weigh-ins and counting points, you and your new friend head to the local Mexican restaurant and share every diet woe you've ever had over chips, salsa, and margaritas. Or, while picking up the book you are supposed to read for the next book club meeting, you get to talking with a stranger who just finished the same book and starts to tells you how wonderful it is. The next thing you know, you're inviting her to join the book club. And, what about the friend you met at summer camp between eighth and ninth grade? You weren't exactly friends from the get-go, because the common denominator happened to be a guy named Rick. Rick manipulated the two of you by claiming he liked you and not her, and then told the same thing to the other girl. When the truth came out, Rick--the dog—got dumped by you and your new best friend.

 Friendships. They begin with a common denominator.

 I have the privilege of having all of those women as friends. Even Lauren from summer camp remains a friend of mine.

 There are childhood friends and new friends. There are also best friends.

 The friendship I have with Danielle, Kat, and Alyssa began with our own common denominator: wine.

 My friends and I have a happy hour, where we get together at least two Sunday afternoons out of the month to share good wine and food and to solve all the problems of the world. Well, maybe not world problems, but typically our own. Join us monthly for my Happy Hour column where you'll find excellent wine and food pairings and get a snippet of our lives.

Let me introduce my friends:

Danielle Bastillia: Danielle is an up-and-coming winemaker in the Napa Valley region. She was part owner for twenty years at Bastillia Wines, but is now the proud owner of Déesse Estate Wines. She takes pride in making small boutique wines using all organic methods, including all natural fermentation. Her wines are stylistically French, and I predict that they will make a huge splash at the Harvest Festival in October when Déesse and Danielle release their first vintage. Danielle is a mother of two daughters (one at Yale and the other in high school). She is very involved in the local community with several charities.

Danielle's favorite wine: "I enjoy the complexity of a good Meritage. I love blending Cab Franc with Merlot and Syrah."

Kat Reilly: Kat is part owner of Christian's *with her husband Christian Reilly in our very own Yountville, where Kat is the sommelier. They also own the five-star* Sphinx *in the city. The husband and wife team make a great pair in the kitchen and on the dining room floor, with Kat knowing exactly how to pair Christian's delicious gourmet cuisine with spectacular wines. Kat and Christian have three children between them, ranging in ages from 6-15. When not at the restaurant, Kat is busy as a mom and wife.*

Kat's favorite wine: "I love Bordeaux style reds. Christian and I once had an amazing bottle of Chateau Chasse-Spleen 1959. Best wine—and night—of our lives."

Alyssa Johnson: Alyssa owns The Vine Gallery *in St. Helena. Not only does she own the gallery, showcasing vineyard art, but she is also a wonderful artist in her own right, as well as a community art instructor.*

She hosts a once-a-month wine tasting and local artist showing.

Alyssa's favorite wine: "I enjoy a good chardonnay. I know that's not very interesting or vogueish, but it's true. And I personally am one of those people who like my chardonnays big, bold, buttery, and oaky. To me, that is a signature California Chardonnay."

Then there is me, Jamie Evans: I am the editor-in-chief here at Wine Lover's Magazine. Besides being an editor and writer, I, too, am a mom. My daughter is nine-years-old and is the light of my life. I also take care of my mother-in-law, Dorothy, who used to date big-time movie stars back in the day, leaving never a dull story to be told in my home.

My favorite wine is Viognier. I like the slight floral tones and the crispness of this soft white on a hot summer's day.

There you have it, the ladies of Happy Hour. I hope you'll enjoy this monthly column about wine, food and friendship as much as I think I'm going to enjoy writing it. As always, we at Wine Lover's *love to hear from our readers.*

Cheers!
Jamie Evans
Editor-In-Chief

***

*T*h*at was it.* Jamie wracked her brain, trying to come up with something new and fresh at the magazine. Her boss—not a creative sort—took the tact of breathing down her neck to bring up the numbers. She diligently studied the demographics that were regularly buying the magazine and ran marketing surveys. As the numbers and research came in over a few months, Jamie took note that nearly half of the magazine's readers were women. She understood the recipe part of the deal. The magazine always printed fantastic recipes and food articles. But most of the time even those were written with a slant toward men, like 'Five Top Grilling Meats,' or 'Superbowl Sunday, Syrah and Snapper,' (the men in the office loved that one, but it definitely hadn't been one of Jamie's ideas). The magazine published plenty of articles on malolactic fermentation, organic growing, cigars and wine, yachts and golf, and what wine to drink while yachting or after golfing.

Yes, there were plenty of testosterone filled articles to feed any man, but what was there for women? Almost half of the readers were women! This excited Jamie. Surveys showed that women and wine went hand-in-hand with the liquid grape being the favored alcoholic beverage amongst the female set. Not to mention that more and more women were involved with making wine, marketing wine, and everything that went with and concerned wine. That was why and how Jamie came up with the idea to do an article on up-and-coming Women in the World of Wine. She chose to address it from the local aspect and started making calls. No better place to begin than in her own backyard of Napa Valley.

Her first call went out to Danielle who she'd met at a charity event for lung cancer. Since divorcing The Bastard (a name they all agreed on when it came to Danielle's ex, Al), she made the decision to finally pursue her dream of becoming a winemaker, a plan she'd squashed deep down for the past twenty years. When married to The Bastard he wouldn't even listen to her winemaker dream. He laughed at her and told her it was nice, but not realistic. Her job was payroll and raising the kids.

Danielle sulked for about three months after discovering *the other woman*. Then she found it far more satisfying to get royally pissed off and went after The Bastard with guns loaded and blazing. Three years ago, Danielle exemplified a woman scorned, and her anger fueled her desire to make fine wines. Now she planned to enter the Harvest Wine Festival in October. A gold medal would put a smile on her face and show her ex exactly who she was—*a winemaker extraordinaire.* Jamie knew that Danielle was headed for greatness and had no qualms about putting the as yet unknown winemaker in her article.

Danielle turned Jamie on to Kat. Kat and her husband Christian ran an incredible restaurant in wine country, *Christian's*. They also owned the popular *Sphinx* in San Francisco. Christian's genius with turning ordinary food into delicacies, combined with Kat's extensive knowledge of wine, made them the perfect pair and *Christian's* was a major success.

Jamie hadn't been into *Christian's* herself; money woes kept her within a tight budget these days, and when a little extra did turn up, she spent it on her daughter Maddie or her mother-in-law Dorothy. After Nate's death, Dorothy had declined rapidly and now suffered from, at best guess, dementia. Jamie was determined to provide Dorothy with the best care she could.

Nate's brother, David, insisted on putting her in a home, but Nate and Jamie promised to take care of her as she aged. She knew that the last thing in the world Dorothy wanted was to live out her last years in a retirement home.

Jamie called up Kat and, after some convincing, she'd finally agreed to do the photo shoot and article. Danielle had mentioned that Kat worked an extremely busy schedule with the restaurant only being open for a year, and that she could also be a bit standoffish. However, after talking with her on the phone for almost thirty minutes, Jamie found that she warmed right up, and a kinship developed quickly between the two.

Then there was Alyssa. It turned out to be just one of those things where you meet someone and there is an instantaneous connection, almost as if you've known each other from another life. Jamie met her while window-shopping in St. Helena on a lazy Sunday afternoon with Maddie. They'd wandered into Alyssa's gallery. She immediately started talking to Maddie, and Jamie—always a sucker for anyone who was nice to her kid—knew she could become friends with Alyssa. The two women wound up talking about art, and it hit

Jamie that she would be the perfect addition to the article.

Alyssa's artwork captivated both the connoisseur and the average tourist, but she was humble about her work and, in Jamie's opinion, didn't charge enough for it. Alyssa was Miss America pretty, with mocha colored skin and delicate features. Her warm brown eyes invited you in, but there was also a tinge of sadness in them, something Jamie could certainly relate to. Alyssa turned out to be the hard one to convince, but Jamie promised her that what she did with her vineyard paintings for the community and for women in general was important and needed to be featured in the article. Alyssa finally agreed. Granted, Jamie had done most of her convincing over dinner and wine with the group, but that night also cemented a friendship among the women.

At first, the four of them would all meet sporadically for dinner, an occasional movie, a card game. But then they thought, why not get together regularly? The response and success of Jamie's original article about these women bumped up the magazine's numbers with the female population. Women were reading *Wine Lover's* along with their usual women's magazines. At least they were in their part of the world. An idea came to Jamie, and she suggested that their get-togethers should be over wine, where they could talk about the wines that they were drinking and what they would pair them with. The other three loved the idea—any excuse for friendship, food and wine sounded good to them.

Their time spent with each other consisted of a bit of gossip, sharing secrets, the occasional shedding of tears, and always a ton of laughter. Jamie chronicled these get-togethers, which took place every other Sunday evening, beginning at the cocktail hour of five o'clock—*The Happy Hour*.

At first, they tried coming up with some kind of group name like The Decanted Divas, which was sort of fun, but a bit too corny. They tossed around Grapevine Girls, but that one reminded them all way too much of *The Golden Girls*. Jamie had said, "We might all be middle aged or close to it, but I'm thinking we're not ready for bingo down at the senior center. I'm not going for Grapevine Girls."

They almost chose The Vineyard Vixens--Danielle's suggestion-- but every time any one of them said the word *vixen* it started a chain of laughter bringing tears to their eyes. "It is funny," Danielle said. "Me a vixen? Please! My husband left me because he was bored with our sex life." She laughed again, but Jamie and the others knew that it wasn't as funny to Danielle as she tried to make it.

"Screw it, we don't need a name," Kat said, unclipping her light brown hair and letting it fall to her shoulders. "It's like a happy hour."

They all nodded in agreement and made a schedule as to who would host happy hour on which Sunday.

The hostess would choose the wine and recipes for the evening. The rules were: no chug-a-lugging (these were tastings, not frat parties), and no driving home buzzed (which occasionally happened to one or more of them, and Kat's husband Christian was available to act as a taxi service if needed).

Tonight was Jamie's night and, as usual, she was running late. It didn't help that Jamie always chose some impossible recipe that typically called for some ingredient she'd never heard of. But she couldn't help herself because as she looked through her cookbooks on the Fridays before her Sundays, she always found a mouthwatering photo that accompanied a complicated recipe. The wine part was easy for her, though. Wineries from all over sent wines to the magazine and *someone* had to sample them. Of course Jamie reciprocated, writing them up in the *Happy Hour* monthly column.

Today was no different as far as the recipe. She'd chosen Duck a la Orange. Already five after four and the duck was in the oven, but she had yet to make the saffron potatoes. Nora still hadn't shown up. Even though times were tight and she'd let go of the cleaning service, Jamie had had to hire Nora to take care of Dorothy while she was at work and to help out on happy hour Sundays. Nora wasn't the best housekeeper, even when she bothered to clean and clear clutter at all, but she always made sure Dorothy had her meals and was happy. And Jamie appreciated Nora's sportsmanship. Taking care of Dorothy came with a certain ... um ... weirdness. God bless her, but Dorothy truly believed Nora was Dean Martin.

While Jamie searched the cupboard for saffron, Dorothy came in, wearing a poodle skirt, a white blouse, and a bow that pulled her long gray hair taut. Her blue eyes, exactly like Nathan's and Maddie's, blinked rapidly. "Hi, honey. Has Dean called? I thought we had a date."

"No, Mom. I'm sorry. He hasn't called. But he should be here soon."

Dorothy laughed girlishly and did a twirl as well as a seventy-seven year old woman could manage. Actually, her twirls were still quite good. Dorothy, who'd been a dancer in her younger years, had also worked in Hollywood for some time. Rumor was that after she divorced Nate's dad, she'd partaken in a few scandalous affairs with notorious hot shots and bad boys in the entertainment business. Now, a tendency to fall back into yesteryear had left poor Dorothy not only believing that Nora the housekeeper was Dean Martin, but there were days that she imagined that the UPS driver and mailman were Frank Sinatra or Elvis. Yes—Elvis. Jamie loved the outfits she donned for her *dates* with Elvis.

"Where's Nathan? He should be home by now. School is out." Dorothy looked at her wrist, at the watch that wasn't there, and tapped it. "He is supposed to come straight home. Dinner will be ready soon." She shook her head. "That boy."

Jamie walked around the kitchen counter and put her hands on Dorothy's shoulders. "Mom. It's me. Jamie. Nathan is gone. Remember? He is an angel now." She swallowed hard. Dorothy frequently forgot that Nate was no longer with them, something Jamie wished she could do. Countless times she wished she could live in Dorothy's world, a world where Nate still existed.

Every time she heard her husband's name, a weight pulled down on her heart. Her breath shortened and sorrow closed her throat, but Dorothy couldn't understand.

"Jamie! Yes. You are such a nice girl. I always liked you. You are so much better than that Ann Marie that Nathan thought he wanted to marry. You came home with him and it was a ray of sunshine walking through the door. Dino thought you were a doll. You need to call Nathan and tell him to come home. He's been gone too long."

"I know, Mom. You're right. Why don't you go watch some TV and I'll let you know when Dean shows up?" Nora had better hurry her butt up, because Jamie's sweet mother-in-law needed a boyfriend.

"Good girl. I'll do that. Will you bring me some sherry while I wait?"

"Of course."

Four-thirty rolled around. Maddie would be home any minute from her Uncle David and Aunt Susan's place in Marin County.

The doorbell rang. "Nora!" Jamie yelled half exasperated, half relieved as she opened the door. Nora scurried past her, removed her purse, and laid it on the sofa. She then said something in Spanish that Jamie thought to be an apology—either that her brother or brother's wife was sick and needed help. It went something like this. "Lo siento. Mi wife de mi hermanos esta esicky."

"Your esposa is sick?"

She smiled and shook her head. "No. Es mi hermano."

"Hermano? *Hermano?* Hermano?" Where in the world was the Spanish/English dictionary at? In her office upstairs.

"Es mi brother."

"Your brother esta infermo?" Oh yeah, *hermano* is brother. Should have known that.

"Su esposa." Nora crossed her arms and looked at her with this 'you are so dumb' expression.

"His wife?"

She tossed up her hands, nodded, and headed for the kitchen, where she gasped at the mess Jamie had created and immediately began cleaning. This was how their relationship went. They spoke Spanglish to each other, with Nora basically in control and typically aggrieved with Jamie. Nora was almost always late and sometimes didn't show up at all (on Sundays). But she always had a fabulous excuse and she definitely knew that there was no way in hell Jamie was ever going to find someone to clean her house (sort of) and take care of Dorothy for two hundred dollars a week, as well as make the trek out on her Sundays. She'd wedged Jamie between a rock and a hard place, and she knew it. So Jamie dealt with it.

As Nora scurried around the kitchen attempting to clean it, Jamie checked on the duck and decided to turn the heat up a little. The potatoes were boiling but she still hadn't found the saffron. Maddie bounded in the side door off the kitchen, loaded down with shopping bags. "Hi, Mommy."

Jamie stopped the saffron search and wrapped her arms around her daughter. "Hi baby. Where're Uncle David and Aunt Susan?"

"They said to tell you that they had to get back to the city because they have a dinner or something tonight."

"Oh." Jamie peered out the kitchen window to see David's Mercedes pulling out of the driveway. This seemed to be becoming the norm with Nate's brother. Maddie's visits with her aunt and uncle typically meant gifts galore. Then when David and Susan would bring her home, they would visit for less than ten minutes, say hi to Dorothy, and leave. Today they hadn't even bothered to get out of the car. With a sigh and frown, Jamie shook her head. Unbelievable. A heart to heart with her husband's brother was overdue and necessary. "Look at you. Looks like you got a few things."

Maddie smiled widely. "Check this out, Mom." She opened a bag and took out Ghirardelli chocolates, a purple cashmere sweater and a pair of True Religion jeans. "Aunt Susan bought them for me. She said they'll be perfect for next fall. Her personal shopper picked them out just for me. And Uncle David took me to the bookstore and he got me a bunch of new books I can't wait to read. They're in my suitcase at the door. Can you bring it in for me? It's kinda heavy."

"Sure, sweetie. Sounds like you had fun." A tightness crept into her shoulders and neck. The jeans alone had to have cost over a hundred dollars.

"I had a great time. We saw the new movie with Matt Damon in it, and then last night we watched *Mamma Mia* again on DVD, and we ate at Auntie Sue's favorite restaurant. It was the best Mexican food ever," she squealed.

"That's wonderful, honey."

"Where's Grandma? I want to tell her about it, even though she won't remember."

"Waiting for her suitor."

Maddie smiled. "Who is it supposed to be tonight?"

"Dean of course."

Maddie rolled her eyes. "Should have known. Oh, my gosh. I can't believe I almost forgot, but the best part this weekend was that Aunt Susan got a horse."

"She got a horse?"

Maddie nodded. "It's amazing. He's soooo beautiful and sweet. He's sorrel, which Aunt Susan said means like a reddish brown, and he has a blaze on his face, and he jumps!"

Jamie remembered that Susan grew up riding horses, and as a young woman rode on the show jumping circuit. When her prized horse had been injured badly and had to be put down, she'd gotten out of the horse world. Apparently she'd gotten back in. "Great. That's wonderful."

"It is, Mom. She said that I can come and ride with her sometimes. I want to go again next weekend. They said that I could. Aunt Susan even said that she'd get riding lessons for me!"

The muscles in Jamie's neck and shoulders tightened further. "Honey, I think that's great, but we need to talk about this, and right now my friends are coming over."

"But, Mom. I can tell you're going to say no."

"I didn't say no. I said that we need to talk about it, but not now."

"But I want to."

"Nevertheless, I need you to either go in and watch TV with

Grandma, or read one of your new books, or find something to do in your room. We will discuss this later. I am expecting company soon." Jamie stood up straight and then, oh no, that smell. *Burning.* The duck!

"Señora Jamie!" Nora yelled.

"I know, I know." Grabbing hot pads off the counter, she pulled open the oven to see that things were only a tad crispy but not burnt. She took the duck out and pulled at a wing. Hmmm. Not at all appetizing and nothing like the photo in the cookbook.

As if on cue, Nora grabbed the hot pads and the duck from her and dumped it into the trash. She headed to the fridge and took out cheeses and some fruit, and went to the cupboard for crackers. Jamie turned off the stove. So much for duck a la' orange and saffron mashed potatoes.

"Mommy." Maddie placed her hands on her hips.

"Not now, Maddie."

Jamie turned in time to see her storm off toward her room. Great way to welcome the kid home, but Susan and David obviously weren't doing her any favors. Horses! Now it was horses!

Jamie kicked the trashcan and Nora's eyebrows went up in scorn. "I know. I know. Don't look at me like that though."

Nora seemed to understand her this time as she turned away and sliced up the cheese. Jamie gave up trying to play blue ribbon hostess, and went upstairs to change out of the T-shirt that was now covered in orange sauce and the jeans she wore every weekend. Fifteen minutes later, the doorbell rang and she dashed down the stairs. Peeking in the kitchen, she saw that Nora had covered her butt. She passed her and Dorothy staring at the boob tube in the den. Nora had even given Dorothy a glass of wine. Jamie smiled weakly at Nora, who shook her head at her, as Dorothy reached for the housekeeper's hand. "Gracias," Jamie whispered.

"Mas dinero. Queiro mas." Nora rubbed her fingers together.

Jamie shrugged her shoulders and walked to the front door, knowing exactly what Nora wanted.

The friends all rolled in together.

"It smells . . ." Danielle wrinkled up her nose.

"Burnt," Jamie replied. Her friends laughed and followed her into the combined open family room and kitchen. "Sorry, but uh, no duck a la orange for you." She waved her hand over a tray of cheese and crackers, grapes, apple slices and strawberries. "Dig in. It's gourmet, I assure you."

"I don't do duck anyway." Danielle smiled and reached for the bottle of Viognier in the ice bucket. "You try too hard. You should know by now that we aren't a difficult crowd to please."

"Look who's talking." Alyssa took a seat on the end barstool and pulled her hair back into a ponytail. She wore a cream colored v-neck sweater that contrasted beautifully with her dark skin. "What was it you served last time? Veal scallopini?"

"We were drinking Italian wines," Danielle replied.

"Personally, I am with Jamie on this. I get sick of the gourmet food." Kat handed Danielle the corkscrew at the end of the counter.

"Sure," Jamie said. "Christian's food is so horribly boring."

"No, of course not. But you know it's nice to have something simple sometimes. And it's better on my waistline. I swear my husband doesn't know how to cook without using a cup of butter and cream in every sauce." She pinched her waist. "And it shows. Just look at my ass. I could hardly squeeze into these." She turned around and patted her butt. "And I won't even show you the excess baggage hanging over these suckers. Thank God for loose fitting blouses." She ruffled out her blouse. It was on the larger, longer side, which as far as her friends were concerned was totally unnecessary. Kat seemed to have a skewed image of her body shape. "Not to mention black. Thank God for the color black."

"Please. You look great," Danielle said. "Here." She'd uncorked the wine and poured glasses for each of them. "So I have some news."

They all leaned in over the kitchen counter

"Yes. What is it?" Kat waved her hands in small circles.

"The Bastard's child bride is preggers again!"

Kat almost spit out her sip of wine. Jamie's went down the wrong way, causing her to cough for a minute, and Alyssa's eyes widened.

"I know. How stupid! First Al knocks her up while screwing her behind my back and she has twins. They're barely three and *now* another one is on the way." Danielle picked up her glass and swirled the light golden contents around.

"How do you feel about that?" Jamie asked.

"Feel about it?" Danielle laughed. "I think it's fabulous." She swallowed another sip of wine. "Wait a minute, you all thought this would drive me batty again? No seriously, this is the best news I could get. When I heard, all I could think about was a fifty year old Al having to change more diapers, being woken up in the middle of the night, and then going through all the toddler stages again. *Times three*." She held up three fingers and grinned. "It's perfect revenge for me. I only have two years until Cassie leaves the roost and then I can travel, go back to school if I want to, and really grow my winery. Al is starting over at fifty. He has all of these babies to deal with and raise. I mean, what if she leaves his aging ass? He'll have to pay Stacey up the ying-yang."

Jamie could see her point but also couldn't help feeling sorry for another baby whose dad wouldn't exactly be father of the year. Not the way Nate was.

"What about the girls? Does Shannon know? Or Cassie?" Kat asked referring to Danielle's sixteen and twenty-one year old daughters.

"Cassie knows and she's not saying much, but that's no shocker. These days she doesn't say much anyway. I think this will probably affect her harder than Shannon. You know, Cassie has always been daddy's little girl and the competition has stiffened with Stacey and then the twins and now a new baby. If this new baby is a boy, that will only make things worse for her. Al always wanted a son more than he wanted his daughters."

"Funny enough though, she always defends him because he gives her whatever the hell she wants. She's learned how to work him and he gives in to her. I am always telling him that spoiling her with clothes, money, and a car isn't the way to raise a happy, self-sufficient child. She hates me right now, because I told her that she had to get a job this summer." Danielle popped a strawberry in her mouth, washing it down with a sip of wine. "I know it might sound mean or wrong, but I can't help hoping that Al's new family at least brings Cassie back to me."

"What do you mean?" Alyssa asked. "She's your daughter. She may be acting like a teenager, but I think her actions are normal. I didn't like my mom all that much at sixteen either."

Danielle nodded. "The problem is that everything her dad does is wonderful. That's only because of the money and gifts. I know that I shouldn't take it personally, but it's hard not to. Everything I do is wrong in her eyes. Every time she speaks to me it's in this adversarial tone, like I'm to blame for all the wrongs in her life and in her world. As if I'm to blame for the divorce! In her eyes, I might even be the one to blame for Stacey and the twins and now the new kid. The other day she suggested that I needed new clothes and a makeover. She even muttered something about how her father might have stayed if I'd worn better clothes!"

"She did not!" Jamie said.

Danielle shrugged. "I don't know. I wouldn't want to do it all over again, but tell you what, I do miss the days when I was on a pedestal. This too shall pass, right? And Shannon will be home next month. I never went through any of this with her. Maybe she can talk some sense into her sister. What about you all? What's going on in your worlds for the last couple of weeks? I feel like I've been out of touch working in the lab and getting ready for harvest."

"I found out my mother is coming to visit for the summer." Kat lifted her glass up to toast. "Woo hoo, doesn't that sound like a reason to celebrate?"

"From everything you've told us, it sounds like a reason to drink," Alyssa replied, and refilled Kat's almost empty glass.

"Venus is coming?" Jamie asked.

"Yes. Birkenstocks and Ram Das aplenty. She suggested I get a wheat grass juicer and told me where I can order the freshest, most clorophylled wheat grass. She hinted that I may possibly want to start growing it myself."

"Oh, no." Jamie picked up a piece of cheese.

"Oh, yeah. And I'm making you all go to Bikram yoga with us. It's only about a hundred and five degrees in the room, and they say you usually stop puking after the first few sessions if you drink lots of water. My mother will tell you it's so powerfully Zen."

"Sounds like a blast. She's coming for the entire summer?" Danielle asked.

"We're still negotiating the terms," Kat replied. "That's my big news, and of course, Perry has another new girlfriend. This one is even old enough to buy alcohol. The boys say she's twenty-two, and she is not a stripper but a receptionist in a hair salon." She touched the ends of her shoulder length, chestnut colored hair. "The best part is that the Sperm Donor told me that she was a doctor. When I met her, I actually asked her where her medical practice was located."

"Nuh uh. No you didn't," Alyssa said.

Kat shrugged. "I couldn't help it. Poor thing says to me that it's not a practice but a salon."

"What did the Sperm Donor do?" Jamie asked.

"Turned bright red, looked at me like I was pure evil, and grabbed Barbie by the arm while he yelled for the boys to hurry up."

"Priceless." Jamie walked over to the opposite counter and grabbed a bottle of Pinot Noir from the Oregon coast to open.

"Now we know Danielle's and my latest turmoil, how about you two?" Kat asked. "Alyssa? What's up?"

Alyssa shook her head and smiled, setting her glass onto the counter. "Nothing. I don't have anything at all really going on."

The other women didn't know Alyssa the way that Jamie did. The introvert of the group, Alyssa seemed to always tread lightly with them. Even after a couple of years of knowing her, Jamie still felt like she'd only scratched the surface. They always included her. They cared about her. Alyssa knew it too, but evident through sorrow-tinged laughter and soft speech, something held on tightly to Alyssa. Jamie guessed it to be pretty damn heavy for her to keep her guard up all the time. Jamie, for one, didn't believe her when she said that nothing was going on.

"Nothing at all?" Danielle asked, eyebrows raised. "No man, or men, or any art sales? How is the painting going?"

Alyssa shifted in the barstool. "Okay, yeah. You know, I'm working on a new oil."

Jamie clapped her hands. "Stop being so humble. Tell us about it."

"It's another one of the little boy pieces."

"In the series?" Danielle asked.

"Yes."

Alyssa had painted two paintings so far of a small African American boy. In the first, he looked to be about a year old crawling through a field of grapevines. His skin lighter than the soil on the ground, his eyes happy, a sweet toothless smile on his face. The grapes around him were golden hued, and Alyssa captured an innocence and beauty with the sunlight raining down on the baby and the grapes. In the next painting she'd done, the child looked about three, but it was clearly the same child. Anyone who saw the paintings recognized that. This one showed the toddler on his toes, reaching up to pick a purple grape.

"What's this one like?" Jamie asked.

"You'll have to wait. When I'm finished, you all need to come by and see it. I think it's my favorite," she replied.

"Do you know the child that you paint?" Danielle asked.

Alyssa took a sip of wine and shook her head. "He's a part of my imagination."

"You know what I think?" Kat said. "I think Alyssa wants a baby."

"Ha! No way. I'm not the marrying, family type. I'm not."

They all eyed her, and Jamie wondered if her other two friends had the same thought . . . *Was she trying to convince herself or them?*

"You may be the smartest of us all. You know what? I've always been really interested in drawing. I'm not great at it, but I like it. I was thinking about dropping in on one of your art classes," Danielle said. "I'm on the Harvest Festival committee and I have an idea in mind for the poster. I might actually try and do the artwork myself."

"I'm starting a new class in two weeks on Wednesdays from six to eight. I'll give you a discount. I know the owner." Alyssa chuckled.

"I would love that. Maybe we can grab a bite after."

"Oh do that. Come by our restaurant. I work Wednesdays and Christian has come up with this terrific new menu. Everything is fresh, organic, super good." Kat clucked her tongue.

"It's a plan. What about you, J? Can you meet us?" Alyssa asked.

"I wish I could. But not with Dorothy and Maddie. I can't go."

"Can't Nora come by?"

"No. She won't do extra nights. I've asked." Jamie didn't want her friends to know about her difficult financial situation.

"Bummer," Kat said.

"I know. Sorry." She popped a grape into her mouth. "You know, Danielle, I can relate a bit to your woes with the Bastard buying off Cassie."

"How so?"

"Maddie's aunt and uncle dropped her off right before you all arrived and of course, they've trumped me again."

"What did they do?" Danielle asked.

"Horses. Susan has gotten back into horses and offered Maddie riding lessons."

They all stared at Jamie. She nodded. "Yep."

"Without asking you?" Alyssa asked.

"Uh huh."

"Wait a minute. They live in the city. Where's the horse?"

"Correction. They live in Marin County. My guess is that the horse is at some pretty posh place. I can't compete with that."

"You can't be driving her to riding lessons there. It's too far and what's with not talking to you first?" Kat reached for the wine. "What is it with all these people who think they have to buy a child's love?

Don't they get that it won't last? It's not for real? Yuck. That's exactly how the Sperm Donor works it too. It's disgusting."

Jamie sighed. "This thing with Maddie and them, it bugs me. It's not like Nate and David were super close. Sure we got together and hung out sometimes on the holidays, birthdays, that sort of thing, but Nate had some issues about David and his obsessive need for material things."

"Isn't that an attorney thing?" Kat asked. "I mean aren't they notorious for always wanting more?"

Jamie frowned. "Not Nate. Sure we had nice things but my husband's first priority was his family. His law practice came second."

"I'm sorry. I didn't mean Nate, it just slipped out." Kat picked up her wine glass.

"It's fine. Nate and I always thought David married Susan for her money. She isn't exactly, I don't know, down to earth. She is Ms. Upper Echelon of Society. Kind of affected, but I'm torn. I feel like David is a connection to Nate for Maddie and she loves going with them."

"What nine-year-old wouldn't? If they treat her like a princess and spoil the hell out of her, of course she wants to go with them." Danielle shook her head.

"I know that. I get that. What I do about it without being the bad guy is another thing. Maybe I'm paranoid. I just can't help but feel as if they're coveting my child. It's like they want her for their own. Does that sound, I don't know—do you think I'm freaking out?"

Kat crossed her arms. "No. It sounds like a mother who loves her child. I'm sorry, but they sound like assholes. They don't have kids, right?" Jamie shook her head. "Okay, that's their issue not yours. I agree it's not fun to be the bad guy, but c'mon, pony up. No pun intended, but seriously, that's what being a parent is all about. I say you have to put your foot down, or they're going to create a little monster and when they're finished with her, you'll have to deal with it."

"Kat's right. They can't have her all the time. She's yours. It's that simple and I have a solution." Danielle smiled smugly. "Tyler Meeks."

"Who? What?" Jamie shoved the plate of cheese and crackers to the side.

"Tyler and his two sisters run the Napa Valley Riding Center. Place is five minutes from here. You pass it all the time."

Jamie nodded.

"I hear he is an awesome teacher. His oldest sister gave my girls lessons when they were little and he was a teen at the time. I recently read in the paper that he now runs a horsemanship for the handicapped program and he's also giving lessons to kids. He is *really* nice to look at, too. At least he was at seventeen. I can only imagine him ten years later." She wiggled her eyebrows.

"Danielle!" Jamie threw a grape at her.

"What? You don't notice hot guys? Come on. Even the young ones are fun to look at, and now he's legal. Hmm, maybe I'll go take some riding lessons from him myself."

"You are so bad," Kat said.

"Yeah and you're not?" Danielle smiled. "And don't you look at me like that." She pointed at Alyssa. "I got a feeling you got more diva in you than you let on. You all act like a bunch of old women. Get with the program. Good wine, hot guys, and sex. That's what I want to talk about, because God knows I'm not having any." She glanced at all of them. "Oh. No one else is either? Old women. Goddamn. We need to get crazy. That's what we all need. And you Kat, you're the married one, I suspect you're at least having sex. And your husband with that Irish lilt? The dirty talk must sound so melodic."

Kat picked up another handful of grapes and pelted Danielle with them. Jamie and Alyssa followed suit.

"Now that's better!" Danielle said, laughing. "It's not sex, but at least it's fun." Before long they were all in a fit of laughter tossing grapes and acting like schoolgirls. Pure escape and total fun. And that was Sunday happy hour.

CHAPTER SIX

Danielle

*D*anielle took out the bottle of wine, now aged for a little over two years. This could be it. The one. The winner. Her first bottle of *Déesse*. *Goddess* wine. The grapes had begun as Bastillia grapes and, if Al had honored his marriage vows a few years before, would likely have gone into a Bastillia wine. Doubtful, though, that the Bastilla wine would have been *this* wine, because *this* wine had been hand-crafted in artisan fashion by Danielle herself.

Guess it was a good thing after all that Al had cheated and left her for Stacey—the vixen—who'd evil-eyed Danielle at that charity event over three years ago as if *she* were the witch. Now the twenty-something luscious redhead had to keep up the image for good old Al these days—an image that took a big hit when his *big* news wove its way through the valley. Stacey could have Al's money and the paunch around his waste-line, as well as his lame sense of humor.

Al had been *unsatisfied*. That one stupid word brought Danielle to tears many times over the last few years, wondering if she'd really aged all that badly. She didn't think so. At forty-five, she thought she was still attractive. Men glanced her way and even smiled at her. Her friends told her she looked a lot like Julianne Moore. Not a compliment to turn down. Granted, it came from Jamie, Kat and Alyssa, but still.

Now when the word *unsatisfied* entered a conversation or crossed her mind, all she could do was laugh. *Unsatisfied*. Yeah well how about now, Al? How satisfied are you with two toddler girls in diapers running around whining and crying all the time, and a baby on the way? She doubted Al was getting much *satisfaction* these days from Stacey. The woman had to be exhausted. After seeing Stacey and babies in the grocery store the other day, she'd actually felt sorry for her. But thoughts of Al, Stacey, and babies needn't take up residence in her head.

This was her time now, and in some ironic twist of fate, Al's unfaithfulness and aftermath turned out to be a good thing. There were moments when she wondered what it would have been like to be married to someone for fifty some odd years or more, share all those memories, and know everything about each other. Sweet little old people holding hands out on a stroll and such. At forty-five, with no love life and no prospects, growing old alone looked like a possibility, and interestingly enough that didn't scare the hell out of her, like she thought it might.

She held the bottle of wine in her hands and closed her eyes for a moment. This had to be the one. Taking it into her office, she grabbed a corkscrew out of the drawer and inserted it. Twisting it down into the cork, she slowly pulled it up out of the bottle. She took a glass from the cabinet and wiped it out, making sure it sparkled clean. After all, this merited a special occasion. As she poured, Danielle watched the dark purple and red colors of the wine blend together. Setting the glass down on her desk, she allowed it to breathe for a few minutes. They were some long minutes.

A new white candle on her desk seemed to be waiting for this moment like the winemaker herself. Yes, a bit of ambience. Why not? She opened her desk drawer again and rummaged around for matches. Finding some, she lit the candle then sat down in her chair. Her fingers wrapped around the glass stem, she swirled the wine, and with a satisfied sigh studied its color. The color of wine always amazed her, and no matter what anyone said, it was never the same. Even with the same type of wines, the color would differentiate by a smidgeon of a shade. Some reds were deep purple, black almost, some as light as a strawberry color. This wine she held in her hand was a dark blood red. How fitting.

She brought the wine up to her nose and breathed it in. *Gorgeous. Stunning.* The fight for these vines obviously well worth it.

The seductive scent of black currant, ripe plum, and what could be none other than dark chocolate, hit her nose, easing the knot in her stomach. She twirled the glass between her fingers again and then brought it up to her lips and took her first sip. Her taste buds awakened to layers of luscious cassis, dried cherry, sweet tobacco, and anise that coated her palate and lingered. A warmth spread throughout her body and she couldn't help smiling. Her toes curled in utter satisfaction. The wine finished with subtle nuances of earth and spice. Danielle waited a few seconds and took another sip to be sure she hadn't been fooled, because God knew she'd prayed this moment would come. This time after she swallowed the wine, she set the glass down, flopped back into her chair, and started laughing.

How sweet, how sweet, how sweet! She raised her hands in triumph. And that was when she came up with the name for the wine; *Revenge.* It was perfect. This bottle of wine was her revenge. Combined with the name of the winery, Déesse, which meant Goddess, she had the name. Revenge of the Goddess. She hoped oenophiles from all over the world would score it high, and after that she would make a killing. Who knew that her husband leaving her for a younger woman would lead to this? She even thought about picking up the phone and calling Al to thank him. No. She'd do that after her wine had been touted from the West Coast to the East Coast. But she did silently toast him.

Finishing off the glass, she corked the bottle and headed up to the house. Now that she'd savored her time with the wine, she knew she needed to share it with one of her best friends. Hands down, she knew she'd call Jamie.

The winery, a good walk from the house, up and down small hills, might be great for toning her legs, but still winded her. Sometimes she drove the golf cart down to her office and the lab, but today her manager Raul was using it out on the vineyard, and she needed the exercise anyway.

Coming up the driveway, she spotted a car. It had to be one of Cassie's friends because it was parked next to the brand new Audi her father and Stacey had gotten her.

When she made it all the way to the top of the drive, she saw that the car was Shannon's. The kid had made it a day early. But she was supposed to be flying home tomorrow and Danielle had planned to pick her up at the airport. Why had she driven all that way? Danielle had told her that she could use her car over the summer. She wished her daughter had let her know that she was driving across the country alone. She could have been hurt, or kidnapped, or worse. What had she been thinking?

She opened the front door. "Shannon?"

"In here, Mom."

Cassie bounded down the stairs, her long strawberry blonde hair swinging with her gait, a huge grin across her face. "Have you seen Shannon yet, Mom?"

"I just walked in the door, honey. I'm heading into the kitchen to see her. Could you move out of my way? I want to give her a hug."

"Sure. No problem, Mom. I love a family reunion." She rubbed her hands together, moving to the side but right at her mother's heels.

Danielle would have to make sure the kid's pupils weren't dilated because she was sure acting funny. No way was she this happy to see her sister.

Danielle couldn't help smiling as she entered the kitchen, Shannon's back to her. "Hey, kiddo. We need to talk. You're in trouble."

"That's for sure." Cassie smirked.

"What's wrong with you, Cass?"

Cass shrugged still wearing that shit eating grin. "Nothing at all."

Drug testing for sure. "Shan? Aren't you gonna turn around and give me a hug?" Danielle went to set the wine down on the counter as her oldest daughter turned around. Danielle missed the counter and dropped the bottle. Glass shattered and wine went everywhere. Her mouth dropped open and she shook her head. "Oh, my God."

***

Danielle called an emergency happy hour the night after Shannon came home. Her news was too much to handle on her own. She'd thrown together a Mexican-style quiche and at that moment wished they had tequila, not just wine.

"Pregnant?" Jamie's mouth hung agape just as Danielle's had the night before. If that moment hadn't been surreal, then what was? Her twenty-one-year-old daughter had stood, belly protruding, flashing solemn green eyes that were the only apology. But Jesus Almighty! How was she going to handle this?

Danielle nodded. "Almost seven months, too. The baby is due the beginning of August." She set out a plate of stuffed mushrooms, plopped down on her butter suede sofa, and poured herself her third glass of the decent Cabernet. She was hitting it harder than usual, but she was hosting and definitely not driving, and drinking a third glass of wine and sharing this new chapter of her life with her friends seemed to be the answer—the only answer.

"So she couldn't even consider not having the baby now," Alyssa said. She reached across the glass coffee table for her glass of wine.

"No. This, my friends, is a done deal." Danielle scooped some mushrooms onto her plate. Food along with the wine and friends comforted her a little. Soft jazz played in the background. Danielle's house was a custom five thousand square foot vineyard dream. Unlike Jamie, Danielle had done all the decorating herself and both the inside and outside replicated a Tuscan hideaway.

"She's been pregnant for all this time and never told you?" Kat's eyes widened.

Danielle shook her head. "Not a word. Not one word. I've talked to that kid I don't know how many times over the past several months. I talk to her at least twice a week. Ask her about school, her job, if she has a boyfriend. I don't know why she didn't tell me when she first found out."

"What's she going to do?" Jamie asked. "I mean is she planning on keeping the baby? What about her last year of college?"

Danielle shrugged. "I tried talking to her about it, suggesting adoption might be a good way to go. My God, she's at Yale on scholarship. She's lined up to graduate with honors, and wants to go to law school. Before she left for school, she'd shared with me that it was her dream to become a Supreme Court Justice. This changes everything." She choked back emotion. Alyssa touched her shoulder and smiled sympathetically. Danielle tried to smile back. "I'm sorry. I'm a little in shock. I can't believe that my brainiac of a child could be so fucking stupid as to get herself knocked up."

"Is there a guy? Obviously there is a guy, right?" Jamie asked.

"No. No guy. My valedictorian is pregnant and who's the father? He's some exchange student she met from Italy and he has now, of course, flown the coop." Danielle waved her free hand in the air.

"Ah, an Italian guy," Kat said. "No wonder. Trouble. Regular Romeo, huh?"

"No shit, Dick Tracy." Danielle shot her a dirty look.

"I'm sorry, Danielle. I don't mean to make light of this. It's got to be difficult. Has she been in contact with him?"

"I haven't gotten that far with her yet. Our conversation last night was slightly tense and when I saw her becoming upset, I did the only thing I could do." Her friends all looked at her. "I wrapped my arms around her, and told her that I loved her and that I would support her."

"Wow," Alyssa said in a whisper.

"Where is she right now?" Kat asked.

"Meeting with her dad. You better believe it won't be long before I get a call from him. I'm sure I'll be the one to blame. I'm sure he'll be delighted."

The sarcasm wasn't lost on her friends. The Bastard blamed Danielle for everything that had gone wrong in their marriage, anything that went wrong with their daughters, and especially for the problems he'd recently acquired with the IRS over his business dealings. Blaming her because, he claimed, Danielle hadn't taught him how to run the books. As if she were supposed to sit him down and give him a tutorial on accounting after he'd screwed her over!

Al's *real* big problem was that Danielle had made out in the settlement in a way he hadn't planned on. She'd gotten half of the vines—the best vines. She'd been able to prove that she'd been the brainchild behind Bastillia Wines. Al managed to get the large distribution deals across the country, but it had been Danielle who worked hand in hand with their employees and helped to cultivate wine into art. Al liked to talk the talk and play big man winery owner, but it was Danielle who truly understood wine from the soil on up, and she now had the means and was in a position to prove it.

"Screw Al," Jamie said.

"Not my job anymore." Danielle laughed and so did her friends. The mood lightened a little.

"Do you know what's next with Shannon?" Alyssa set her glass down and leaned back into the sofa.

"She told me that she already scheduled an appointment on Thursday with a doctor out here and planned to deliver the baby here. That's pretty much as far as we've gotten. Right now it's like walking on eggshells with her. I guess I kind of need to let it settle." She sighed. "Enough about my drama. What's going on with you?" She looked at Jamie who sat stunned. "When we talked on the phone the other night it sounded like you made the decision to take Maddie over to check out the riding lessons, right?" More wine and another long sigh. "I can see you all don't want to change the subject, but humor me. I'm tired, frustrated, and don't want to think about my problems right now."

Jamie nodded. "Okay. I did. I called and I'm taking her next weekend. In fact, my sister-in-law called and they, of course, asked if they could have Maddie for the weekend, but I told them no, that we already had plans. Then Susan said that she wanted to take her to riding lessons. I was so happy to be able to come back and tell her that *I* was already taking her to riding lessons." She smiled and smugly crossed her arms in front of her.

"Good," Alyssa said. "Sounds like you're moving forward, keeping your daughter tuned more into you than her aunt and uncle."

"What about you, Kat? Venus still coming to town?" Danielle

asked.

"She's coming all right. Three weeks and my dear beloved mother will be here." Kat emptied her glass, and stood. "Hey, hate to be a buzz kill, but looks like your girls just pulled up."

Danielle stood. "Jeez. They said they'd be home after ten, after everyone went home. It's only nine."

Jamie and Alyssa stood too. "That's okay. I have an early morning meeting," Jamie said. "I have to get Maddie up extra early and take her to morning care."

"I should get going too. I'm a bit tired. I also have some things I need to take care of early tomorrow." Alyssa set her glass down.

"Come on. Stay. The girls won't mind, and you know I want you to stay." More than anything, Danielle was afraid to be alone with Shannon. Then there was Cassie who seemed to be reveling in the fact that her sister had one-upped her on the, *Oh boy, you are in a world of shit* chart. No, Danielle preferred the company of her friends, their wine, and the food to her girls right now. But her pals were already heading to the door with their purses and insisting they needed to leave, obvious that they didn't want to get caught in the crossfire of pregnant daughter and soon-to-be grandmother.

Last night and all day, Danielle had tried to process Shannon's pregnancy; the ramifications, the possible positives, the many negatives. But not once, until that very moment that her best friends were checking out on her had the thought crossed her mind that in less than three months she was going to be a grandmother. Now it did, and suddenly Danielle felt very old and she knew that even if her daughter might be ready for this, which she doubted, she seriously wasn't ready at all.

CHAPTER SEVEN

Jamie

*J*amie left work a half hour earlier than usual to get Maddie from the after-school program and to her second riding lesson, taught by a perky, long legged blonde twenty-five year old. The woman was fantastic with Maddie—soft spoken, easy going, but firm on safety and focus. She was a perfect fit for her little girl. What wasn't so perfect about the riding lessons was the expense. Jamie, already stressing over what to do with Maddie during the summer while she worked, knew that day camps were costly, but leaving her at home with Nora and Dorothy seemed cruel. She'd have to figure it out and make it work, along with the riding lessons.

When she'd inquired about the lessons, she'd spoken to a different young woman who had told her the lessons were thirty-five dollars an hour. But when she'd brought Maddie out for her first lesson last weekend, Gwen told her that it was fifty dollars for the hour. Jamie had been shocked and said something to Gwen about the price difference. Gwen apologized, saying she wished she'd known who had told Jamie this because they'd raised their prices over two weeks ago.

Jamie would normally not press the issue. Maddie wanted the lessons, and Jamie wanted her to have them. Not only because it made her feel like she finally had more control over her child than her in-laws, but because Maddie had fallen hard for horses. For Maddie to fall for anything was a big deal.

Jamie had taken Gwen aside while Maddie brushed down a paint horse named Patches. "But I was told that it was thirty-five, and fifty is a lot more. I'm kind of on a budget." It was a nice way of saying that she was flat-ass broke. She knew if she put a pencil to paper that she'd be in the red every month, and she was. She chose not to pick up a pencil or paper. She'd borrowed money off of credit cards and even had a couple of unsecured loans at high interest rates. It had been difficult getting banks to loan her money after Nate died, and when the economy tanked, things got even tighter. The medical bills piled up and, truth be told, she knew that she and Nate lived a pretty high life before he got sick. A life that included five-star vacations, designer clothes, expensive dinners out, and all sorts of lessons for Maddie, like piano, ballet and tennis—none which ever stuck.

Then Nate had gotten so sick and the insurance hadn't covered the experimental drugs they'd tried. Yes, he'd had life insurance. A half million dollars, which at the time sounded like a lot, but when there are medical bills upwards of six figures and a mortgage to pay and private tuition for Maddie, and now Dorothy to take care of, making ends meet was getting harder each day. Jamie knew she should sell the house, put Maddie in public school, and do what she could to save some cash. Paying for riding lessons did not fall into the saving cash category. But Maddie didn't deserve to have her entire life change because her mom was deep in debt.

Jamie had gone ahead and asked Gwen what she could do about the cost of the lessons.

"You'll have to speak with Tyler. He'll be here next week."

While Maddie attended her second lesson, Jamie put some steel in her backbone and headed to the boss' office to discuss the issue. The ranch was pristine with three large barns, housing rows of stalls in them. The pungent smell of manure wafted through the air combined with hay, soil, and something floral. It might have been neroli orange blossoms or maybe jasmine? She wasn't sure. From what Jamie could see, there were also three large arenas, one with jumps in it. Olive and orange trees were scattered all over the property. A good-sized log home stood in the background with a front porch swing included. Kind of like a Norman Rockwell painting.

Tyler Meeks' office was at the end of the main barn, opposite a large tack room.

Jamie expected to round the corner and walk into the office to find an attractive man. After all, Danielle had mentioned he was a looker. She'd seen plenty of attractive men in her day, but none of them had taken her breath away like Nate had when they'd met. None of them until that very moment when she laid eyes on Tyler Meeks. *Wow. Oh wow.*

Tyler Meeks looked up from the papers on his desk. His hair and skin were sun-kissed and golden, his green eyes were the color of the Mediterranean Sea, and his lips were shaped perfectly with a little bow meeting in the middle. He had a three-day shadow, and Jamie knew that her thoughts were downright ridiculous. Movie stars looked this good, not horse trainers.

And then it hit and it hit hard. Guilt. More guilt. First off, Tyler Meeks was at least ten years younger than she was, and secondly she was a married woman. Technically. Sort of, anyway. Well, she should have been. She wanted to be. Why couldn't Nate be here right now? To watch his little girl ride a horse? To not care if her riding lessons cost them thirty-five dollars or a hundred dollars? And in those strange few seconds looking at Tyler Meeks and preparing to argue about his prices, she felt tears spring to her eyes.

"May I help you?" Tyler asked. He picked up a remote control and turned off the TV in the corner. "Sorry. I like Judge Judy," he quipped.

"Yes. Maybe. I hope so." Jamie swallowed and collected herself. "I'm Jamie Evans." She reached across the desk as Tyler stood and shook her hand. "My daughter Maddie is taking lessons from one of your instructors. Gwen."

"Nice to meet you. Gwen is very good with the youngsters. She's taking my place with the kids right now. I've got my hands full just running the place."

"Yes, Gwen seems to be really great. My daughter is very excited, and she loved her first lesson. She's out there right now getting ready again." She paused, her fingers clasping the band on her purse tightly. People didn't make her nervous. She was an editor-in-chief. She handled people all of the time. But this guy made her nervous.

"Great. I'm sure you and your husband will find that we have a great program here. Our focus is on safety first and developing a real passion for horses."

"I'm not married. My husband passed away." Now why in the world had that come out? She never said stuff like that, especially to strangers.

"I'm sorry." His face reddened a bit.

"No. Please. Thank you." She couldn't sound any more ridiculous if she tried.

"I thought that, well, that's a beautiful ring." He pointed to her hand.

She glanced down at the marquis diamond surrounded with tiny emeralds (her birthstone). Her wedding ring. Jamie knew she'd better get to the point before this situation became any more strained. "I'm here because of the pricing." He raised his eyebrows. "You see I was quoted one price by one of your employees and then when I brought Maddie for her first lesson, I was told it was another price."

Tyler clucked his tongue. "What were you initially told?" He sat back in his chair.

"Thirty-five dollars an hour." She looked down.

"Then that's what it is. If one of my employees told you that, then that's what it is. What did you pay last week?"

"Fifty."

Tyler stood again, reached into his back pocket and took fifteen dollars out of his wallet, handing it to Jamie.

"No. No. It's really not that big of a deal."

"I think I'll be okay without the extra fifteen. Please take it." He walked over and placed the money in her hands. Something terrifying went through her. Something she vaguely remembered as lust. And as she looked from the dollars in her hand up into those sea green eyes, she thought for a second there that he felt what she was feeling.

"Thank you," she said. "I better go watch my daughter." She pointed to the opening of the office, but she didn't move. It was almost as if some force stronger than her own will kept her there in the presence of this illegally gorgeous young man.

"Why don't I walk out with you? I have a horse I need to check on. Mare colicked last night. She's a stoic one. Had the vet out and he oiled her, gave her some Banamine and we walked her for hours."

Jamie had no clue what he was talking about, but it sounded good to her and she nodded with a smile.

"You don't ride, do you?" he asked, glancing sideways at her.

"No. I mean I like horses. I think they're beautiful, and I've ridden, you know on the trails, like when you go on vacation."

Tyler laughed. "Right. You get a poor old nag who gets one rider after the next until she finally breaks down."

Jamie frowned.

"No. I don't mean that what you did was wrong. Lots of folks who go on vacation take those rides. Let me guess. Was it in Hawaii?"

She nodded. "Maui." A distinct memory flashed through her mind of riding up through Haleakala on her honeymoon with Nate, his face golden from the sunlight, almost translucent. He'd looked like an angel. The image of him like that, breathing in the tropical fresh air of the island, looking so peaceful and content, was engraved on her soul. She could never forget that day. Whether or not she rode a poor old nag she had no clue, because all she'd thought about that day was how lucky and happy she was to be married to Nate.

"I've never been there, though I'd like to go some day. Lots of responsibility here and with my parents passed on, and neither of my sisters wanting to deal with this place anymore. So it's all mine." He smiled and dimples creased both cheeks.

Wouldn't you know the man would have dimples too?

"Hey I have an idea. Why don't we saddle up one of the horses and give you a chance to ride a real horse. I mean a real nice horse."

"No, no. I can't do that."

"Why not? I think you'd enjoy it. You can ride Pickles. He's one of my good old boys and won't do anything nasty. Come on. Your daughter is out with Gwen. I can give you a bit of a lesson."

Jamie shook her head. "No. I can only afford Maddie's lesson. And I thought you didn't give lessons any more. That's what you said."

"I won't charge you. And I make a few exceptions. Come on. Give it a try."

"I'm not exactly dressed for it."

Tyler eyed her from the ground up and back again. She felt her face heat up. Why did it feel like this guy was undressing her with his eyes? Did he make moves like this on every woman? What was she? The poor widow that he could now put his smooth cowboy moves on?

"I see what you're saying. First of all, you would need some boots."

She was wearing a pair of clogs because she had not been able to find her tennies that morning.

"The jeans are fine and unless you have some real affinity for not getting that particular T-shirt dirty, then that's okay too. I'm sure one of my sisters or one of the instructors has a pair of boots that'll fit you. Hang on a sec and let me peek in on my mare and see how she's faring."

How could she say no to that kind of enthusiasm? Jamie didn't think Tyler was going to take no for an answer, but she tried one more ploy. "I'd really like to watch my daughter take her lesson."

He stopped walking and turned to her. "You're afraid."

"I am not."

"See it all the time. Stop worrying. Your daughter is in love with the horses already. I'm pretty sure of that. If I know anything, I know that when little girls start begging moms for riding lessons that it's a done deal, and there is no going back. At least not until she hits high school and discovers boys."

"Comforting."

"True, though. I say you ride my horse. I'll give you a short lesson. Then you'll have a bit of an idea as to what Gwen is teaching your daughter. The two of you can have some fun later on talking about it. Who knows? Maybe you'll like it so much, you'll want to do it again.

You're going to have plenty of days out here to watch your little girl ride a horse. Shoot, before you know it she'll be pleading with you to lease or buy her one."

Why couldn't Maddie have picked a sport like soccer? "I guess I'm sold. I'll ride your horse."

"Good." He stopped in front of one of the stalls and opened the door. Inside was a beautiful palomino, all golden with a light blonde mane and tail.

Jamie stood there awed. She had always found horses to be gorgeous. And she had wanted one as a kid at some point. But they'd lived in the suburbs and her mom had no interest in horses—only a fear of them. Jamie lost interest.

She watched as Tyler gently stroked the mare and spoke softly to her. "How you feeling, mare? Better? You gave me a scare. Let me listen to that big old gut of yours." He put his ear to the side of her stomach and listened, then walked to the other side of her and repeated his actions. "Good. Nice gut sounds, and looks like you passed your oil. Good kid." He scratched behind one of her ears.

Something about watching him with that horse shot that lustful feeling straight through Jamie again—all the way down to her toes. She didn't need to be riding his horse. She needed to get out of there and fast. This was supposed to be about Maddie, not gawking after some hot guy who wanted to give her a riding lesson. Twenty minutes later, she found herself up on a bay Quarter horse, walking around one of the arenas on the ranch with Tyler giving her instructions like, "Get your heels down. Sit up straight. Tighten up your right rein, and good job keeping him on the rail." She rode for about forty-five minutes and the longer she rode the horse, the more she realized how much fun she was having. When they were finished, she rode the horse back to the crosstie area to tie him up and followed Tyler's instructions.

"Take your right foot out of the stirrup. Good. Now lean your body over the horse and kick out the left foot. Now push off and slide down."

Instead of sliding down, Jamie tripped and fell right on her butt. Tyler laughed, and she started laughing, too. He held out a hand to her and pulled her back up. "You okay?"

She nodded. "My nickname is obviously not Grace."

"Ah well. You did good. You'll get off him better next time. Your daughter is over helping Gwen rinse off the horse." He pointed to a set of wash racks on the other side of one of the arenas where she could see Maddie spraying off a horse and laughing.

"There will be a next time, right?"

"Oh, no," Jamie said. "I don't know about that. Like I said, I can't really afford it."

He nodded. "Did you like it? If you could afford it, would you do it?"

She stood there for a few seconds thinking about it. "Yes. You know, I think I would. I wanted to ride as a kid and I think it would be fun and good for me too."

"I have an offer. Saturdays I run a horsemanship for the handicapped program. I'm always needing volunteers, and all you have to do is help the kids brush and saddle the horses, and then a team of two to three people lead the horse and kid around."

"I don't know if I could do that."

"I can teach you. It won't take long. I could also knock off a few more dollars from Maddie's lessons."

"You do this for everyone?" She smiled.

"Only the pretty ones." He winked at her.

"Ah." She didn't know how to respond. Was he coming on to her?

"You seem like a nice woman, and it's obvious you've had some rough times. Let me help."

"Pity service."

He sighed. "If you're helping me help some handicapped folks, I don't think that I am pitying you. I believe in helping others. Or are you too proud to accept that?"

She crossed her arms and studied him. He was right. She had no room to be too proud, and helping others *was* a good thing. And if it meant that Maddie could do something she loved a little more often, then who was she to say no?

"When do you want me here to start my training?"

CHAPTER EIGHT

Alyssa

*A*lyssa closed the gallery to prepare for her art classes, taking up the largest area in the three sectioned-off gallery spaces. She covered the paintings and floor with a tarp, just in case.

She set up chairs, easels, and all of the supplies. Alyssa loved the way the rich earthy scent of her oil paints with their acidic overtones assaulted her senses, signaling that call to arms—pick up that paintbrush!

Five people, including Danielle, showed up for the Wednesday evening art class. It was a mixed group with an age range from nineteen to seventy. They were a good group, all interested, and some even showing talent as Alyssa had them do the first sketch—wine or vineyard related—which would later become their first oil.

After a demonstration period and then some questions and answers, the artists went to work. This was Alyssa in her element. She put on some old jazz classics to add ambiance. Snapping her fingers in time to Ella Fitzgerald, she moved around the room, offering advice and guidance.

She stood over Danielle. "I like it. You're pretty good at this."

Danielle looked up at her and smiled. "You think so?" Alyssa nodded. "Thanks."

"You okay?"

"Sure. I'm good," Danielle replied. "Better. I'm doing better."

Alyssa wasn't convinced. Maybe she'd talk to her at dinner. There was a lot on her plate right now, but Alyssa wouldn't push her. If anyone respected privacy, she did. The things that hurt her the most were the ones she was least likely to talk about. The past was gone and it could not be changed, so why bother sharing it anyway? It was easier to shove it aside, try and forget about it, and move on.

Two hours later, the artists put away their supplies, thanked Alyssa, and headed back to their everyday lives. Danielle helped her put chairs and easels away and take down the tarps.

"That was great." Danielle held up her sketch of a wine bottle and a slab of cheese surrounded by grapes. "I needed that. Some time away."

"Good," Alyssa replied. "I'm happy you could make it over. You have some real talent."

"Speaking of talent, you said that you had a new painting you were working on."

"I'm not quite ready to show anyone. It's missing something. I can't tell what. I feel it though. It'll come to me. I promise you'll be the first to see it when I'm ready."

"You artists," Danielle quipped.

"I know. We can be a bit strange about our work. They're like children, I suppose. You want to protect them right?"

"Isn't that the truth." Danielle walked through the gallery, stopping in front of Alyssa's oils of the little boy in the vineyard. "This child, he looks so real. You had to have had a photo or a model to do this."

"No. The pictures are in my head."

"And you've never seen this boy before?"

"No."

"You are truly a talent, my friend." Danielle tucked her dark red hair behind her ears. "Shall we go eat?"

"Sounds good."

Danielle headed for the door, her back to Alyssa who reached out and touched the cheek on the boy in the painting, almost as if saying good night—good night to a ghost.

***

Kat

Kat spotted her friends come in and seated them at the best table in the house. *Christian's* had a different flair than *Sphinx* did. It had class like their place in the city, but cleaner lines. Black and white and Tiffany blue were the primary colors. A fireplace sat in the middle of the restaurant giving off a warm glow during the winter evenings. For the summer months, Kat placed candles inside the hearth. On the walls were black and white photos of Christian in various cooking motifs, some with him and Kat and some with his daughter, Amber. There was one with her boys in it as well.

"Hi, ladies. What can I get you to drink?" Kat asked after her friends sat down in one of the booths.

"What would you recommend?" Alyssa asked.

"For you, I have a great Chardonnay from a local winery owned by a Latino family. Kind of a neat story. Dad started out working in the fields years ago and made his way up the ranks. Now he owns his own winery."

"El Sueño, right?" Danielle asked. "Great family and, yes, the wines are fantastic. Why don't we have a bottle of that?"

"Perfect. And I'll also bring you out a delectable herbed goat cheese and mushroom tart. It's delicious."

"And low cal, too," Alyssa said.

"Of course!" Kat hurried off to get the wine and put the order in for the tart. She'd planned to serve the girls herself if she couldn't join them. It was after eight on a Wednesday and things were slowing down. The scent of garlic and rosemary filled the bustling kitchen as four cooks worked alongside Christian.

"Mushroom tart," she said to her husband who was overseeing his sous chef, Renaldo. He patted him on the back. "I'll get it."

Kat pulled out a chilled bottle of the Chardonnay from the wine cooler and started to head back out into the restaurant.

Christian put a hand on her shoulder and stopped her. "Can I talk to you?" he asked.

She grimaced. That was a tone she hated. "Now?" She held up the bottle of wine.

He nodded. "It'll only take a minute and its been weighing on me all day."

She sighed heavily. "What is it?"

"It's Jeremy," he said.

She knew it. Hours, and occasionally days, would go by without Christian coming to her with some complaint about one or both of her boys, and like tonight, he always picked the most inopportune moments to accost her. It was almost like he waited to attack when her defenses had no choice but to be down. For goodness sakes, she was trying to pour wine for patrons, and now her friends were waiting on her. It had been three days, and she'd held her breath, hoping that they could make it through a week without some squabble about her sons to bubble over. "What now?"

"He had on my socks again."

She eyed the wine, intentionally avoiding her husband's gaze. "He had on your socks again?"

"Yep. I know they were mine too because I put my initials on them, and when I saw him with them on, I asked him to take them off."

"Did he?"

"Yep. But he sort of tossed them into the middle of the floor."

"Uh huh."

"Kat! What are you going to do about this?"

"I guess he needs new socks. I'll get him some."

"No. He needs to respect me and not take my things. And Brian? I had to ask him four times to take out the trash yesterday. Four times."

"He's fourteen."

"But four times?"

"What do you want me to do?"

"Consequences, Kat. Those boys need consequences or they won't get anywhere in life. They won't. You have to give them boundaries and expectations." He crossed his arms.

"I will talk to them, but right now I think we both have jobs to do."

He nodded, seemingly somewhat satisfied.

Kat had learned that blended families were nearly impossible. Marriage to Christian had not been what she thought it would be. The night he proposed—out on a sailboat, with the gourmet food, good wine, and beautiful flowers—it hadn't occurred to her that things might be anything but smooth sailing for the two of them. She hadn't thought that the kids might be a problem.

There was no love lost between the three boys in her life. They weren't ever mean to each other—there was no yelling or anything like that. But from Christian, it was these daily jabs that made her feel like she sucked as a mother, and from the boys it was constant questions as to why Christian was such a jerk to them.

She put on a smile and walked back out to Alyssa and Danielle's table. Opening the wine, Danielle said, "You okay, hon?"

"Perfect. I am absolutely perfect." She poured their wine, maintaining grace and her smile, knowing that if she told everyone else that lie long enough, then she might start to believe it too.

CHAPTER NINE

Danielle

*D*anielle sat next to Shannon in the doctor's waiting room. How surreal and strange to be seated next to your twenty-one-year-old pregnant, unmarried daughter. And yet, why was that so strange after all? Twenty-one-year-old women got pregnant all the time, and many of them were unmarried. But none of those other women were Danielle's daughter.

Shannon didn't want her to come. Danielle practically had to beg to join her. They sat quietly flipping through women's magazines and trying hard not to act tense inside the waiting room filled with pregnant women. All Danielle wanted to do was hold Shannon's hand, make her little again. Start all over. Wouldn't it be great to have a start over button, one you could pull out of your purse when things got screwy, press the button, and viola—take a trip through time and make some changes? But what would she change and how would she change it? So many things. But would the outcome be different? Who knew? It was all silly banter playing in her mind while seated next to her *unmarried twenty-one-year–old pregnant daughter*.

Danielle knew they needed to talk—really talk—about what was happening. Their talks had been fairly benign thus far. Any time Danielle tried to bring up the idea of adoption or contacting the father in Italy, or what Shannon's plan for the future might entail, it turned out the same way—with Shannon either in tears or simply stating that she didn't want to talk about it. For the past few days, Danielle stuck to topics like the wine she was making, and what was happening on *Grey's Anatomy*, and even the weather. Talk about surreal. They'd talked about the weather as if they were strangers, not mother and daughter. How had all this happened? They used to be so close. They talked about everything under the sun. Danielle didn't outwardly admit that she had a favorite child. She didn't. Not really. But the bond between her and her oldest child was special. Unbreakable, so she'd thought. Cassie had always been loud, pushy, obstinate, and rebellious. Not Shannon. She'd been a mommy's girl from day one. They had so much in common, were so open with one another. And now—they talked about the damn weather.

But dammit they did need to talk about it. They really did. This was not going away. There was a baby growing inside of her daughter, and they *had* to talk about it. Maybe today after the doctor's appointment she'd take Shannon to lunch and they could sit down and discuss things like rational adults.

"How did you find this Dr. Fry, honey?"

"I asked for a referral from my doctor back east and he searched around for me and gave me this guy's name. But when I called, they said I'd be seeing a different doctor. I don't know, something about the practice being sold."

"It's good that you've been seeing a doctor regularly."

Shannon looked at her mother as if to say, *do you think I am an idiot?* Just as she opened her mouth to probably say this exact sentiment, her name was called. Danielle stood up to go in with her. Shannon looked back at her. "I'm a big girl now, Mom."

Danielle looked down and bit her lip, forcing back tears. Yes, she was a big girl now, wasn't she? "I know, honey, I really wanted to come in and maybe hear the baby's heart beat."

Shannon paused and then reached for her hand. "I'm sorry, Mom. Come on."

A few moments later, in the patient room with the smell of antiseptic and the temperature set at freezing, Shannon wore the paper gown and thin blanket. Danielle sat in the chair against the wall behind the door, pretending to read an article about holistic health pros and cons.

A knock at the door signaled the doctor's arrival. His back was to Danielle as he entered. He was tall with graying hair. He shook Shannon's hand and introduced himself. He then turned around. Danielle reached out her hand to shake his and as he did so in kind, he caught himself. "Danielle Peters?"

"Mark?"

"You two know each other?" Shannon asked.

Danielle knew she was blushing. "Yes. From high school. I'd heard you became a doctor. But I thought you moved to Washington, D.C."

He nodded. "I did. I've only been back for a few months. Divorce. I bought the practice here from Dr. Fry."

"That's great. Gosh. It's been a long time."

"It's really great to see you."

Shannon cleared her throat.

Mark . . . Dr. Murphy turned to Shannon. "I'm sorry. It's been quite some time since I've seen your mom. You are her mom, right?"

Danielle nodded.

"Hey, I have a great idea. Why don't the two of you go out for coffee and catch up? Right now, I'd kind of like to, you know, get this over with."

He turned from Danielle to Shannon and changed his tone. "Of course. My apologies. So, feeling good? Any problems?"

"No problems. I feel fine," Shannon replied.

"Good. I've gone over your chart and have spoken with your doctor back east, and we agree on the protocol he had going with you."

"Good," Shannon said. "I feel great and on board with the protocol and very sure of what I'm doing. Can we just get things done here? I'm tired."

Danielle glanced at her. She was acting off. It had to be because Danielle was in there with her. She was making her nervous.

"Of course. Let's go ahead and give you an exam, see how things are going."

"You know, I'd like to hear the baby's heart beat, but I think I'll step out for the other stuff," Danielle said. Suddenly she wanted to be as far away from the exam room and Shannon and Mark as possible.

"Sure." Mark took out the Doppler and placed it on Shannon's stomach.

The room filled with the sound of the baby's heartbeat racing along, and it hit Danielle hard. "That's the baby. That's my grand baby."

Shannon took her mother's hand. "Yes, Mom. It is."

Danielle had no idea she would have such a reaction. She brought the palms of her hands to her face, cupping her mouth and nose, her eyes wide. The baby was very, very real. The little heartbeat was echoing through the room, racing, thudding along.

"Sure is, Grandma," Mark said. "Maybe you two want to record it and take it home for your husband?" He looked at Danielle.

"Nah," Shannon said. "Neither one of us is married, and I think my dad has enough *baby* stuff of his own on his plate. His new wife is pregnant *again*."

"Ah. Okay." Mark smiled sheepishly at Danielle.

"You know, I don't think I want to be called Grandma," Danielle said.

"We can discuss that later," Shannon said. "Can you go so he can examine me now?"

Danielle excused herself while Mark finished the exam. She was in the waiting room when Shannon came out. "Dr. Murphy would like to see you for a minute."

"Me? Why?"

"I don't know."

Danielle walked back through the doors. Mark stood around the corner writing out a prescription. He looked over at her and smiled.

"I know this is kind of strange," he said, "and because it is, feel free to say no. Like I said, I've only been back for a few months and it's good to see you, and I was wondering if you *would* have coffee with me? I thought your daughter's idea sounded good. And because we're old friends and everything, I suggested to her that she see my colleague. He's wonderful. Top notch. Dr. Jeffers."

Danielle was speechless.

"I understand if you don't want to. I really do. It is different meeting this way again after all these years."

"I'd love to," Danielle blurted.

Mark's smile grew wider. "Great. That's great." Now he was blushing. "How about next Sunday afternoon? I have to be out of town for almost a week, so…"

"I can't. I have plans. Instead of coffee, would you want to have dinner?" She could not believe she asked him that, but Mark Murphy hadn't changed a whole lot since high school, except for the gray hair and a few lines around his eyes. Her heart raced, and she could hear the blood rushing through her ears.

"Dinner is great. I have a conference to attend that I leave for tomorrow, but I'll be back next Thursday. How does Friday night work for you?" he asked.

"Perfect. Next Friday it is then." She handed him her card with her phone number on it.

"I can get the address off Shannon's chart."

"Okay."

Danielle smiled as she opened the doors to the waiting room.

CHAPTER TEN

Jamie

"Pick up his leg and clean out his hoof. Like this." Tyler picked up the leg of the chestnut colored horse named Popeye and cleaned out the hoof with a pick. He set the hoof down and handed her the pick. "Your turn. Do the other side."

Jamie wrinkled up her nose. She didn't mind brushing the horse, or even spraying him with a mist of fly spray. But she didn't know about picking up the leg of a thousand pound animal and cleaning crap out of his hoof. She wrapped her hands around the lower part of the leg and tugged. The horse did nothing.

"Lean into him a bit," Tyler instructed.

She did. Nothing. She pulled and tugged. "Come on!"

Tyler knelt down and showed her again how to do it. "Easy."

"Easy for you," she said, frustration building. Jamie tried again. The horse continued with his standstill. Jamie stood up. "He doesn't like me."

"That's not it. He doesn't think that way. He might if you'd abused him."

"I haven't."

"Horses are herd animals, and like all herds, there is a pecking order. I hate to tell you, but you're not high up on his list. He's got you buffaloed."

"What do I do about that?"

"Take charge. He isn't convinced that you're in charge." Tyler smiled.

"You think? Of course I'm not in charge. He outweighs me by about eight hundred seventy-five pounds."

"Yes, but your brain is larger than his. He's smart, don't get me wrong. That's a big mistake most people make. They think that horses are big, dumb animals, but that's not even close to true. He's smart enough to know right now that you don't have the confidence to pick up his hoof."

"I have confidence. I'm an editor-in-chief. I am a boss. I'm a mom."
Who was this guy to tell her that she didn't have any confidence?

"I'm not saying that you aren't all those things and more. But
horses sense energy. If something is off with you, then he doesn't
trust you, and he has to trust you before he'll respond to you."

"I'm open to suggestions here."

"Is there something bothering you? Or someone? Some kind of
problem, where you need to stand up to someone?"

"What, are you psychic?" she asked.

"No. But he is." He pointed to Popeye.

"Please."

"Stay with me on this. If you have an issue that requires you to
belly up, then see yourself doing so. Take care of the problem in your
mind, and then try and lift his hoof again."

Jamie sighed. "You're kidding me, right?"

"Nope. Close your eyes and do what I said."

"This is all very strange and sort of New Agey."

"Not at all," he replied. "Do it."

Jamie did as the horse whisperer suggested. She knew the
problem currently on her plate was her brother-in-law and his wife
and their attitude toward Dorothy and her. With her eyes closed,
she ran through a scenario of talking with David and defending
Dorothy, telling him that he needed to help take care of his mother
and not be such a jerk. It did feel good, even if it was all in her head.
When she finished, she opened her eyes and saw Tyler standing
there still, a half smile on his face. "What?" she asked.

"Nothing. Now go ahead and try."

She bent over, took the leg again, and after asking him three
times to pick up his hoof, the horse did.

Tyler applauded. "Good. Now do the other two. When you're
done there, his saddle is the darkest one in the tack room, in the
corner on the middle stand. His pad is lying on top of it. It's navy
blue with black diamonds around it. Can't miss it. I'll be back. Kids

should be arriving soon." He walked away.

He *walked away*. Great. What was she going to do now? Hoof pick in hand and hands on hips, she eyed Popeye. The horse actually appeared to be giving her the once over. Jamie took a look around. There were a handful of teenagers and adults tacking up horses and getting ready for the program children to arrive. She didn't want to look totally helpless and inept, so she went to Popeye's other leg and gave it a tug. To her surprise he lifted it up. Maybe there was something after all to this horse whisperer stuff. After twenty minutes of hoof picking and locating the right saddle, which was not easy to lift and haul around, she began to feel in need of help again. Where was Tyler? He was nowhere in sight so she gave it her best shot and took hold of the unwieldy hunk of leather. It took some serious effort, but she did it. Popeye grunted as it landed on his back.

"Sorry," she said.

Now to figure out how in the world to fasten the thing. There was a long leather strap and then the woven cotton part that Jamie knew was the cinch. She'd seen other people do this. She could do this. Where was Tyler? He was supposed to be helping her. Some help!

"Need some help?" she heard him ask.

She jumped, not hearing him come up behind her. "Yes." She turned around and saw that Tyler was with a boy of about thirteen and someone she assumed was the boy's mom.

"Jamie, this is Wilson and his mother, Petra."

Jamie stuck out her hand. "Sorry, my hand is kind of dirty."

Petra smiled. She was tall with long dark hair pulled back into a single braid, and light brown eyes that were as warm as her smile. "That doesn't bother us." She shook Jamie's hand.

"Jamie. Jamie. That is a nice name," Wilson said, cocking his head to the side. He gave the horse a pat. "This is Popeye, Jamie. Popeye."

"Yes, it is, and I could use some help with Popeye's saddle," Jamie replied.

"Should we help her, Wilson?" Tyler asked wrapping an arm around his shoulders.

"Yes." Wilson nodded while Jamie and Petra stood back from them. Wilson watched intently while Tyler cinched up the saddle, wrapping the latigo strap through and around the leather insert.

"My son is mentally challenged," his mother explained to Jamie. "He's thirteen, but emotionally he's only about five years old. He's a very sweet boy and he loves the horses. I can't tell you how grateful I am for this program and for people like you and Tyler who work with these kids. This is the highlight of Wilson's week. He sees so many doctors and therapists that coming here is a break for him. Our big fear is congenital heart failure, because he has a hole in his heart. But we take it day by day and bringing him here is a joy for both of us. It really is."

Jamie took in what this brave woman told her. She often asked God why these things happened to such good people. She didn't know the answer, and maybe it was as simple as 'that's just life.' Or maybe there was something more to it. Maybe a child like Wilson brought out the best in people. As Tyler lifted the boy up onto the horse, he smiled widely saying, "Look, Mom, I'm a cowboy." For a moment, Jamie knew she was witnessing something powerful and true in Wilson's smile.

"Jamie, come on over to this side," Tyler instructed. Jamie walked around to the right side of the horse. "Now you'll stay to the right of Wilson and help him maintain his balance by holding his legs. I'll lead Popeye around and, since we're low on staff today, Mom is going to get on this side with me and hold the left leg."

For thirty minutes, leading Wilson around on Popeye, Jamie forgot her financial problems, her worries over Dorothy, and how she planned to deal with her brother-in-law and his wife. Her focus was all about making sure Wilson had a good time up on the horse.

After Wilson, there was a little girl named Juliet, and after her, another little boy named Shawn. Three hours of tacking up, leading kids around, and putting horses away, the adrenaline still rushed through Jamie. One of the best parts of the morning was that she could spot Maddie every so often helping out with her teacher, Gwen.

At lunchtime, they all gathered around one of the shady willow trees on the grounds. Maddie was full of her own news. "Mom, I cantered today. After I helped Gwen with the kids, she gave me a lesson on Roadie and I cantered."

"That's wonderful, honey. I can't wait to watch you."

"I wish I could have a horse," Maddie said.

"Some day, babe."

Maddie kissed her on the cheek. "Can I go get a candy bar out of the machine in the tack room?"

"I guess. But don't get used to treats around here."

"You're the best mom ever."

Jamie laid back in the tall grass. Sure, she was saying that now, but from what Jamie had seen from the teenage children her friends had, being "the best" didn't last in your children's eyes. If she was lucky, she had three more years of being "the best" and then there would be that huge downgrade to "the worst." From all appearances, that stage lasted anywhere from four to seven years. Great. She was really looking forward to *that*.

A light breeze blew across the ranch and Jamie daydreamed of horses and children. Her sweet daydreams turned a tad erotic when Tyler waltzed into her thoughts while she dozed. The man had a body and a smile and, oh, those eyes! Why did he have to be so young? Why did he have to be . . . period? Jamie did not want to think about undressing Tyler Meeks or kissing him or doing anything else for that matter.

"Must be a good dream," Tyler said.

Jamie's eyes shot open, and she saw that he was leaning over her. "No. I wasn't dreaming. Nothing. It was about nothing."

"You had a nice smile on your face for nothing."

"Really, I wasn't thinking anything at all."

"Okay." He shrugged and again walked away.

Jamie gritted her teeth. She hated to admit it, but Tyler was getting under her skin.

CHAPTER ELEVEN

Kat

*I*t was a warm Saturday afternoon and for the first time ever, really, Kat felt like she was connecting with her six-year-old step-daughter. Granted, she'd known the little girl for three years now, but Amber's mother, Emily, made sure to label Kat as the scary step-monster as much as she could. The irony was, Emily would drop Amber off on a whim, without notice, claiming she had to fly off to wherever for work. As if her company didn't have a schedule drawn up prior to the day before, or the day of a necessary business trip? What, they would just come to her a few hours before she needed to be at the airport and tell her that she had to go to Timbuktu on business? Please! Kat hadn't fallen off of the turnip truck recently, if ever. She knew that the word *dumbshit* was not engraved across her forehead, but every time Emily called, she and Christian would take Amber.

Kat realized that she should confront the woman about boundaries and schedules. But it really wasn't her place. It was Christian's. The blended family management thing could be a real bitch. Not like the nuclear family didn't come without complications. Marriage alone was difficult—nothing at all like the ideal happily-ever-afters that played out on movie screens. Add children to the marriage, and things tended to get a bit muddier. Take that idea and throw divorces into the mix, remarriages and all the kids involved. The result tended to be dysfunction junction. Ah, yes, the making for a Valium addiction. But Kat didn't pop pills. Sure, she had herself a glass of wine in the evenings (some nights that glass was larger than other nights) while working at the restaurant, and she usually had two or three when with her friends, but she wasn't dependent on any chemical. She'd even given up smoking.

Blended families meant trying to balance it all while walking on a tightrope with fifty-pound weights in each hand. As a mom and wife, Kat loved her whole family, including her step-daughter. But as a woman, Kat found that loving them all and trying to make it work was often a detriment to her sanity. And taking Amber in on a regular basis, without upsetting Christian with a discussion on why Emily needed to have better boundaries, was one of those elements contributing to her mental chaos. And then there were the boys, the Sperm Donor, and Christian's delicate feelings around all of that. Ay, yay, yay. Yes. The balancing act weighed on Kat quite a bit.

Kat held onto Amber's hands as she pulled her around the pool, her little fingernails shining hot pink from the polish they'd painted on earlier, a huge grin spread across her angelic face. Jeremy dove into the deep end, his body tanned and lean from all the working out, while Brian hung out in the Jacuzzi, his longish hair hanging in his eyes, still holding on to the attitude he'd copped that morning—completely insulted that his mother wouldn't even consider buying him the new Apple laptop. And here she'd thought he'd always be sweet and that the proverbial teenage wasteland wouldn't become a part of their relationship. Wishful thinking!

"Can you toss me into the deep end?" Amber asked.

"No, sweetie. You can't swim that strong yet."

"I'll catch her," Jeremy said, his blue eyes shining.

Maybe there was light at the end of the tunnel after all. Did Jeremy really want to play big brother?

Amber beamed. "You will?" Obviously she was as shocked as Kat.

"Yeah, sure! C'mon, Mom, toss her."

"Okay. One, two three!" Kat pumped Amber up out of the water with each count and on three tossed her across to Jeremy. Water splashed all over as he caught her.

Then Brian jumped in from the Jacuzzi, spraying water all over them again. "Hey, I'll catch her, too," he grumbled. At least a grumble was better than the full-on aggrieved attitude.

"Cool," Kat said. "Mind if I take a break for a minute? I'll go make us some sandwiches and grab some sodas." Is this the way normal families worked? If so, Kat could live with it. Too bad Christian wasn't there to see how good the boys could be with Amber, instead of him behaving like they were children with the mark of Satan on them.

"I want turkey and cheese," Jeremy said.

"Me, too," Amber yelled out.

"No cheese," Brian said.

"I know," Kat replied. As if the kid had just picked up the bizarre habit of no cheese. Of course, he'd eaten pizza all day long. But cheese in any other form? Forget it.

She toweled off and walked back to the house, the whole time listening to the kids laughing and playing in the pool. Maybe she should have a pool party. Invite her friends and their kids. Yes. Maybe that was exactly what everyone needed. Brand new pool. Hot summer on the way. A party. Perfect. Maybe she'd even do it while her mother was visiting. Could she invite her dad too, or would that be too awkward? She couldn't really have a party and not invite her father. She'd ask him and see how he felt about it. If he was uncomfortable, then she'd do it when her mom wasn't here.

Peaches, their golden retriever, was on the couch when she opened the French doors to go back inside. The retriever jumped off and sulked away when Kat gave her one of her looks. "You know what, you lazy bum, you and Squeak need to go outside and play. Where is she?" she called the aging Chihuahua, who ambled into the room probably thinking she was going to get a treat. Instead Kat booted them out and went into the kitchen to make lunch.

She'd just finished the last of the sandwiches, grabbed some chips and sodas, and started back outside when both dogs went a little berserk, Squeak with her little yip and Peaches with her low bark. "What the heck?" She opened the back door and caught herself.

"Hey, Kat." It was Perry and some long legged, young blonde. *Typical.*

There stood Kat, hands full of a platter of food in her Land's End bathing suit that was not covering up her cellulite the way she'd hoped the hipster bottoms would. "Hi, Perry. What are you doing here?"

"Can you shut those dogs up? What the hell is wrong with them?"

"They're doing their job." Using her hip, Kat opened the handle on the door and ushered the dogs inside. She must have been a lovely site—her rear end hanging out, balancing food, and an awkward hip movement to get yip and yap in the house. She forced a smile as she turned back around. "Now, why are you here?"

"I'm picking up the boys." He wrapped an arm around the blonde, and ran a hand through his thick, dark hair, his dark brown eyes twinkling with their ever mischievous glint. "This is Beta."

"Hello," the child said with a Swedish accent.

"Hi," Kat replied. "Where's Inga, or Iris, or…"

"Indie," he interrupted.

"Yeah, Indie. Where's she?"

"We broke up."

"Ah," Kat clucked. "Nothing like jumping right back in the saddle, huh? So you're here for the boys, but you're about three hours early."

"I called and left a message for both boys on their cell phones and also on your house phone. Beta and I are going down to Cabo for a few days and our flight leaves tonight, so I can't take the boys to dinner. I'd figure I'd take them to lunch."

"I just made them lunch." She looked down at the sandwiches, "I guess you better refigure."

"I'm sure they'd prefer going out. They're out at the pool?" Not waiting for Kat's reply, he headed that way with the blonde in tow.

Kat tried to keep up with them while also attempting to balance the full load of lunches. "You know, it would have been nice if you'd actually waited and talked to me. We have plans."

Perry shrugged. "Looks to me like you're swimming. Not much in the plans department."

Blonde Beta giggled.

"Wait a minute." She hated when he did this.

"Dad!" It was Brian of course.

"Hey, bud. Hi, Jer."

"Hey, Dad." He didn't have the same enthusiasm at the site of his father that his brother did.

"Toss me again," Amber whined in Brian's arms.

"Nah, our dad's here."

Kat watched as Brian handed Amber to Jeremy and climbed out of the pool to dry off. It was no use even trying to interfere now. The hero had arrived. Brian walked over to him and gave him a high five and a hug. "What's up?"

"Not much. Waz up with you, G?"

The Mister Cool act was so disgusting. Kat could get wanting to be the kid's best pal, but at some point, didn't Perry feel the need to act at least a little parental? Dumb question. The answer was quite obvious.

"Same old same," Brian said. "You know, just kicking it."

"Right on. Right on. Get dried off. I'm taking you guys to lunch. Come on. Go get dressed. You too, Jer. Put the kid down and get out. This is Beta. Say hi."

"Hey," Brian said, in a different tone than he'd used to greet his father. Maybe he was tiring of his dad's girlfriend turnstile after all.

"I can't go, Dad," Jeremy said, still holding on to Amber.

"What do you mean you can't go?" Perry crossed his arms.

Kat looked from her son to her ex-husband.

"I have a friend's birthday party to go to."

"Call them up. You can't go. You're going with me. I drove an hour out here to take you guys to lunch. There'll be other birthdays with friends. Let's do this."

"You can't do that," Kat said.

"Bullshit. The kid is going with me. I haven't seen him for a couple of weeks, and I'm going to be gone for a few days. I want to hang out with him." That glint he'd had in his eyes turned from mischief to venom. Perry always lived up to his reputation as a snake.

Kat stood up tall, nearly dropping the lunch. "Could you please watch your language? And you know what? No. Jer doesn't have to go with you. The plan was for dinner tonight. You changed the plan, Jeremy agreed to dinner, but he has a birthday party to go to. He's not hanging out with you, *G*. You can take Brian for lunch." She made her eyes into little hateful slits. When dealing with a snake, sometimes it took acting like one too.

"Maybe you guys should check your messages sometimes," Perry said.

"Maybe you shouldn't expect to change everyone's schedule to fit your own whenever you feel like it. Have fun in Cabo." She gave Brian a hug. "Have a good lunch, honey."

"Nice pool. Restaurant must be doing well," Perry said.

Kat got the subtlety of the remark. "We're fine. You must be doing okay yourself. Graphic designers are in demand obviously. Cabo isn't exactly cheap, and the boys mentioned you bought a new Porsche." Perry owned his own graphic design firm in San Francisco with many of his contracts coming from major businesses all over the country. Kat had been there when he'd started the firm, and even helped him by doing all of the administrative work. Now he was a success, and she admittedly hated that.

"Let's go, Bri." Brian, the bimbo, and the Sperm Donor walked down the patio steps and headed off to their lunch. "Later, Jer."

Kat stifled a smile. The guy was such a jerk. He had two sons, and he routinely tried to get out of his obligations in supporting them. Sure, he wanted the perks of having the boys, of playing the hero father in front of his girlfriends, but that's where it ended. After that little scene, though, she was sure of one thing. Jeremy was getting as sick of him as Kat was. There was no birthday party that afternoon; Jeremy was free to do as he pleased.

Kat was glad Jeremy saw his father for what he was, but it still made her sad. She turned to see Jeremy pulling Amber around the pool like he had earlier, and although there was this near triumphant feeling knowing that Perry didn't completely win this time, it was tempered by what she understood had to be the effect on Jeremy. She knew what it was like to be abandoned by a parent. But at least in her case, she'd been an adult when it had happened. Jeremy was still a kid, and Kat couldn't help notice a loss of innocence in his eyes as he realized how truly superficial his father's love was.

"Hey, you two. Come get your lunch."

Amber wrapped her arms around Jeremy and said, "I like you. You're fun."

He twirled her around and the water sprayed out from the ends of her feet. "You're okay, too, Monster. I think we'll keep you around." He boosted her onto the steps, and Kat wrapped a towel around her.

"Thank you," Kat said.

"No, thanks, Mom," he replied.

They hung their feet over the side of the pool and ate their lunch. They'd have to talk about what had happened. She wouldn't allow Jeremy to wallow in feelings he probably didn't completely understand. But for now, the three of them would dangle their feet in the water and revel in the fact that, although it was a strange one, they were indeed a family.

CHAPTER TWELVE

Alyssa

Alyssa didn't know why she couldn't tell her friends last week about the letter. She'd even thought of telling Danielle about it over dinner after art class, but she couldn't. Why couldn't she be open like the other three? Who was she kidding? She knew exactly why. Alyssa knew she couldn't tell them because it would mean taking her three pals back to the very beginning, and then they would wonder why she hadn't told them before. The past was so painful, and one of the things she really loved about Jamie, Danielle, and Kat was that they knew when to back off. They weren't friends who tried to pry you open as if you were a closed mollusk with some precious jewel inside. And Alyssa was simply not prepared to be that honest with them, or even with herself.

She dabbed her paintbrush into a rose color and blended it with a deep red hue. Sade played over the sound system in her studio. Coffee brewed, filling the room with its earthy aroma. The space nestled behind the gallery was too small to hold her classes in, but worked fine for her own time at the easel and canvas. The painting she was working on now was taking on a darker tone than the ones she'd already painted of the boy with no name.

It was almost seven. She'd gotten there early, because she hadn't been able to sleep. She'd tossed and turned and thought over the letter that she hadn't responded to.

In a few hours she'd put away her brushes and open the gallery for tourists and the few locals who came by every so often to see if she was carrying anything new. This place was her sanctuary, and a place where honesty dwelled. That was the worst part about having such good friends and not telling them her secrets; the feeling that she was being dishonest with them. They'd shown her their troubled sides, their woes, and she hadn't shown them hers. Look at Jamie and the problems with her brother-in-law, losing Nate, and now having to take care of her mother-in-law, too. Then there was Danielle and everything that was going on with her and her daughter. A pregnancy. A baby. Tough stuff. And Kat. Although she played it up like not much bugged her—her ex, her husband's ex, and all the stuff they dealt with daily with the kids and the restaurant—Alyssa saw through Kat's tough exterior. All of it ate at her. Maybe Kat kept some things quiet like she did?

Alyssa set her brush aside and grabbed the wine glass that she was using as a prop. She placed her hand across the top of the glass and studied the lines in her hands and the light, the peach of her palm that bled into a soft caramel color. She picked her brush back up. She'd already painted the glass on the table in the painting, and now she began to paint a hand—her hand covering the top of it. Before long, hours rushing by, she realized that it was almost ten o'clock and time to put her artwork away to open the gallery up. She sat back for a moment and admired her work. It showed her hand covering a glass of red wine, as another hand reached out for the glass. It was a child's hand. The boy's hand. She wasn't finished with the painting, but she'd started to paint in the little boy's face reflected in the glass. She'd named the painting "Protector."

She took off her smock and washed her hands, then poured herself a third cup of coffee. Time to open. Alyssa walked to the front glass doors and unlocked them. She turned her sign around to read that she was open. The mailman showed up a few minutes later with a certified letter for her to sign. She thanked him and took the letter back into the gallery. The second one now.

How had he found her? Alyssa closed her eyes, memories flooding her, one after the other. The letter in her shaking hands, she read it. How would she handle this? Alyssa had no answers. What she did know was that everything she'd tried to protect, everyone she'd tried to protect, all the lies she'd told and the words she didn't say—none of it mattered now. The truth was about to rain down on her and everyone around her.

CHAPTER THIRTEEN

Kat

*C*hristian came up behind Kat and wrapped his arms around her, nibbling on her neck and then her ear. She squirmed. "Careful. I'm dicing tomatoes." She held up the knife.

"I like it when you're feisty." He took the knife from her hand, set it down on the counter and kissed her hard. Then he twirled her around and said, "Let me help."

"You sure?"

"Yes, I'm sure. What are we making for the girls?"

"Pasta with pancetta, goat cheese, and spinach in a light cream sauce."

"One of my favorites. Simple, but bursting with flavor." He smiled.

When he did, when he really smiled that way like he was truly happy, Kat couldn't help feel that everything was right in the world. His smile took her back to the moment they met, the wine, the dinner, and of course the love-making. These days, though, the lovemaking wasn't often. It was rare that all three kids would be out of the house and time would present itself—time and no resentments. That morning, there had been no kids around. And after a mimosa brunch with more champagne than orange juice, a little flirtation, the realization that all the kids were gone--one thing led to another and before long they spent some time kissing, fondling, loving, and definitely not resenting. And, in the aftermath, the resentments tended to stay at bay as well. Even later in the kitchen, while prepping—no resentments. The orgasms alone meant that they would have at least twenty-four hours of peace between them.

And then . . .

"Emily called me yesterday."

Whenever Christian mentioned his ex's name, the hairs on the back of Kat's neck stood on end as a warning signal. Warning! Warning! Duck and cover! "Uh, huh." This was Kat's typical response when Christian mentioned Emily.

"She and Baron are getting married." He continued dicing tomatoes.

"That's great. Maybe she'll mellow out on us a little."

"They're moving to the city."

"San Francisco?"

He nodded.

"That's only an hour away. No big deal, right? We'll still have Amber on the weekends and most holidays."

He stopped dicing. "Emily wanted to know if Amber could come and live with us."

"What? Full time?"

"Would that be a problem?"

Kat shook her head in disbelief. "Wait a minute. Your ex-wife wants to give her child up for most of the time? What kind of mother does that?"

"She's pregnant."

"How convenient. What, so just because you get pregnant with a new man's kid, you give the old one up to the ex-husband and his wife?"

"We have two kids here already. I don't see the problem."

"My kids aren't the point. The point is that Emily uses us. She uses Amber too. Despite having bad-mouthed me to Amber for the last three years, she just dumps her on us whenever she feels like it. The other day was the first time I finally felt that Amber and I had a connection. I mean, the poor kid thinks I am the wicked witch of everywhere, not just the east. And now *Emily* expects me to come in and do the hard work that she doesn't want to do? Even though she thinks I am so horrible, she wants me to do the job and you don't have the guts to at least tell her that. Call her to the table, Christian. She has used us time and again and made certain that we never have any time alone together."

"As if your ex and your sons don't do a good job of that themselves."

Kat didn't have a come back. This was their problem. Neither one knew how to edit, how to not say every little thing they felt. If they weren't saying exactly what they thought and felt, then they were working hard to tuck it in a neat corner and pray they could keep it there. Invariably they couldn't. Thus, resentment.

Kat went to the refrigerator and took out the spinach. "I can finish this."

Christian set down the knife and looked at her. "You're going to play it this way then."

"I'm not playing anything. *You. We* are being played."

He walked out of the kitchen and yelled back, "I'm going to the restaurant."

"You do that," she mumbled, trying to keep herself from crying. She nicked her thumb good with the knife while chopping the spinach, and that's all it took to bring on the water works. "Damn!" she whispered loudly, knowing that Christian was still in the house and that she didn't want him to see her cry. Never let them see you cry, right? Why did they play this stupid game with one another? Their anger wasn't about each other. Not really.

She heard the garage door close and the sound of the engine as he backed out. She sighed heavily and went over to her iPod and put on some Pearl Jam. For some reason, it always made her feel better, and she didn't have time to sulk. The girls would be over shortly. She needed to put on some makeup and appear together, even though inside she felt like she was completely falling apart.

***

"I think I'm a manic or bi-polar or something like that," Kat said. Danielle, Alyssa and Jamie looked at her, wearing various expressions of either amusement or disbelief. "No, really, I think so. I can be depressed all week about this and that, and then I plug in my iPod and dance around the house while I'm cleaning or fixing a meal, listening to 'Better Man.' Even after I've had a major fight with Christian, all of a sudden I feel good, even great."

"'Better Man?'" Danielle asked.

"By Pearl Jam," Jamie answered.

"Oh," both Danielle and Alyssa mouthed.

"Yeah, so 'Better Man,' dancing like a lunatic, like a chick in college on Ecstasy. Then the next song right after that is 'Don't Give Up' by Peter Gabriel. You'd think I would have set my iPod so that all my 'up' tunes would play and not be mixed in with my downer tunes. When Peter Gabriel starts belting out lyrics I start bawling like a baby, so I have to turn it back to 'Better Man' to feel better."

"Can I ask you something?" Alyssa said.

"Yes."

"What is it about 'Better Man' that makes you feel better?"

"Maybe you're menopausal," Danielle said.

"I'm only forty. Don't you think that's kind of young?"

"You could be peri-menopausal," Jamie said.

Kat frowned and looked at Alyssa. "I don't know why the song makes me feel better. Maybe it's the music, maybe it's Eddie Vedder's voice, maybe the lyrics. I really don't know."

Danielle reached across the picnic table for Kat's hand. They were sitting in Kat's backyard, facing the swimming pool, the waterfall splashing into the pool, the odor of chlorine filling the air. "What's going on, Kat? This isn't about a song, and I don't think any of us believe you're manic."

That's when the waterworks really started and they didn't stop for several minutes. By the time they did, her three friends had scooted in closer. Danielle still held her hand. Jamie had an arm around her and she leaned her head on Alyssa.

Kat choked back a sob and sighed. "I'm sorry. I'm really sorry. I'm being ridiculous. Maybe it is just menopause."

"Kat? What's going on?" Danielle asked.

She sighed heavily and then let it all spill. "It's everything. It's me. It's Christian. The boys. Their dad. Emily and Amber. Sometimes it's all so exhausting. You know, Jeremy is seeing a counselor now. I took him last week after the Sperm Donor came by with his latest girlfriend and Jeremy didn't want to go with him. He lied, saying that he had a birthday party to go to, and I covered for him. Then we talked and he told me that he is so afraid of turning out like his dad—of using women and being a liar. He said that at times he's even thought about killing himself because the last person in the world he wants to wind up like is his father."

"Oh no!" Danielle said. "No, honey, you know he doesn't mean that. I mean about the killing himself. He's a teenager. They go through this stuff."

Kat shook her head. "No. No. I don't think he would ever do that, but obviously he needs to talk to someone. For him to tell me this and tell me he feels that depressed is huge. I had to help him. The counselor did say he was depressed and wants to put him on anti-depressants. I don't know, though. I don't know how I feel about them." She wiped her face with the back of her hand.

"They worked for me," Alyssa said.

They all turned to her.

She nodded. "I've taken them in the past. They do really help. Don't discount them yet. Some people do need them, and probably in Jeremy's case, it's temporary. As he finds his way into adulthood and discovers that he is nothing like his dad, but his own person, then it's likely he can come off of them. How does he feel about taking them?"

"He says he'll do whatever I want," Kat replied. "We're pretty close. For a few years there, it was tough, but now, as he's heading into his senior year, there's been a change and we've grown close again. He trusts me, I think. He doesn't have that with anyone else."

"What about Christian? What kind of role does he play? Can the boys talk to him about things?" Jamie asked.

Kat laughed sarcastically. "No. Christian's relationship with the boys is strange. I call Christian's issues with the boys the cave man syndrome. You know, he don't look like me, talk like me, walk like me—he no part of me. He part of Sperm Donor."

Alyssa shook her head. "That is a pretty antiquated, silly way to think. You really believe that's how he feels?"

"Yes I do. I know it sounds stupid, but the real deal is that the boys and Christian don't have much in common—nothing really. Christian grew up an outdoorsman. His grandfather taught him to hunt. His father taught him how to build things. His uncle taught him how to fight. Christian could probably win on *Survivor*. I keep telling him to try out. Guy can take some twine and a paper clip and he'd figure out how to feed a clan."

"Just because he can feed a clan doesn't mean he can handle a family," Jamie said.

"What can I say?" Kat said. "He makes me laugh. I mean really laugh, and you all know it takes a lot to make me laugh." She smiled.

"But what about your boys, Kat?" Danielle asked. "Does he make them laugh? Does he make them happy? You three were a package deal. Christian knew that."

"Yeah. I know. Guess I failed to think it all through before we got married. When it comes to the boys, it doesn't work. He doesn't get them at all, and they don't get him at all. For as much a caveman as Christian is, my boys are of the new era, the new age—they're videoettes. I gotta take the blame for helping them to achieve techno guru status. I haven't always been the best at setting rules."

"Oh for God's sakes, Kat. I have lots of friends with teenage boys, and you're not the only one battling the video game addiction. You can't put all that on your shoulders. They're good kids, right? They get good grades, and I know Brian plays tennis, doesn't he?" Danielle let go of her hand.

"He does."

"And isn't Jeremy in wrestling and on the debate team at school?" Jamie chimed in.

"Yes. He took second at the state championships last year. He says next year he wants to join the water polo team."

"Then I'm sorry, but Christian needs to get a grip here. This isn't so much about you. Time for your big boy to grow up and stop sulking that the boys belong to another man. That's just bullshit to deal with it. He's acting like a spoiled brat. Tell him to find something he can do with the boys. At the least suggest they have a movie night. He married into this family, now he needs to take the helm." Danielle's neck reddened. "Seriously, you are not a referee, or a babysitter. You are a wife and a mother, and a friend, and a sommelier, and we love you, and your husband needs to get with the program."

Kat nodded. "I know. At times I think Christian wants to be a dad to them, but then he gets all weird because Brian is so close to his dad, so he backs off."

Danielle snapped. "Look at me." Kat took her eyes off her wine glass. "Stop making excuses for Christian. I did it for Al for years and look where that got my marriage. You've got to tell him, hon, you've got to tell him to step up."

No one said anything for a minute. Jamie broke the silence. "I think Danielle's right."

"Me, too," Alyssa said. "I don't think he needs to try and take over and play Dad with the boys. Sure, if he'd been around since they were young, but they were what, eleven and thirteen when you got married?" Kat nodded. "Being daddy is out of the question, but he *can* be a friend to them even if they have nothing in common."

Kat wiped away angry tears. Her friends were being honest, but that didn't mean their words didn't hurt. "I miss what we used to have. It was fun and easy. Well, maybe it was never easy, but at least we had fun. And now I feel duped, because when we first dated, Christian used to take the boys to ball games and to the restaurant and the city and the park. They did have good times together."

"What do you think happened?" Alyssa asked.

Kat shrugged. "I don't know. Maybe we both got complacent. Maybe we all got too busy. We opened the restaurant out here. We moved with him from Oakland to Napa. That was a big change for the boys." Kat twirled her empty wine glass.

"I'm not going to say it again, my friend. Last time you'll hear it from me, but stop making excuses. Talk to your husband." Danielle poured more wine for everyone.

"We do have a lot to talk about. On top of it all, when we moved out here, Christian's ex, Emily, followed us. I think at the time she did it to get under our skin and it worked. But now, Emily is moving back into the city because she's pregnant and getting married."

"How is Christian taking it? You guys won't see Amber as often, will you?" Jamie asked.

"Just the opposite. Emily wants us to have Amber for the week, and she'll take her on the weekends."

"What?" Danielle said. Boy did she wish she could kick Christian in the ass. Her friend didn't deserve what he was dishing out.

"Yes. I learned this a couple of hours ago, thus the big fight and "Better Man.""

"Oh," they all said in unison.

"What are you going to do?" Alyssa asked.

"What can I do? He's my husband. She's his daughter, and as weird as it can be around here with all the family blending that goes on, I don't think I have a choice."

"You have choices," Danielle said. "Maybe ask Christian to get his own place for awhile and then he can come back home when he's all grown up. That's what I'd do."

"Really? That's not an option. Not at all. I see where you're going here, and yes I agree I need to have a talk with my husband. And yes, I also agree he acts like a petulant child when it comes to my boys, but Danielle you've been married and divorced. You know the pain that comes with it. I've already been through it once before, and this time I promised myself that before I headed down that path again that I would do everything possible to make my marriage work. It may not be ideal. But what marriage is? No matter what the situation is around here, I love my children and I love my husband, and I will do whatever the hell it takes to make it work. So back off."

Danielle sucked in a pocket of air. "I'm sorry," she said quietly. "I was only trying to help."

Kat closed her eyes. "I'm sorry, too. And I know. I know how much you care and want the best for me, and I love you for it. I really do, but I think this is one of those times when I have to sort it out on my own time."

"I think I want more wine," Jamie said. "Um, like a bottle. Yeah. A bottle for each of us."

"Works for me," Alyssa said.

Kat and Danielle looked at each other and started laughing. Jamie and Alyssa, wide-eyed, followed suit, grateful things hadn't completely blown up between their friends. After a few minutes of their laughter with the tension dissipating, Kat finally said, "I *did* always want a little girl. It won't be that much harder, right?"

"Not until she gets her period and turns into a teenager. Then she'll go all ape shit on you and that's when you can send her back to her mother. Even her dad will want that," Danielle said.

"Speaking of daughters, how is Shannon?" Jamie asked, wanting to shift the focus a little bit. She sensed Kat's exhaustion.

"Big. Very big and grumpy and still not talking a lot. It drives me crazy, but what can I do? We need to have a heart-to-heart. I don't know what to think. Maybe she isn't ready to talk, but she better get ready soon because she gets bigger every day. I have to tell you something kind of good though. I have a date."

"What?" Kat said.

Danielle told them all about running into Mark again.

"You're going on a date with your daughter's gynecologist?" Alyssa laughed. "There must be some law against that."

"Yeah! You think?" Jamie chimed in.

"Funny. Ha, ha. *No.* He referred Shannon to his colleague. And it's only a dinner date with an old friend."

"How much of an old friend?" Kat asked. "I mean how much of a friend was he?"

Danielle knew she was blushing. "You know me too well."

"There's this sparkle in your eye. That's all," Kat replied.

"He was my first."

"Your first?" Jamie asked.

"Yes. You know. Sex."

"Oh. *Oh.* Interesting." Jamie heaped another pile of pasta onto her plate.

"This is more than interesting. This is juicy. Do tell. Is he good looking?" Alyssa asked.

Danielle smiled and closed her eyes for a second. "Yes, he's attractive." She nodded. "Very. He is really handsome."

"You got the butterflies, didn't you?" Kat asked.

Danielle bit her lip and nodded. "I did. I do right now just talking about him."

Jamie clapped her hands, Kat laughed, and Alyssa pointed at her and said, "You go girl."

"It's kind of strange." Danielle twirled her pasta around with her fork.

"No, it's good," Kat said. "Really, really good for you."

"Speaking of good looking men, you're taking Maddie to riding lessons, aren't you?" Danielle looked at Jamie.

She nodded.

"Well?" Danielle motioned her to continue. "Have you met Tyler?"

She nodded again.

"Look at her." Kat pointed at her. "Cat got your tongue?"

"Yes, he is a nice looking *young* man."

"That's all she's going to give us? 'Yes he's nice looking.' Notice I left out the 'young' word. Jamie, you aren't no grandma," Alyssa said.

"Hey," Danielle piped in. "Ouch. Nana-to-be here."

"Yeah well, you don't count. You're like the freak of nature who found the fountain of youth," Kat commented.

"Whatever. You don't have to tiptoe around it," Danielle replied. "Back to Jamie and the cowboy. I think there is more to it than our blonde bombshell does tell. Dish, Blondie."

Jamie giggled.

"She's giggling," Alyssa said. "Oh my God. She's giggling."

"I rode his horse."

"What? You rode his horse? Is that a euphemism for something?" Danielle teased.

"Not even. He talked me into riding his horse while Maddie had a lesson, and I had fun. I liked it. And I volunteered for the Horsemanship for Handicapped program that he runs on Saturdays. Then I rode his horse again. He's giving me riding lessons once a week."

"Do I smell romance in the air?" Danielle asked. "A little passion? A little heat? Some lust." She rubbed her hands together.

"No. Please. I rode his horse. *Twice*. That was it. That's all there is to it."

"Maybe ride him," Kat said.

"Kat!" They all looked at her.

Jamie frowned. "You are all so impossible. Ride him. Jeez." She shook her head and swallowed the rest of her wine, and then she couldn't help herself but started giggling again.

"You should think about it at least. I mean if just thinking about doing it with him, makes you giggle like a girl, hmmm . . . what it might be like. You know you're thinking about it." Kat sliced into the peach pie she'd baked that morning. "Dessert? Coffee? Think about it, J. You deserve some fun."

"Leave me alone and give me some of that pie," Jamie replied.

They all opted for the pie and some decaf. Picking up their plates, they followed Kat into the kitchen. "I think we're quite a crew. Look at us. I'm getting another child, Danielle is dating her daughter's OB-GYN . . ."

"Hey, I am not. I explained already."

"Uh, huh, and he was the one who got you naked at sixteen. Very tantalizing, and now Jamie is riding horses and lusting after the cowboy."

"Kat." Jamie rolled her eyes and rinsed her plate.

"Sorry. I'll stop." She smiled wickedly. "For now. What about you, Alyssa? And don't tell us there's nothing to report. I know you have a life. We're your friends. Spill the beans. Give us the goods.

Tell-all time. You must have a secret lover, or you robbed a bank. Something."

"I do have something." Everyone looked thoughtfully at her, all stopping whatever they were busily doing in the kitchen. Until she saw the looks on their faces, she didn't actually believe she'd said the words aloud: "I have a child. A son. He's eighteen. His name is Ian."

***

WINE LOVER'S MAGAZINE
When Life gets Crazy...
By
Jamie Evans

Life is like a roller coaster. There are ups and downs and twists and turns. Things come at us from every corner, every direction. Just when you begin to think that life is predictable, you can be thrown a curve ball and things get crazy. It seems in the past month, our Happy Hour discussions have tended to be about life's never-ending rollercoaster ride. When the ride dips low and then chugs up hill, it's not easy. It's saying, "No," when you want to say, "Yes," or saying "Yes," when maybe you should say, "No." It would be nice if the coaster had one long stretch of straight ahead and at an easy pace.

Alyssa, Kat, Danielle, and I are on that coaster that does loopdy-loops, from aging parents to surly teenagers, blended families and new families. Not to mention that romantic possibilities for at least one of us looks to be on the horizon.

One thing that I know for certain is that when life gets crazy, the best way I can think of to handle it all is by getting together with friends, sharing a bottle of syrah, and piling high a plate of pasta with goat cheese, spinach and pancetta in a light cream sauce. It's like stepping off the uncontrollable ride for a few hours and taking a deep breath. Check out the pasta recipe straight from Kat's kitchen in this month's issue. Cheers!

Jamie Evans
Editor-In-Chief

CHAPTER FOURTEEN

Alyssa

Alyssa steadied her hands by taking hold of the water glass in front of her. She'd arrived at the restaurant twenty minutes early. She'd gotten ready two hours earlier. Did she have too much makeup on? Was her dress conservative enough? Motherly? It was at least ninety degrees outside. She'd finally decided on a light teal colored summer dress with a scoop neck.

The restaurant she'd chosen, Hurley's in Yountville, was neither fancy nor underrated. It was simple, elegant, and served excellent food.

When she'd told her friends about her son, she'd felt such relief.

After reading the letter, she phoned the number listed in it. When she heard the young man's voice for the first time—her son's—she'd instantly been awash with regret. After agreeing to meet with Ian this week, she'd gotten off the phone and closed the shop. For the rest of the day, she didn't answer the phone, afraid of who might be on the other end this time, and she worked late into the night on the painting—*Protected*. She had so many questions for Ian and one of them was, had he felt protected growing up? But how could she ask him that, and if he gave her an answer other than yes, how would she react to that?

Alyssa recognized him the moment he walked through the door. She gasped. He was built like her father—tall and lean—even a bit too thin. His eyes were a deep hazel color like her own, his skin darker than hers. She felt a confusing mix of excitement, relief, and joy that were combined with fear, sadness, and regret. She grabbed onto her chair to steady herself.

He walked directly over to her. "Alyssa?" His voice was deep and his handshake firm.

"Ian?"

He nodded and smiled. "Hi."

"Hi." There weren't hugs and tears, but a soft hello and smile were a good start as far as she was concerned.

"How was your flight and drive? Did you have any problems?" she asked, knowing he'd driven a rental car out to the wine country. She'd suggested picking him up, and had wanted to, but Ian hesitated. Alyssa decided that since this was their first meeting together, she would allow him to call all the shots.

"Good. The car is nice. It's a hybrid Camry with a GPS system. My dad wanted to make sure I didn't get lost. I've had my license over a year now, but he was carrying on at me before I left about not driving over the speed limit, and you know, come to a complete stop at the stop signs. All that." He laughed again—a nice hardy laugh. "And he wanted to come with me. I begged him to let me go by myself. I can't believe he actually did. It took some convincing. Flight was good. Easy, fast."

Alyssa immediately liked this kid. The mention of his dad though, put an even deeper hole in her center. "That's what dads do, you know. They have to watch out for you."

"Yeah, and my dad worries a lot about me."

The waitress came by and asked if they'd like something to drink. Ian ordered an iced tea and so did Alyssa. She watched as he sweetened it with two sugars, exactly how she took her own tea. "How long have you been looking for me?" she asked.

"Not long. My dad actually found you some time ago, I guess. He thought maybe I'd want to meet you someday. My parents always told me I was adopted. Actually I come from a really big family. There are seven of us and five of us are adopted. You could say we're the original Brangelina family. Except none of us look like Angelina Jolie or Brad Pitt." He laughed again.

Alyssa liked the fact that the kid had a sense of humor. "That must be kind of neat. A big family." It made Alyssa happy to know that he'd been raised in a large family. She had a half brother from her dad's first marriage, but they'd never been close, and he was about twelve years older than she was, so she never spent much time with him growing up. He lived in Michigan now and they saw each other during occasional family gatherings. He'd never known about her pregnancy. Actually, none of her family had. Her parents had been in Tuscany that year with her grandparents while she was at college. They'd never understood why she'd switched schools the following year, but she'd convinced them it was because she thought she could do better at NYU and wanted to go into journalism. "How do you like it, being in such a large family?"

He smiled again, warm and goofy and youthful. "You know, it's got some good things about it and some not so good. We don't have a mansion, so we fight a lot over bathrooms and food and you name it, but there is a lot of love. After my mom died, it was good that we all had each other."

Alyssa nearly choked on her tea. "Your mother passed away?"

His eyes watered and it was obvious he was fighting the emotion. "Almost four years ago. Drunk driver."

"That's awful. I'm so sorry, Ian." Alyssa brought her hand up to her mouth.

"Thank you. It was awful, but Mom was a very special lady and, even though we miss her, she'd be really mad at us if we sat around sulking about her."

The revelation that Ian's mother had been killed placed even more guilt on Alyssa. In some roundabout way, she felt responsible for the pain that he had suffered.

The waitress came by again and asked them if they were ready to order. Neither had even opened the menu. They briefly scanned it, and both opted for the Kobe beef cheeseburgers. When the waitress left, Alyssa asked, "And how does your dad feel about you meeting me?"

He twirled his straw in his glass, and took a minute before answering. "He wanted me to. He said that I needed to. I had to. Like I said, he had already located you through public records."

She waited for him to elaborate, but when he didn't, she replied. "Good. It sounds like you get a lot of support. That's really good." Ian came across as an honest, gentle kid. Alyssa couldn't help but like him. Even more than that, she wanted to take him in her arms and comfort him when he'd told her about his mother's death. She wanted to tell him that she wished she'd been there when he was one, two, three, twelve—all of it. But it was so very obvious to her that his parents had done a wonderful job raising him and at least one of Alyssa's questions had been answered: she knew that her son had felt protected growing up. The heavy weight she'd carried around for all of that time finally began to ease. Even breathing felt lighter.

"I'm glad you decided to find me." The waitress placed their burgers in front of them. "Well, you came all of this way. I am sure you have a lot of questions for me."

He set down his burger. "I do, but I'm not even sure what they are right now. I mean, I had some in my head while getting here and then you know, now I meet you, and it's kind of changed, and I'm not sure what to ask."

"What changed? I'm not sure that I understand."

He took a drink from his tea and cocked his head to the side, with his palm resting on his chin. "This is gonna sound weird but, even though I wanted to meet you, I also really wanted to not like you." He sighed. "I'm sorry if I'm blunt, but my mom always told me to be honest. She kind of put the fear of God in all of us. And now I kinda feel like she's always watching me, keeping me straight." He laughed.

"As they say, honesty is the best policy."

"I don't know if you can understand, but I thought if I met you and didn't like you, then it would be this huge validation for my parents, especially my mom. I don't know how to describe this and the only thing I can think of, which isn't right at all, is that it's almost like cheating. By meeting you and liking you and finding out that you're not some horrible lady, I feel like I'm cheating on my mom." He cast his eyes away from her.

"That makes a lot of sense. But I don't think liking me invalidates who your parents are to you and what your mom means to you. She sounds like a wonderful woman. Like she was an amazing mother."

"She was awesome." He lit up and for some time told her all about his mom. Louise Thomas did sound like a great woman, and Alyssa wished she'd had the privilege of knowing the lady who'd helped raise Ian.

Over the next several hours, Alyssa and Ian got to know each other a bit better. Alyssa took him to her studio. They drove over to Sonoma Square about thirty minutes away and had coffee and dessert. She learned about his four brothers and three sisters who were all from various backgrounds. Two of them were even from different countries. One brother was from Mexico and one sister from Indonesia. They truly did sound like the original Brangelina clan. He told her about his first year of college at UCLA and his interest in majoring in film. He also told her about some of his friends, some girlfriends, sports he enjoyed. All in all, Ian had a pretty normal life, and Alyssa was thankful.

He also never once asked her about his biological father and what had happened. He told her that his parents had said that she'd given him up for adoption because she'd been too young and not financially equipped to raise him. Alyssa agreed that was true. This was what she'd told the adoption agency, and she'd chosen not to meet Ian's adoptive parents.

Ian followed Alyssa back to her house that evening, where she made her best fried chicken, mashed potatoes, and a fruit salad for him. He ate every bite, and the hole in Alyssa's heart began to sew itself up. "You're staying at a hotel?" Alyssa asked.

"Yes. The Best Western. My dad made the reservation. I have to call him as soon as I get there."

"Why don't you stay here with me? I have room."

He nodded. "Maybe I could. I should call my dad and see what he thinks."

Alyssa wanted to remind him that he was almost nineteen and he didn't need his father's permission. Throughout the day, Ian had brought up his dad quite a bit, and Alyssa was feeling uneasy about

Ian's adoptive father and wondered if he might be more overbearing than protective. Worries resonated in the back of her mind, and she tried to ease them by reminding herself that Ian had grown up happy and healthy and that Ian's father's reactions to meeting her was normal. "Sure. I'll rinse the dishes, and I'll have some Chunky Monkey."

"Yeah! My favorite. You know that Beastie Boys song?"

"'Brass Monkey?'" Alyssa said.

Then in unison, they sang, "That chunky monkey." Ian pointed at Alyssa who cracked up.

"You like the *Beasties*? Cool. Know what my favorite movie is?"

"What?" she asked.

"You'll never guess, cause it's so random."

"Try me," she replied.

Ian turned around, his back to her and then flipped back toward her, chin ducked, lips puckered and eyes at half-mast. She slapped her knees. "Uh uh. No way! *Zoolander*!"

"You're good."

"What's not to love about Ben Stiller?"

"Seriously," he replied. "Besides Jack Black, he's probably the funniest white guy around."

"I think I would agree with you. Now, go call your dad, and I'll get the dishes. Afterwards, I'll see if you can guess my favorites."

"Deal," Ian replied.

While in the kitchen rinsing the dishes, Alyssa could hear Ian's voice drop as he spoke to his father. She didn't want to eavesdrop, but sensed that something wasn't quite right. She leaned against the wall closest to her small den where he'd gone in to make the call. "No, Dad, I haven't told her yet. No. You don't need to fly up here. I can do this. No. She's super nice. Yes. I like her. She's a good lady."

Alyssa sighed. What was it he needed to tell her? What was Ian's dad so concerned about?

"Okay. I will. Yes. Okay, Dad. I know. I know you're worried. I feel fine. I really do. I'm good. I'm a little tired. Yes, I'll call you back.

I love you, too."

Alyssa hustled back into the kitchen.

Ian came in a minute later. "My dad says that if it's okay with you, then I can stay."

"Good, it's a done deal. Here's your ice cream. Want some hot fudge on it? I already put it in the microwave."

"Sure."

She got the fudge out of the oven and poured some on their ice cream. They took their dessert and sat down on the couch in front of the TV. "Your family is good?"

"Yes." He'd grown quiet. "Alyssa, I have to tell you something."

"Okay." She felt nauseous.

"I got sick a few years ago, before my mom died."

"Sick?"

He nodded. "Yeah. Real sick, actually. I had cancer. Leukemia. Then it went into remission."

"Oh." It was difficult to find the right words to say as a mixture of emotions began running through her. "It's good though that it's in remission, right? That's good, right?" The feeling in her gut told her this was not good. He didn't say anything and the reality of the silence hit her. "It's back. Isn't it? Is that what you're telling me?"

He nodded. "Yes. I found out two weeks ago, and they wanted to start chemo immediately. But I needed to contact you first."

"I'm so glad you did, but the leukemia. Tell me about this." She clasped her hands together to keep him from noticing that they were shaking. Her body from the inside shook all over as if a freeze was coursing through her.

He nodded. "This is going to sound bad, and I don't know how to make it come out right. I did want to meet you and I am happy that you are so great, but I had to find you." He sighed. "My doctor says that I need a bone marrow donation and he says that I have the best chance for a match through a relative—especially a sibling—and I totally understand if you don't want to be tested, and I wouldn't blame you. I'm sorry to spring this on you. I didn't know what else to do and my dad wanted to come but I had to do this by myself. Do you have any other children? Could you be tested?" His words poured out in a rush.

Alyssa took his hand, shoved away her own fear at the sight of his. She quickly realized that Ian needed someone strong to lean on in that moment, and she was his only option. "Hey, hey. Okay. It's gonna be okay. I don't have other children. I don't, but of course I'll be tested. Absolutely."

Ian—her son—wrapped his arms around her. She held him tight and something clicked so strong inside her in that moment, something she'd never felt before. A fierce need to rescue, save, *protect. To protect* this boy.

Her boy.

CHAPTER FIFTEEN

Kat

It was a two-for-one Wednesday. Kat was picking up her mother from the airport at one o'clock, and Emily was dropping Amber off that evening. Kat wasn't entirely sure how she'd get through the day, but as with everything that went on in her life, she'd make it. It wasn't that Kat didn't love her mother, but the mother she had today was not the mother of yesteryear. It was the mom of her childhood that she missed and longed for.

Kat's mom had been the Brownie troop leader for both her and her younger sister, Tammy. She was the room parent, the field trip driver, and the stay-at-home mom who made scraped knees better with a swipe of the washcloth and a kiss. Their Oakland home wasn't anything elaborate, but it was always spotless. Mom had been the one to sit and do homework with Tammy and her, drive them to and from dance classes to piano classes. She'd been supermom.

And Dad worked. He was a car salesman and a damn good one. Kat remembered when he was promoted to the GM position and he took them out to the best Chinese restaurant in the city before going to see the Benji movie. The four of them watched *Happy Days* and *Laverne & Shirley* together. They had a dog named Spot and a cat named Tiger. They even had a frigging gold fish that they had named by all putting names in dad's baseball cap and randomly selecting one. Mom's name won. It was Guru. *That* right there should have been a sign. Kat was eleven at the time and Tammy had been nine--and Mom had already begun *enlightening* herself. She watched that yoga woman on PBS everyday. She started reading books by Ram Dass and Shirley McLaine—who quickly became her idol. But she didn't do much more than that until Kat was out of the house, married to the Sperm Donor and involved with two babies.

Then it happened.

Kat's mother just packed up one day, gave her dad a hug, thanking him for loving her and providing for her for all those years, but informing him that she needed more. *More!* Her mother needed more what? Oh, lest it be forgotten that by this point, Dad owned his own lucrative dealership. Mom had enjoyed all the luxuries that went along with a little money in the bank. Things like cruises, designer clothes, nips and tucks in sagging areas, and a lot of relaxation. As far as Kat had been concerned, the *more* that her mother needed shouldn't have had anything to do with "broadening the soul's horizons," but *more* of visiting her grand children, for starters. That would have worked out well, and filled her up. They don't move to ashrams, become yoga instructors, and name themselves after a fucking planet.

But, no! *Her* mom left behind *her* father who quickly turned into a shell of a man. It was only recently that he'd begun to live again. She'd also served Kat's sister, Tammy, up on a silver platter to Kat. Tammy had some issues. Actually quite a few.

Kat's sister had not been able to escape the clutches of painkillers. At twenty, Tammy had been in a serious car accident while driving around late at night with another addiction—bad boys. She'd broken her pelvis and back. Those hours, days, and weeks in the hospital spent watching her baby sister suffer were memories Kat loathed. But it was the days after Tammy went home, went through painful physical therapy and emotional upheaval, that Vicodin, Percocet and Darvocet became her sister's best friends. And as Tammy's best friends began to control her life, Mom looked more and more to her new age wisdom, turning a blind eye to Tammy's problems. And Dad became the consummate co-dependent. He provided Tammy with money, a place to live, clothes, a car, food, medical insurance—whatever she needed. Kat's dad was a good man.

The times spent with her dad were some of the best times in Kat's life. They would see a movie together once a month. As kids, he took her and her sister to this old school diner for breakfast every Saturday morning before he set out to the dealership. If he got home in time before they'd gone to bed, he always came into their bedroom and tucked them in, kissed them good night, and told them stories.

Kat wondered if Dad knew that her mom would be in town for the summer. She should tell him, just in case they ran into each other. Dad had uprooted when Kat moved with the boys and Christian to Napa, just as Christian's ex had. Apparently, everyone had decided Napa was nicer than Oakland. Yeah. No brainer there.

She wasn't sure how her father would react to the news, but she probably owed it to him. Her fingers crossed, she hoped this wouldn't throw him off kilter. Mom had gone off the deep end and lost herself in incense and mantras, but Dad on the other hand, had actually found himself.

"Hi, Mom," Brian walked into the kitchen, interrupting her memories, and headed directly to the fridge where he opened the carton of milk.

Before he got the carton all the way up to his lips, Kat cut in. "Do not even think about it if you want to live another day. Use a glass."

He frowned and went to the cupboard. "Grandma coming today, huh?"

"Yep. I have to head out in a bit to go get her. Hey, why don't you come with me? We haven't hung out for a while. I miss you." More and more, Brian had been *hanging* (his word) with his dad. School was out for the summer, and between Dad time and his video game addiction, Kat hardly saw her younger son.

"I can't. Dad and I are going to play tennis and then see a movie. Take Jeremy."

"Jeremy is over at Guy's house. They've each got a few more volunteer hours to do for their required senior year community service. Guy's mom arranged for them to work down at the shelter for the afternoon, which by the way, you should get a jump on. Don't wait until right before your senior year to cram in sixty hours of service."

"I know." He nodded.

Kat doubted he'd heard a word she said. "But Bri, you've spent a lot of time with Dad lately, and I'd like someone to drive with me, and I'd like it to be you. We always used to talk and joke, and it'll be fun. We can get burgers on the way. Your grandma would be so happy to see you. Come on. You can go play tennis with your dad another day."

Brian gulped down his milk and turned to his mom. "What is it with you?"

"Excuse me?"

"Yeah. You have a problem with Dad."

"I don't have a problem with your father."

"Whatever." Brian started to walk out of the kitchen.

"Brian Patrick! Come back here."

She heard the aggrieved sigh down the hallway. "What, Mom?"

"Get in here. You can't say something like that to me and then walk away. I think this is something we should talk about. But first, you need to change your tone with me."

"What tone?" He walked back into the kitchen and grabbed an apple from the fruit bowl.

"That one." She pointed at him. "That smart-ass sarcastic tone, like you think you own the world and I am only here as one of your many servants."

He stared at her like she was crazy.

"What do you mean I have a problem with your father?"

He sighed again. "Like every time I make plans with him, you get all weird."

"I do not."

He nodded. "You do, Mom. You kind of freak out."

"Actually I never say a word about it. I should, considering that neither your father nor you, for that matter, seem to have any consideration that we have a schedule set up. So far this summer, it's been all too laisse-faire and I haven't pressed the issue."

"Yeah, cuz I'm old enough to make those decisions."

"Who told you that?"

"Dad. He said that since I'm fourteen I can decide who I want to live with even."

The heat rose to Kat's neck. Blood rushed through her ears and every nerve set on edge, but instead of blowing up, she took a deep breath. "That's not entirely true, Bri. It really isn't. Family courts make those decisions, and that decision has been made. You live here, and you visit your dad."

"You know that Dad still loves you." Brian took a large bite out of the apple.

Kat closed her eyes and sighed. Wasn't he too old for this? Sure, kids always wanted their parents back together, but she and Perry had been divorced for almost five years. "No, he doesn't, sweetie. I mean not in the way that you think." *How does one negotiate these waters?* "Sure, as a friend." *There was a blatant lie.* "But honey, your daddy does not love me anymore, and I don't love him." Brian frowned. "I mean, I love him for giving me two of the best gifts in the world—you and your brother, but that's it. I'm sorry."

"Whatever. But Dad does love you. He told me so himself. He says that you're the best thing that ever happened to him, and he's sorry he ever hurt you, and he totally takes the blame, and if he ever had another chance . . ."

Kat held up her hand. "Bri, there isn't going to be another chance with your dad. I loved him once. I love him for you guys and that's it. I'm married to Christian now, and that's who I love."

Brian looked down. Kat placed a hand under his chin and lifted it to look at her. "I'm sorry, baby. I am."

He sucked back his breath and nodded, his eyes watering with a combined look of sadness, anger, and fear. Divorce stuck forever. In fact, the word divorce alone should be defined as an emotion and not an event. Kat could see that for her youngest son, this emotion took front and center in his heart and mind regularly. And God, if she didn't ache in return because of his pain. If she could only take it away, eat up the darkness for him, and rid him of it.

"Whatever, Mom."

"Come with me today. Please. We can talk some more. Instead of burgers, let's stop off for dessert lunch. Remember when we used to do that when you were little? When we had mental health days?"

That got a smile out of him. When the boys had been younger, there was the occasional school day that she would denote as mental health day. Instead of school and nutritious meals, the day was all about sleeping in, eating junk, and having whatever dessert their hearts desired for lunch. For Brian, it was usually a hot fudge Sunday. "Hot fudge . . . You know you want to." She wiggled her eyebrows at him.

But before Brian had a chance to answer, the doorbell rang. Kat made it to the door ahead of him, ready to go on attack, knowing that it was Perry. "Hey, Kit-Kat. The kid ready? We're cruising out to play some tennis, and..."

Kat stepped out front of the door and shut it behind her. "I know your plan, but I want to tell you something . . ."

Just as Kat started into her tirade, Brian opened the door. "Hey, Dad. I'm ready."

Perry slapped him on the shoulder. "Good deal, bud. I'm gonna squash you on the court."

"Right." Brian smiled and his face lit up. Kat failed to do that these days—light up her child.

Perry turned back to Kat and smiled. "You were saying."

She smiled back. "We need to talk."

He winked at her. "Anytime, Kit-Kat. Anytime. Let's go, man. Knock some balls around."

Brian turned back and waved weakly at his mom. "I'll be home by dinner, okay? Maybe we could do dessert lunch tomorrow. Love you."

"I love you, too." She swallowed back the hurt, sucking it deep down. As she went to shut the front door, another unannounced, unwelcome guest pulled into her driveway.

Emily.

Kat pulled herself together and watched in horror and amazement as the woman went around to the back of the car, took Amber by the hand, grabbed two pink Polly Pocket suitcases, and practically dragged the child to the front door. "Good, I'm glad you're home."

"Hi, Emily. Um, I thought you were coming by tonight."

Emily stood up straight, tucked her long brown hair behind her ears, and straightened her khaki skirt. "Our schedule has changed. The movers came early, and I really need to be there with them, without any disturbances." She glanced down at Amber who looked like she'd been crying and was ready to start again. "Here are her things, and I won't be able to get back this weekend. But next weekend we'll pick her up on Friday. I'll call Christian with the details." She bent down and pulled Amber into her. "You be a good girl for your daddy and Kat. Mommy loves you." With that, she turned on her loafers and headed back to her convertible.

Kat looked down at Amber who was now sucking her thumb and watching (most likely in terror) her mother leave. Kat took her by the hand and opened the front door. They could get her suitcases later. The last thing this child needed to see was her mother pulling away as she abandoned her, which was exactly what the self-centered bitch was doing. "Hey, sweetie, have you ever had a dessert lunch?"

Amber shook her head.

"Well, today you're going to, and it'll be the best lunch of your life. I promise." Kat stooped down, picked Amber up and twirled her around. "Did you hear me? Do you hear what I am saying? Dessert lunch! It's crazy. It's wild and it's gonna be the best!"

Amber giggled and so did Kat.

CHAPTER SIXTEEN

Jamie

Nora arrived thirty minutes late, as usual, but Jamie had prepared for it this time. "Buenos Dias, Nora," Jamie said.

Nora didn't reply, but instead took out a small piece of paper from her purse and unfolded it. Jamie recognized it. It was the check she'd written her last week. "El cheque es no good. Bounce, bounce, bounce." Nora made a motion like she was bouncing a ball on to the ground.

"No. No. I don't think so. You sure?" Jeez. Jamie had hoped this wouldn't happen. She'd written the check on Sunday as always and crossed her fingers that Nora wouldn't go to the bank until Tuesday. Tuesday was the day her check from work went automatically into her checking account. "When did you go to el banco?"

Nora stared at her.

Great. The game. Here she was going to play *the game* with Jamie, and they were talking money. For once could they not play the stupid game of, *I don't understand what you are saying to me, even though I really do?* "Okay. Donde. No. Que. No. Quein did tu visita to el banco?" She asked motioning with her fingers like they were walking and knowing that her Spanish was pretty much all wrong, but she had to at least make the effort.

Nora raised her eyebrows. "Hoy."

"Today?"

Nora nodded. "Hoy. Sí."

"What? No. That's wrong. It has to be wrong. You wait here."

What Nora was telling her couldn't be. She couldn't be overdrawn. She headed toward her office and nearly crashed into Dorothy who came around the corner out of her room. "Hello, darling girl. I was wondering if you could get me an appointment at the hairdresser today? I have a big date tonight." She smiled and did a little curtsy.

"Guess who with?"

"Not now, Mom. I have to take care of something with the bank."

"What do you have to take care of with the bank? Tell Nathan to do it. He's the man of the house. He can handle whatever it is. Come in my room and see what I'm going to wear tonight. It's so pretty, and it's all for Dean. It's purple with organza. I want to wear a purple flower in my hair."

"Not now. I will in a minute."

Dorothy frowned. "Jamie, that's enough. Go and tell Nathan to do it. That's what men do. They take care of the finances, and you are take care of the house. That means me and Maddie, too."

How was it she could be so coherent about some things, but could never remember that Nate was no longer alive? Jamie grabbed her gently by the shoulders. "Mom. I am *the man* now. I do all of it. Nathan is gone. We have had this conversation. I will come and see your dress in a minute, and I will see about getting you a hair appointment, but first I have to deal with an issue with the bank." Dorothy frowned. Jamie hugged her tightly seeing that she'd hurt her feelings, but what was she supposed to do? If Nora's check didn't clear that morning, something was seriously wrong. Jamie knew that she'd scheduled all of her bills to go out that day through online banking, and she'd set up her mortgage to automatically pay on the first of the month.

Nora followed Jamie, flagging the check at her as they went down the hallway. "I needed dinero. I needed para mi familia. You needed a pagar mi ahora. I no coming no mas. You paga mi."

Jamie waved a hand at her. "I know. Uno momento. Please wait. Por favor." She shut her office door, sat down at her desk and sighed while her computer booted up. When she finally signed onto her banking site, she gasped. "What the…?" Oh no. Jamie saw that she was a thousand dollars overdrawn. Yes, things were tight, but how could this have happened? Her first thought was that someone had stolen her identity or had somehow gotten access to her checking account. That had to be it. Going over the withdrawals everything looked normal. Until she got to the mortgage payment. "How stupid! How could I have been so stupid?" she said out loud.

She opened up her desk drawer, found the bill file, and located the mortgage company's statement. She dialed the number on the payment coupon, went through the five minutes of prompts and listening to her balance, her pay off, et al., and then after seven or eight minutes of listening to ridiculous elevator music and commercials about American Bank, Jamie was ready to come unglued. Finally a person came on the other end—a real live, freaking human being. Imagine!

"American Bank. Can I have your account number and name please?" the woman on the other end asked.

Jamie gave up all of her info again.

"How may I help you today, Ms. Evans?"

Jamie explained. "You see, well, actually it's kind of funny. I do online banking with my bills and I did them over the weekend, and I paid you guys twice, and I don't have the money in my account to pay you a double payment. I'm not sure how I did that. I guess I wasn't paying attention. Stupid, I know, but can you help me?"

"Hang on a moment please." Jamie could hear the clacking of computer keys through the phone.

"It shows here that your payment went through fine with us."

"Yes, with you, it did. But um, I have quite a few checks that came out after yours and the bank did not clear them. See the first five hundred overdrawn they cleared, but after that they didn't and they're charging me something like thirty-three dollars per bounced check."

"I'm sorry about that, ma'am."

"Thank you. So can you refund me that extra payment?"

"We can't do that."

"What do you mean you can't do that? You have to. That's my money."

"That's our policy, ma'am. We can't do that."

"You have to do that. That's my money! I didn't mean to pay you twice and now I'm being penalized by my bank and it's costing me three times as much with all of these bank charges."

"I'm sorry, ma'am, you'll have to take that up with your bank."

Jamie clinched her fists. "Can I please speak to a supervisor?"

She endured another three minutes of crappy music and then a man came on the line. Jamie explained the entire scenario again.

In a southern accent the man said, "Gosh, ma'am, I sure am sorry about that, but you see it is our policy to apply anything over and above the payment you make toward the principal on the home."

"Can't you just, with a few key strokes, make a change to that policy? Can't you please refund that money?"

"No, ma'am. I can't do that."

Jamie sighed. "I'm kind of in a financial crises at the moment. I'm sure there is something you can do for me."

"What I can do, ma'am, is wave any late fees you may incur say next month. So say you happen to be after the grace period, I can make sure you won't be charged if that turns out to be the case. Will that help?"

"No that won't help. I'm never late, and I don't want to start being late. You have to put that money back into my account, and then I can pay you on time in August. But I'm on a fixed budget right now, and I need that money to get through the month."

"I really am so sorry, ma'am, but there is nothing I can do to reverse that."

Jamie shut her eyes tight. *Think.* Think. Nate would have asked her to ask herself what was the outcome she wanted here. She wanted the damn money back into the account. That wasn't going to happen, so what was the next best case. Wait a minute. Something the manager said hit her. "Okay then, can you at least make that over payment go toward my next month's payment? That should be doable, right?"

"No. I can't, ma'am."

"You're kidding me. Why not?" Jamie was starting to lose it.

"It's not our policy. You would have had to have written two checks for that to happen. One for this month and one for next month. But the good news is that you now have that extra money applied to your principal. That is always nice to know, isn't it? A little security in that."

"No there isn't! I don't care about the damn principal. Not right now! I care that I am overdrawn by a grand, that I'm being charged by my bank for every draft now, and that I won't have any money in the bank for another week. I need to get groceries and my mother-in-law needs her hair done." She knew she sounded frantic.

"I understand your predicament, ma'am. I really do, but there is nothing that I can do for you. That is our policy."

"Screw your policy and screw you!" Jamie slammed the phone down and read over her online statement again. How totally ridiculous. That was her money. Now she was running late.

Jamie came out of the office with both Nora and Dorothy standing there obviously eavesdropping. "You paga mi."

"Yes. I will pay you today in cash. Okay? Got it? Make her lunch and take care of her. I have a meeting." She was way too exasperated to even try and speak her broken Spanish. She grabbed her purse and headed out the door. How she was going to pay her, especially in cash, she had no clue. But she'd figure it out. Right now she had to drive into the city and have lunch with her brother-in-law, David. Maybe it was time for David to step up and help out financially with his mom. One area she and Nate had not been smart in was financial planning, but who plans for their husband to die at thirty-five? She certainly hadn't.

But he had died. And now, as Jamie headed out onto the 101, tears blurred her vision and she had a long talk with Nathan, asking him over and over again the same question until she was shouting it.

WHY?

***

Nate's brother, David, sat across from Jamie looking suave and self-satisfied. He had the same blue eyes that her husband had, but David was nowhere near as good looking or as decent as Nate. He was rounder, balding, and there was a look in his eyes that Nate had never had—greed.

David had chosen a trendy fish and chips place near the wharf. "I'm not sure what you're asking me for, Jamie. You and Nate agreed to take Mom on as she aged. This is a discussion we had a long time ago. Susan and I never planned for my mother to stay with us. We both have careers, and Mom has always lived in Napa Valley."

Jamie pushed aside the fried food, unable to stomach much of anything. "I have a career too, and a daughter that I'm raising on my own, and yes, we did have this discussion when Nate was alive. But that has changed. I'm not asking you to move Dorothy in with you, but I could use some financial help."

"What about the money from Nate's life insurance?"

Jamie shook her head in disbelief. "Wait a minute, this is *your* mother we're talking about. And as far as the life insurance or any monies left to me from Nate, that's a joke. We spent most of it trying to keep him alive."

"I told you both that was a waste of time, and that you would have been better off spending that time together doing things with each other and Maddie."

"My husband, *your* brother, wanted to live. And I wanted him to live. We were willing to do anything if we had even the remotest possibility of making that happen."

David leaned back in his chair, a cool breeze coming off the bay. "Here's what Susan and I are prepared to do. My wife is looking into a few facilities both here in the city and out in Napa. When we find a home that is suitable for all of us, then we can place her there."

Defeated, Jamie didn't reply at first. "I'm not looking to put her in a nursing home. I am only looking for some financial help. I have someone who comes in daily and helps us out."

"I'm not paying for your housekeeper, Jamie."

"She is not just my housekeeper. She makes Dorothy's meals,

helps her dress, watches over her, and she's been very good with tolerating Dorothy's rapidly declining mental state."

"Yeah well, her mental state." He shoved a French fry into his mouth, and while still chewing, continued, "All the more reason for her to be in a nursing home. Don't you think that would be best for you anyway? You could get on with your life." David's cell phone rang and he answered.

Jamie looked out at the wharf, boats weaving side to side as a steady strong breeze filtered through. Men on fishing boats tugged in their nets and yelled back and forth to one another. The silver water cupped into small white caps with flecks like gold coins bouncing off them as the sun peeked through the myriad of clouds, reflecting its rays on the water.

David bantered with the person on the other end of the phone about some brief. She couldn't believe this guy was remotely related to the man she'd been married to. She had a gut feeling that David's wife was calling the shots in this situation. If he made waves and Susan took off for better things, then David would see his posh lifestyle go down the drain. He made decent money, but he didn't come from the kind of money his wife had.

He hung up the phone. "I have to run." He tossed down enough cash for his half of the lunch. "It's been hard times for everyone, Jamie. Money is tight for us too these days. We'll do what we can. I'll have Susan call you when she finds something, and to set up some time when we can have Maddie for the weekend. Good to see you." He bent down and gave her a kiss on the cheek. "Take care."

On her way home, she ran the conversation over and over again in her mind. She called David every name in the book and drove faster than she should've. She couldn't believe she'd taken the day off work to get nothing accomplished.

She had signed Maddie up for horse camp that week praying that check wouldn't bounce, too.

She parked at the ranch and got out. Tyler had the group of kids seated on the grass while he and another instructor put on a puppet show. Jamie sat down next to Maddie who took her hand. Jamie squeezed it. Tyler caught her eye and smiled. The story they told with the puppets had something to do with two cowboys, a sheriff and one very smart horse—smarter than the cowboys or the sheriff. Tyler did funny voices and all the kids laughed. Jamie laughed too. It was a nice diversion.

"All right gang, see you all tomorrow at eight. Don't forget to take home the craft that you made with Gwen, and remember we're going to have a little quiz tomorrow on the anatomy of the horse, so look at the worksheet I gave you. You can go and get your things."

"My stuff is in the club house, Mom," Maddie said.

"Okay, babe. I'll wait."

Maddie sprinted off with another little girl. Tyler came over. "She's a great kid."

"Thanks. She looks like she's having fun."

"Definitely. How about you? Are you enjoying the lessons and the volunteer work?" he asked.

"It's great. Pretty rewarding. I had no idea that the horses could be such a deep connection for some of those kids."

"Wait until you've done it for a while. The growth with the kids is awesome. I'm hoping to expand the program."

Maddie ran up next to her mom and gave Tyler a hug around his waist, surprising Jamie. "Thank you, Tyler. I had a lot of fun."

"Me too, kiddo." He ruffled the top of her hair. "See you tomorrow, and then for your riding lesson, and Saturday for horsemanship?" he asked Jamie.

"I'll be here." She smiled and grabbed Maddie's hand as they walked to the car.

"He's so cool, Mom. He let me brush *his* horse, Buster. But one of his horses died the other day like daddy did." Maddie got into the car.

Jamie opened up her door. "What do you mean?"

"His one horse, Flame, was really, really old and he had something in his legs where it was hard for him to walk any more, and the vet came and gave him a shot so he could go to Heaven."

"Oh. How sad." She knew how hard it must have been on Tyler to have one of his horses put down. Surely it hadn't been the first time. The guy had grown up around them, but Jamie had seen him with his animals and knew how much he loved them. She doubted it had been easy.

"Do you think horses go to heaven like Daddy did?"

Jamie nodded. "Sure I do."

"Maybe Daddy is riding one right now. Wouldn't that be neat? When I feel sad about Daddy, I'm going to think about him riding a horse in Heaven and I think I'll feel better. A shiny white horse with a long silver mane and tail, that's the kind of horse Daddy has in Heaven, and he prances."

"Like a horse for a king or queen," Jamie said.

"Yeah. That's perfect, Mom. I still miss Daddy, but sometimes it's hard for me to remember him until I look at a picture of him. Do you miss him?"

"I do. A lot. I like your idea though. I could see Daddy riding the white and silver horse in Heaven and having a lot of fun." Jamie bit down hard on the side of her mouth, working to keep her emotions at bay. Maddie didn't talk often about Nate, but Jamie's therapist had told her to expect that Maddie would have questions and want to talk about him. As hard as it might be, as time passed, Jamie knew she needed to be strong, honest, and supportive of her daughter. It was no time to reminisce and be melancholy.

"I think I'll call Uncle David and tell him about it."

Jamie cringed. "Why don't we wait to do that? Maybe we can let it be our special vision of Daddy."

Maddie looked out the window and didn't say anything for a minute. Jamie almost took the words back, realizing that she shouldn't try and get in the way of Maddie's feelings and relationship with her aunt and uncle, but at the same time knowing what jerks they really were. Eventually, Maddie would discover that herself. People didn't change. "I like that, Mom. We'll keep it our secret, like

Daddy has a secret horse world in Heaven on Prancer. That's the name of his horse."

Jamie smiled and nodded. "I think that is wonderful. I love it."

"Maybe we could draw pictures with Daddy on Prancer in Heaven."

"Maybe we could." Feeling better, Jamie couldn't wait to get home, get everyone dinner and take a long hot bath.

Turning down her street, her stomach sank. There were two police cars parked in front of her house. Oh no. Was she in trouble over the bounced checks? No. Oh *no*. What if something happened to Dorothy or Nora?

"Mommy why are there police cars here?" Maddie asked as Jamie pulled into her driveway and spotted Nora chatting wildly to the police.

"Stay here, honey." Jamie jumped out and approached the group. "What's going on?"

Wild eyed and hands flailing, Nora was carrying on in Spanish to one of the cops who seemed to understand her as he stood there nodding his head. He held up a hand to her and turned to Jamie. "Dorothy Evans is your mother-in-law?"

"Yes. Why? What's happened?"

"Your housekeeper called us and said she got out of the house and that she has mental problems. Is this true?"

"Oh, my God. Yes. If she's lost, she won't know how to get home. We have to find her."

CHAPTER SEVENTEEN

Danielle

*T*wo hours before Mark was supposed to pick her up, Danielle had nearly every piece of clothing she owned spread out on her bed. She tried a handful of things on. None of them made her happy. Some made her look fat, others slutty, others like a church lady, others like she was heading to the office, and others that screamed, *Married!* One thing was for sure, Danielle needed a new wardrobe. She flopped down on her comforter, right on top of the pile of clothes, closed her eyes and, with a big sigh, wondered what in the hell she was doing. Having nothing to wear had to be a sign. It just had to. At forty-seven, she had no business going out on a date with her high-school sweetheart. Maybe if she didn't think of it as a date, but rather a dinner with an old friend, that would make it easier to find something to wear. She certainly never had this problem when she was going to dinner with her friends. Yes, think of Mark as an old friend. Sure.

"Hey, Mom." Cassie came in the room.

Danielle opened her eyes. "Hey. What's up?"

"Do you have any money? I'm going to the movies with some friends tonight."

Danielle propped up onto her elbows. "Yes, I have money but maybe we should back-track here. How about the idea of asking me if it's okay for you to go the movies with your friends, and how about you telling me what you're going to do for me to earn the money I will consider giving you for the movies. I notice you still haven't made much progress on the job hunt."

Cassie put her hands on her hips and gave her mother a blank look.

"I'm all ears."

"Mom."

"Yes?"

"Come on." Cassie tossed back her strawberry blonde hair.

She sighed. "Here's the deal. Yes, you can go to the movies and, yes, I will give you the money, but tomorrow I planned to go to the nursery and pick up some flowers to plant in the pots on the front porch. So you can do that with me, and that's how you'll pay me back. Then I suggest you drive into town and pick up and fill out as many job apps as you can."

"Mom," she whined.

"It's not negotiable. You and me—nursery and then gardening. I'll even give you a little extra, and why don't we get some lunch together. Then you can go job hunting on a full stomach."

"I guess so."

"My purse is on my dresser. You can take twenty."

"I need a little more for gas."

Danielle sighed and sat up. "Fine. Take forty and we'll negotiate a few more chores tomorrow."

"Thanks. Hey what's up with the clothes?"

Danielle picked at her fingernails and stood up. "Nothing. I'm going out to dinner, and I can't find anything to wear."

Cassie smiled. "You have a date, don't you?"

"No. No, I don't have a date. He's an old friend."

"No, he isn't. Shannon told me. He's that doctor and you guys went out in high school."

"Where is Shannon?"

"She said she was going to the farmer's market. Don't change the subject. It's *so* a date, Mom. Sweet." Cassie began picking up articles of clothing and quickly discarded several pieces, shaking her head. "No, no, no. Oooh. This is nice, Mom. Really nice. Wear this." She held up a slinky black dress. One that Danielle deemed as over the top—much too sexy.

"Really? Why that one?" The dress was pretty. She'd bought it during the mourning process after the divorce—on a whim. She'd passed a boutique in St. Helena and saw it on a mannequin. She'd felt so ugly and undesirable, and the dress screamed, *Take me and*

I'll make you pretty again! She'd plunked down the three-hundred dollars for it on the one card that Al had forgotten to cancel. *Oops.* She'd taken it home, hung it up, and let it sit for what was now over two years. It was a wrap dress with a slight ruffling that followed the low cut neckline. Made of silk. Very chic, but a bit too low cut.

"It's hot, that's why."

"I don't know that hot is what I'm going for."

Cassie's mouth dropped. "Don't be lame, Mom. Of course hot is what you're going for. Now put it on."

For some reason, she listened to her teenaged daughter and put it on.

"See. That is way hot."

Danielle looked in the full-length mirror in her bathroom. Not bad. "Don't you think it's a little, you know, I mean, my cleavage is kind of out there?"

"No." Cassie rolled her eyes. "Jeez, Mom, you've got great boobs. I say when you got 'em, flaunt 'em."

"Nice, Cass. That's real special."

Cassie shrugged. "I didn't get so lucky. Must've inherited Grandma Bastillia's boobs. I have to wear padded bras to even look like I have any."

"You have a beautiful figure, Cassandra."

"I don't have boobs."

"Good news for you then is that they will never sag."

"I know, because I am going to have a boob job when I turn eighteen."

"No you're not."

She nodded. "Yes I am. I was thinking, too, that I'd have a little tattoo of a hummingbird right over my areola. Get it? Don't you think that would be cute?"

Danielle stared at her and debated this one in her mind for about five seconds. She did not have time for the argument and went with the old *pick and choose your battles* mantra. The boob job talk with the nursing hummingbird would have to take a rain check. "What shoes do I wear with it, and should I wear jewelry, too?"

Cassie helped her mom finish picking out the outfit for the evening and even helped her with her hair and makeup. Danielle was taking one last look in the mirror when the doorbell rang.

Cassie ran down the stairs, beating her to the front door. "Gotta get a look at the goods."

"Be nice."

She turned back and smiled at her mom as she swung the door open. There was Mark. He looked handsome and almost as nervous as Danielle was. He wore a pair of dark slacks, a striped aqua and grey button down, and a dark grey sports coat.

"You look great," Danielle said.

"And you, you're gorgeous."

Cassie cleared her throat. Danielle quickly introduced her and told her to have fun at the movies and not to be out past midnight. "Right. Now you kids have a good time, too," Cassie said.

Danielle shook her head and walked with Mark to his car. Mark opened up her door, and before long they were on their way to *La Toque* in the quaint town of Rutherford.

The restaurant was stunning, reminding Danielle of a French country inn with its large wood framed chairs covered in brocade cushions. An enormous stone fireplace stood on one wall, and in the center of the restaurant was a refectory table with a sprawling floral arrangement of lavender and purple calla lilies.

Mark ordered a bottle of Champagne and they agreed on mussels in an orange salsa broth for appetizers. He toasted her with his glass of Champagne, holding it up in the candlelight, his blue eyes shining, and she remembered getting lost in those eyes as a girl. They were still damn easy to get lost in. "To you, to old friends and loves, and new beginnings."

They clinked glasses and took a sip. After a few more sips, conversation turned back to those good old days. "You know, I thought about you a lot over the years," he said.

"You did?"

He nodded. "Why wouldn't I? You were my first. My first love and my first." He waved his hand in a rolling position.

This admission took Danielle by surprise. Mark had been on the football team, the academic decathlon and student council. Girls loved him. She loved him. "Me? What about Catherine Ketchum."

He shook his head. "No."

"But she told everyone . . ."

"Cross my heart. Scout's honor."

"Then, Rachel Whiting? Not her, either?"

"Not her, either. It was you, Danielle." He took her hand.

"I, well, why didn't you tell me that then? You knew you were my first."

He shrugged. "Stupid young guy stuff. Me playing big man."

"Huh."

He nodded. "Have you thought about me?"

"Yes, of course. We did date for what? Almost an entire year and obviously a lot happened during that year." She smiled. He smiled back at her making her stomach turn over and sending electricity down her back. How odd that the feelings you could have as a sixteen-year-old—particularly that feeling of lust—could be exactly the same some thirty years later.

"What happened to us?" he asked.

"If I remember correctly, you went away to college and I stayed here and was a senior in high school. That's what happened. Then your parents moved away from Napa, and I guess we kind of drifted apart from each other."

"Right."

The waitress came over, suggested some specials, and took their wine orders. Danielle decided on the ricotta porcini ravioli in a wild mushroom sauce, while Mark had the pork confit with creamy polenta.

"The years in between . . . How were they?" he asked.

She sighed and set her Champagne down. "You know how life is. There have been some good years, some not so good, and, well, it's this up and down thing. Life."

"True." He laughed. "How long were you married for?"

"A little over twenty years. I was traded in for a younger model."

"That guy is a fool." He took her hand and squeezed it.

She smiled and felt heat rise to her cheeks, as she glanced down at her plate. "But I have my two gorgeous daughters who I love, and I am now pursuing some of my own dreams."

"Like what?"

"I am currently making my own wines."

"Really?" His eyes opened wide. "Impressive. I am seriously impressed."

"Don't say that until you try them, but I have to tell you that I do think they're pretty good. I'm entering the fall festival in October. Fingers are crossed that I come away with some awards."

"Look at you. I'd like to try some of your wines some time."

"Why don't you come for dinner next week?" She crossed her legs.

"I'd love too. Wednesday is my early day at the office. How does that work?"

"That works great."

From there, the dinner went smoothly as they continued to talk about her wines and his practice. It was good to feel relaxed around a man, and strange at the same time. This was a real date. A real first date, so to speak. The food was delicious and the company was ever so desirable. It couldn't get any better.

Over a shared peach cobbler, Danielle decided to ask about his past thirty years away from the wine country.

"I obviously went to medical school back east. I met my ex-wife there. She was a dermatologist, or studying to be one at the time. We moved to Connecticut and had our practices there. It was nice, really."

"What about children?"

He grew quiet and sat back in the booth. A sadness crept into his baby blues and Danielle sensed that she shouldn't have gone there.

"We had one. A son. Riley. He died when he was six. He got MRSA. It's a streptococcus virus. Here we were, his two parents, doctors, and our son got and died from MRSA. He had a cut on his knee, a scrape really. You know boys playing out on the playground. I think it was kickball, and he fell. I don't know." He cleared his throat. "He didn't go to the nurse, just got back up, wiped off his knee and kept playing. His mom had a late meeting that night and I had a delivery, so the babysitter had him for dinner and she didn't get him into a bath. By the next morning the wound was infected and he had a fever. Things happened quickly after that. Within three weeks he was gone."

"Mark." She took his hand. "I am so sorry. So sorry."

"My wife Marci and I, well, things changed. You know, we loved each other, but this sadness and pain took hold of our lives and stayed there. We would try and pretend it wasn't there, and we even tried to have another child but with no luck. Marci felt guilty for even trying to get pregnant, so I didn't suggest fertility drugs or any alternatives. I only wanted her to heal. And I wanted to heal, but together we couldn't do that. And trust me, we tried for ten years. Finally she found someone that she thought she could love and who could help her heal. Someone who wasn't going to be sad along with her all the time. This guy made her happy, and that was all I wanted. We parted as friends and still are, but we knew we couldn't stay married and be happy. Not with each other anyway."

Danielle was speechless. This man had been through so much more than she could ever handle. To lose a child would be by far the worst thing ever.

"I do think I can find happiness again. I do. Moving back here was a step in that direction. And it would appear the fates have stepped in and made sure that you and I connected again."

"I'm glad they did."

"Me too. Ironic in the way they did so." He laughed. "So how is your daughter?"

"She's good. Bigger everyday. The pregnancy was a shock to say the least."

"She's a brave young woman. There aren't a lot of women who would do what she does."

Danielle wasn't quite sure what he meant. There were a lot of young, single women who had babies every day around the world, but she nodded and finished off her wine.

"And how about you? How are you coping with all of this?"

"What can I do? She's my daughter, and she's made this decision and I have to support her. I love her and she is an adult, so there isn't much I can say or do, but I sure would like to talk with her some more about it. She's rather closed off and seems to be out of the house as much as she can be."

"She'll talk. Give her time. I conferred with her new doctor and he agreed that the specialist I recommended is the right guy for this."

"Excuse me?" She set down her glass. "Why does Shannon's baby need a specialist?"

CHAPTER EIGHTEEN

Alyssa

Alyssa lit the candles in her cottage, placed the shrimp salad in the center of the table, and took out the bottle of Sauvignon Blanc. She loved this cottage. It had a guest room, an office and her bedroom. The place wasn't much over fifteen hundred square feet, all decorated in shabby chic and painted in a light lemon. Alyssa liked to keep fresh flowers in the house picked from her garden and she used candles to brighten the mood.

As Alyssa finished arranging a bouquet of daisies and blue bonnets, her friends came in one by one. Kat gave Alyssa a hug and immediately took a glass off the counter. "Looks wonderful as always," she said.

"Thank you." Alyssa poured the wine. They sat down at her table and looked at each other for a few seconds. "Long week?" Alyssa set her glass down.

Everyone sort of laughed and nodded. "Pretty much," Kat said. "But before we get into my stuff, we've been dying to hear how your lunch went with your son. Ian, right? Didn't you get any of my messages? I called you a few times this week."

"Me, too," Jamie said.

Danielle raised her hand. "What gives? You don't return our calls. And you cancelled art class."

"I'm sorry. Of course I do return calls, but well, something came up," Alyssa replied.

"What?" they all asked.

"I went to Los Angeles to meet Ian's family."

"What?" they all said a bit louder this time.

Alyssa nodded. "I didn't plan it. He came here and we had lunch and he's a great kid." They all smiled seeing the glow that had taken over their friend. They'd never seen Alyssa look so exuberant. "We have a lot in common. He likes to draw, and he's a writer and a musician. He's just finished his first year at UCLA and wants to major in film. Then he said that his dad wanted to meet me and wanted me to come down to Los Angeles with him."

"So you did?" Jamie said. "That was brave."

"Seriously brave," Kat said.

Danielle sat stunned.

She shrugged. "It wasn't easy, but I wanted to. I was curious about his family and where he lived and where he'd gone to school. I wanted to know all that I could."

"How was it?"

"Great. His dad is a nice, nice man. And his brothers and sisters, and aunts and uncles are all very sweet people. They truly welcomed me with open arms."

"How about his mom?" Jamie asked.

Alyssa told them about her and how she'd died. For a minute, no one said anything. Kat broke the silence and said what everyone else was thinking. "Alyssa, you're not getting in too deep too soon, are you?"

"What do you mean?" she asked.

Kat shrugged. "I don't know. It all seems pretty fast to me. I mean you couldn't even tell us about the fact that you'd had a child, and we've been your good friends for the last three years. Then Ian comes into your life and suddenly you're meeting his family. With his mom gone, I think that there is a concern as to what Ian expects your role to be and maybe what you want to be to him."

Alyssa took a sip of the wine. It tasted like pears and grapefruit. "I don't need to analyze this and I don't need my friends to analyze this. I need you all to be happy for me."

"We are, honey. I think what Kat is saying is that we don't want to see you get hurt." Danielle looked across the table for some support from Jamie, who nodded.

"I'm fine. I don't have any intention of replacing the family he has or the mother he had. Things are going fast. They have to. We don't have a choice. The thing is, Ian has leukemia and he needs a bone marrow donation. I'm going to be tested, and if I'm a match then I am going to donate to my son."

No one said anything for a moment. Kat broke the silence. "Leukemia? I'll be tested too. You never know." She wasn't sure what to say. No one else seemed to know either.

Jamie and Danielle nodded and said they would also go in to be tested.

"Thank you. Thanks for understanding," Alyssa said, overcome by her friends' compassion. She turned to Danielle. "I don't know what you and Shannon have discussed about her child--if she plans to keep the baby or what. But I am telling you that after living all this time wondering what my child was doing, how he was doing, all I can say is that she should keep the baby."

Danielle didn't say anything. She was not ready for this. Not at all. She simply nodded.

"Danielle?" Jamie said.

"Uh huh."

"What is it? You okay?"

"I'm fine. Tired is all." After just learning about Alyssa's son, the last thing she wanted to do was talk about the baby and what Mark had told her. She hadn't even had the opportunity to speak with Shannon about it. She'd gone to the city with her best friend from high school for the weekend, and Danielle expected her back the following day.

"I don't mean to tell you or Shannon what to do, but meeting Ian has changed things, changed me. I think for the better. I know him being sick is heavy, but I can't believe that I'm going to lose him now. There's a reason for all of this. There has to be," Alyssa said.

"I believe that, too," Danielle replied. "He sounds like a great kid, and you know we'll do anything we can to help."

"Thank you." Alyssa offered them each shrimp salad and stood up to grab the garlic bread out of the oven.

They all piled the salad onto their plates and thought about what to say next. They ate quietly for a moment.

It was of course Kat who broke the silence. Her timing impeccable as usual. "I'm having a pool party for the Fourth. I've been wanting to have a party, and now with my mom here and Amber with us, I think we should have one. Everyone bring their families. We can do it potluck style," she said, shifting in her seat.

"Works for me," Jamie said. They all nodded in agreement. "How is it with Venus and Amber both with you?"

"Crazy. Venus is crazy. You'll see. I don't need to say a word. I'll let you all decide for yourselves."

"Speaking of nut jobs, I had lunch with my brother-in-law," Jamie said.

"Uh oh, just by the tone of your voice that doesn't sound too good." Kat piled some more salad onto her plate and refilled her wine glass.

"No, it wasn't. I tried to talk to him about Dorothy and the way she is deteriorating and said that I could use some help with her."

"Has she gotten really bad?" Danielle asked.

"She actually got lost the other day."

"Lost?" they said.

"Yes. Nora was watching one of her soap operas and Dorothy got outside and took a two-mile walk down to the Starbucks, dressed to the nines. Can you believe she walked that far? Two miles! The police were at my place when I got home. It was like a scene out of *Cops*. Then this older black man brings her home in his car and he's laughing when he gets out. Comes and tells us that she's sure he's Sammy Davis Junior."

"She knew her way home though? I mean enough to give him directions?" Kat asked.

"I know. I don't get it. I'm happy she made it home but now I've had to pay Nora more money until I figure something out. I hate to leave her at all."

"Why don't you hire someone new?" Danielle asked.

Jamie sighed. "I'm a little tight on money right now. She's about all I can afford."

"Did you tell your brother-in-law about what happened?" Danielle asked.

"No. This was after I met with him. Same day though. And since he'd already told me that he thought we should place her in a home--which I promised Nate that I wouldn't do, and I know it would kill her—I thought it best not to tell him about the incident. She may be losing it, but Maddie and I are the only family she has. David and Susan never visit, and he doesn't seem to care."

"What jerks," Alyssa said.

"Oh, honey, I am sorry." Danielle hugged her. "I didn't know things were tight for you. I wish you'd talked to us. Maybe we can help."

Jamie bit her lower lip and shook her head. "Please. You don't need to be sorry. You have a full plate yourself. I can take care of this. It *will* get better."

"I say we all have some heavy stuff these days. We're a sorry lot, aren't we?" Kat asked rather tipsily. She held up her glass, "Here's to life, love, and all the other shit in between."

The women toasted one another, grateful that one thing that stayed consistent in their ever-changing lives was their friendship.

Wine Lover's Magazine
Constants
By
Jamie Evans

In the last column I wrote about life being like a rollercoaster and all the ups and downs we go through. This month over wine and an amazing shrimp salad that Alyssa made at her lovely home, my friends and I continued to deal with life's numerous curve balls.

The uncertainty of life got me thinking about the importance of constants in our lives. Constants can be anything from the bills in the mailbox, to needing gas for the car, to loving family members and caring for good friends. The not so fun things like the bills and the gas—the givens—can be annoyances at best and utterly depressing at worst. However, they are there. There are no surprises when it comes to these things. We know that we need money in the bank to acquire even basic needs, and when money isn't easy to come by, then we have to figure out if we need to change our lifestyle to keep up with the basic constants in life.

Loved ones and friends are what I consider joyful constants. There are times when even the most wonderful of constants can cause pain and heartache, but that overall feeling of love and warmth given and received from them makes the bad times tolerable. Without these joyful constants, we would never understand love and humor, or pain and sorrow.

The bottom line about constants is that they are dependable. They are there—always. I'm happy at the end of the day (even when I open up the bills) knowing that I have three constants in my life who make me laugh, who bring out the worst and the best in me, and who make me a better woman. They are my friends. So, this week, take some time to call the constants in your life and toast to them, whether they are your friends, siblings, parents, or even pets . . . give your dog a hug and toast him for being your best friend!

And since good food and wine should be a constant in your life, try Alyssa's shrimp salad with a glass of crisp Sauvignon Blanc.

CHAPTER NINETEEN

Danielle

*I*t was Monday afternoon, and Shannon still hadn't returned from the city. Nor had she answered any of her mother's calls. Danielle was beside herself, so instead of going to the lab or the winery to work, she cleaned the house. She didn't just pick up. She took an old toothbrush and scrubbed grout. She waxed and polished the hardwoods on her knees, organized the bathroom and kitchen cupboards, and then, after eating a quick tuna fish sandwich, braved Cassie's room.

Danielle had a rule where Cassie's room was concerned—never go in. The reason for that was that she might never find her way out. It was a maze of clothes, cups and plates, books, CD's, DVD's, papers, and empty junk food wrappers. She should've made the child clean, but the energy required for that argument was more than what it took to live with it. She did have to give the kid props for doing a great job gardening with her on Saturday.

However, a cloud of guilt hung over Danielle as her youngest daughter had tried hard to make conversation with her, telling her about the movie from the night before. Through it all, Danielle feigned interest, wanting so badly to be present. It was rare that Cassie shared with her on that level any longer. Then she asked her about her date with Mark and all Danielle could tell her was that it was fine. Soon thereafter, Cassie put her earphones back in her ears and did what she normally did—shut her mother out.

Danielle had been relieved. All she could do was play out in her mind what she wanted to say to Shannon. The conversation they needed to have was coming, and as soon as her daughter came through the door it would have to happen. In the meantime, she would organize Cassie's room and hopefully alleviate the guilt she felt for not paying proper attention to her on Saturday.

After determining what were clean and what were dirty clothes, she began folding the clean pile. But when she opened the drawers of Cassie's dresser to put them away, she realized she would first have to sort through *that* clothing, fold it and then make room for the other clothing. Some of this stuff had to be too small.

Halfway through cleaning out the middle drawer, her hand found something *non-clothing*. It was round and plastic and she pulled it out, already with an idea as to what she'd found. She closed her eyes and sat back with a big sigh. In her hands she held a packet of birth control pills.

***

Danielle heard the back door slam and set the baby photo of Shannon back on the mantelpiece. She'd been standing there for at least twenty minutes looking at baby pictures of both girls. How easy it was then. If only she could go back, hold them in her arms. Now she wasn't even certain she knew the two young women living in her home. They were virtual strangers to her.

"Hi, Mom," Cassie said and headed for the kitchen.

"Hi, Cass. How was your day?" *Keep cool and don't lose it.*

"Fine. I think I got a job at In-N-Out, which is, like, so humiliating because if my friends see me I'm gonna die, but no one is hiring, and you're stuck on this job thing. Anyway, so my day basically sucked."

Danielle started in for the kitchen. "Cassandra there is something I need to talk to you about." She cringed. *Never use her full name like that.* The cat was now out of the bag that this was one of those conversations that would not exactly be fun.

Cassie stood there, her mouth full of chocolate chip cookie and placed a hand on her hip. "Sure, Danielle, but can I go change first? I'm going swimming at Hannah's house."

"Don't call me Danielle, and, no. You can have a seat."

Cass rolled her eyes and plopped down on a barstool at the kitchen aisle, twisting it from side to side. "What's on your mind, *Mom*?" she asked between mouthfuls of cookie. "I already know what you're gonna say, cause, like, you've already said it before. I got a job, okay? We good? Or do I have to go plant more stupid flowers with you? That was fun."

Amazing how one moment (especially when the kid needed money) she could be sweet as honey and the next, surly and truculent. "I found something that belongs to you today." Danielle stood on the opposite side of the kitchen aisle.

"Okay." Cassie sighed and looked out the window. "What did you find?"

Danielle reached into her shorts' pocket and pulled out the birth control pills. "I think these are yours."

Cassie's eyes grew big and her face red. She stood up and crossed her arms. "You were looking in my stuff! I can't believe you were looking in my stuff!"

"Wait a minute. How old are you? The last time I checked you were still living under my roof and you're a minor."

"That's beside the point. You can't go through my things."

"You know what? I can. But it's not like that. I didn't go snooping in your things, Cass!" Danielle's stomach swirled. She tried hard to push the emotion aside and not get wound up.

"Whatever! God!" She shook her head and started to walk away.

"Cassandra Rose Bastillia, don't walk away from me!"

Cassie stopped and turned to face her mother. Danielle still knew the right tone to hit to get her youngest daughter's attention.

"What!"

"Sit down." Cassie slunk back and sat down. "I was not snooping. I got tired of seeing your room in a state of disaster. Looked like a hurricane plowed through it. Since I know your idea of cleaning your room is shoving your crap under the bed or stuffing it in the closet, I decided to do it for you. By the way, I expect it to stay exactly how it is. We can discuss that later." She sighed and reached for her daughter's hand. Cassie didn't pull away, but she kept her hand limp and didn't respond by squeezing her mom's hand back like she would have when she was a little girl. "I found the pills in your underwear drawer when I was putting clean pairs away."

"Oh."

"Yeah, oh." The next part of the conversation was about to get tricky and Danielle wasn't quite sure how to handle it. Very delicately because one of her kids was already knocked up. "I take it you're having sex then."

"I don't want to talk about this with you." Cassie looked down.

"I got a news flash for you, kid. This isn't exactly a conversation I want to be having either."

"Good. Then I can go." She fidgeted in her chair.

"No. Just because we don't want to have it, doesn't mean we don't need to have it. Are you having sex, Cass?"

"Duh."

"Okay." Danielle's stomach dropped. "Since when?"

"I don't know, Mom."

"You don't know?"

"No, and I don't know why that matters."

"You're my daughter and it matters because I love you and having sex isn't something to be taken lightly. It should be a mutual decision between two *adults* and hopefully *adults* that are in a loving relationship."

"God, Mom, when did you leave planet Earth? Get real. Everyone *does* it. I don't see the big deal and I'd think, considering Shannon's situation, that you would at least be happy I was responsible enough to get on the pill."

This wasn't going how Danielle wanted. Cassie had her there. And she knew she was being a hypocrite. She herself had had sex with Mark at sixteen. But she'd been in love with him, or at least thought she was. "Is there someone? Someone special?"

"No."

Danielle blew out a bunch of air and leaned back in the chair. "Honey, you do know that birth control pills are not foolproof and they don't prevent diseases."

"I'm not an idiot. I take the pill and I make the guy wear a condom."

That was sort of a relief. "Oh." The next part was going to be even harder. "Okay, but Cass, by the way you make it sound, you've had sex with a lot of guys."

She shrugged. "A few."

Could she just die right there? Could someone please put her out of this misery? "A few? All from your school?"

"Some."

"Jesus, Cassie, aren't you even remotely concerned about your reputation? What people might think or call you?"

"Are you saying that I'm a slut?"

"I didn't say that, but, honey, if you're having sex with more than one guy and that gets around, which it always does, then, yes, there are people who may say that. Doesn't that bug you?"

"No. I'm not a slut. I'm careful. Like I said, everyone does it."

"If everyone told you to jump off a bridge would you do that?" She raised her voice.

Cassie stood up and walked up the stairs. "Get over it, Mom."

Danielle started to follow her. As she did, the front door opened and Shannon came in. Cassie's door slammed and Danielle turned and looked at her oldest daughter.

"You know, don't you?" Shannon asked.

Danielle had been wanting to have this conversation all weekend with Shannon, but after what had just transpired with Cassie, she wasn't up to it. She looked to the top of the stairs. Cassie wasn't opening that door. She looked back at Danielle and tossed her hands up. From one kid to the next, but they both needed to be dealt with, so while one was simmering the other one was now in the hot seat. "Yes, I know. Mark told me. He had no idea that I didn't know, and what I want to know is why I didn't know? Why haven't you told me about the baby? And how long have you known?" She didn't stop with those few questions, already fired up from Cassie, Danielle continued.

"Have you thought about this? Really thought about this? Your career? Your life? Do you even remotely understand the challenges that you and this child are going to face? And what about a relationship for you in the future? Do you think that there's a man out there who will want to take this type of challenge on? What *have* you been thinking?"

Shannon didn't reply for a minute. She tucked her long red hair behind her ears and quietly answered her mother's tirade. "I figured first we'd get past the initial jolt, you know, of me being pregnant and all." Her words rushed like a fast flowing river caught on a current headed for the falls. "I'm sorry, Mom. I wasn't ready. I wasn't ready to talk to you about this, and, yes, I have thought a lot about what I am doing. That's all I have thought about for months."

"Don't you think this is something we may have wanted to discuss when you came home? Actually this should have been talked about as soon as you found out. Your pregnancy should have been discussed with me *when* you found out. This is bigger than you coming home and announcing that you're pregnant. This is quite a bit bigger. This is about a child who is going to have special needs. Your baby has Down Syndrome. Do you get that? I don't know if you realize what you're getting into. Do you want that kind of burden?" Danielle wished she could take it back the minute she said it.

"Burden? Is that how you feel?" Shannon crossed her arms. "And don't talk to me like I'm a child. Of course I get what Downs is, and I am totally aware of the challenges we'll face, but a burden, Mother?"

Danielle closed her eyes and shook her head. "No. I ... Look, even if the baby didn't have special needs, raising any baby is no easy feat. I don't think you've thought this out all the way. What I'm trying to say is that, even if the baby didn't have Down Syndrome, you are in for a lot more than you realize. I struggled even though I had your father in the house. I can't imagine what it would have been like to do it alone. I know women do it, but I see Jamie struggling with her daughter, and I know it wasn't easy for Kat, and I don't want that for you. With this baby it will be that much harder."

"How about me, Mom? How about what I want? What did you expect me to do?"

"You had to have known for a while."

"Yes. I've known since I was four months along."

"Then why? Why did you decide to go through with this?"

"With *this*? *This*," she said as she rubbed her expanding stomach, "is my son. And it wasn't easy to make *this* decision. It really wasn't. But did you forget your faith? The same one you taught me? This baby is a life, and I know it won't be easy. But what if this is what my life is supposed to be? What if this baby is the best gift I could ever ask for? You assume this will be horrible and terrible and so hard and that I'm throwing my life away. How do you know that this child isn't going to give me the life I am supposed to have? As far as I am concerned, this baby is a gift from God, and I am not going to destroy his life or mine. I know what I'm doing. I want this baby, and I'm going to love him and take care of him. I have enough faith that God will carry me through. I think you might want to try that out. Faith, Mom. That's all it is. I believe in him." She pointed to her belly. "And in me."

"Shannon, please."

"Please, what? This is my life. My son. And I'm sorry if you don't agree with it." Shannon shook her head. "I'm going to lie down."

"Wait, honey. I'm sorry. I want to talk about this."

Shannon headed for the stairs and didn't turn around.

Danielle put her face in her hands. Her mind racing. Why couldn't she talk to her daughters any more? Maybe Shannon had been right. What did Danielle expect her to do about it now anyway? She should be proud of the kid. She had fallen back on her faith, and how many times recently had Danielle wished her youngest would do that these days? She was a hypocrite. That's all there was to it. Confession. She would go to confession. She would talk to her priest. Now there was something she hadn't done in ages. Yes, she was definitely a hypocrite. This whole situation was going to take far more than a few Hail Mary's and saying the rosary. This was huge. Had she expected Shannon to abort this baby? No. She shook her head. But the life that both of them would have now . . . what was it going to be like?

"Smooth, Mom."

Danielle wiped the tears away and looked up to see Cassie standing over her, her arms crossed in front of her. "What?"

"Nice going. You're scoring all sorts of points these days."

This was the last thing she needed. "You heard that?"

"Yes, I heard."

"Then could you please leave me alone?"

"Sure." Cassie let her arms dangle to her sides. "But has it occurred to you that this life-changing event might be the best thing that's ever happened to Shannon? It might be what makes her into the person she's supposed to be. Like maybe having sex with different guys might make me the person I am supposed to be." Her smile was as sarcastic as her tone.

If Danielle had the strength she would have stood up and smacked the kid across the face. "Cassie, for once, just shut-up. Please," she said quietly.

"No. I'm serious. And how do you know that taking the pill won't be the best thing in the world for me? Obviously Shannon didn't take it and look what happened there." She rolled her eyes.

"Cassie, shut-up! You don't know when to stop, do you? You just keep going and going. Is this the way you speak to your father and *Stacey*?"

"Get over it. You're so bitter about Dad and Stacey. Let it go."

"Let it go. Yeah. You know what, Cass? I think it's time you go. I think you should head on upstairs, pack your things, and call your dad and let him know that you're moving in with him and his wife and your two baby sisters. I will no longer take your abuse in my home."

Cassie stood there stunned. "What? That place is a madhouse with freaking Elmo crap everywhere. No. I'm not moving there."

Danielle got up and took Cassie's keys from the counter, then walked to the kitchen and picked up the phone.

"What are you doing?" Cassie yelled. "You can't take my keys! Dad gave me that car. Give them back."

Danielle dialed Al's cell phone while Cassie continued to rant on. When he answered, she calmly told him. "Your daughter needs you."

"What? Is it Shannon? Is she okay?" Al asked.

"Not that one. The little banshee in the background screaming that I can't take her car keys away or tell her to move in with you. Well, she's wrong. Here's the deal, Al, Cassandra will be moving in with you and Stacey for the rest of the summer. We can reassess the situation in September."

"You can't do that. We have to go back to court for that kind of decision."

"Bullshit! Listen here, Cassandra is disrespectful, obnoxious, and downright mean to me. I won't tolerate it any longer."

"Put her on the phone. I'll talk to her."

"No. You'll talk to her tonight over dinner at your house. You better call your wife and ask her to make up a room for Cassie, and then you better have your ass here to pick her up in one hour, or else I'll bring her myself."

"I'll be there," he said. "But we're not finished discussing this."

She hung up the phone. She didn't want to do this. She didn't want to send her child over there, but she knew that if she didn't do it, things would not change. Cassie needed to see the chaos and the dysfunction on the other side of the fence. But still. Was she being too harsh?

"You're a bitch! I'm never coming home!" Cassie stormed up the stairs and slammed her door.

Well, then. There was her answer. Tears blurred her vision. She momentarily wondered if she'd done the wrong thing. What if Cassie never did come home again?

CHAPTER TWENTY

Jamie

Wednesdays had become Jamie's favorite day. It was the day she left work fifteen minutes early and went out to the ranch for a riding lesson. She told herself that the real reason she liked Wednesdays so much was because she loved the horses and going riding. She also liked Saturdays because that was when Maddie took her lesson and Jamie helped with the horsemanship for the handicapped.

So far she'd done a decent job convincing herself that her good mood on Wednesdays had nothing to do with her riding instructor. Nothing at all to do with Tyler Meeks. Nothing to do with his amazing teal colored eyes, or his strong arms, or that wavy blonde hair that she wanted to run her fingers through, or the soft voice he used with his horses, and with her.

She cringed, twisting from side to side in her swivel chair behind her desk, chewing on her pencil. She was almost finished editing the last article for the September issue of the magazine. This one was about the resurgence of Bordeaux wines and how the traditional red wines coming from California were taking on more of the French style—less jammy, fruity rather smoother with less alcohol content in them. It was a trend Jamie appreciated. That was the kind of husband Nate had been—complex, smooth, understated in a way. Not like pretty-boy Tyler who had a way with animals and, by all appearances, women too. Not that she'd ever witnessed Tyler come on to anyone. He was always respectful and polite and the occasional comment or look that she took for possible flirtation, she chalked up to Tyler just being his charming self.

"Blah," she grunted. She finished her article and scooped her things into her briefcase.

On her way out to the ranch, she called to check on Maddie. Fortunately, Maddie had made a good friend at the ranch named

Skylar, and they lived close by. Jamie liked the little girl's mom, Beth, and they had scheduled regular play dates. Beth picked Maddie up after horse camp and kept her while Jamie planned to take her riding lesson.

She dialed Beth's number on the blue tooth, and a moment later she was talking with Maddie. "Hi, Mommy. Can I spend the night with Skylar?"

"Did her mom ask you?"

"Yes. She said it was okay. Please."

Beth's voice came over the blue tooth. "It's fine with me, Jamie. I'm running some errands right now, and then we'll head home so they can play. Why don't you take the night off? Skylar has some clothes that'll fit Maddie, and I'll drop them at camp in the morning."

"You sure?"

"Positive."

As much as Jamie wanted to have dinner with Maddie and spend time with her, in some ways it was a relief. She'd just been able to cover the overdrafts from the past week only two days ago. After paying a bazillion dollars in overdraft charges, she immediately went to the grocery store and rationed for the week. Dorothy wasn't too complicated and would be happy with PB&J and some carrot sticks. This would work fine for Jamie too, and that way they could have the hamburger tomorrow night and she'd be able to slide one more dinner in there. The budget and rationing thing sucked, but so far she'd kept it from affecting Maddie. However, Nora had upped the ante and had her husband, who spoke better Spanglish with Jamie, call her and tell her that she needed more money if she was going to continue watching Dorothy. There hadn't been much of a choice. Dorothy's escape to the coffee shop to hang out with Sammy Davis Junior had made both Nora and Jamie nervous wrecks. The good news was Nora stopped watching her daily soaps and followed Dorothy around like a warden.

But to meet that higher wage for Nora, Jamie was down to taking cash advances from her Visa card. She knew she should see some type of financial counselor. She made a decent living, but it didn't cut it any longer. Medical bills, mortgage, credit cards, and the plain old cost of living was causing her a great deal of grief and sleepless nights these days. Being out with the horses gave her a couple of hours of reprieve.

Once at the ranch, she used the bathroom to change into her jeans and boots. She hurried up and took out the horse she rode, Dune. He was a gorgeous palomino Quarter horse that had been one of Tyler's champion working cow horses a half a dozen years ago, and now, at fifteen, he spent the better part of his days teaching beginners like herself.

Tyler spotted her and waved. "Hey, Jamie. How's it going?"

"Good, and you?"

"I'm good. Listen, you're going to ride Washington today. Dune had some chiropractic work done this morning and could use the day off, and I think you can handle Washington."

"You really think so?" Jamie had seen others ride Washington and he was a nice horse, but she had noticed he would occasionally spook. Tyler usually only put the intermediate riders on him, and she didn't know if she was quite ready.

"I do think. You've got good balance and, sure, he can be a pill sometimes, do a little jig, but don't give off any fear, keep your seat in the saddle, heels down and contact on the reins, and you'll be good. I already got him tied up on the ties, so go ahead, groom him up and get the saddle on."

"Okay." That was part of riding. Tyler's was not one of those fancy places where grooms and stable hands did all the work and all she had to do was get up on the horse and ride. The grounds were pristine, the barns gorgeous, but riders were expected to work, and Jamie had found that to be a significant part of the fun and relaxation for her. Plus, in only a few weeks, she'd built up some biceps and lost a few pounds. She was able to fit into her size fours again and liked that very much.

Horse groomed, saddle and helmet on, Jamie led Washington

over to the step stool and got on the horse. Tyler was already at the arena waiting for her.

"Today, since you're on a new horse, what I want you to do is start by breathing and relaxing up there. Let him walk both directions on a semi-loose rein and stretch his legs a bit while you allow yourself to get a solid feel for him. Sit back on your pockets."

After a few minutes, Jamie began to relax some. The horse moved smoothly, and she got fairly comfortable with him.

"Good job," Tyler said. "Get your heels down a bit more. Yup. Now steady your hand. Beautiful."

The way he said the word beautiful. Hmmm. No daydreaming on the horse. But for a few seconds, Jamie couldn't help thinking he was calling her beautiful. It was a nice little daydream but before she got carried away with it, someone ran into the back of one of the metal sheds with the water truck. Washington spooked, lurched to one side, and Jamie lost her balance and came off, landing first on her right elbow and then onto her rear.

"Damn," she yelled.

Tyler dashed into the arena. "Whoa, whoa." Jamie pulled herself up, rubbing the sore elbow that was already swelling and managed to get to the side of the ring. It was then that she noticed that her hip smarted, too. Tyler quickly got a hold of the loose horse and came over to her. "You okay?"

"Smarts a bit."

"Let me look."

She showed him the elbow, a bruise already appearing.

"Gonna be black and blue. Let's get some ice on it. Raul!" He yelled out for one of the stable hands who quickly came running over. "Put him up for me. I've got to get some ice for Jamie here."

Raul nodded and took hold of Washington's reins, leading him away. The horse had a truly remorseful look in his eye. Jamie gave him a pat on the face with her good hand and told him that she knew he didn't mean it.

Walking back to Tyler's office, Jamie said, "See? I told you that I wasn't ready for that horse."

"You were ready. That was a fluke thing. Anyway, it looked to me like you'd lost your focus for a minute. Like you were off in another world. I've told you that you can't ever lose your focus."

She knew her cheeks were turning pink. If he'd only known what world she'd been lost in. Maybe taking these riding lessons wasn't such a grand idea.

Once inside the office, he looked at her arm and elbow again. "I don't think it's broken, but you might want to have an x-ray. It hurt?"

"Like hell."

"Hang on." He went over to a cabinet above his desk and took out a bottle of whiskey and poured her a shot. "Here." He held it out to her.

"Thanks." She took it. Normally whiskey wouldn't be her thing, but the elbow throbbed, and maybe it would ease the pain.

Tyler then went over to his fridge, got a scoopful of ice from the freezer and placed it in a plastic bag. "Sit down." He pointed to the sofa that had seen better days and sat down next to her. He took her hand gently and with his fingers, lightly went up and down the arm. Even through the throbbing pain, his touch sent all sorts of sensations all over her body. Ones she hadn't had in a very long time. Maybe it was the whiskey. That seemed safe to chalk it up to. She was afraid to ask what he was doing. His fingertips reached the elbow joint and his eyes met her. "Hurts here, huh?" He frowned.

"Oh, yeah."

"I've seen a lot of broken bones. I think you bruised it up pretty bad, but I don't think it's broken." He took the ice pack and set it on her elbow. She flinched. "I know it's cold. But you have to keep it on for twenty minutes." Again, his blue eyes met hers and her stomach danced around.

Then Jamie did something she never thought she was capable of doing. Injured or not, with her free hand she touched the side of his cheek and kissed him hard on his lips. For a second, there was no real response, but before she knew what was happening, he was kissing her back just as hard. Jamie forgot the elbow, forgot that she barely knew Tyler, forgot that he was her riding instructor, forgot that he was ten years younger—she forgot all of it.

Jamie laid back on the couch. Tyler pulled himself away and looked at her, but before he could ask her if she was sure, or before he could tell her he was sorry, and before she could change her mind, she reached for his belt buckle and he rapidly unbuttoned her blouse. "Your elbow?" he whispered.

"It's fine." She pulled him into her, kissing him longingly the entire time they undressed one another. Jamie hadn't felt this kind of desire in so long and, as far as she knew, there was no one else in the world but the two of them. He helped her out of her jeans and his lips caressed her breasts, a hand between her thighs. Jamie let out a soft, husky moan.

His lips moved down to her stomach. Jamie tilted her hips up. "Please."

Tyler moved up and inside her with a gentle ease that made her wrap her arms around him and pull him in deeper. Her fingernails dug into his back as he rocked back and forth slowly. Then together they began moving at a rapid pace that left them both breathless. Within moments, an electrical sensation--a warm glow all over the body took hold of Jamie and she came. It was only then that Tyler released himself. "Oh, Jamie. Oh, God." He eased himself off of her, looked at her, and then kissed her passionately, eliciting the same desperation she'd felt when she'd began undressing him.

It took a few minutes before the full realization of what they'd just done settled into her. She still felt the afterglow, but the reality that they were not the only two humans alive all too rapidly flooded back. They were in the real world.

"I uh, I . . . Oh my God. What . . . ?" she couldn't even form a complete sentence or thought. She started grabbing her clothes. Now the elbow hurt.

"Wait a minute. Sit down and take care of that elbow. What are you doing?" he asked.

"I have to go."

"Jamie. No. Have dinner with me."

"I can't. Maddie. I have to get Maddie," she lied.

"Have dinner with me tomorrow then. Come on. We can't forget what just happened."

"We need to. Forget it. Just forget it. That was crazy. I don't know what that was."

"That was a bit crazy, but damn if that wasn't best crazy I've ever had." He smiled, flashing those dimples of his.

"No. It wasn't. I mean, yes, it was fantastic. I have to go." Jamie grabbed her boots and ran to her car barefoot with Tyler right behind her.

"Don't be silly. Come and have dinner with me."

She stopped and turned to face him, her head lowered. She nodded and sighed. "Tomorrow. I'll have dinner with you, but this? What we did? This didn't mean anything. It was the whiskey and I was hurting and you were nice and…"

"I'll see you tomorrow. Why don't you come here around seven, and I'll fix us a meal."

"Fine. Seven." She just wanted to get out of there and away from Tyler.

Jamie drove home. There was no real thought. She tried hard to block out that she'd attacked Tyler and had sex with him. Then the tears came--a flood of them, and then surprisingly, between the tears, was hysterical laughter.

What had happened to her? What had come over her and what in the world had she been thinking? She was a slut, a bimbo. No, she was a grown woman who hadn't had sex in over three years and who lusted after a man who was seriously, seriously gorgeous and her body took over her brain. It happens. No. She was a slut.

She argued with herself the entire drive home, never coming to a solid conclusion about what in the world she had just done—or who she really was.

CHAPTER TWENTY-ONE

Alyssa

*A*lyssa was in Los Angeles with Ian's family for the second time. She'd come down mid-week to be tested to see if she was a match for Ian, and also to get to know his family better. At first it had been a little awkward. Everyone was nice to her, but the situation being what it was, it couldn't be anything but strange.

Ian's family lived in the Fairfax district of Los Angeles in a good-sized, older Spanish-style home that had been in Ian's mother's family for years. Half of the seven children that had been raised in the home were now grown and living on their own.

Alyssa liked and had the utmost respect for Ian's father, Charlie. He was warm, kind, soft-spoken, and a strong father. He had to be. She really admired that he'd been raising these kids on his own for the past few years since losing Louise. One thing she'd noticed about the family was that they talked about their mother quite a bit. The house was filled with lots of love. Family photos hung on the walls and were displayed on side tables. Like Alyssa's parents, Louise had been white and Charlie was black. They were a multi-cultured, multi-faceted family.

Touring the house with Ian, Alyssa picked up a photo with his mom and him in it. "Your mom was really beautiful," she said. The photo was taken at the beach when Ian was about ten, Louise's dark brown hair was tied back into a ponytail with long strands coming out of it and blowing in the wind. Her arms were around Ian as she stood behind him, and they were smiling—happy. Her brown eyes were content, confident, and loving while Ian leaned back against his mom. "Could I make a copy of this?" she asked.

"Sure. I can scan it in my computer, I guess." He appeared perplexed. "Why would you want a picture of my mom and me?"

Alyssa set the photo back down on the side table next to the tan suede sofa. She thought for a second. "Connection. You and I have formed a nice connection and I wish I'd had the opportunity to know your mother. Sometimes we need a reminder of how to be great, why we should be our best. The way your family speaks of your mom, I get the feeling she gave her best all the time, and I'd like that reminder."

What she didn't tell him was she also wanted a reminder that she'd done the right thing by giving Ian up for adoption. Ian had been brought up in the right place.

Ian picked up the photo. "I'll scan it now and set it on the kitchen counter. I'm going to go throw the ball around across the street at the park with my brothers and some of their friends. Have you had a burger yet?"

"No. I'll head out and grab one. You're feeling okay then? I mean to go play ball?"

Ian smiled. "It's not tackle, or even rough at all. Yeah I get tired, but I think I can handle it. I like being outside."

"Okay. Have fun. Be careful." Was she sounding like a mom?

Ian laughed and shook his head. "Yeah. I know." He gave her a brief hug and jogged up the wooden steps to make the copy.

She took in the house with its white stucco walls, archways, and wrought iron chandeliers. The furniture was worn but comfortable. The house spoke *family*. They even had two cats—a calico and an orange tabby—and a chocolate lab named Cocoa. Ian's family, as diverse as they were, looked to be the most normal family on Earth. Now she had to help make sure Ian spent a long life with them.

Alyssa made her way out back. Like the house, the backyard was comfortable. There was a decent size lawn with a koi pond off to the side, lots of green foliage, and a small rose garden. Charlie and his brother, Darren, had been busy making hamburgers for the family.

The barbeque where Charlie stood flipping burgers was set up on the patio with a large square table and umbrella in the center. His brother stood next to him, drinking a beer.

"Hey, Alyssa. You finally gonna eat something?" Charlie asked.

"I was waiting to make sure the kids got theirs first. I wanted to be certain you had enough."

"Girl, I didn't raise all of them without learning how to plan meals," he replied.

His brother, Darren, laughed. "Shoot, your kids alone can eat everything in that kitchen and then some. Once their friends pile in, forget it." He glanced at Alyssa. "You're lucky you getting any."

"He's full of it. Don't listen to him. I know exactly what I am doing. I didn't listen to my wife telling me how to do everything all those years for nothing."

"You actually listened to your wife?" Alyssa asked. "I didn't think most men did that."

Darren winked at her. "When Louise spoke, we all listened."

"Amen. Or she'd whoop ass. Man, that woman could make a fuss when she needed to." Charlie scooped Alyssa's burger off the grill and onto a bun.

"Beer?" Darren asked. She nodded. He grabbed the plate from Charlie and handed it to her, pulling the chair out from the patio table while she sat down.

She looked up at him. "Thank you." She could tell they were brothers, not only their polite manners, but because they looked so much alike. Charlie seemed to have about ten years on Darren, and she guessed he was in his early forties despite his strong build. He reached over into the cooler and took out a Sam Adams, opened it, and gave it to Alyssa.

"Whatever she did, she must have done it right. You have a great family, Charlie," she said. "Thanks." She held up the beer to Darren.

"They're faking it because you're a guest." Darren took a sip from his beer.

"Now, there you go again, telling lies. I may be older and fatter, brother, but I can still take you."

"Uh huh."

Charlie sat down with them and popped open a beer.

They bantered back and forth a bit longer and Alyssa enjoyed the show, but she knew there was something bigger here than men having fun. She knew they wanted to talk to her, and she waited for their cue.

After more small talk, Charlie set his beer down. "Alyssa, we got the test results this afternoon." He sighed.

She could tell it wasn't good news by the way he said it. "So soon? I thought it would at least be a day."

"Ian's doctor rushed it," Charlie said.

"I'm not a match am I?"

Charlie looked down and Darren said, "No."

Charlie leaned across the table. "I know you've already done a lot here, Alyssa, and I can't thank you enough."

She looked back and forth from Darren to Charlie. "What is it?"

"The doc still says that the best matches come from blood relatives, like your parents, any blood siblings, or, since you weren't a match, then maybe the father. The doctors say that a sibling is usually the best bet."

Alyssa sat back and didn't say anything for a minute. She nodded. "My parents don't know about Ian. They were in Tuscany when I had him, but I can call them. And siblings…" She knew that Ian had at least six siblings out there. "This is hard."

"We know," Darren said. "You don't have any other children?"

"No. I don't."

"What about the biological father? Do you know where he is, or if he has other children?"

Alyssa set her half finished beer down and mustered a smile, and then glanced away before looking back at the men. "Look, I don't want to sound cold or selfish here, but can I have some time alone? I need to think for a bit. I really have some stuff here to process."

"Of course," Charlie replied. "I know how hard this must be. Here we've come at you out of the blue and stirred up a lot in your life in a very short amount of time. Take some time."

"Thank you. I think I'm going to take a drive. I'll come back in the morning though. We can talk some more about this then. I know time is of the essence."

Both Charlie and Darren stood. "Thank you again." They each gave her a hug.

She took the photo Ian had scanned and left. She spotted Ian with his brothers and their pals playing their game across the street. She decided not to bother them. He looked to be having a good time, smiling, laughing, and living. Watching him, Alyssa knew what she had to do.

***

After leaving Ian's home, Alyssa took a long walk by the beach, the sand between her toes cool, soaking in everything that had happened to her over the past weeks and the myriad of feelings she was now coping with.

After watching a Southern California sunset that filled the sky with shades of purple and red, she headed back to her hotel room at the Marriott where she'd had enough hotel points to stay in a little suite. It was nice with a kitchen, couch in one room, and then the bedroom in the other. She paced back and forth in the room for several minutes and picked up the phone twice, once actually sitting down to dial. She still remembered the phone number, if it were the same number that it used to be.

But she couldn't do it. Not yet. How would she explain this? She'd run far and fast from Terrell, breaking off their engagement without a very good explanation—she'd told him she wasn't ready, and he'd told her he didn't understand. How could he? He suggested they live together and he'd wait. But she'd told him that she didn't know if she would ever be ready. She'd left him behind with a broken heart and she'd boarded a plane to the West Coast and kept her secrets buried deep inside her. How many nights had she laid awake wondering if she should've told Terrell the truth?

She wanted to be able to tell Charlie and Darren that she'd called the father and that he would be tested to see if he was a match. She knew that for her to get what she needed from Terrell, she would have to tell him the truth, or at least a part of it. How strange life was. How ironic. There was so much truth to the six degrees of separation theory. The last thing in the world Alyssa ever expected was for that night to come full circle and force her to face her past head on.

Alyssa decided to go down to the hotel bar and have a drink. Beer or wine wasn't going to be strong enough to relax her at all, so she ordered a whisky and nursed it. While sitting there, watching people, couples go in and out of the bar, holding hands, cuddling up with one another, anger overcame her. She could have been a half of one of those couples. She shot back the drink.

"Easy there."

Alyssa looked up to see Darren standing next to her.

"Hey. What are you doing here?"

He sat down opposite her at the small table. "I was worried about you. Charlie and I got to talking about how difficult this all has to be for you. I remembered you said that this was where you were staying and since it's on my way home, I thought I'd stop by, see if you needed anything, see if you were doing okay. I was planning on giving you a call to see if you'd come down and have a drink with me, but you beat me to it."

"I guess I did." She tried to smile at him. The waitress came by and Alyssa ordered another drink.

"I'll join her," Darren said. "Must have all hit you pretty hard."

She nodded. "It's not Ian or Charlie and the family. It's something . . ." she sighed, "I have hidden something from people I love, from myself really, for so long, and now it's come back to haunt me and I don't know how to deal with it. But I know that I have to."

"This have to do with Ian?"

"Yes."

"Do you want to talk about it with me? I can keep a secret." He smiled his big, beautiful smile that lit up his entire face and, for a second, Alyssa forgot the pain that she was in.

The waitress came back with their drinks and Alyssa took a long sip. Setting the glass down, she studied Darren for a minute and then she did something she hadn't done in years: she trusted a man.

"Four years ago, I was engaged to a man, and a few weeks before we were to be married we had an engagement party. I actually planned to tell him the following day about Ian. What I wasn't prepared for was that my fiancé's best friend, whom I'd never met, would be someone that I really had met. Someone that I once knew." She took a long drink from the whiskey. "I thought I would never see this man again. But I did. And I met his lovely wife, and found out they had five children with another on the way."

Darren listened and encouraged her to go on.

"This man—James—who was my fiancé Terrell's best friend, is also Ian's father."

Darren's eyes widened and he studied her for a second before responding. "Are you serious? What did you do? Did this guy know you'd had his child?"

She pursed her lips together and shook her head. "No," she finally replied.

"Why?" he asked, his eyes narrowing. "Why didn't you tell him?"

She closed her eyes tightly for a second, images racing through her mind. When she opened them, she blurted out her painful secret. "Because he raped me."

Darren's jaw dropped. "Alyssa, my God, What did you do?"

"I broke off the engagement, and I didn't tell Terrell the truth. This man had been his best friend since childhood. At the time I felt that if I could get away from the past and not let anyone know about it that would be the best way to handle it. Now it's caught up with me."

"I hate to ask this, but how did this happen?"

"The rape?"

He nodded.

"It was one of those situations you hear about on the news, and maybe that was partly why I never told anyone. I wasn't sure anyone would believe me in the first place. I was eighteen, a freshman at

Colombia. My parents were abroad, and for the first time in my life, I felt like an adult, you know? I wanted to major in art, and I had a closet of an apartment that I shared with another girl. Things looked good. I was out grocery shopping one night and that's where I met *Jimmy* at the grocery store off campus. He bumped into my grocery cart. He was good looking, funny and charming, and a few years older than me, and I thought that was sort of cool. He joked with me in front of the fruit tables for fifteen minutes, chatting before he asked me out. I said yes, of course." She remembered everything like it was yesterday.

Darren shook his head.

"He took me to an expensive restaurant and we talked all evening and I liked him. But then he started coming on to me, and I wasn't ready for that. I hadn't had a lot of experience with guys. I was a virgin and never dated much in high school.

After dinner, he drove over the Brooklyn Bridge. I asked him where we were going and he kept saying that it was a surprise. I knew I was in trouble when he parked in an alley. I told him again that I wanted to go home, but he told *me* that we were there to get to know each other better and I would get home when he got me there.

"That's when he lunged for me, ignored my cries and pleading for him to stop. He tore my clothes, not caring what I said. Finally I gave in because I had *no choice*. Six weeks later, I found out that I was pregnant, and I made the decision to have the baby and give him up for adoption. The best part is that when I spotted him at our engagement party, he acted like he didn't recognize me." Alyssa was surprised that she didn't feel like crying or choking on emotion. She didn't feel as though she were suffocating—something she'd felt time and again when she thought about that night. Telling the story to Darren was almost like talking about a book she'd read or a movie she'd seen. The distance of it all, and time seemed to make it easier, and she let out a relieved sigh.

"You've been carrying that, *all that* for this long?" he finally said.

"Yes," she whispered.

"Alyssa, you don't need to carry it alone any longer. You are so brave, woman. Unbelievably courageous."

"You can't tell Charlie or Ian. Please."

"No. I know. I won't. But I can help you through this. You should not do this alone. That bastard needs to be called out on it, and, whether or not he is a match for Ian, he needs to pay some restitution."

She shook her head. "Darren, I don't need a hero here. I am grateful you want to help me, but I don't need you going to battle with this man. All I want is for him to be tested, and if he is a match, for him to donate the bone marrow. I don't need anything else."

He sat back. "If that's what you want."

"There's one thing, maybe," she said.

"Anything."

"Maybe you could make the initial phone call to get his number and then call him."

"It's done. I'll do whatever you need."

"Thank you." She smiled, and in so many ways felt relieved. After finishing their drinks, Darren walked with her to her room. They planned to meet in the morning. He gave her a kiss on the cheek and started back to the elevator.

"Darren?"

He turned around.

"Will you stay the night with me?"

CHAPTER TWENTY-TWO

Kat

*K*at was dreaming--something about a waterfall in Hawaii and eating pineapple. Nice, but then a monkey was at her side tugging on her arm and saying her name in a small voice. Maybe it wasn't Hawaii after all. Were there even monkeys in Hawaii?

"Kat, Kat, Kat. My bed."

"Your bed?"

"Uh huh. I wet it. I'm sorry."

Slowly Kat realized this was no longer a dream and the tugging on the T-shirt she slept in wasn't coming from a monkey. It was Amber. Kat sat up. "What is it, honey?"

"I wet my bed," Amber said in a quiet voice.

Kat slid out of her bed, Christian softly snored. Not much woke him, especially after a long night at the restaurant. She took Amber's hand and led her into the bathroom. They both blinked their eyes several times as Kat flipped the switch and assessed the situation.

"I'm sorry," Amber said again, tears pooling in her big eyes.

"You don't need to be sorry. Accidents happen. Let's get you out of the wet jammies and clean you up." Kat helped her out, ran some warm water in the tub and wiped her off, and then dried her. "Go get in bed with your daddy, and I'll change your sheets."

"Thank you." Amber hugged her hard. "I don't wet my bed too much, but sometimes I do. Mommy says it's when I'm tired."

"I am sure you were very tired. Now go and get in bed."

Kat stripped the sheets off the twin bed in Amber's room. The urine had soaked through and there had been no protective sheet on the bed. Amber had stayed with them plenty of times and never wet the bed, so Kat hadn't prepared for this. It took her a good fifteen minutes to get it all cleaned up and she knew she couldn't put new sheets on until the following day. So she went back to her bed where a little girl and her daddy slept. When Kat lay down,

Amber immediately scooted up next to her and began twirling Kat's shoulder length hair in her fingers. Kat realized that she was becoming this child's mother and, oddly enough, she welcomed it. Amber felt as much her own as the boys did to her, she remembered that tomorrow Emily would be coming to pick Amber up for the weekend, and she sighed.

In the morning, she woke tangled up in the soft white sheets and brightly striped duvet cover, with Amber's arm across her shoulders. Divine smells wafted from the kitchen. Coffee, for sure, and was that vanilla and butter in the air? Christian was making his famous Grand Marnier French toast. How lovely. Oh, and bacon. Kat loved bacon. Who didn't love bacon? What was he trying to do? She'd be signing up for Weight Watchers after this morning.

Kat eased Amber's arm off of her and rolled over. What a sweet face to wake up to. Tangles of blonde hair whisked across her little heart-shaped face, her long dark eyelashes covering the pretty hazel eyes that now looked at Kat with trust and love. She had no idea that she would fall so deeply in love with this child and so quickly. Yes, she'd known her for years, but their relationship had always been strained because of Emily's brainwashing. Usually Amber only wanted to be with Christian when she'd come to stay, but it was different now. Amber was smart, and Kat sensed that the girl felt abandoned by her mom. Kat silently agreed that Amber was right: Emily had dumped her and moved onto a new life, a new family. That felt familiar.

She thought of Venus, who was probably off on her morning hike and then headed to yoga and meditation. So much for the oodles of time that she'd promised to spend with them. Since she'd landed, her mother had been on the hunt for yoga studios, spas, organic food markets, psychics, and New Age bookstores. Today, though, after Emily picked up Amber, Kat had agreed to join her mother in a yoga class, and then supposedly Venus had some big, fun surprise in store for her. Kat didn't have much time for surprises. Saturday night was a big night at the restaurant, and Christian would need her there. Since Amber had moved in, they'd decided to hire another sommelier, and Kat had cut her work at the restaurant in half.

Amber stretched and yawned, sleepy eyes blinking. "Hi, Mommy."

"No, honey, it's me, Kat."

"But you are a mommy."

"I am."

"Can I call you Mommy Kat?"

Kat pulled her close and hugged her. "Of course you can." Mommy Kat—funny, but cute.

"Something smells good," Amber said, and sat up.

"Sure does. Maybe we should head into the kitchen and see what's going on." She took Amber's hand and they walked down the long hall of their ranch-style home. The house was done up Southwestern style with jute rugs, lots of leather seating, and bench stools in traditional hand woven kilims in colors of sea foam green, bright orange, and dark brown. While the house had been in escrow, Kat and Christian had taken a long weekend jaunt to New Mexico and fallen in love with the Southwest style and flare.

The smells from the kitchen grew stronger--garlic and onion were in the mix now. And there was laughter. Who was Christian laughing with? Her mother? Yes. Shit. Her mother was probably filling his head with her stupid New Age crap. Wait a minute, more laughter. Jeremy? He was up before ten o' clock? It was only eight-thirty.

"Hey, guys," Kat said, interrupting what seemed to be an inside joke as Jeremy, Christian, and her mom stifled their laughter. "Looks like I'm interrupting. What's going on in here?"

Amber let go of her hand and ran to Christian, wrapping her arms around him, "Daddy, Daddy, what are you making?"

"French toast. And, no, you are not interrupting. Your mom was telling us about the time when she dressed as a punk rocker on Halloween and showed up at your high school to pick you up."

"Mom! Did she tell you that it wasn't Halloween yet?" Kat made a face at her mother, who looked bright and cheery with her auburn hair (colored by natural dyes) pulled back tightly, and her makeup (all mineral and natural) applied perfectly. Kat ran her hand through her mussed, brunette hair that she'd noticed had a few grays popping through, and wrapped her comfy terry cloth robe tightly around her, moving toward the coffee pot.

Her mom waved a hand in the air. "Please. It was a week early. I loved the costume and thought you'd think it was funny."

"No. I was mortified, especially when Chad Becker who I had a huge crush on saw you and you winked at him."

"I was only having fun."

"What's a punk rocker?" Amber asked.

Christian laughed. "Yes, Nanny V, do tell us what a punk rocker is?"

"I wasn't just any punk rocker, you know."

"No, Mom. We are so not going there." She poured her coffee.

"Who were you, Nanny?" Jeremy asked.

Kat turned to him, surprised to see him dicing tomatoes. "What are you doing?" Kat asked. "And why are you up?"

"He's chopping tomatoes for me," Christian said.

"I'm up because Christian woke me about an hour ago and asked me to take out the trash and come help fix breakfast." He answered without his usual sarcasm and Kat squinted suspiciously at him. Jeremy shrugged. "I didn't mind."

Maybe the anti-depressants were working. After talking it over further with the counselor, Jeremy's pediatrician, and Christian, they'd thought giving it a go was a good idea. Kat was skeptical of the tact that Christian wanted to take with Jeremy. Christian told her only two nights earlier that he planned to start getting the kid up and busy. First, she didn't believe that he'd even take a real interest. Then when he continued on with the banter of how a kid needs to get going early, needs focus, needs something to accomplish, she felt like he was jabbing at her as if she didn't push the boys hard enough. Christian's ideas were always fairly good and his heart was in the right place, but the way he implemented things sometimes came across as harsh to Kat who had grown up in a pretty gentle, peaceful environment. Christian's idea of waking a kid up typically meant a shake of the shoulder and the words, "Get up, get going. Make something of yourself." The response this typically got from the boys was major complaining.

But this morning, Jer looked content, and far be it for Kat to rock this boat.

"Nanny V, what is a punk rocker?" Amber asked again.

"Yeah and who were you?" Jeremy asked.

"Have you ever heard of Sid and Nancy?" Her mom smiled devilishly and winked at Kat, who shook her head.

Christian raised an eyebrow.

"No," both kids replied.

Kat whispered in Christian's ear, "Am I dreaming this?"

"Nope, and everything is almost ready." He gave her a kiss on the cheek and pat on her butt.

"Too bad Brian isn't here," she said.

"Why would he be here with us where you actually have to try and participate in a family, when he could be with Disneyland Dad and get whatever he wants, whenever he wants it?"

"Chris . . ."

"It's true, and you know it." He put the French toast under the broiler to caramelize the Grand Marnier.

"See, Nancy had this horrible addiction to..."

"Okay, Mom. Amber is six. I don't think she needs a history lesson on Sid and Nancy."

"I want one though," Jeremy said.

"We'll rent the movie," Christian said.

"Seriously? There's a movie?" Jeremy dumped the chopped tomatoes into the pan.

"Sure. You and me tomorrow night when your mom is out with her friends. Whose house is your little soiree at this time?"

"Jamie's."

"I'd like to go," her mother chimed in.

"No you wouldn't. I mean, we just get together and talk about our kids and stuff. I think you'd have more fun here having movie night."

"No, I wouldn't. I want to meet your friends. I'll plan it. I'll even make a tofu dish to bring."

"You don't need to do that."

"I insist."

"Okay. Great." How was she going to convince her mom to stay home?

"Mom, Christian said that I could come work with him at the restaurant and make some cash," Jeremy said.

"Really?" She glanced at her husband, now whisking eggs for the omelets.

"Sure. I could always use a dishwasher."

"Wait, you said that I could also chop and dice and stuff," Jeremy said.

"I did and, yes, you can. I'm teasing, Jer. But you might have to wash a dish or two."

"That's cool."

Was this really her family? Kat looked around the room: Christian and Jeremy getting along like two peas in a pod, and Amber calling her Mommy Kat. Her mother was still as nutty as ever, but maybe she could deal with it for one happy hour with her friends. It could turn out to be entertaining. If only Brian hadn't chosen to spend the night at the Sperm Donor's, they'd all be here. Well, there was also Dad. She'd avoided talking to him about Venus, but he knew she was here because her sister Tammy had told him. She'd see if they could have dinner together in the coming week, to make sure he was okay and that the simple idea of her mother's mere presence in town hadn't shaken him.

They sat down to eat and everything looked as good as it smelled.

Her mother toasted them. "To my beautiful family. May you honor the light from within."

"Here, here," Christian said, holding up his orange juice. "To the light within."

Oh, Brother. Kat looked at Christian who winked at her and nodded. "Absolutely. Lights ablazing all from right here." She pointed to her heart. "Right from within."

***

The heated yoga class about killed Kat. She sweated out at least two gallons of water and wanted to puke twenty minutes into it, then grew dizzy in between downward dog and upward dog for the fifteenth thousand time. And this was supposed to ease the mind and take away stress? Sure, it'd take away the stress all right, because if you made it out alive, your ass would be so kicked that you'd have no choice but to go back to bed and sleep for at least a full day. Kat was not afforded that luxury. One thing the grueling hour and a half of yoga did do was take her mind off of Amber's departure with Emily. She'd left after breakfast and it nearly tore Kat's heart out when Amber said to her mom, "I don't want to go. I want to stay with Mama Kat and Daddy."

"You'll be back. Now say goodbye." Emily tugged on her hand.

Christian intervened and scooped Amber up into a piggy-back. "Now you go and have fun in the city with your mom and Baron. Kat and I have to work tonight anyway, but we'll come and pick you up on Tuesday."

Amber pouted. "I wanna stay here and swim with Jeremy and play with Nanny V."

"She's swimming?" Emily asked.

"Quite well," Kat replied. She rubbed Amber's leg. "Now, honey, you go and have lots of fun with your mom like Daddy says. We'll see you in a couple of days."

Amber nodded as tears slid down her face. Kat had to go back into the house while Christian buckled Amber into the backseat of the car. It was only three days, but she didn't know if she could make it either. How come Emily had all the control? She'd been the one who'd made up all the rules in this game, pulled all the heartstrings.

Selfish, conniving . . .

Oh, yeah, but that yoga, that took the anger right out of Kat and filled her up with sore everything and total exhaustion, and she had an entire evening of work to look forward to.

After showering at the yoga studio and putting on a little makeup, her mom, looking chipper and practically glowing, hooked her arm in Kat's. "Wasn't that fun?"

"Terrific."

"Good. I'm happy you enjoyed it because I bought you a membership."

"You did what? Now why would you do that?" Kat unraveled her arm from her mom's.

"Because you need some stress relief. Look at you."

"What's wrong with me? And how do you figure sweating the piss out of me releases stress? I'll have to drink six gallons of water just to make it through the day."

"Yes, you will. Maybe not six, but water is what cleanses us, inside and out, keeps us clean, pure, and in touch with the earth and all of its glorious gifts."

"Bullshit."

Her mom looked at her like a wounded puppy. "It is not. I don't understand you, Kitty. You are so negative. You have beautiful children, a husband who adores you, a successful business, good friends, and all you do is complain."

They reached the Jeep and got in. Kat didn't comment for a minute. She didn't want to comment, because she knew the truth and the truth just happened to be that it was her mother who was her problem. "Mom, I'm sorry. I feel a bit edgy about Amber leaving with Emily, and the yoga was tiring, so I didn't mean to take it out on you." Kat swallowed hard, deciding to go back to her old adage of maintaining the balance, not rocking the boat, keep everyone happy so no one gets hurt.

"I understand, Kitty. It's fine. I'm excited for you to start regular yoga classes. We can go every morning while I'm here. That will give you a good start. And they say it takes twenty-eight days for a person to form a new habit. We'll have lots of time together and you'll form wonderful new habits. Now for the surprise. We are going to *The Grapevine Meditation Center* to align our chakras. You will feel amazing afterwards and all your energy channels will be flowing and connecting! This is so great, isn't it?"

"Yes, Mom. It's great." Kat bit her tongue and followed her mother's directions to *The Grapevine Meditation Center,* working to maintain her focus on the light from within.

CHAPTER TWENTY-THREE

Jamie

*J*amie sat at her outdoor table with her friends, trying hard to pay attention, but her mind was elsewhere.

Danielle laughed at something Kat said about her sons.

"They're charming boys, Kitty. You were no sweetheart when you were a teenager either," Venus said. She'd joined them for the evening, and Jamie found it was nice. Their conversations tended to stay lighter and easier with their guest there. She knew that a lot had happened in Alyssa's life over the past week. She knew that Alyssa hadn't been a bone marrow match for Ian, but she didn't know what the next step was. They hadn't had an opportunity to discuss it.

"Teenagers and grown children. That's a party all in itself," Danielle said, her voice tinged in sarcasm. "You can set up all the boundaries you want and all the rules. In fact you have to. I get that, and I agree with it, but let me tell you something." Danielle trained her eyes on Jamie. "Take Maddie. She's what, nine now?"

Jamie nodded. "Almost ten."

"Right and she's a sweet kid, isn't she? Loves her mom."

"She's great. Sure, she has an occasional meltdown, but so far so good."

"You ain't seen nothing yet, sister. So Maddie throws a little tantrum now and again. Danielle looked at Kat. "Remember when it was all oohs and ahs and that little baby, then toddler then young child was all cute and cuddly and sweet?"

"Ah yes, those were the days." Kat laughed.

"Right. I hate to say it but those days are rapidly racing to a halt, J. Before you know it, they'll be long gone. The next thing you know, you'll be dealing with surly attitudes and a vocabulary that consists mainly of grunts and an occasional *whatever*. This is when you'll find yourself drinking not just one glass of wine at the end of the day. You know, for a little stress release. Oh no. One won't do it. You'll need two or three when the kid starts sneaking out and lying to you and possibly piercing her belly button or trying to get a tattoo of a hummingbird on her boob, or getting on the pill, or getting knocked up."

Everyone glanced at each other. Alyssa mouthed the word *hummingbird* to Kat who shrugged and shook her head.

Danielle continued on her tirade. "And while you're on your third glass of wine at night, you'll begin having cryptic, pathological thoughts wondering if that sweet child of yours taking up two hundred fifty square feet of your home is really the spawn of Satan." She shook her head and took a full gulp of wine, setting it down hard on the table.

"I'm telling you right now, it sucks to be a parent of a teenager. And word to the wise, be sure you have your hairdresser appointment booked every four weeks, because that's how often you'll be going in to cover up those grays. I believe the years from thirteen to eighteen sprout grey hairs on mothers as if the hormones being emitted from the little demons are like bags of fertilizer attracted directly to the roots of your hair. And, I don't even want to give you a heads up on what those five years do to your face." She touched the side of her eyes. "Crow's feet right here. Popping up like crevices in the fucking Sahara desert. I'm even considering Botox. Never thought I'd say that." Danielle picked up the wine again and finished it, then reached across the table and poured herself another glass.

"You're scaring me," Jamie said. "And, hon, maybe you should have some water or some coffee."

"No. Wine is good. Being buzzed, drunk, numb, whatever, is good for now. Thank you very much."

"I'll drive you home tonight," Alyssa said, and Danielle nodded.

"Danielle is right, J." Kat smiled. "You should be afraid. Be very, very afraid, of little demon spawn, right, Mom? I think you can relate with me and Tammy."

"Of course not. Face it all head on. It's a wonderful, divine challenge. Living at the ashram has taught me that communication is so important. You must have that with your children. For instance, no one likes to talk about sex any more, as if it's a bad thing. Sex is a wonderful thing." Venus reached for the platter of salmon and put another piece on her plate.

"Mom, no. Not sex. We don't want to talk about sex."

"I don't understand why you're all so squeamish talking about sex." Venus set down her wine.

"Mom?" Kat implored.

"What? You must realize, darling, that I have had a lot of sex. I had you and your sister. You don't think that is the only sex I ever had, do you?"

Danielle laughed, Jamie smiled, and Alyssa shook her head.

"Yes, mother, but you are my mom. Can we not discuss your sex life?"

"You're such a prude and it's obvious you're not getting enough of it yourself."

Kat's jaw dropped. "Jesus, Mom."

"I'm serious. You're always uptight, snapping at Christian. The man adores you. The two of you need to be getting it on a lot more. I even heard on Oprah that Dr. Oz says that orgasms extend your life span and keep your stress levels way down."

"I don't watch Oprah," Kat said, pouring herself some more wine.

"That's obvious. You really should. You don't need more wine, honey, you need a lot more nooky. It'll help you burn some of those extra pounds in the hip area."

"Thank you, Dr. Ruth. And how the hell do you suppose I make that happen? There are three kids in the house, and then there's you, in and out all the time. We have no privacy."

"Lock your bedroom door."

"Easier said than done. I, for one, don't feel like hanging from the chandeliers while Snoop Dog is playing from one room, and Papa Roach from the other. And as far as Amber goes, I think she needs a little security right now. I'm not going to lock our door, because she may need us."

"I think she's a buffer between you and Christian, because you don't want to deal with how angry you are at him for not stepping up and being the dad to the boys that you wanted. So now you're going to be the mother to Amber that her mother hasn't been to her, so you can one-up your husband."

"And I think you're full of shit. You and all your theories. Just because you ran off and went all Hare Krishna on us, certainly doesn't qualify you as having a degree in psychiatry. Maybe you should analyze yourself, Mom, and all the ashes you left in your wake when you decided to go and *find* yourself."

Venus sat back and smiled. "I will think about that. Thank you for pointing that out."

"Oh, Mother!"

"What?"

"Nothing."

"You should consider a lock on that door and start having more sex. Look at your friend. She's happy as a clam. She must be getting it a lot, and recently too, I'd say. Maybe three or four times this week, right?" Venus leaned her elbows on the table. "Which is it, love. The magic number. Three or four?" She looked directly at Jamie who turned bright red.

"Me?"

"Yes, you. Of course you. Not my daughter. From what I can tell, you appear to have harnessed your inner sex goddess and you've done it quite well, I might add."

"I, I . . ." Jamie couldn't say anything. Everyone was staring at her.

"Jamie? Is there something you want to share with the rest of us?" Danielle asked, a smile spreading across her face.

Jamie put her face in her palms. "Oh, God," she groaned. Looking up, she nodded and said, "Yes, okay, yes. It's true. I am having sex everywhere and all the time."

There was a collective gasp.

"For how long?" Kat asked.

"With who?" Alyssa asked.

"I think I can guess," Danielle said. "It's with Tyler Meeks."

"The cowboy?" Alyssa asked.

Kat nodded. "The *younger* cowboy."

Jamie closed her eyes and leaned back in the chair, allowing everyone to toss out their questions. She opened her eyes and slammed her hands down on the table. "Yes, yes, yes. Okay. It's with Tyler. And it's the best damn sex I've ever had. We did it in his office the other day and then in every room in his house and even in the hay barn, and I love it. I really love it, but I am so damn miserable I don't know what to do."

"What?" Venus asked. "I'd say you're doing it. Don't do anything else, but it."

Kat shot her a look. "Pipe down and listen for once. Otherwise you can walk home. I don't want another word out of you tonight."

Venus frowned, dejection all over her face, but she kept quiet.

"Details," Danielle said. "We want details."

Jamie told them about the fall off the horse and what had ensued directly after in Tyler's office.

"You little hooker, you," Danielle said. "Huh. I love it. Cool. Okay so that was the first time. The sex guru here says there's been at least three or four times this week."

Jamie felt the heat rise to her cheeks. "More like seven or eight. I am a little hooker, aren't I?"

"Girl! Oh yeah you are," Alyssa squealed. They all laughed.

"When did you find time for all that?" Kat asked.

"She made time," Venus cut in. "It was important."

Kat shot her another dirty look.

"The night after the first time, he invited me to his place and . . ."

"What's his place like?" Kat asked.

"It's nice. It's clean and lots of Western art and all rugged-like with leather sofas and chairs. And he can cook, too. I mean it all smelled great, but we didn't exactly eat dinner."

"Who gives a shit what his place is like! What's he like?" Danielle slurred.

Jamie knew she had to be bright red by now. "He's wonderful," she whispered. "Oh my God, he's amazing. I think I've lost my mind."

"This is great," Kat said. "Good for you."

"No. Not really." They all looked at Jamie, waiting for her to continue. "It's these nightmares I'm having. One minute I'm in bed with Tyler, the next I've lost Dorothy again. In the worst one, I lost Dorothy because I was busy, you know, being with Tyler and Nate came home and caught me in bed with the cowboy. Horrible! It's Nate. I feel like I'm cheating on him." Jamie took a long drink from her wine.

"Nate is gone, sweetie," Danielle said.

"I know that! Don't you think I know that?" Jamie snapped at her. "Everyday I wake up and I think maybe it's all been this horrible nightmare and then I roll over and the man I planned to spend the rest of my life with is not there. I know better than anyone else that he's gone, but I don't want him to be gone. I want him here where he belongs. Where I can hold him and make love to him, not Tyler. I want Nate here to kiss Maddie good night and tell her bedtime stories. I want him here to help me make decisions about Dorothy and to tell me what to do while I'm financially going down the drain. Don't you think I know that he isn't here? But he's here." She pointed to her heart. "I'm sorry, I am so sorry." She looked down, shaking her head. "I feel so, so guilty."

Danielle finally spoke. "Of course Nate is in your heart, and feeling guilty is understandable. You're not the kind of woman who goes to bed with just any man. You know we were all teasing you, honey. You are not a little hooker. Not at all. We were funning."

"But I don't love Tyler." She sniffled. Alyssa handed her a tissue and she blew her nose.

"I don't think you have to love him," Alyssa said.

"Think about this for a minute." Kat set down the bottle of wine. "What if the tables were turned? What if you were the one who had passed away?"

Jamie looked up at her, mascara smearing on her face. Danielle wiped it away with her fingertips.

Kat nodded. "Yes. Say it was you and you're living on the other side. Heaven or whatever you want to call it."

"Nirvana," Venus piped in.

"Whatever. There you are with your pretty angel wings." This got a smile from Jamie. "You're dancing around and things are pretty good in this new place, except for one thing. Every time you check in on Nate, he's miserable. He can't let you go. All he does is think about you. He cries himself to sleep, he wakes up needing you. He pretends that everything is fine. He takes care of Maddie and his mom, and for their sake pretends that everything is fine. But he is not fine. He is *miserable.*"

"It would be awful for me."

"Even with your angel wings in your happy heaven, it would be awful for you to see the man you loved so bound up in the past that he could no longer live in the present. And say, he meets someone. A nice lady who treats him well, and who really likes him. Someone who could probably take good care of him and Maddie. And he likes her and they get together and their sex is fantastic and a little bit of Nate starts to let go of a little bit of Jamie. Wouldn't you want him to continue having the happiest, most positive human experiences he could? That's what he would want for you. Don't you owe it to yourself, to Maddie, to Dorothy and especially to Nate?"

Jamie stared at Kat.

"I know I am supposed to be quiet," Venus said with tears in her eyes, "but, bravo! Bravo! Oh, my girl, you *do* get it. You really do."

Jamie stood up, walked over to Kat, and leaned over to hug her. Kat stood and hugged her back. "Thank you," Jamie said.

"It's okay to live and love again. It really is," Kat said.

Jamie pulled away, wiped her face, and looked at her friends. "I think I needed that." She drank a little wine and then asked, "Now who wants to hear about the hot sex?"

Everyone laughed and Venus popped open a bottle of champagne. "You can count me in."

***

Wine Lover's Magazine
Summer Love
By
Jamie Evans

Living in Napa Valley during the summer is HOT. I'm not only talking about the weather. The wine country is full of new loves and old loves, as tourists flock here to our quaint valley to wine taste and experience the allure and romance that Napa is known for.

Summer loving has become a popular topic for my friends and me lately. What exactly is love? How do you fall in love and then keep it? Everyone has a different idea about how that's done. Some think sex is the answer, others believe it is all about communication and family bonds. We haven't come up with any solid answers, but the conversations have sure been fun!

In this month's issue, take time to read over our Summer Loving section, find romance in your home, add some spice to your sex life, and, as always, have a good bottle of wine with you while falling in love and staying in love. This month's wine pairing and recipe comes from my kitchen, and it's one of my favorite summer meals: Salmon in Miso Sauce with a refreshing glass of Viognier.

CHAPTER TWENTY-FOUR

Danielle

*D*anielle had done it to herself again. Taken on more than she could chew. Why had she agreed to help organize the Harvest Festival? Her official role was to put the media and marketing together between the wineries and the consumers who would be paying top dollar to come and taste the finest Napa and Sonoma had to offer. It entailed talking with each winery owner or their winemaker and organizing their marketing pieces. She would then condense down the information to a paragraph for each one, and put them together in magazine format. She also had to hire someone to do the graphics. This would be no cheap endeavor. Her budget for it was three grand—not a big budget considering the expectations involved, so each winery would have to pitch in. She looked at the list of her contacts and spotted the one name she knew would be there—but had hoped wouldn't: Al Bastillia. Of course *The Bastard* would be entering Bastillia wines. Their wines had been in the festival for the past twelve years. Why would this one be any different? One could hope though, right?

Danielle traced the outline of the design of her Deésse label. The artist had done a splendid job. The label showed the profile of a beautiful woman, her naked backside exposed, long red hair flowing over her shoulders, and a strip of gold coming up from the bottom of the label and encircling the Goddess. It hadn't been cheap, but it was a work of art. Danielle loved the concept of the Goddess, so she'd penciled out an idea and taken it to an experienced artist. She would have asked Alyssa to do the artwork, but between flying back and forth to Los Angeles to see her son, Alyssa was already bogged down.

In some ways, having to do so much herself was working out well. During the day, Danielle was able to busy herself with the festival and keep her mind off of her own difficult issues. But at night, there was nothing she could do but think about them.

Cassie was still out of the house. She missed her terribly, but knew that her daughter needed to get the message loud and clear that Danielle was done taking her crap. Did that make her a cop-out or a bad parent?

The other situation keeping her up at night, and keeping her on the verge of a migraine, was that she longed to support Shannon and understand her better. She wanted to reestablish the connection that they once had—that incredible bond that she missed so much. She still had not been able to tell her friends about the baby's condition. It was all a bit too much to deal with. Telling them would make it a fact, and Danielle didn't know if she was ready to accept any of this situation for the reality that it was.

She took a stroll through the small winery warehouse. French Oak and steel barrels were stacked on one side of a long row and the other side contained boxes of her first vintage that was already packed and ready to go. She smiled and said hello to a handful of employees working there. They were a good group who respected and cared for her as she did for them. Most of them left Bastillia after the divorce and came to work for her.

The warehouse smelled of must, oak, and fruit—smells she'd never tire of. They were of the earth. Harvest would begin next month, and Danielle would be right in the midst of the workers. It was an exciting, if exhausting, event.

She walked outside and headed over to the main building where daily wine tastings were offered. She'd just opened up this area and, because her place was off the beaten path and because one had to pass Bastillia to get here, many tourists didn't make that extra mile to her place. Compared to Al's Disneyland of wineries, hers was small potatoes. But! But she'd still *won* the best crops and she would use that to her advantage. Better believe it. Once oenophiles started tasting the wine, Deésse wines would no longer be small potatoes.

Danielle stopped and admired the small but elegant building before reaching it. It had an old-world, Tuscan feel to it and replicated her home on top of the hill. She recognized a car pulling up and smiled. Mark.

He got out of his Audi with a picnic basket, and Danielle couldn't help feel the smile on her face spreading. The man was full of surprises. She'd been distant when she had first heard the baby had Down's, but Mark had called daily. Somehow he managed to be supportive without being pushy, and she'd grown to rely on his calls. Then one day last week he hadn't called, and Danielle missed him, wondering if she'd finally pushed him away. It turned out that he'd had a difficult delivery and was in the hospital all day and had gone to bed there exhausted. He'd sent her roses the next day.

"I didn't expect you. What's this all about?" she asked.

He handed her a bouquet of wildflowers and kissed her cheek. "I finished early for once and thought, what better way to spend my time than with you? I know how busy you are, but I figured I'd take a chance, see if we could have lunch together."

She crossed her arms. "Lunch, huh?" She coyly twisted a piece of hair that had fallen from her ponytail. "What you got in there?" She tried to peek in the basket, which he placed a hand over.

"No peeking. So, lunch?"

She smiled. "Everyone does need to eat. Come on. I have the perfect spot. Let me get something real quick." Danielle hustled into the tasting room and asked her pourer Carmella where a blanket might be.

Carmella was a petite Italian lady of about fifty who had a ton of flair and exuberance. She outsold the three other pourers who rotated shifts at Deésse. At that moment she was pouring for an older couple and describing the nuances of the Chardonnay they made at the winery. She shrugged. "I have one in the back seat of my car out back. You can use it."

Danielle came around the back of the bar and kissed her on the cheek. The older couple watched curiously. "Thank you." She handed her the flowers. "Would you put these in a vase for me?" She grabbed a bottle of chilled Chardonnay from the wine fridge behind the bar and two Styrofoam cups.

"Don't mind her. She owns the winery. Owners tend to be a bit whacky in these parts," Carmella told them.

They laughed while Danielle formally introduced herself and shook their hands briefly. Then she sprinted out back for the blanket. How funny that just seeing Mark there made her behave like a girl again.

"I thought you'd changed your mind," Mark said when she came back.

"No. I was getting this." She held up the blanket. "And this." She presented the wine with the two paper cups around the top.

"Nice. Good idea. From the looks of it, you're planning a leisurely lunch."

"I could use a break," she replied, though what she really needed was a few more hours in her day. But a handsome man with a picnic basket and flowers didn't pull up in a gal's driveway often. At least not in this gal's driveway. "Follow me."

They hiked through rows of vines for almost ten minutes. "Hey, I said lunch, not a hike," Mark commented.

She stopped. "I figured if you could go through all that trouble to put lunch together, then I can go the extra mile for the perfect spot. Don't tell me you're out of shape, doctor."

"No. Maybe a little." He laughed. "I could probably spare ten pounds."

"Couldn't we all," she said. "Only a few more feet." They walked up an embankment, stopping under an old willow tree.

"Beautiful," Mark said, setting the basket down and reaching for the blanket.

"It is, isn't it?" The view before them was of her property, dressed in colors of sienna, gold, light and dark greens and browns. "Like an artist's painting."

"It is an artist's painting though." He sat down on the blanket and patted the spot next to him.

Danielle handed him the wine and corkscrew. "What do you

mean?" Mark put the corkscrew into the wine and twisted, opening it while Danielle held out the cups. "High class, I know," she said pointing to the cups.

"Nothing but the best, baby. That's what I like about you." He smiled and memories of their youth flooded her. It had been his smile that had gotten her underneath him thirty years ago, and damn if it wouldn't work again. "What I mean about the view being done by an artist is exactly that." He leaned back on his elbows and turned to his side, holding up his cup. "To a leisurely lunch."

"Cheers." She touched her cup to his, and they each took a sip.

"Nice," he said. "Mhhm, do I taste pineapple? Maybe a little toffee or hazelnut."

"Ah, what do we have here, a connoisseur? Very good, Dr. Murphy."

"I'll admit I do have a passion for wine, so when you told me you were a winemaker, I was thrilled, but I was also secretly worried."

"Worried?"

He nodded. "I couldn't help wondering what I would do if your wine wasn't something I liked."

"So you're not a connoisseur, but a wine snob." She punched him lightly on the shoulder.

"Maybe a bit, but this," he held up the cup, "this gets huge points. I'm thinking a ninety-seven."

"I don't even think Parker gives a ninety-seven on anything."

"He hasn't tasted your wine yet, now has he?"

"True." She opened up the basket. "What do you have in here?"

"Let's see." He took out two sandwiches on foccacia bread. "My specialty. Grilled veggies, spicy sausage, and feta cheese."

"You can cook too?"

"Yes. This. This is what I know how to cook." He handed her a sandwich. "And I can scramble eggs too."

She laughed.

"And, I sliced us some strawberries, a little honeydew melon, and I couldn't resist so I stopped by Bouchon and bought some lemon bars for desert."

"You are after my heart, aren't you?"

"I am," he replied, a serious note in his voice.

She hadn't expected that. Not really. It was good. Heart-racing-and-beating-out-of-her-chest good, but still, kind of overwhelming. "This is so nice, Mark. Thank you."

They sat in silence for a minute, eating. The sandwiches were delicious. Danielle set hers down, and took a sip of wine. "We got sidetracked. Back to the artist and the view and the painting. I had a feeling we were going down a Socrates route."

"I don't know about that." Mark laughed. "I was talking about God."

"God?"

"Yes. I have a lot of faith. After losing my son, I couldn't find solace anywhere except when I prayed. I can't explain it, because I was never a religious man before that. I'm still not. Not really. I'm a spiritual man, I guess you could say." He held out his cup and she poured him some more wine. "I'm a doctor. I'm supposed to be all about science, but I'm not that guy. You don't deliver babies for twenty-some odd years and not come to believe in God. You just don't. Maybe it sounds corny, but I see God everywhere I look, in everything I see. And this landscape here in front of us is His artwork."

Danielle sat up and took his hand. "That's beautiful. I . . . I don't know what to say. It's lovely."

"What about you?" he asked.

"Me? On God?" He nodded and she sighed. "I still have my faith, and I believe, but I have to admit I struggle sometimes."

"We all do."

She shrugged. "I grew up Catholic, and now I guess I'm what they call a cafeteria Catholic, stopping in on holidays, going to confession when I'm at my rope's end and know I've done something horrible, like kicking Cassie out for being surly and disobedient. And I've alienated my oldest daughter for hiding the truth from me for so long."

"Oh yeah, the sin of parenting. That one will get you in a lot of trouble with the man upstairs."

She laid back on the blanket and relayed the story to Mark. "I feel so rotten. Like I'm not being a mother at all to either of my girls."

He lay down next to her, the two of them looking up under the tree. "I think you did the right thing with Cassie. That may sound strange coming from me because I've lost a child and I would do anything, tolerate anything, to have him back with me. But Cassie is a teenager, and you're her mother. If you allow her to talk to you like that and run all over you, she's going to think she can do it to other people who might not be so forgiving. You never know when her words and actions could get her into trouble. Besides, you've dealt with a hard blow recently and, if you ask me, Cassie is looking for attention, and her timing sucks."

"You could say that."

"Not to mention, she does have a father and from what you've told me he's been less of a father and more of crux—someone she can get whatever she wants from, whenever she wants. Maybe this time spent with her father will teach him what it is to be a dad. Or maybe she'll learn how to appreciate you more. Of course, I'm a gynecologist, not a psychiatrist, so I don't know if you should take my advice on this."

"Of course I want your advice. Go ahead."

"Your gamble is a good one, and I think it will pay you in dividends."

"God, I hope so. But what about Shannon?"

He sat up and faced her. "This you may not like as much."

"I want to hear it anyway." She'd almost forgotten how good it was to have someone—a male someone—to bounce things off of.

"Give her time. The young woman I met seemed mature, responsible, and intelligent. I think you have to come to terms with the idea that your daughter is an adult and this is *her* choice. You may not agree, and you may not like it, but, if you want to rebuild your relationship, you have to love her and her baby through this. Support and love. That is what it's all about."

"How did you learn all of this?"

He took her hand. "When you lose someone you love, particularly a child, you rethink, reevaluate everything in your life. You realize that it really all comes down to love."

Danielle couldn't speak. Mark brought his hand to her face. Looking into her eyes, he kissed her softly on her lips. It was sweet, slow, and understanding, almost as if they had been lovers for decades. She sat up and leaned her head on his shoulder. "Thank you," she whispered.

They finished off the wine and food, and lay back down under the tree, holding hands and talking late into the afternoon.

CHAPTER TWENTY-FIVE

Jamie

*T*uesday morning felt like a splash of cold water had been thrown in Jamie's face. She'd woken up late and had to scramble to get out the door to work, but just as she was about to leave, Nora stopped her. "Me no mas. No mas working for you."

"What?" Jamie shook her head. "Oh, no, you're not doing this to me today. I understand, and I'm trying to find some more help for Dorothy. This is about Dorothy?"

"Sí. Dorothy. Mi no quiero cuidado no more."

"I know it's hard to care for her, but please! And Maddie will be going to her friend's house in an hour so she won't be here much longer. Skylar's mom is picking her up."

Nora looked at her sympathetically and then spoke in English. "I'm sorry, Señora Jamie. I no more take care of. I afraid. I love her and you and Maddie but no more. My daughter es have baby and I take care of her now. I go now. You no needed pay me for last week. I see it not much money for you now."

"No, no, no. I pay you. I pay you more. Lots more. I'm working on it. I'll take care of it." She grabbed Nora by the shoulders. "Please stay. Don't go. Please. I need you today."

"I sorry. My daughter needed me for the doctor." She hugged Jamie hard. "Bye, bye, Señora Jamie."

Jamie stood frozen as she watched her housekeeper and her mother-in-law's caretaker walk out the door. She wanted to cry, scream, and throw something, but already late for work, she didn't have time for a temper tantrum. No. She had to get Dorothy dressed and take her to work with her. First she had to get Maddie taken care of. She called Skylar's mother and explained that she was in a bind. She agreed to let Jamie drop Maddie off as soon as she could.

Jamie got her up, poured Maddie a bowl of cereal, and said, "Hurry, babe. I'm really late. I'm taking you to Skylar's."

"Okay, Mommy. But can I watch *The Saddle Club* while I eat?"

"No time. Eat, dress. We have to go. Chop, chop."

Maddie frowned but did what she was told as Jamie hurried to Dorothy's room. "Mom." Jamie shook the sleeping woman lightly. "Mom?"

Dorothy stirred. "Good morning. How lovely. You are such a pretty girl. Who are you again? I mix you up with Doris Day and Sandra Dee all the time."

"Mom. It's me, Jamie, and we have to get up and get going."

"Where are we going?"

Jamie thought about this for a minute. What would motivate Dorothy to get a move on?

"We are going to see a lot of your old friends today. We can have lunch together and maybe Dean will be there, or Sammy Davis, or who knows? *Who does really know?* We might spot Frank Sinatra out and about. Let's just make it an adventure."

"How fun! But what will I wear?"

Jamie wasn't about to let her get into the closet and use up the precious minutes they had over the day's attire. She quickly rummaged through the closet and pulled out a pretty, floral sundress for her. Dorothy was thin and the dress looked nice on her. Jamie pulled her hair back into a bun, dabbed some blush on her cheeks, and put lipstick on her. She poured her a cup of coffee in a to-go cup and handed her a banana and a piece of toast. Jamie checked her watch and swore under her breath. It was a short week because July Fourth was on Thursday, and she had a lot to take care of.

She got Maddie to Skylar's house and pulled into her parking space in front of Wine Country Corp., the parent company of her magazine. She spotted the big boss' car, and her first thought was that this couldn't possibly be good. It wasn't their quarterly meeting and Evan Michelson was not the type of man or boss to drive in from the city just to check in. Had she missed something? Forgotten something? She glanced at Dorothy. Damn. Time to take a deep breath and get her head on straight.

"Mom, this is where I work. There are some important things for me to handle and I'm going to need you to be patient. I'll set you up with some magazines in our conference room."

"Will anyone I know be in this conference room? I hope Rock is here today. Are we at NBC or Paramount? It looks so different. What have they done to the place? It's smaller. I know Rock is homosexual and all. Everyone knows it, but we don't talk about it though. He is such a dear. Maybe he could join us?"

Jamie was in *trouble*. "Okay, Mom. Let's go."

As she entered the offices, Jamie's assistant Adrienne came around the corner and grabbed her by the shoulder. "Evan is here and it's not good." Then she looked Dorothy up and down. "What is she doing here?"

Jamie glared at her. "Where is he?"

"In the conference room and they're all waiting for *you*."

"They?"

Adrienne nodded. "He has all the staff writers and the department editors. You're late."

"Take her into my office. Give her some magazines and a juice or something and keep an eye on her. *Please*."

Adrienne mustered a smile. "Sure," she said with a tinge of sarcasm.

"Mom, this is my assistant and she is going to take you to my office. I'll be there soon."

"Hello, Jane, it's lovely to see you again."

"Jane?" Adrienne mouthed, aware of Dorothy's mental issues.

"If I had to guess, Mansfield."

"Who?"

"Google her." Adrienne was not quite thirty, big busted, had long poofy blonde hair and a thing for tight blouses and pencil skirts. No wonder, Dorothy decided she was Jane. But for all her outlandish outfits and wild makeup, Adrienne was good at her job.

Adrienne was right. Seated at the long glass topped conference table were her editors and staff writers. Evan sat in her seat at the helm. He looked up as she hurriedly walked in, and found a seat. "Good morning, Jamie. Nice you could make it."

"I'm terribly sorry. I was unaware that we were having a meeting."

No one looked at Jamie. They were all reading the papers in front of them.

"You do know that your work day typically begins at eight in the morning?"

"I had a family emergency."

"Oh?"

"I did. What is this all about, Evan?"

He straightened his expensive silk tie, and his dark eyes lit up. "We at Wine Country Corporation have decided to do some restructuring. Obviously in light of difficult economic times, we've had to take a careful look at the bottom line. Wine Country's in-home tasting and purchases are growing at a steady pace still, but sales are down with the magazine here."

Jamie clenched her fists under the table. Technically, sales were only down by a small percentage, and she knew what this was all about. She'd called Evan last month about revamping the magazine and targeting it more towards women. Her idea was to add columns on beauty and health, include more recipes, a book club section, and base all of it on wine related products. Evan told her that men were still the ones who spent more money on the types of wines the magazine usually covered—collector's wines, the more expensive wines. The irony there (and she did know where he was headed) was that the in-home wine sales his company made via a multi-level marketing program sold mediocre wines for high prices to the average Joe who didn't know enough about the wines to know any better. Evan purchased the wines from sell off lots and had them bottled by his own label *Wine Country Gold*. Even the name was cheesy. Jamie watched the numbers, and Evan had been putting more money into that business and letting her and the magazine run themselves. She could see the writing on the wall.

"My partners and I have decided that we are going to transition the magazine into what will now be called *Wine Country Gold*. I hate to be blunt, but there is no other way around it. Some of you will be losing your job." He glanced up, and something caught his eye out of the conference room. The group opposite Jamie also looked up. "Excuse me but does anyone know who that old woman is?" Evan asked.

Jamie spun around. She jumped up. Dorothy was outside the glass walls of the room, peering in. Jamie got up and opened the door for her. "Mom? Mom? What are you doing?"

"I'm looking for Jane."

She took Dorothy's hand, and brought her into the conference room, pulled up a chair next to her and sat her down. Everyone was silent and watchful. She cleared her throat. "Um, this is my mother-in-law Dorothy and uh, part of the family emergency I mentioned. Okay." She turned back to Evan, mustering a smile. She didn't want to say more about Dorothy if she didn't have to since Evan's mouth was already slightly open. "You were saying, Evan?"

He shook his head. "Yes. I was saying that some of you will lose your jobs *here*, but I want to stress the opportunity you could have by becoming one of *Wine Country Gold's* consultants. You could earn more than you have been earning at your writing jobs and would have the possibility of receiving new cars, trips, all sorts of wonderful incentives. It's only a hundred-and-fifty dollars to join. That is the deal I'm giving you all. This is a one-time opportunity, though. We typically bring in our first level consultants at two-hundred and twenty-five dollars. Do the math, friends. That is a seventy-five dollar savings." He smiled as if he was delivering the best news possible.

Jamie thought she might be sick.

Dorothy raised her hand and Jamie shoved it down. "I was wondering if anyone has seen my friend Jane around? And, you are looking a bit pale today, Yul," she said to Evan.

"Yul?"

"She's confused," Jamie said but as difficult of a situation that she was in, she almost couldn't help laugh. The bald Evan *could* possibly pass for Yul Brenner.

"I have a question." Jamie asked while everyone around her squirmed in their seats.

"Shoot." Evan pointed at her.

"You're saying that some of us are losing our jobs…"

"Not you, Jamie. *Wine Country Gold* has other plans for you. You will have a list on your desk by tomorrow, and you can handle the terminations and present the severance packages."

"That wasn't what I wanted to ask you. What are your plans for the people who keep their jobs? If I'm hearing you correctly, you're closing the magazine."

"Jamie, you are not hearing me. That is *not* what I said. We will be restructuring, and those writers we keep on will be writing articles strictly about Wine Country Gold wines, where they come from, how the company was founded. Things like that."

"Basically you're turning us into a marketing department for the wine tasting business."

"If that's the way you want to put it. Before I made this decision, we were outsourcing the marketing, but I feel this is a perfect fit for such a transition."

There were grumbles from the group. These people were writers, not marketing gurus. They researched their stories and cared about what they wrote. What Evan was suggesting would never work, because this wasn't how these writers thought. What a condescending jerk-off.

"There's Jane now. Bye-bye." Dorothy stood and headed to the door.

Jamie spotted Adrienne rushing down the hall.

"I couldn't have said it better myself," Evan said. "Good-bye, everyone. Jamie will be going over the details with everyone here tomorrow morning."

Her employees, many of them friends, stayed frozen in their seats. Jamie tried to go after Dorothy, but Evan stopped her as they reached the door simultaneously. Adrienne approached Dorothy and began talking to her. Thank God.

"You need to do something about your family emergency, Jamie," Evan snarled.

"I'm sorry." Flustered and angry, she tried to keep her cool.

He handed her a large packet. "I'll expect everything to be carried out by tomorrow afternoon before the holiday weekend. All the information you need is here, and you're lucky I don't fire you for this mishap." He waved his hands in the air. "I've already had my secretary schedule a meeting with you for next week so you can apprise me of the decisions made. I would suggest that everyone, even you, look into becoming consultants for *Wine Country Gold*. It's a great way to earn extra income and, regretfully, I've had to make pay cuts across the board. Including you."

Jamie stood speechless as Evan Dickhead walked out of the offices.

The conference room broke out into cries of outrage. Jamie's head spun. They looked to her for answers and she had none. Not a one. She finally faced the dozen employees. She reached into her wallet, pulled out her company American Express card, and held it up. "I have no answers. I don't know what in the hell just happened here. But I was thinking that we all deserve a day off. Anyone up for lunch at Domaine Chandon?"

CHAPTER TWENTY-SIX

The Fourth

Alyssa unloaded her car full of desserts for tomorrow's Fourth of July party. She'd done her best over the past day to do anything and everything to keep her mind off of what she had to do. But after baking three different fruit pies, a batch of brownies, chocolate chip/macadamia nut cookies, and a strawberry cheesecake, her mind went back to the facts she had to face.

Kat was in the kitchen making potato salad when Alyssa walked in, her arms loaded with bags. "Jeez, girlfriend, what do you have there?"

"I know. I got carried away. There's a couple more bags in the car."

"Brian! Come here and help Alyssa." He didn't answer.

Alyssa set the bags down. "I can get them. You don't need to call your son."

"I don't think so. He can help. Bri!" Still no answer. Kat walked back into his room where Brian laid flat on his back in bed, listening to his iPod. Kat pulled the earphones away from his ears and his eyes shot open. "Mom! What up? You scared me."

"Go grab a couple of bags out of Alyssa's car for me." He stared at her blankly for a few seconds. He pushed himself off the bed, shoulders slumped, hair in his eyes, and lurked past her. He grunted what sounded like a possible hello to Alyssa. "Say hello, please," Kat instructed.

"I did," Brian replied.

Kat walked around in front of him, pushed his shoulders back, and brushed the hair out of his eyes. "Try again. This time louder with a little enthusiasm." Alyssa stifled her laughter. "This is good practice for you. And Alyssa is a friend, so she can take it. We'll call this etiquette 101. *How to say hello to guests.* Something you learned at five, but due to the undeveloped frontal lobe, this 'Hello, how are you?' thing, must have gotten lost in the dark abyss between Akon and *World of Warcraft*."

"I don't listen to Akon, Mom, and WOW is lame."

"What is this? He speaketh in full sentences! How blessed are we? Thank God, because it was taking a lot of effort for me to decipher caveman grunts." Kat put an arm around him.

Brian shook his head. "Hello, Alyssa. How are you?" he said clearly and politely.

"I'm great. Thank you for asking. The bags are in the trunk of my car."

"I've got them. Stay and entertain the peanut gallery," he said.

"He has your sarcastic wit, I see." Alyssa walked over to the kitchen island. "May I?" She held up a spoonful of the salad.

"Of course, and, yes, my son is a regular Adam Sandler. What do you think?"

"About the potato salad or the kid?"

"The salad."

"It's excellent and the kid is pretty great too. He's just a teenager."

"I do know this. If Jeremy hadn't gone through it first, I'd be pulling my hair out. But he seems to have reached the other side. You know, it's true that their frontal lobe isn't fully developed until they're in their twenties. It does explain a lot."

Alyssa laughed. "Where is Jeremy?"

"With Christian. They're in the backyard, digging the hole to bury the pig for tomorrow."

"That's huge, isn't it? That they would do something like that together?"

"Not only that. Yesterday, Christian let the sous chef take over and I managed the restaurant, while the two of them went hunting together for the pig."

"That's great, Kat! They're bonding. That must make you happy."

"It really does. For so long, I've been hoping that somehow, someway, my sons and Christian would bond. I don't know if it'll happen between him and Brian because Bri is so busy worshipping his father. I don't want to be the one to highlight all the shit that he's done or hasn't done. I can't even ask Brian what time his father will be picking him up without getting my head bit off!"

"I think that's one of those situations where you have to stay totally neutral. It's a no win deal. But who knows? I bet you never thought Jeremy and Christian would develop a close relationship."

"You're right. Part of me believes it has to do with Amber. It might sound strange, but I think she has sort of cemented us together. Jeremy is nuts about her, loves tossing her around and teasing her, and Christian appreciates him playing big brother to his daughter."

"Funny how a kid can do that. It's kind of the same with me."

Brian came in and set down the desserts. Kat looked at the three bags and back at Alyssa. "How many people do you think we're having? Looks to me like you have enough here for a regular bake sale."

"I needed a distraction."

"Am I done now?" Brian asked.

"Yes. Why don't you go outside with Grandma and Amber and help with the decorations in the back."

"Do I have to?" He grimaced. "Nanny V goes on and on about some of the weirdest stuff. The other day I had to hear all about how living in *the now* keeps us centered, and how we should enjoy *the now* because it's all we have. I don't even know what she meant by *the now*."

"She means the present, and, yes, you do have to go help."

"Mom . . ."

"Five bucks. Do it for five bucks."

"Ten," he said.

"Seven," she replied.

"Okay."

Brian went out the French doors. Kat turned to Alyssa, "Chapter thirteen in the parenting handbook states that bribery, although not always the best parenting method, is very effective, especially in a time crunch."

Alyssa laughed.

"I'm guessing you need to talk. What's so heavy on your mind that you had to turn all Betty-Crocker-on-steroids on me?"

Alyssa plunked down at Kat's kitchen table. "It's heavy."

"What isn't heavy?"

"Right. You know how you were saying that Amber is kind of like the glue around here for the family? Well, Ian has become the glue for my heart. And when I found out I wasn't a match for the bone marrow, I knew I had to do something. I had to look into every possibility. I called the father. Actually, Darren, who is Ian's uncle did it for me."

"What did Darren say?"

"Darren told him that he had a child with a woman eighteen years ago and then explained the medical situation."

"What did the guy do?"

"There's more to it."

"What do you mean?"

Alyssa closed her eyes for a second. "Ian's father date raped me."

"Alyssa!"

"He did, and I told Darren this. He was the first person that I ever told. Darren didn't let on that he knew, though, when he made the call."

"That must have been so difficult for him. And for you."

"It was. But I think that the father handled it the only way he could."

"What happened?"

"It took Darren some convincing on his part, but he got him to agree to be tested. Of course, the father is demanding a paternity test. Darren told him that they'd pay for that, and they could go from there after the results came back."

"And did they?"

"It was rushed through, and it came back positive. I was a virgin when it happened, so no surprise there."

"I can't even imagine what you've been through and how you've dealt with this all of these years by yourself."

"It hasn't been easy, but it's helped to have friends like you."

"All the same, you should have told me, told us, we could have been there for you."

"I couldn't. I was ashamed, and I thought if I buried it deep enough that I could leave it there and forget about it. I was wrong. The father's blood tests came back and he wasn't a match. But the doctors are saying that Ian's best chance is if he has any siblings, and he does, Kat. James—the father--has six other children."

Kat reached for Alyssa's hand. "What are you going to do?"

She sighed heavily. "I'm going to go to New Orleans and confront him. He has to have his kids tested. He has to see if one of them is a match."

"How do you think he'll respond?"

Alyssa looked down. "I can't even think about that right now. All I can think about is helping Ian get well."

"Ian's family knows everything?"

"Darren obviously knows, and Charlie has been told that we called the father. It was Charlie who phoned me today and said that he wasn't a match. I told him I'd be in contact with the father to ask him to have his other children tested. I'm flying out the day after tomorrow."

Kat squeezed her hand. "I'm going with you."

"No. No. You have your family and your restaurant. You can't go."

"My mother is here. She can help with the kids, and I've only been working at the restaurant part time anyway these days. You've done so much alone, Alyssa. Let me be there for you. Please."

Alyssa nodded. "Thank you."

***

The Fourth of July party was in full swing and Kat was beside herself. She'd had no choice but to invite her father. He'd called and asked what their plans were, and she'd invited him. What else could she have done? She'd warned him about her mom.

He insisted it would be fine, saying, "That chapter of my life is closed, and I think your mother and I can be perfectly cordial toward one another."

Hopefully that would be the case, because Kat had watched her mother eye her father nervously for the last hour. He'd stayed on one side of the pool, drinking his Tom Collins and chatting with Danielle and Mark. Shannon had come along with them, too, looking huge and uncomfortable. And Cassie had surprised all of them by showing up on her own.

Kat noticed that her dad looked a little extra spiffy. He'd worn a Tommy Bahama shirt that Kat and the family had given him on his birthday, a pair of khaki shorts (with the shirt tucked in no less, and a belt—not typical for her dad), and instead of his usual socks and tennis shoes, he had on flip-flops, which even Kat had to admit gave him a bit of an edge on the coolness factor. Plus, if she didn't know better, Kat could've sworn he may have used some Grecian Formula because his normally almost all silver head of hair looked less silver today.

Kat's mother sat at the other end of the pool at another table, drinking strawberry daiquiris and chatting with Jamie, who had brought Maddie and Dorothy. Dorothy thought that she was at Lucille Ball's house and she kept referring to Kat as "Lucy," even though Danielle was the redhead.

"Lucy, darling, would you bring me one of those wonderful drinks this nice lady is having?" Dorothy pointed to Kat's mother.

Venus winked at her and stood up. "I think I'll make my way over and say hello to your father."

"Mom, do you think that's a good idea?"

"Yes, I do. Go get this lovely woman a drink, Kitty."

Kat eyed Jamie. Maddie and Amber were splashing around in the pool having a great time. "Mom, stay right here, and we'll be back with your drink," Jamie said.

Christian walked by with a beer in hand. "What do you think? A half-hour and I'll have the guys help me dig out the pig?"

"Perfect." Kat patted him on the shoulder. "Can you keep watch for a sec? Jamie is going to help me in the kitchen." She nodded her head toward Dorothy.

"Love to," he replied.

"Rock, darling, did you bring your partner today?" Dorothy asked, as Christian sat down next to her.

Christian almost spit out his beer. "Not today, Love."

Jamie and Kat laughed all the way back to the kitchen. A minute later, Danielle joined them. Alyssa had stopped by briefly, having to run to catch a plane to L.A. to spend the holiday with Ian and his family. She and Kat would meet in New Orleans the next evening.

"What's the pow-wow all about?" Danielle asked.

"My mother is going over to talk to my father. This could end the party right here," Kat said. "I need to make up some more daiquiris. Dorothy wants one."

Danielle peeked outside. "Your father is shaking her hand."

"That's civil," Kat replied.

"I'd say so," Jamie said.

Kat went to the fridge and sliced some more cheese and placed it on a plate with crackers and salami. "Maybe I'm freaking out over nothing."

"I think so," Danielle said, as she started another pitcher of daiquiris.

"I'm sure she'll bore him with some kind of technique that teaches him how to achieve his dreams." Kat turned to Danielle, trying to forget that her divorced parents were having a conversation that could easily turn into a fight. "I like Mark."

"Me too," Jamie said.

"Good, because so do I. He's great. I mean, he is really great. We're having fun together, and I haven't felt so comfortable with a man ever. Not even after twenty-one years with Al."

"He could be *the one*," Jamie said.

"Slow down. Way down. We're hanging out, taking it slow. Don't be rushing me to the altar." Then she smiled. "But if things keep going this way, who knows?" She shrugged. "Speaking of men, where is Tyler? We were hoping you'd bring him."

"The ranch is having a hoedown. He wanted to come with me and meet everyone, but he's in charge there. I'll probably stop by the ranch when I leave here, but it's hard with Dorothy." She frowned.

"You okay, J?" Danielle asked.

She bit her lower lip. "I quit my job."

"What?" Kat asked.

Danielle looked at her.

She told them all about Evan's restructuring nightmare. "I can't work for someone like that. Not in good conscience. I can't. So, I quit."

"What are you going to do?" Kat asked.

She shrugged. "I don't know actually. I also put the house up for sale."

Danielle hugged her. "It'll be okay."

Jamie pulled away. "It has to be. Right? Sunday, I'm taking Dorothy over to that Vineyard Escape. I hear it's a great retirement community, but I have to go and talk to my brother-in-law again. He's such a cheapskate, but I know I can't afford a retirement community. Sure, I can get another job, but Maddie and I are going to have to downsize quite a bit."

"I might have a temporary job for you," Danielle said.

"I don't need a handout, but thank you."

"No, I'm serious. The Harvest Festival is sneaking up a little too quick for comfort. I'm supposed to have people lined up to do a television spot for a commercial. I'm terrible in front of the camera, and you know so much about wine."

"You're a winemaker," Jamie replied.

"I know, but what I mean is that you have knowledge not just about wines, but about foods, and beauty treatments, and all sorts of interesting things. You could help me write the spot and if you *star* in it, there's a thousand dollars in it for you. I know it's not much, but it'll help with moving costs, I'm sure."

"You should do it, J," Kat said. "You're super photogenic. Do it! You never know what might come out of it."

"You'd be helping me out," Danielle pleaded.

"Fine. Yes. The money will help with the move. I've actually already had an offer on the house."

They finished making the pitcher of daiquiris and took one back to Dorothy.

"Good timing, ladies. I have to go dig out a pig." Christian kissed Dorothy on the cheek.

"Always the gentleman. Such a shame you're gay," Dorothy said.

"It really is." Kat winked at him. She glanced over to see what was going on between her parents. Her mother was polishing off her drink and her dad was now in the pool laughing. Kat sighed, relieved.

Christian was getting Brian and Jeremy out of the pool to help with the pig and Mark got up to join them. The women followed, curious to see the action. What action it was! Men, heaving and hoeing, grunting and slaving away. The women went to work, putting out the side dishes, plating the shredded pork onto platters, and setting everything up buffet style.

Food, fun, friends on the Fourth. Nothing better.

Jamie wanted to leave, so that she could make a quick stop to see Tyler, but Maddie and Amber had been having so much fun that neither one wanted the other to go.

"Can Amber spend the night, Mommy?" Maddie asked.

Kat frowned, knowing then that she wouldn't see Amber for a few days. She would be leaving for New Orleans in the morning, and Amber's mom would be picking her up and still have her even after Kat returned.

"I think that's a great idea," Christian said.

"Thank you, Daddy." Amber threw her arms around Christian and then Kat. "Thank you, Mommy Kat." Her heart melted yet again.

She put some things together for Amber and sent her off. She hated to see her go, even if it was with Jamie. It was the same feeling she'd had for years every time the *Sperm Donor* would pick up the boys—a combination of fear and a slight sense of loneliness.

Some of the guests had left already, and Kat scanned the area for her mom and dad and Jeremy, but couldn't find them. Christian took her hand, "I get you all to myself tonight."

She smiled, thinking all she wanted to do was climb into her bed and get some sleep. After putting on a big party, and now having to still finish packing, the last thing she had on her mind was romance.

The sun started to set, so everyone climbed up to the top of the hill behind the house to watch the fireworks. Kat and Christian sat with Danielle and Mark.

"Was Cassie in the movie room with the other kids?" Kat asked.

"I don't know. Come to think of it, the last I saw her, she was back in the pool swimming after dinner."

"So was Jer," Christian said.

Danielle and Kat eyed each other.

"They were awfully flirty with each other," Kat said.

"I noticed," Danielle replied.

"Brian?" Kat called out.

"Yeah?" He was a few feet away sitting with one his pals from school who he'd had over.

"Did you see where your brother went?"

"I dunno. I think he's still swimming."

The fireworks started with a display of gold shooting up through the air. Oohs and ahs echoed from onlookers as spirals of color blasted out and danced in the night sky. For those fifteen minutes, all Kat could think about, (and probably Danielle, too), was what their two teens might be up to.

The fireworks ended and people started their hike down the mountain.

Danielle leaned into Kat. "You thinking what I'm thinking about our kids?"

"Only that they could be getting it on with each other anywhere within a few mile radius?"

"Pretty much."

Brian trotted past them while his friend threw him a football. "Careful, Bri, you could trip and . . ." Before Kat finished the sentence it was too late. Brian tripped, fell, and tumbled partially down the hill. Kat screamed out and tried running after him the best she could. Christian beat her to him.

Christian knelt down next to Brian, who was moaning. "Okay, son, hang on, hang on a minute here."

Brian cried out. "It hurts!"

"What hurts? Tell me what hurts," Christian said calmly.

"My leg. My leg it's killing me."

One of their friends handed Christian a flashlight and he shined it on Christian's leg. Kat gasped.

Mark bent down and took the flashlight from Christian. "Let me take a quick look, and then we're going to get you down the hill and go from there, deal?"

Brian's body shook. Kat's mind spun. Mark shone the light in Brian's eyes and then over his body. He turned to Christian. "You get on one side and I'll get on the other and let's get him down the hill."

Christian nodded.

Mark handed the light to Danielle. People were crowding around them. Christian asked them nicely to move out of the way while Danielle flashed the light ahead of them.

"It's going to be okay, sweetie," Kat assured him. In the dim light, she could see tears coming down his face.

"It hurts, Mom."

"I know." She tried to sound as calm as Mark and Christian. Danielle took her hand and they made it down the hill and back into the house.

Once in the light, Brian started to shake. "He's a little shocky. Get me a blanket," Mark ordered. "Let's get him to the hospital. It'll be busy in the emergency room tonight, so I'll call and get you in. I can follow you."

"Would you?" Kat asked.

"Sure. Not a problem."

Danielle squeezed Kat's arm. "I can get the other kids home and clean up. I'll let your mom know what happened."

"Thanks. Don't worry about cleaning up," Kat said. Danielle waved a hand at her. "Just leave it. My car keys are on the hanging thing, the . . . God, I don't know what you call it, by the door." She'd almost forgotten about her mother. Oh and Jeremy. Too much to think about. "Jeremy."

"I'll find them and tell him, too. Go on with Brian and Christian. Don't worry. Call me when you can."

Mark kissed Danielle and told her he'd be back to help her as soon as possible. They got Brian into the car. His shaking had lessened, but he was still in quite a bit of pain.

"Can you call Dad?" Brian asked.

"I will, honey. Let's get you to the hospital first."

A couple of hours later, x-rays revealed that the break, although bad, wasn't as bad as they had all initially thought. Brian had broken the leg in two places, but the good news was the breaks were clean and surgery wasn't needed. Kat could finally sort of relax.

Brian was now occupied watching the FX channel while the cast dried.

His dad finally returned Kat's call. "What do you mean the kid broke his leg?"

"I don't think I need to translate broken leg for you, do I?"

"What the hell were you letting him do?" the Sperm Donor asked. "Weren't you watching him?"

"You're kidding me, right? He's a teenage boy and he was catching a football and tripped. I thought you might want to know. He's not two anymore, and this could happen on your time, my time or some other parent's time. Get off your high horse, Paris."

He sighed. "I'm in Palm Beach, Kit-Kat."

"Good. Stay there and don't worry about it. I'm sure if you send him a video game, he'll be happy and you can be the good guy as always. I have to go." She hung up the phone and went back into Brian's room.

Christian asked Kat if she wanted to get a coffee. She looked at Brian. "Go, Mom. I'm fine."

"You sure, honey?"

"Yes, Mom. Did you talk to Dad?"

So much for that needy creature up on the hill only a few hours earlier. "Yes. He's out of town for a few days. He says he'll call you tomorrow."

"Oh. Okay."

They headed to the cafeteria. Mark had gone back to their house to get Danielle, and Kat's mind was now free to wonder where her other son had been all evening. She dialed Danielle's cell number and gave her the full report. "Any news on your end?"

"I found them. They were in Jeremy's room hanging out. They seemed to be just talking but I can't say what, if anything, occurred before that. I did tell them that they needed to come out of the room. I plan to have a talk with her about why it isn't okay to hang out in a guy's bedroom. Even though I'm sure that will go in one ear and out the other."

"We'll have the same talk with Jer."

They said their goodbyes, and after Kat and Christian sat down in the cafeteria with their coffees, Kat said, "I can't go with Alyssa tomorrow, not with Brian like that."

"It's a broken leg, babe. He'll be fine. I can take care of him."

"But what about when you're at the restaurant?"

"Your mom is there, and you'll only be gone for a couple of days. We can manage. Brian will be fine. He's in good hands. I promise you that I'll take care of him."

"Why the change of heart?"

"What do you mean?"

She shrugged. "I don't know. Since we've been married you've pretty much steered clear of developing real relationships with them. Sure, you've been around, but it's not like you've reached out to them. But lately you've been bonding with both of the boys. It's nice."

"I know. I can't tell you why exactly. I'm sure if some shrink got a hold of me, I'd discover it's some archaic issue in my psyche because the boys belong to another man."

Kat looked up at him from her coffee, astounded. "You're not serious, are you?" She'd been right all along!

He sighed. "I don't know. I know they're good kids. They're your kids, and I can't complain. But I haven't been able to connect. They don't look like me, or act like me. They're nothing like me."

"That's nutty, Christian."

"Maybe, but I've realized that I have a choice in this. I can choose to have a relationship with the boys and to become their friend. In the process, I know it will make you happy, and in turn we'll all be happier. I know what family means to you, and watching you with my child and the way you've taken her in and the way you love her, I thought that maybe it's about time I do the same thing with your kids."

"Our kids," she said.

"Our kids." He smiled. "You'll go tomorrow. Alyssa needs you."

As much as Kat didn't want to leave an injured Brian behind, she did know that he would be in good hands. She'd worry, but she'd go. In some ways she felt relieved, because it would be nice to have someone besides the Sperm Donor acting as a parent. "I'll go."

"Good."

"On a different note, though, since we're sharing parental duties, I need you to have the sex talk with Jer."

He groaned. "Which talk would that be?" He laughed. "How not to have it?"

"What does that mean?" she asked defensively.

"Nothing."

"I thought maybe you were implying that we don't ever have sex." He raised his eyebrows.

"You are."

"I wasn't, but . . ."

"Christian, we had sex two weeks ago."

"Two and a half. Seventeen days actually.

"You're counting? Since when did you start counting?"

"I'm not some freak, okay. But we have only been married for a few years and every two to three weeks is not that much."

"Oh my God, you sound like my mother."

"I'm not trying to sound like your mother. I'm saying that I would like to make love more often, and now with Amber in our bed, it's complicated things a little more."

"We do have three kids in the house."

"We have a lock on the door. We used to have sex every day. Remember? Sometimes two or three times."

"Yes. But that was the lust period. The falling-in-love period. Now we're in the real world."

"But couldn't we bring a little of that back? A compromise, maybe." He pinched his fingers together.

"What are you thinking?"

"I'm thinking a few times a week might make me happy."

"A *few times* a week! Where do we find time for that? You are such a guy. Are you not happy? Is that what you're saying?"

"No, goddamn it, Kat. Why are we arguing about this? I love you. I'm your husband, and I am a man, and I want to be with you. Is that a crime?"

She didn't say anything for a minute. "No. It's not a crime. I don't know what's wrong with me. I feel overwhelmed. I feel like I can never get it all done, and sex eats up time, time when I have things that need to be getting done."

"It's time to do me. It's time invested in our relationship, Kat. You know what we need? We need a vacation."

"What about the kids? What do we do with the kids?"

"We have family and friends and they all do have other parents."

"I don't want to send them with their other parents."

"I know, but I'm not talking about a week. Even a weekend away would do us some good. Think about it. Okay? Take the days you're with Alyssa, try to relax some if you can, and think about a weekend away together."

"Okay."

"Good. And I'll talk to Jeremy."

"Thank you." They got up from the table and Christian took her hand while they walked back to Brian. Kat's mind sputtered. She knew her husband was right, but it didn't change the fact that Kat had lost her sex drive.

CHAPTER TWENTY-SEVEN

Alyssa

Alyssa was grateful that Kat had joined her despite what happened to Brian. Without her friend there, she thought she might chicken out and not go to see James. She also worried that he wouldn't show up.

Darren asked her, almost begged, to let him go with her, but she said that it was something she needed to do on her own, and that Kat would be with her. Meeting James face to face would be a part of her healing.

But what if he didn't come? He would come because she had tricked him. She'd spent quite a bit of time over the last week researching James. Alyssa had learned that James was the owner of several jazz clubs in New Orleans and in other parts of the country. Since Katrina, he'd lost a great deal of money and was trying to sell off some of his clubs or find investors to help him open clubs in other areas.

Kat made the initial call, telling him that she was the assistant to a possible investor who was only in town for a day and who would very much like to meet with him. James offered to have her come to his offices, of course, but neither Kat nor Alyssa thought that prudent. Kat insisted that Alyssa needed to meet him at a nearby coffee shop.

Alyssa stood in front of the mirror and noticed how much she'd aged in the past month. Lines creased around her eyes and bags that weren't there before stood out, making her look older than she cared to. She finished putting on her makeup and came out to see Kat leaning back on her bed, probably as tired as she was.

Kat opened her eyes. "You ready?"

She shrugged. "I suppose as ready as I'm ever going to be."

"I'll be right there for you. You'll be fine. Say what you need to and get out. It'll be okay. I know it."

They walked out of the boutique hotel and headed west to the coffee house in the French quarter that they'd staked out earlier. They were intentionally a few minutes late, not wanting him to have a chance to see her first and leave.

"Do you want me to go in with you?" Kat asked when they reached the shop.

"No. Wait out here. I can do this."

Kat hugged her and Alyssa slipped through the front doors. The smells of greasy food and coffee hit her and her stomach gurgled. The restaurant painted in light pinky peach with black accents tried to be twenties retro-chic looking. It failed. The colors and the smells swirled together and Alyssa swallowed hard, trying to keep the nausea at bay.

She spotted him in a booth near the back, sipping coffee. Her heels clicked against the scuffed hard floor. James looked up and spotted her, recognition crossing his face, and then terror.

She sat down across from him. "Hello, Jimmy," she said, using the name he'd called himself back then. "Surprised to see me?"

He stared at her. "Who . . . ?"

"You're not going to ask who I am and play that game you played so well a few years ago, are you? You knew then who I was, and you know now who I am."

"I have a business meeting."

"I'm the investor, although I'm also not the investor."

"What do you want?" He squirmed.

"I'm Ian's mother."

"I know."

"You do have a memory, then. I'm sure when Ian's uncle mentioned my name to you, it rang a bell. And you're Ian's father."

He didn't reply.

"You're not a bone marrow match for our son."

"What do you want?" he asked.

"The best chance that Ian, our son, has at finding a match is from a sibling."

James stared at her and then started shaking his head. "No, no, no, no. You are not asking me to have my children tested."

"Yes, I am."

He nearly choked on a sip of water. "I can't do that. I can't. I can't. I have a family and I don't want my wife to know anything about this. Or Terrell. He can't know that you and I dated and had a child together. I'm sorry, but they need to find another donor."

Alyssa leaned across the table, her hands no longer shaking. "Listen to me, you son-of-a-bitch. We didn't date. You took something away from me a long time ago, and it's doubtful that you ever looked back, ever thought about me."

He tried to interrupt.

"No. It's my turn. I have had to live with that night for the last nineteen years. Every day. I think about that *night*. The night that you raped me."

"Wait a minute now," he retorted, his face turning red. "I didn't . . ."

"Don't go there. *You* did *rape* me. The word *no* meant nothing to you." She noticed a couple staring at them, and she tried to lower her voice, but rage took over every part of her—rage that she'd kept pent up for almost two decades. "How about my crying and begging you to stop? Remember any of that? I do. You've taken too much from me already, but you won't take my son away from me now. I have a relationship with a child that I have missed for years, thinking that if I looked at him it would only bring me more pain and memory of that night that you *raped* me.

"But I was wrong, and now it's time for you to make amends so that, in some small way, you may be forgiven. I don't care what you tell your family about Ian. All I care about is keeping him alive. It's a blood test. That's all your kids need, and if there is a match, we can go from there. Maybe you'll get lucky and none of them will match Ian's marrow and then you can walk away and forget about all of this. But, if you don't do this, if you don't test your kids, then I will tell your wife, and I will tell Terrell why I left him right before our wedding day. I don't care who it ruins."

She stood up. "You *will* do everything you can to save my son. Your children can be seen tomorrow afternoon by Dr. Preston here in town." Alyssa had chosen the doctor so that James couldn't find a loophole.

A sadness and fear crept into his eyes. He slowly nodded. "Where is he located?"

She gave him the doctor's address. "The results will be back within forty-eight hours. Where can you be reached?"

He handed her his card. "My cell phone."

She took the card and walked out. Kat came rushing over from across the street. She'd been waiting as promised and immediately hugged Alyssa. They started walking silently, and Alyssa finally spoke. "He'll do it. He'll have his children tested."

Kat hugged her again. "You did the right thing."

"I did the only thing."

CHAPTER TWENTY-EIGHT

Danielle

*D*anielle didn't like this one bit. She'd shown up at the Starbucks out of curiosity because she thought Al might be trying to send Cassie back home.

He'd called her up and insisted they meet in person. What could be so damn important that they couldn't have discussed it over the phone? She shut her eyes, hoping Cassie hadn't done something stupid.

"You okay, Danielle?" It was Al.

She opened her eyes and nodded, looking up at the man she'd been married to for twenty-one years and feeling almost as if she were seeing a stranger. It wasn't that he'd changed all that much. Yes, he'd put on about fifteen pounds, his hair was grayer, and the lines on his forehead were more prominent. "I'm fine. Want to sit down. What has Cassie done?" she blurted.

He shook his head. "Nothing. This isn't about her."

"Oh. Good. Thank God," she sighed. "What is this about then?"

"Hang on. I'm going to get a coffee. I'll be right back."

Maybe he wanted to discuss Shannon and the baby. Danielle hadn't asked Shannon if she'd told her dad about the baby's condition. It wasn't something she cared to do, or felt it was her responsibility to do. Mark's talk with her out under that willow tree had stirred up some good old common sense. As hard as it still was to simply let go and accept Shannon's position, she was doing it a little at a time, day by day, and she'd noticed their relationship improving. Tonight they'd even planned to go out to dinner together and maybe see a movie if Shannon wasn't too tired.

Al sat back down, his large hands around the coffee cup—hands that held her own for many years. But there was no more love between them, no more hate, just nothing.

He didn't say anything, his eyes shifting around the Starbuck's.

"Al, you wanted to see me," Danielle finally said. "What is it? You want to talk about Shannon and the pregnancy?"

He nodded. "We probably should talk about that."

"Okay."

"What do you think?" he asked.

"I think it doesn't matter a whole terrible lot what I think. Shannon is an adult and she's made a decision to have the baby," Danielle replied.

"Without a father, though."

"Without a father. Women do it all the time." Danielle got the feeling that Shannon had not told him about the baby's condition. Seemed it was as hard for her daughter to tell her parents as it was for Danielle to confide in her friends about it.

"But what will she do? Do you know what her plans to finish school are, or how she is going to support this baby? I'm not going to support her and the baby because, as you said, she's an adult now. She should have really thought about what she was doing when she got pregnant."

Al hadn't changed under the magical powers of his younger bride. He was still uptight, critical and anal. "People don't typically think when they're in the throes of passion, now do they Al?" She cocked her head to the side and smirked.

He didn't say anything.

"Shannon has been raised with good values, and I trust she's going to be fine." Was she giving herself that speech, or her ex-husband? And was she trying to prove she was the adult here, or did she really believe what she said?

She took another sip of peppermint tea and sat back, thinking for a second. She did believe it. She'd raised her daughters well, and now it was their turn to test the waters of life on their own. All she could do was sit back in the life boat, and hope they would fair the waters that lay ahead. Danielle stared at her ex-husband who looked so completely uncomfortable shifting back and forth in his seat. "Is that it, Al? Is that what you needed to see me for? I am really busy with the festival details and my business, so I need to be getting back."

He reached for her hand and grabbed it as she started to stand. Surprised she looked at him. "I want to help with the festival. I have some ideas."

She slowly sat back down. "Since when? Al, I've known you for twenty-five years and I don't remember a time where you ever showed an interest in charity work, or festivals, so I find it hard to believe you want to help with the preparations for this." She stared hard at him.

He reached for her hand again but she pulled away before he could grab it. "I messed up, Danielle. I really screwed up." He shook his head and looked down.

"What? What do you mean?"

When he looked back up at her there were tears in his eyes. "I can't do this. I can't. Stacey and the babies." He brought a hand to his forehead. "I made the biggest mistake I ever made by cheating on you and being with her. She's making me miserable. You and me, we had such a great marriage, and we've had so many good times. We've raised two daughters together. We built a company. And I screwed it all up. We did have it all, didn't we? I'm so sorry. Can you forgive me? Would you ever . . . ?" He looked at her, his eyes pleading.

Oh, how pitiful.

Three and half years ago she might have said, "Come home and we'll see a counselor." But now? Danielle stood up and grabbed her purse. "I forgive you, Al. I did that a long time ago. Now go home to Stacey and your babies."

"But can't we talk about this?" he asked as she stepped away.

She turned back. "No. There is nothing to talk about. Go home and be a husband and a father. You lost that right with me. Don't make the same mistake twice."

Danielle walked out of the Starbuck's. She should've felt like a million bucks. She'd finally gotten what she'd wanted from Al. He was remorseful and close to begging her to take him back. But instead of feeling elated, Danielle just felt sorry for Stacey—who now had to live with him.

CHAPTER TWENTY-NINE

Jamie

*J*amie held Dorothy's hand as they walked down the hall of Vineyard Escape. So far, so good. It was clean and bright, but not hospital-like. It did appear to be more of an apartment or condo complex, except that there were only elderly people around, other than the staff, and a lot more wheelchairs.

"And this is our restaurant." Their host, Samuel—an older, obviously gay man—spread his arms wide and showed them a large, comfortable-looking room filled with booths and a few tables. It did look like a restaurant but all the meals were included in the cost of living here. "Our residents can come in at any time of the day, and we have a full wait-staff waiting to serve them. There are many wonderful selections on the menu." Samuel snapped his fingers. "Theresa, Theresa." A young blonde woman looked up from behind a hostess stand. "Hi. Could you please bring us a menu, doll?

"As you can see, these are not cafeteria-style plates. We serve gourmet meals and even offer wine and beer for those residents who are allowed to imbibe. And there are special menus for those with strict dietary needs. But that isn't the case with your mother, now is it?"

"No." Jamie perused the menu and it all sounded wonderful.

"Also, whenever you or one of your other relatives would like to stop in for a meal, we make it easy for you by charging it either on your monthly statement, or giving you the option to pay at the time."

Jamie nodded again. This place was not going to come cheap. Quality never did. Dorothy looked approvingly at the restaurant, but Jamie knew that convincing her brother-in-law was going to be tough.

"Let me show you the apartments now," Samuel said, "and then we'll move on to the spa."

"Spa?" Jamie asked.

"Of course. Don't you think that after years of taking care of people, of working day in and day out, that a daily spa treatment should be in order? Your mother deserves that much."

"Yes, of course." Shoot, Jamie wanted to move in.

"Alrighty then." They went down a short hall and Samuel unlocked the door to the apartment. It was quaint and nicely furnished and decorated. It held a good-sized kitchen, family room, a bedroom, and bathroom.

"We don't have stoves or ovens in the apartments. We can't have anyone burning down the house. Hence the restaurant. Of course there is always room service. And each resident is assigned their own resident assistant and the R.A. makes sure their residents are eating and are happy." Samuel flipped his hand.

"Who is this for?" Dorothy asked, leaning into Jamie.

"Maybe for you, Mom. Do you like it?"

Dorothy's face screwed up in confusion. "It is nice, but I like living with you and Nathan. That's where Dean comes to visit me. And I really like that little girl who sits by me and watches TV with me all the time."

Jamie hugged her. "I know, Mom. Let's look around some more, okay?"

"I guess so," she replied, sounding worried.

Samuel escorted them to the spa. The place was like a resort complete with manicurists and hairdressers.

"This is a nice place," Dorothy said. "Am I getting my hair done here?"

Samuel glanced at Jamie. "That's a wonderful idea, Mrs. Evans. Let me see about an appointment." Samuel walked over to the receptionist. They talked for a moment and Jamie saw the woman nodding. Samuel came back. "Lorraine can see you right now, as a matter of fact." Samuel escorted Dorothy to the hairdresser's chair and Dorothy looked happy as a Cheshire cat. Who knew such a simple pleasure like getting your hair done could bring so much joy?

"I'll show you the rest of the spa and the pool area, then we can go on back to my office where we can talk business." He rubbed his hands together.

The rest of the place was as impressive. The spa was done up Spanish-style, with arches and soft lighting. Classic guitar played on the speakers. There were a dozen treatment rooms offering everything from body wraps, massages to facials and acupuncture. Apparently you didn't need to die to go to heaven. You could just move into The Vineyard Escape. This place made getting old look like fun.

But heavenly fun came with a price. As Jamie sat opposite Samuel in his office listening to all of the benefits of living at The Vineyard Escape, her eyes kept going back to that monthly expense of seven thousand dollars that jumped off of the contract form.

"Keep in mind that the price includes twenty-four hour nursing staff, her resident assistant, rent, two spa treatments a week, meals, and maid service."

"Uh huh," Jamie said, taking it all in. "Samuel, I'll be honest with you. I love this place and I would love to have my mother-in-law live here, but I don't have that kind of money. I . . ."

"Do you have any family members who could help you? We could allot her only one treatment a week, but we do feel it is crucial for the happiness of our residents to go to the spa at least weekly. They deserve to be happy in their latter years and that is what we provide."

"I appreciate that. I can talk to my brother-in-law and see, but I doubt he'll be willing to help me out with this."

"He can come by and take a look at the facility. Why wouldn't he want the best for his mother?"

"I agree. Thank you."

"Here's my card and please call if you have any questions. It's been a delight."

"Should I pick her up at the spa?"

Samuel nodded. "I'll escort you."

Samuel walked her back down to the spa. The hairdresser was dousing Dorothy's new updo in hairspray. When she saw Jamie, she spun around in the chair. "Look, honey. Look over there." Dorothy nodded her head toward a gentleman sitting two chairs down getting his haircut. "It's Frank and he keeps smiling at me. I *am* beginning to tire of Dean."

Samuel looked at Jamie. "That's Harry. Not Frank."

Jamie shook her head vehemently. "No. No it's not. That is Frank Sinatra, and we'll take the apartment."

***

The contracts on the house had been signed and Jamie had thirty days to pack away a decade of memories, find a place to rent for herself and Maddie, and get Dorothy settled into her new home.

Tyler had been spending a lot of time with the two of them, and Maddie had basically fallen in love with him. Jamie was still in lust, and the jury was out as to whether or not she could, or would, fall in love with Tyler. He was a great guy, handsome, had a lot to offer, and the sex—well, no brainer there. And she'd sort of gotten over feeling like she should be wearing a scarlet letter. The problem for her was still the age thing. Say they did get together—officially—for the long haul. She would age a lot faster than he would, *and* men never seemed to age the way women did. Why was that? A man could get all grey and be considered debonair, but on a woman it was just plain old, *old*. And then Tyler would find a new woman, someone hot and young. What a miserable thought. Maybe she should break it off with him before that happened, before they got any closer. But she didn't want to give up riding, and she didn't want Maddie to give up riding, and dammit, she really didn't want to give up Tyler. But she didn't know if she could fall in love with him, and Jamie wanted to fall in love.

Tonight, Tyler was taking them all to dinner, including Dorothy, who referred to him as John Wayne. He didn't mind at all and actually enjoyed humoring her. But before any fun time could be had, Jamie needed to see her in-laws. They'd been ignoring her phone calls, her texts, her e-mails all pleading for help with Dorothy. And she'd had enough. So today she had dropped Maddie at the ranch, and was blazing her way toward the city where she planned to drop in on David and Susan. This time she wasn't leaving without getting them to agree to pay for Dorothy's care.

When she pulled up in front of their two-story Marin County mansion, she almost turned around. A valet came up to her to park her car. Ah, a party at the Evans' home! How nice. Guests were getting out of their cars dressed to the nines and Jamie had on blue jeans and a J. Crew T-shirt. "Ma'am, would you like me to park your car?" the valet asked again.

She hesitated. "Yes. But close by. I won't be long." Screw it. She'd driven this far, and if these people could throw afternoon fetes that afforded caterers and valets, they could most certainly afford to help Dorothy.

A burly man dressed in a tux and gripping a communications radio stopped her at the door. "Invitation?" He eyed her up and down.

"I'm related to the Evans."

"Do you have an invitation?" he asked again.

"No, I don't have an invitation. I'm here to see David and Susan Evans."

"This is an invitation-only party. You'll have to come back."

"I'm not coming back. I want to see David and Susan Evans right now."

Walkie-talkie tough guy radioed something and before long another hulk came on the scene. Jamie tried to stay rational. "I am David's sister-in-law and I am here to see him about his mother. It is vitally important. Life or death." She nodded for emphasis.

Hulk One and Two looked at each other, whispered something, and then Two left.

"Where's he going?" Jamie asked.

Number One crossed his arms and stared at her, or at least she assumed he was staring at her from behind his dark sunglasses. Invited guests heading into the house shot her curious glances, and Jamie did her best to flash them polite smiles.

A minute later, Susan appeared dressed in a light, flowy, off-the-shoulder, floor length chiffon number, her blonde, highlighted hair done in a perfectly coiffed updo, her beady green eyes trained on Jamie. "Jamie, we weren't expecting you. We're having a private gathering this afternoon for Senator Mast."

"Right. I won't take up a lot of your time, Susan, but we need to talk about Dorothy."

"Oh." She waved a hand at her. "I've found her a lovely place here in the city. They have on-staff doctors and nice rooms. It's perfect and well within the budget. I planned to call you about it, but we've been busy. I'll get to you this week."

"You have a budget? That's interesting. But you're not getting back to me this week. Here's the deal. I found Dorothy a place in Napa Valley that is superior, close by me—since I'll actually take the time to visit her—where she can still enjoy freedom and be respected for the fine woman she is. I have told this to David, and I'm now telling you. I do live on a budget and these days it's getting tighter. You, on the other hand, can apparently spring for parties for corrupt politicians." A few guests stopped, curious as to who the crazy lady in the jeans was. "You and David owe her. I have friends who are journalists for some very prestigious papers, including *The Wall Street Journal, The New York Times, The Los Angeles Times,* and *The Chronicle.*" This was all complete bullshit, but by the horrified expression on Susan's face, Jamie knew she was buying it. "I've been thinking about doing an article with my friend from *The Wall Street Journal* on aging parents, and about the children who do and do not take care of them. I'd hate to name such high profile figures like you and David, and I'm sure Senator Mast would be mortified to know that people like you who neglect their aging parents are some of his major contributors."

Susan took a step back, her face paling. "I'll be back in a moment," she whispered.

Ten minutes passed and Jamie started wondering if she was calling her bluff. But then David appeared and handed her a check and some documents.

"What's this?" Jamie asked.

"That's a hundred grand, and my mother's life insurance policy. I am signing it over to you, along with power of attorney. It's worth a million dollars. That should take care of her. Now go away, Jamie. We'll be calling you to visit Maddie. We do expect to be seeing her more often in light of our generosity."

She walked away with a smile and muttered, "Over my dead body." There was no way in hell Jamie was going to expose Maddie to those people ever again.

"Forgive me, Nate," she said as she got into her car.

She looked toward the bay as a summer shower started to come down, and she laughed. David and Susan's little soiree in the garden was getting drenched. Pity. She pulled out of the circular drive and spotted a full, bright rainbow. A sudden sense of peace came over her, and she wondered if it was Nate's way of letting her know he approved.

CHAPTER THIRTY

Kat

Kat smiled at the sight of her dad's red VW Beatle in front of his house. When he'd made the decision to move out to Napa to be closer to Kat and his grandkids, she'd been overjoyed. Her dad badly needed a change. She'd begged him for years to sell the house she'd grown up in, the one where her mom had left him behind to sulk and fret.

Dad's home was small, over fifty years old, but quaint and set against a small wooded area. She went around to the side door off of his kitchen, knowing when she walked in that the familiar smells of coffee and must would hit her—a smell Kat liked because it meant new memories for her dad, and it actually felt more like coming home to her than if she had still lived in the old house in Oakland.

Kat shut the back door and Dad's cat, Roy, slunk over and rubbed his orange body between her legs, looking up at her and mewing. "Hi, Roy." She picked him up and scratched behind his ears. "Where's Dad?" Usually when she entered her dad's place, CNN blared from the television.

Roy mewed again. "Haven't you been fed?" She set him down, took his food from the cupboard, and poured some in his bowl. He wolfed it down. It was only eleven o' clock and Kat knew that Dad typically got up around eight, and after getting his breakfast fixed, gave Roy his. The cat shouldn't be starving.

Something didn't feel right. "Dad?" she called out. There was no answer. Maybe he was out back in his garden, but he would have heard her drive up and walked around front. Maybe one of his golfing buddies picked him up and they had an early tee time, and he'd just forgotten to feed Roy. Of course it had to be something like that, but had he also forgotten to lock his back door?

Kat wandered though the house. "Dad?" she called out again. As she entered the family room, she heard music coming from the hallway. He must be in his bedroom reading and couldn't hear her with the music on. She headed down the hall then she stopped in her tracks, her jaw dropping. *Unbelievable.* Clothes were all the way down the hall and laughter was coming from her father's bedroom. Not just *anyone's* clothes or *anyone's* laughter, but her *mother's*. Her mother was at her father's house and, from the sounds coming from the room, they weren't catching up on old times—at least not by talking, anyway. Horrified, Kat turned around and got the hell out of there as fast as possible.

***

An hour later Kat pulled into the bookstore's parking lot. Her mother sat on a bench in front of the store looking happy as a freaking clam. "Hi, honey. Thanks so much," she said, sliding into the front seat.

"Get the book you wanted?" Kat asked. Jeez it must have been a wham, bam, thank you ma'am session. Eww! How could she even think like that? They were her parents. Gross! And talk about manipulation. That morning her mother had asked her to drop her at the bookstore, knowing that Kat needed to run some errands, and then to come back and pick her up. Dad must have been waiting in the parking lot when Kat had dropped her off, because they hadn't wasted a minute.

"They didn't have it." She frowned.

"Really? That's too bad. You've been waiting here this whole time for me then?"

"No, no. I browsed around, but didn't find anything."

"Huh. You, the avid reader, didn't find a book to read? There must be a million books in there. A million alone about New Age stuff."

Her mom shrugged.

"Why are you lying to me?"

"What do you mean?" she asked, and cracked the window.

"I know. I know you were with Dad. I went there to visit him and

I heard you and I saw your blouse on the floor, which, by the way," she glanced at her mom, "isn't even buttoned right."

Her mom looked down and fumbled with the buttons, obviously flustered. "Oh."

"Mom, what the hell is going on?"

She sighed. "When I saw your father at the Fourth of July party, it was like seeing him for the first time. I don't know. I can't explain it, but regret and sadness washed over me. I was so sure he'd be angry with me, but then we started chatting. He's so different now, so relaxed and at ease with himself. He seems happy, and I'm at such a good place in my life, well, things happened from there. He called me, and then we texted each other all weekend."

"You're texting each other?" Kat hadn't even gotten that whole texting thing down.

"Yes."

Kat didn't know if she wanted to laugh or scream at her. "I don't believe this."

"Why does this bother you so?"

"Why do you think? Why, oh why, would this—you and my dad together—bother me in the least, Mother?"

Her mom sighed. "I know I've made a lot of mistakes, and I know I hurt you, and your dad and your sister when I left, but you have no idea what it was like for me, for so many years."

"Like? Like! I have pretty good idea. Let me see, you lived in a nice house, ate good food, had friends, kids who adored you, and a husband who would do anything for you. Yeah, that sounds shitty to me, Mom."

"I know how you feel and what you think."

"No you don't."

"I needed more. I needed to feel like a woman again and not a mother or a wife, but a woman."

"What the hell does that mean?" Kat asked.

"I needed to be on my own, to grow spiritually, emotionally, mentally."

"And you couldn't do that with my father?"

"No, but now I am at a different place, and I think I could."

Kat pulled the car over, staring straight ahead.

Her mom was looking down. "What is it with you? Why do you feel so, so, like you have to control everything? Not everything can be controlled. But you keep trying and it makes you miserable. You are totally miserable. You couldn't control me then, not now either, and you can't control anyone else."

Kat closed her eyes and tried to absorb this. Oh fuck it. Would she ever be happy holding it all in? Nope. She started out calmly. "I'm guessing, Mom, that you're basically calling me a control freak?"

"Yes, Kitty, I guess that I am. You try and control your husband though sex, or in your case, through no sex. And you control Brian by bad-mouthing his father, but Brian sees right through both of you. He's not entirely the naïve boy you've made him out to be. That child suffers more than you'll ever begin to realize. He's so torn between the two of you. You don't get to the core of him at all. Where's your core? Is it love or control?

"And now you have this adorable little girl in your home, and I watch you. I see you've fallen totally in love with her. She is the substitute child for what you couldn't accomplish the first time around, or the second, and now you're trying to make her the perfect kid. Good luck with that. The thing is, you have no control where Amber is concerned. She's not your daughter. And sometimes, you must let it all go. You have to breathe, take stock, drink water, cry, and start at zero."

Kat could do nothing but stare at this woman, her mother, who called herself Venus. Was this a joke? After about a minute of the stare off, each waiting for the other to make a move, Kat did. "Fuck you, Mom."

"What?"

"You heard me. Fuck you. You have no idea. No clue of the pain I've suffered, or where I've been, or who I am. Sure it's easy for you to say breathe, drink water, yoga the hell out of your body. Let's talk control, Venus. I never knew you weren't anything but happy and neither did Dad. Always smiling. That was my mom. You're still always smiling. It's hard to tell what's real with you. But then you drop the bomb on us, thinking because we were all grown-ups that we could all handle it, and you go all transcendental on us.

"You leave a young woman—your daughter—who almost died in a car accident. You leave her addicted to pain pills and hand her over to me while I'm dealing with two toddlers and an asshole husband. But that isn't the worst of it. No. You left a husband who did nothing but work his ass off all his life and worship you, and now you decide that a life of reconciliation is the new and right life for you. Your new life.

"You know what your new life left for me? A sister who to this day still can't cope with the real world and a father who just got his life back. So again, Venus, fuck you!" Kat wiped hot, angry tears form her face.

Her mother's eyes watered.

"And one more thing, if you hurt my dad again, ever, I will never, never forgive you. You better think twice about what you're doing with my father."

Venus didn't reply. Kat turned out onto the main road and they drove the rest of the way home in silence.

CHAPTER THIRTY-ONE

The Blow Up

"We found a match," Alyssa said. The four friends had taken their happy hour to Christian's Restaurant where they wined and dined, catching up with each other. The colors of blue, black and butter in the restaurant mixed with the candlelight, casting shadows and a soft, comforting glow about. Smells of gourmet food and grapes from their wine added to the coziness of the evening. Danielle, Kat and Jamie looked at Alyssa. "The father. Ian's father has six kids and one of them is a match. His six-year-old. A little girl."

Danielle glanced at Jamie. "You found the father then?"

"Yes." Alyssa had made the decision not to tell Danielle or Jamie about the rape. At least not yet. Kat and Darren knew and to her that was enough. It wasn't about keeping it a secret any longer, or even about shame. Now it was about letting it go and letting it lie.

"Six kids?" Jamie asked. "He didn't know about Ian?"

"No. I never saw a need for him to know, but now, I had no choice."

"It's good. That's good. There's a match," Kat said, reaching for her water.

"What about the father's wife and kids? Do you know what he told them?" Danielle asked.

"No. I don't. And I don't care to. I'm happy that we can go forward. I'm leaving tomorrow. I'll be back and forth. I have a gal taking over at the gallery and an instructor coming in to teach the art lessons. Ian will have to be in the hospital for a few weeks. They need to kill as many of the bad cells as they can, but in the process it also destroys good cells and his immune system will become very vulnerable. It's going to be a process. Once the doctors accomplish that, the little girl donates the marrow."

"What's it going to be like for the little girl?" Jamie asked, thinking of her own six-year-old.

"Most donations don't involve any surgery. Doctors typically request a peripheral blood stem cell donation, which is non-surgical and outpatient. But in Ian's case, marrow was requested. That means the procedure for the little girl will be surgical. At least it'll be done as an outpatient."

"I've heard it's horribly painful," Jamie said.

Kat shot her a dirty look. If Jamie had only known what Alyssa had been through.

"No. I know most people believe that, but the doctors explained that pieces of bone are not removed from the donor in either type of donation; only the liquid marrow found inside the bones are needed to save Ian's life." Alyssa sipped her wine. "Don't get me wrong. I feel bad about this and, yes, the little girl will have some difficulties from the procedure. She'll have to take a medication for several days prior that could cause her to have headaches, bone or muscle pain, nausea, insomnia or fatigue." Alyssa tried to ease her conscience knowing that these symptoms would disappear one or two days after donating. "She might also feel some soreness or pressure in her lower back and perhaps some discomfort walking for up to three weeks." She hated that this wouldn't be a cakewalk for Ian's sister either.

Jamie cringed. She was happy for Alyssa and Ian that they'd found a donor, but if it were her daughter who had been a match, she didn't know if she could allow her to do it.

Alyssa could read Jamie's face. "I know it sounds bad, but the doctors say it won't be, and there is a strong chance that Ian will come out of this healthy."

"I understand," Jamie replied.

"Does Ian know who the donor is?" Danielle asked.

"No. The donor's parents and Charlie, Ian's dad, felt it unnecessary. And so do I."

"That's his sister, though. If Ian has five siblings, doesn't he have a right to know who his family is?" Jamie asked.

"I think that's a real personal decision," Kat remarked. "I'm sure that Ian's family has their reasons, and to me it sounds as if everyone is on the same page about the issue."

Alyssa gave Kat a slight smile. She was becoming annoyed with Jamie, but she had to remind herself that Kat was the only one who knew all of the intricacies involved with the situation. She realized that without telling Danielle and Jamie everything, she'd have to give them the benefit of the doubt. For a second, she thought about telling them about the rape, but Kat saved her.

"The family seems to have it under control, unlike my family who is skidding *out* of control. At least my mother and father are." She picked up her glass of cabernet and polished off the rest of it.

"What are you talking about?" Danielle asked.

"My parents are sleeping together."

"What?"

"Yep." Kat told them the story about catching her parents in bed together. "The aftermath was ugly. I blew up. I mean, I went nuts. I told my mom exactly how I've felt for years, about her leaving my dad, her new life, all of it."

"What did she do?" Danielle leaned back in her chair.

"Moved in with my dad."

"Whoa," Alyssa said.

"I'm sorry, Kat, but honestly I don't get what the big deal is. I know it's kind of weird to think about your parents being together, but come on, I would think that would make you happy." Jamie took a bite from her salad.

"The big deal is that my mom broke my dad's heart, and left me to pick up the mess she left behind with both my dad and my sister."

"But your dad is a grown man. I know it must have been awful to deal with when she left, but what they do now, well, it's not up to you. It's not your responsibility to take care of any of them at this stage of the game. If your mom and dad want to fool around together and you think your mom is going to break your dad's heart again, you cannot take that on."

Kat stared at Jamie. "You don't get this at all."

"Wait. I think you're taking this wrong. I understand your point, but at some juncture, you have to let go of everyone else's problems. It's seriously not your job to make them happy." Jamie was feeling uncomfortable. So far tonight she hadn't scored any points amongst her friends. "But what do I know? I'm not walking in your shoes." She tried to make light of it because everyone had grown quiet.

"No. You're not. And I kind of find it interesting that you of all people would tell me to let go of something." Kat knew she should stop right there, but her damn emotions insisted on getting in the way. "Nate has been gone now for three years and you're still hanging on to him."

"That's unfair, Kat," Danielle cut in. "It really is."

Kat nodded. "I'm sorry, J. I am."

Jamie stood up, tears in her eyes. "No, that's fine. I have to go."

"Jamie," Kat pleaded. "I'm sorry."

Jamie waved a hand at her and walked a few steps. She turned around. "You have no idea what it's like to lose someone that you love. No idea. Your mom may have changed over the years, but she's still here with you. She's still your mom, and she is *here*. Don't compare my feelings and the loss of my husband to losing control over something you never had control over in the first place," she said and walked out of the restaurant.

***

Changes
By
Jamie Evans

This will be my last column as Editor-In-Chief of Wine Lover's. *The magazine will soon be changing form, and I am making some changes too—from leaving my position here at the magazine to moving from my home of seven years. I felt it apropos that this month's issue be about* change. In some ways, it's good to know that nothing stays the same. In other ways it's quite frightening.

One thing I do know for sure is that change is always happening, and there's no point trying to halt its movement. As you read this month's issue and tackle changes, be them small or big, think about how you handle change. Do you do it alone? Do you accept it or fight it? How often does it move in and out of your life?

I'd love to hear from readers and receive your replies on the topic of changes, but as with everything, I'm changing. Thank you for reading Wine Lover's. It has been a pleasure to be a part of your lives, even in some small way.

Cheers,

Jamie Evans

CHAPTER THIRTY-TWO

Danielle

Danielle took Shannon's hand and pulled her up from the couch where her daughter sat watching the Food Network. "Come on, honey. We've got somewhere to go."

"Where?"

"It's a surprise."

"Mom, I'm tired and my back aches and I don't want to go anywhere."

"And you're cranky, but I forgive you because you're eight months pregnant. But we have a baby on the way, and I realized this morning when I got up that we haven't had a baby shower."

"I don't want a baby shower."

"Yes, you do. I'm giving you one, but there are things he'll need," she said as she rubbed Shannon's belly, "that you probably won't get at a baby shower. Like a crib."

Shannon eyes widened and then tears formed in them. She waved her hand in front of her face. "Sorry, I'm a little emotional these days." She smiled.

"Of course you are a little emotional. That's normal."

"Really, Mom? We're going to get him a crib?"

"Yes, and I think we should have some lunch to nourish you and the little guy, and we should talk about his name because calling him, *him,* isn't working for me."

Shannon hugged her mom. "Thank you, Grandma. I didn't know what I was going to do, because I don't exactly have loads of cash, but I do plan to get a job after the baby is here and figure things out with school."

"You don't need to worry about any of that right now. But don't call me Grandma."

"Nana?"

"No."

"Nanny? Grammy?"

"Don't think so."

"Well, he can't call you Danielle."

"Let's think about it. Get your shoes."

Three hours and three thousand dollars later, the baby had a crib, a car seat, a changing table, a comforter, matching curtains, a stroller, a swing, a high chair, a bassinet, blankets, washcloths, a robe, towels, and several sets of outfits.

"I thought you said that I was getting a crib, and that I could get all of the other things from a baby shower?" Shannon took a bite from her steak salad.

"I guess I did go a little crazy, but it's not every day you become a grand . . . I mean a . . ."

"Mom."

"No, not a mom. I've done that. You know what I mean."

"No, Mom, Mom, my water just broke."

Danielle set down her fork and froze for a second. Then her thoughts caught up with her voice. "Oh, my God. Oh. Oh, okay. Let's go. Let's go!"

The waitress came by as Danielle helped Shannon out of her seat. "Is everything okay?" she asked.

Danielle pulled a hundred dollar bill from her wallet and handed it to the waitress. "Gotta go."

"But don't you want the check? I'm sure I owe you change. Was the food bad? Is there a problem?"

"There will be if you don't move!" Danielle yelled. "My daughter is having a baby."

The waitress moved quickly out of the way.

Danielle drove like a bat out of hell to the hospital. Shannon called her doctor, and was told he would meet her there. "I'm scared," Shannon said.

"It won't hurt. That's why they have drugs."

"No, Mom. I'm scared I don't know what the hell I'm doing and that I won't be a good mother."

"You're going to be a great mother. The best mother. I can already tell how much you love this baby. Look how hard you've fought for him. Look at what you've given up just to get him here? And let me tell you something about being a mother. There are two things you will do over and over again as his parent—you will love him no matter what, through the good and the bad, and you will sacrifice time and again to do what you think is right for him. And, Shannon, you've done that already. You will be fantastic at this. I know it."

"Oh God."

"Honey. Stop worrying."

"No. The pain. Oh God. It feels like someone just reached inside me and took my ovaries in a vice. Oh God." She shut her eyes tightly.

"Okay, okay, we're almost to the hospital. Breathe." Danielle tried to remember something useful from her Lamaze class from when Cassie was born, but all she could remember was telling Al to go to hell every time he barked at her to "Breathe!"

"We're here, babe."

Danielle pulled up in front of the hospital and helped Shannon get out. She handed the keys to a security guard, and gave him ten bucks.

"What's this for?"

"To park the car."

"I can't park your car. I'm security."

"Then leave it there."

"You can't leave it here."

She handed him another ten. "Park the damn car! My daughter is having a baby."

"Mom, you are acting crazy."

She smiled at the security guard. "Please park the car?"

He shook his head. "Sure. I'll leave the keys at the front desk."

"Thank you."

The nurse in triage took down some notes and then asked Shannon, "You're sure your water broke?"

Danielle turned Shannon around so the nurse could see her

backside. "I don't know, unless the poor girl peed in her pants, what do you think?"

The nurse looked from Shannon's rear to Danielle like she was fairly insane, then picked up the phone. "I need a bed."

Ten hours later, mother and daughter had walked the miracle mile around the hospital a thousand times because Shannon's contractions had come to a halt and the doctor hoped the activity would get things moving. It was now past ten at night. Danielle's friends had all called, Shannon's father had called, and Mark stopped in several times already.

Shannon was now back in bed, tired and more than a little cranky. Cassie popped her head in. "Hey, sis, how's it going?"

Shannon rolled her eyes and groaned.

Cassie shrugged. "What's on TV?" She started to grab the remote off of the stand next to Shannon's bed.

"Don't you even think about it," Shannon growled. "That's my fucking remote control."

"Sure," Cassie replied sheepishly and handed it to her sister. She whispered in her mom's ear. "She turn into the Antichrist, or what?"

"Cassie," Danielle warned.

Mark came in and motioned for Danielle to come out into the hall with him. "What is it?" she asked.

"I've been conferring with Shannon's doctor, and since she's not dilating, we have to start talking about a c-section. Because her water broke already, we only have a limited amount of time to get the baby out. Do you want one of us to explain this to her or do you want to do it?"

"Maybe the both of us should talk to her. I know she feels comfortable with you. She likes her doctor fine, but I think she really trusts you."

"Let's go talk with her." He put an arm around her.

Danielle nodded.

Shannon wasn't thrilled with the option but understood why they needed to start considering and preparing for a c-section delivery.

Mark told her they could give it a couple of more hours. They could try giving her Pitocin to bring on stronger contractions. Shannon agreed to give that a try. Two hours later, when Shannon was in more pain than Danielle could bear, the doctors stopped the Pitocin. There had been no change.

They made the decision right after midnight to go ahead with the c-section. Danielle called Al to let him know. She was pleased that Cassie had stayed. "It's been a long night already, kid. You want to go home and get some sleep?" Danielle asked her.

"No way. I'm here for the long haul, Mom."

"We've got a few minutes. Let's go grab a soda or coffee or something, then."

Cassie nodded, and Danielle took Shannon's hand. "Hey, baby, we're going down to get a bite and a soda out of the vending machine. You okay?"

Shannon nodded, but didn't look okay. Her eyes reflected the same fear she'd shown when she'd gotten lost in the grocery store when she was five. "Hurry up though," she said.

"We will, sweetie."

They walked down to the vending machine where they bought Cokes and a couple of bags of chips. "It ain't exactly nutritious, but it'll do."

"I lied," Cassie blurted out.

"What do you mean, you lied?" Danielle asked.

"About sex." She opened the soda and took a sip. "I told you that I had sex with a lot of guys just because I knew it would drive you crazy."

"Oh, Cass."

"I'm sorry. I thought you were snooping in my room, and so I got mad and I told you that. I haven't had sex with a bunch of guys. Only one guy. Jordan."

"Oh." Jordan had been Cassie's first real boyfriend two years earlier. They'd dated half of her sophomore year, but he broke her heart when he decided to go to the prom with one of the cheerleaders.

Then he'd gone off to college in the fall and Danielle was pretty sure that Cassie hadn't heard from him again.

"I don't even take the pill anymore. If you looked at the dates on them, you'd have seen that." She teared up. "I thought he broke up with me because I was bad at it. It's not like we did it very many times."

Danielle pulled her into her arms and hugged her tight. "Guys are jerks."

Cassie grunted a little laugh. "Mark seems nice."

"He is nice. He's really nice."

Cassie pulled away and wiped her face. "You're blushing, Mom. You really like him."

"I do."

"Cool."

They started walking back. The fluorescent lighting in the corridor bounced off the stark floors. "Cass, you didn't do anything wrong with Jordan. He's just a dumb guy. The best advice I can give you about guys and sex is that it's really complicated, and no matter how much you think you like or even love a guy, when you throw sex into the mix, it gets even more complicated. On top of that, it's usually the girl who winds up the most hurt by it. Women don't just have sex to feel good physically, and I'm not saying that all guys do, but at your age, that's more the norm than not. But for girls, we tie in a lot of emotion, and we think that having sex with a guy means love. To a lot of women, especially young women, it means a man will love you back, if you sleep with him. That's why it's good to wait. It's good to wait until you're old enough and mature enough to understand the consequences on every level."

Cassie nodded. "I know."

"Good. I hope so. You're too damn young, Cass. It's too much for someone your age. It really is."

She nodded. "Mom, I'm miserable at Dad's. Can I please come home?"

Danielle stopped and looked at her. "Do you think you can

respect me and my rules? Because, honey, I can't have you home if you plan to continue talking to me the way you do and walking all over me. I love you, but I can't have it."

"I understand. Can you give me another chance? I promise not to blow it."

"The babies getting to you, huh?"

"You have no idea. But it's not so much them, even. It's Stacey. For a long time I thought she was so cool and hip, but she's a nag. She nags Dad every second he's around, and then she nags me. I don't have a clue what Dad was thinking."

Danielle simply agreed. "We better get back to your sister."

Shannon was prepped, and then Danielle prepped. Cassie waited in the waiting room, and a few minutes later, the anesthesiologist, Shannon's doctor, and Mark came in. Mark explained the procedure to them both again.

"Mom?"

"Yes, babe?"

Shannon stretched out her free arm and wiggled her hand. Danielle took it and stroked her hair. "I'm proud of you. I am so, so proud of you," she said, and she meant it. Maybe having this baby would not have been her choice for Shannon, but her daughter had convictions, and she'd stuck by them, allowing her faith to lead the way.

She smiled at her.

"Incision has been made," Mark reported.

Danielle didn't want to see the cut on her child. Standing at her head and holding her hand was the best place for her. A few minutes later, Shannon's doctor lifted out a seven-pound baby boy. He held him up. "Here he is."

Mark looked at Danielle. "Do you want to cut the chord?"

"Yes." Danielle did so, and then the baby was quickly examined and wrapped up. Vitals were being taken on Shannon as the baby was handed to Danielle.

He was truly beautiful. Not all red and purple like so many

newborns. His little eyes were closed tight, and Danielle smiled when a little squawk came from him. She ran her finger over his perfect, tiny feet and hands, and she instantly fell head-over-heels, totally in love.

"Can I see him?" Shannon asked.

"In a minute," a nurse replied.

"Doc. I got a drop on the pressure here," another nurse said.

Mark took a look.

"I feel dizzy," Shannon muttered.

Beeps and whistles started going off, and orders were shouted at the staff quickly.

"What's going on? What's going on?" Danielle asked.

A nurse took the baby and put him into the incubator. "Let's get him to the nursery."

"What is happening?" Danielle demanded again, not able to keep the panic out of her voice.

Mark looked up from where he stood over Shannon, working frantically on her. "Danielle, go with the baby."

"She's coding!" the anesthesiologist said.

"Code blue, code blue, 121, code blue 121," went out over the hospital speakers.

Danielle was pushed out of the way as more hospital staff rifled into the room, each of them doing something to help save her daughter's life.

CHAPTER THIRTY-THREE

Alyssa

Alyssa stood over Ian's hospital bed. It would be four weeks before the actual transplant could take place. She'd be traveling back and forth between L.A. and Napa during that time. She knew she was eating up a large chunk from her grandmother's inheritance, but she couldn't think of a better way to use it. She was staying at a residential hotel within walking distance of Cedar's Sinai and, for now, everything in her life besides seeing her son through this was on hold.

His first chemo treatment had been administered that morning, and despite it, he seemed in good spirits.

"Thank you for being here with me," he said.

"I wouldn't be anywhere else," she replied.

"My mom was like that, too. I mean my other mom."

"I know what you mean." It was the first time that Ian had made an acknowledgment that she was also his mother. "I bet you really miss her. Everyone must miss her." Alyssa thought about the copy of the photo of Louise and Ian that she kept in her purse. She'd taken to looking at it daily and saying a silent prayer of gratitude to the woman who'd raised Ian, and also asking her to help heal him. She felt a kinship with this woman she'd never known.

"We do," Ian said. "My dad especially. He's married to his work now, and us kids."

"Do you have a favorite commercial he's made over the years?" Alyssa had learned from Charlie that he wrote commercial jingles and Darren produced commercials. They owned their own lucrative business and were not only brothers, but partners, too.

Ian smiled. "Yeah. I like the one where the kid is in the bath tub with the singing rubber ducky. You know the bubble bath commercial, but the kid can't say rubber ducky. Instead he says wubber yucky."

"I love that one, too." They both started laughing, and before long it turned into belly laughter. When they'd stopped and Alyssa wiped the tears away, she said, "I would think it'll really help you out that your dad and uncle are already in the business. With connections and everything."

"Definitely. I'm super excited about school and writing. I can't wait to get back. I have to get rid of the crap in my body, but then I'm full speed ahead."

Alyssa inwardly hoped that would happen for him. He was bright, talented, and so deserving. Why was it that someone like Ian had to be so sick? In the past few weeks, she'd learned a lot about leukemia and bone marrow transplants. The good news was that Ian seemed to be an excellent candidate because his overall health was good and he was a strong young man. But plenty of things could go wrong, from the cancer coming back to the donation not working.

"I'm writing a script now, you know," Ian said.

"You are?"

"It's a comedy. A caper type. Kind of like The Pink Panther. Love those movies."

"With Peter Sellers. Yeah, me too. Those are great. I would have thought you too young for those."

"No way. My mom loved them, which meant we all had to love them." He laughed. "You and me have a lot in common. It's that biology thing, I guess. I wonder if I would have a lot in common with my biological dad."

Alyssa didn't say anything.

"I'm sorry. I know you don't know where he is and what his life is all about. It's too bad you only knew his first name."

Alyssa nodded. How could she tell him the truth? How could she not? He had a right to know. Maybe he didn't have to know the details around how he was conceived? But James had no right to be in Ian's life. None. Or was she being selfish by not telling Ian? She'd already learned that secrets and skeletons come back to haunt in due time. But shouldn't Ian know that his sister was the donor? And that in addition to her, he had five other biological siblings? She needed to take a walk, clear her mind, but she didn't want to alert him that something was wrong.

"Do you like to paint?" she asked.

"No. I'm not much of an artist. Oh wait, I did do some impressive finger-painting back in kindergarten." He laughed. "Why?"

"You know I'm into art, and I have some paintings that I want you to see when you get out of here."

"What are they of?"

"You'll have to wait and see."

"Oh, you gonna be like that. Okay, then, you gonna have to wait to read my script."

"Deal."

"What's a deal?" Darren walked into the room. "Your dad will be by in a bit. He says give him a call if you need anything. So, what's a deal?" He looked from Alyssa to Ian.

"Alyssa has some special paintings she's going to show me when I get out of here, but she won't tell me what they're of, so I told her she'll have to wait until then to read my script."

"Sounds like a good deal to me." Darren smiled at her. "How are you, kid?"

"Kind of tired now. They give you some of those feel good drugs along with the chemo, so you don't start puking right away."

"Kid has a way with words. What you trying to tell us then, you too tired for a visit?" Darren laughed.

"No way."

Darren handed him a Target bag.

"What's this?" Ian asked

Darren shrugged.

"Oh, man, thanks." Ian took out the set of *Bourne Identity* DVDs. "I love these."

"I know," Darren replied. "That's why I got 'em."

"You the man."

"I know. Want to watch one?"

Ian nodded and Darren walked over and put one of the DVD's into the player. A few minutes later Matt Damon's face flashed across the screen. They all watched the opening scene. Alyssa glanced over from her chair and noticed Ian closing his eyes. She walked over to Ian and placed a hand on his shoulder. His eyes fluttered. "You want to rest?" she asked.

"Maybe."

Darren stood. "We can come back later and finish watching this with you. You should probably rest up for your dad's visit. And I'm sure your brothers and sisters will be by throughout the day."

"Okay. I am kind of tired."

Darren gave him a hug and Alyssa kissed him on the cheek. They both left his hospital room with a sigh and unspoken emotion between them. "You hanging around or would you like to go grab a bite to eat with me? I finished a big account's project this morning, so I'm thinking I can take the day off," he said. "Let him get some rest, and we can drive up the coast for some lunch."

She checked her watch and realized that she hadn't eaten much that day, and it was already after one o'clock.

"Sure. Sounds good."

Thirty minutes later they were seated at a surf shack restaurant in Malibu, eating fish tacos with beer. They small-talked about the beauty of the ocean, the grey-blue waves hitting the sand and crashing against them. They talked about her art and his work, and, of course, they talked about Ian and the family—a family she was beginning to think of as her own.

Alyssa knew something was happening between them. What that was, she couldn't be sure, but she had never, not even with Terrell, felt so comfortable and at ease with a man.

After lunch they took a walk out on the beach and he reached for her hand. She closed hers around his, and they walked in silence listening to the ocean.

The night Alyssa asked Darren to stay with her in the hotel suite had been innocent. She'd needed a friend and he was there for her.

They'd stayed up watching movies and talking. She'd fallen asleep late into the night, and he'd gently woken her and told her to go get into bed. She'd found him asleep in the morning on the couch. After waking, he'd ordered in a big breakfast for the two of them, and then he'd made those phone calls, first to Terrell to get James' phone number, and then to James.

In a turn of good fortune, a woman answered at Terrell's place, and Darren made up a story about being an old friend who had lost touch of James and needed the phone number. At first the woman hesitated, but after a couple of minutes of Darren charming her, she looked it up and gave it to him. Alyssa wondered who the woman was and hoped for Terrell's sake he had moved on. She was certain he had. A man like Terrell wouldn't have remained single for long.

She was surprised Darren was still single, though. Alyssa learned he'd been married once, ten years ago, but after three years of marriage, they'd mutually agreed it wasn't working, and he'd been single ever since.

"Ian asked again about his biological father," Alyssa said.

"What did you tell him?"

"Nothing."

"You did the right thing. Ian doesn't need to know that man."

"Maybe he does though. If not his father, doesn't he have a right to know his siblings?"

Darren stopped and let go of her hand, a breeze off the ocean blew strands of hair in her face that he brushed aside. "Ian has a family. He doesn't need any more complications in his life. He's been through hell and back, and I don't see where getting to know his bio father and siblings is a great thing. Let them be a family and let us be a family." He took both of her hands now. "Leave it alone. It's not up to us to decide anyway. It's up to Charlie, and we know he doesn't want that."

Alyssa nodded. "You're right." She knew Darren was right. Ian had enough to deal with. Getting to know this other family, regardless of all the intricacies, would be too much for anyone to handle. She hoped that Ian would stop asking and things would be left alone. Only time would tell.

They started walking again, and Darren put an arm around her shoulders. She leaned into him, and Alyssa knew that what Darren had said about them being a family was becoming a reality for her. Wrapped in Darren's warmth, she never wanted to leave this safe haven.

CHAPTER THIRTY-FOUR

Jamie

*J*amie slid the tape gun across the box that she'd loaded with dishes. She stood up and stretched. Her back ached. She'd forgotten how exhausting moving was. Dorothy sat at the kitchen table eating some lunch. Right now she was staring off into nowhere, looking forlorn, a feeling that Jamie could relate to. Since leaving the restaurant last weekend, she hadn't spoken to Kat. She'd talked with Danielle who told her that Kat felt awful about what she'd said. Kat had also left her a few messages, but Jamie hadn't returned her calls. She wondered if she was angry at Kat or if she was angry because there was a part of her that knew that what Kat had said was the truth.

Jamie came over and sat down next to Dorothy. "Did you like your sandwich, Mom?"

Dorothy nodded. "We aren't going to live here anymore, are we?"

Jamie put her hands gently on Dorothy's cheeks, looking into her eyes. "No, Mom, we aren't."

"But I like it here. This is a nice place."

"I know. I like it here, too, but I can't afford it any longer. We have to move." Jamie technically could have kept the house after David signed over his mom's life insurance policy, which Jamie could cash in for her if need be. But that was Dorothy's money, and Jamie planned to use it in the event that she lived another decade or more—which was highly likely. Other than her failing mind, Dorothy was healthy. And with Jamie's new plan, Dorothy could live out the rest of her life in the lap of luxury that she deserved.

"Where are we going?" Dorothy asked.

Jamie smiled. "Do you remember that nice place I took you to the other day? The place where Frank was flirting with you?"

"Yes. It was a delightful place. Did you know that Betty was there too? I wanted to visit with her but we didn't have time."

"Betty Davis?"

Dorothy nodded.

"I have good news. You are going to be living in the same apartment building as Betty Davis and Frank!"

"On Fifth Avenue?"

"Close. Yes. Very close." Okay, so it was only about three thousand miles close, but Dorothy had a right to her fantasies.

"You will live with me, too, won't you? You and your adorable little girl, Maddie?"

"No. We can't live there."

"Yes, you can. Don't worry about the money. I'll pay for it," she said smugly.

"I think we would only get in the way when you have so many suitors and friends who I'm sure will be coming around a lot. But Maddie and I will visit you all the time."

Dorothy frowned. "All the time?"

"All the time."

"I suppose that would be fine then. But don't tell Dean where I've moved to."

"Don't worry, Mom. I don't think you have to worry about him finding you."

"I need my nails done."

"I'll do your nails for you." Jamie got up and went to her bathroom. Although painting Dorothy's nails would suck up some time, she could use a break from the packing. She glanced at the clock and saw that she only had a couple of hours left before Maddie and Tyler would be showing up from the ranch. Every night he'd brought over take-out, and helped her pack, as well as taken Maddie back and forth to the ranch. He'd been a godsend, really, and although she had misgivings with Maddie down the hall, they'd fallen into bed every night and made love. However, Tyler had left long before Maddie was up each morning and then returned only a few hours later to take her with him to the ranch.

And last night he said it. Her cowboy had said those three words every woman longs to hear from a man like Tyler Meeks. Lying in each other's arms, after tangling up in the covers for a good hour, he had stroked her hair and whispered, "I love you."

Jamie had snuggled in closer to him and felt his smile when he kissed the top of her head. "And when you're ready, I think you'll love me back."

She'd wanted to say it, wished she could, wished she felt what he seemed to be intensely feeling, but he was right—she just was not ready to love him back.

Jamie found the perfect shade of pink polish for Dorothy and tromped back downstairs. "Let's pretty up those fingernails for you."

"For Frank, honey."

"Absolutely for Frank." Jamie laughed and gave Dorothy a kiss on the cheek. "I love you."

"I love you, too, Sweetpea. I really do." She patted her hand. "You're a good girl."

Jamie had just finished one hand when the phone rang. She picked up the phone and saw on the caller ID that it was from Queen of the Valley Hospital.

***

Kat arrived first, followed by Jamie. Alyssa caught the first plane out, with Ian, Darren, and the rest of the family understanding. She promised she'd be back in L.A. as soon as she could.

Cassie was sitting in the waiting room, her face red and puffy. Al and Stacey were seated next to her looking numb, their eyes tired and faces pale.

Kat asked softly where Danielle was.

Al looked up. "The nursery with the baby."

Kat and Jamie walked quickly through the hospital corridors without saying anything.

Their friend stood on the other side of the plate glass window, walking around with her grandbaby in her arms. When she spotted them, they could see grief and exhaustion strained across her face. She brought the baby over to the window and held him up. She tried to muster a smile for them. Both her friends fought back their tears. A nurse came over to Danielle and took the baby from her. She came out of the nursery. No one said a word as they wrapped their arms around each other and cried together for several minutes.

Finally, Danielle sucked back a sob and said, "She died. She died for eight minutes, and she came back. They brought her back. But now we don't know. We don't know what will happen. She's in a coma and she may never come out of it. They don't know."

"I am so, so sorry," Kat said.

Jamie rubbed her arm. "How about the baby? He's so sweet."

Danielle smiled through her tears. "The baby. I haven't been able to tell you. It's not that I'm ashamed, but scared. I've been scared as hell."

Kat looked at Jamie and then Danielle. "What do you mean, honey?"

"He has Down Syndrome."

Jamie gasped. Kat reached out, placing a hand on Danielle's shoulder.

"I've known but I couldn't tell you yet. I, I needed to process it all."

Jamie rubbed her arm. "You can always tell us anything."

Danielle shook her head. "I know that. But sometimes there are things that no matter how much I love you, you're my best friends, but there are times when it feels right to keep things amongst your family. This was one of those things. I knew I'd have to say something eventually, but I wasn't ready to do that."

Kat hugged her. "We understand."

Jamie thought about the things she'd kept private from her friends. Danielle was right. It had nothing to do with trust or love. "The baby is good though, right? He is just beautiful, Danielle."

"He appears healthy right now. The doctors have told me that as time goes on, we will have a better idea as to how he will develop both mentally and physically. I can't think about that now. I can only think about Shannon and what if . . . ?"

"She will get better," Jamie said. "You have to have faith."

Danielle's head shot up. "Faith? Faith! Where does faith play into this? How is it that God can allow this to happen to my child? My child who had so much faith she believed having this baby was what God wanted, that God would give her the life she was supposed to live. And her faith, a faith I brought her up to believe, now has her lying in a hospital bed where she may never wake up again! Where I may one day have to decide to take out the support and let her go. Faith. I have none right now and I don't know if I ever will again."

Jamie didn't know how to respond, but she knew she'd been exactly where her friend was in that moment and all she could finally say was the one thing that her mother had said to her when Nate was dying. "I'm sorry. I really am."

Danielle closed her eyes for a second, then opened them. "I know."

The three women took a walk outside where they bought coffee from a stand and sat down next to a water fountain. In silence, they let their friend grieve, taking turns holding her and wiping away her tears.

CHAPTER THIRTY-FIVE

Alyssa

*T*here had been no Happy Hour for the rest of July. It was halfway through August, and it didn't look like they'd all be meeting this month either. There wasn't much to be happy about anyway, and between what was going on with Jamie, Danielle, Alyssa, and Kat, time passed quickly. They saw each other at the hospital where Danielle had taken up a vigil, bringing the baby with her and working on the festival project to try and keep her mind occupied. Jamie had taken over most of Danielle's responsibilities for the Harvest Festival. Kat continued to avoid her mother and do what she always did—everything she could for everyone around her, which now included making regular dinners and dropping them off for Danielle and Cassie. Alyssa spent most of her time in L.A., with a few flights back home to see Danielle and Shannon.

Shannon's condition had not changed.

Alyssa now sat in the sterile-looking waiting room at Cedars-Sinai in Los Angeles. Thankfully she was the only one in the room. A family with a toddler had just left, so Alyssa got up and turned off the television blaring Sesame Street. She sat back down in the uncomfortable, taupe chair, and picked up a magazine on the side table next to her.

She tried to read it, but found herself aimlessly flipping through the pages. When would there be news about Ian? It had been hard to watch him grow so weak in the past month and become so sick, but at the same time, he showed such inner strength and courage. He'd told her all about his childhood, his mother, and siblings. What he didn't tell her, Charlie, Darren, and his brothers and sisters filled her in on. All of them were such excellent people, and her son was an excellent young man. He shouldn't have to go through any of this. No one should. Thank God, James and his wife had agreed to allow their daughter to be a donor.

Alyssa knew that at that moment, in the same hospital, in a different corridor, were Ian's sister and her parents. She'd remained quietly in the waiting room while Darren and Charlie went to get a gift for Ian—a video game he'd been wanting for some time. Neither one of them had been able to sit still for long, so she held down the fort and expected them to return any time.

Alyssa hadn't told them that she'd anonymously sent Ian's sister--whose name she'd learned was Jessica—a big basket filled with stuffed animals and Barbie dolls. It didn't feel right that this little girl had to go through this. Again, she wished she could talk with her mother and tell her how sorry she was, but would she really know what to say? Probably not.

She closed her eyes and leaned back in her seat. Drifting into a light sleep, she dreamed of Ian and of Darren. A man's voice startled her awake.

"Alyssa?"

There stood Terrell. She had to still be dreaming. Her ex-fiancé was standing right in front of her.

"What . . . Why are you here?" She studied him. He hadn't changed at all, and her stomach sank at the sight of him. "How, how are you?"

He sat down next to her. "Why didn't you tell me?" he asked.

She sighed. There was no point in wasting words. He'd come here for answers that she owed him. "You know about Ian?"

He nodded. "James told me everything."

"Everything?"

"Yes. Why didn't you?" he asked.

"Because I loved you." He faced her now, and she could see the hurt that she'd caused him still lingered deep inside of him. "I wanted to protect you. How could I tell you about Ian or James? I wanted to tell you about Ian. I planned to, the day after our party, but then I saw James, and . . . how could I? You went on and on about being best friends since childhood. The man is like a brother to you, and when I saw him, I knew there was no way I could destroy that."

"You destroyed my heart instead. Don't you know how much I loved you, Alyssa? I would have supported you, stuck by you."

"I was ashamed."

He sighed. "I wish you had told me. Not James."

"What did he tell you exactly?"

"That you had a date nineteen years ago, and he was probably more forceful than he should have been. That you got pregnant with Ian that night and he never saw you again until our party. He never knew you had a child until all of this happened."

A little forceful. "Yes." That was all she could say.

"I know he can get angry, and I have to wonder how aggressive he was with you."

"I don't want to talk about it. It's in the past. The man has made his amends. He told you. I'm sure he told his wife. Otherwise, his daughter wouldn't be here right now helping to save Ian."

He nodded.

"How did she take it?"

"Olivia is a strong woman. He didn't tell her that it was *you,* and I agree that she doesn't need to know that. But she was angry. She's a good lady, and she knows that Jessica donating the marrow could help this young man live. She knows that's the right thing."

"I wish I could thank her."

"She's a mother, and I'm certain she knows how grateful you are."

Alyssa nodded. "How about you? I don't understand why James told you. I promised him that I would not bother his family or friends. You didn't have to know."

"Maybe he felt he owed me. It hurt bad when you took off. I was torn apart, and maybe for him this was his way of asking for forgiveness."

"*Can* you forgive him?"

"I don't know yet," he replied.

"Me?" she asked. "Can you forgive me?"

"I already have. That's why I'm here. I'm getting married in a few weeks to a nice woman, one who I care about and who loves me."

"That's wonderful," Alyssa said and looked away.

Terrell paused for a moment. "I still love you," he blurted out. "I want you back. Please tell me that you still love me, please tell me there is a chance . . ."

"Alyssa?"

Both Terrell and Alyssa looked up to see Darren standing there. "You okay?"

She nodded.

"He's in recovery. Charlie and I checked a minute ago. A nurse was coming down to get you, but I told her I'd tell you. Charlie is going to his room now to wait for him." He eyed Terrell who stood up. "You want to go to the room and wait for him with us?"

"Yes. Of course," Alyssa said. "I'll be right there. I'm going to the restroom first."

"Want me to wait?"

"I'm fine."

"Okay. You sure? I can wait," Darren said.

She shook her head. "I'm fine. I really am."

Darren nodded and left quietly.

"There's no chance, is there?" Terrell asked.

Alyssa shook her head. "I'm sorry."

His head dropped. He sucked in a low breath, leaned forward, and kissed her gently on the cheek. Then, quietly as he'd come, Terrell stood and walked out the door.

CHAPTER THIRTY-SIX

Kat

Kat sat across from her dad, sipping a glass of wine with their late lunch at the restaurant. They sat on the trellised patio underneath the twining grapevines and evening jasmine. The dull heat of the day mixed with the wine, making Kat a little sleepy. The mountains in the background shone golden from the beating sun. Even in the middle of a hot summer, Napa Valley was one of the most beautiful places in the world. The smells of the valley alone were heavenly from the fruit and rich soil that filled the air. Kat popped an olive from a local grower into her mouth.

Jeremy was serving them and proud of it. Christian had promoted him to server, and she'd watched Jeremy and Christian grow closer over the last month. Brian was still in his cast and, even though Christian worked hard to take care of him when Kat was in New Orleans to be with Alyssa, he still remained a bit standoffish toward his step-dad. On the up-side, Christian continued to keep trying, so not all hope was lost.

"Kitty, we need to talk," her father said.

She held up a hand, knowing this was coming, knowing he'd been sent to be the peacemaker. "Mom put you up to this."

"No, she didn't. I am doing this on my own, and I need you to listen and stop being so stubborn." He frowned and the creases around his hazel eyes deepened.

"Dad, there's nothing to talk about."

"That's not true. I have stood by for years and watched you hurt, watched your sister hurt, and let myself sulk and hurt while you took care of me and everyone else. I moved out here knowing you'd be close by to take care of me. For years I wasn't much of a father or a husband."

"Come on, Dad! What, is she brainwashing you to believe that? You were the best dad in the world and the best husband. I don't know what you're talking about."

He took the bottle of chilled Chardonnay from the ice bucket and refilled his glass. "When your mother left, I was heartbroken. That's true. And I didn't do right by you. You stepped in and did it all for me and Tammy, and I was comfortable with that. But Kitty, I am a changed man. I'm no longer a man who needs to be taken care of."

"I know that."

"I don't think you do. There are some things in my past that I am not proud of. Things that drove your mom away."

"What are you talking about?"

Jeremy came by with a basket of bread. Kat shooed him away. "Not now, Jer."

"Your mother held the family together. I know I worked many hours to provide, but she was the glue. I knew she wasn't happy with all of the hours I worked, how I always showed up late for things, or not at all."

"You were working."

"I know, but that was an excuse for me, too."

"I don't understand," she said.

"I used my work as an excuse, because I didn't think I was worthy of such a fine family. I felt the only way to hang on to your mother and you kids was through providing a living."

"Exactly. Dad, you didn't do anything wrong."

"Honey, I did." He sighed and looked away from her for a few second before continuing. "When you and your sister were in high school and so busy with your own lives, your mom needed me, and I pushed her away because I didn't know how to be there for her. I had an affair, Kat."

Her stomach tightened and her hands started shaking. She reached for her wine. "What?"

"I did, and God bless your mother. She tried for years after that to move forward with me, but it was too much for her, and she finally left me." Kat couldn't respond. "Her leaving wasn't really her fault. She deserved better, and if she hadn't left, I wouldn't be who I am today. That is, a pretty happy old fart."

"I am so confused." She swallowed her wine, trying also to swallow back all of the confusing thoughts rushing through her mind. What he told her explained so much, but she didn't know what to think, or where her allegiances sat, or how to handle any of it. She was an adult. She should know how to handle this. "What about now? Now you've been forgiven and she comes back to you, and it's all fine?"

"Not entirely, but sort of. I know that time does heal. And time away from one another has seemed to heal both of us. I love your mom. I always have and I always will. If we wind up back together, that would be wonderful, and if not, it's not in the cards. But, honey, it's not up to you to worry about us, or take care of me and be angry at her. It's not. I'm a big boy and she's a big girl and she loves you with all her heart. And so do I. I think what I'm asking here is for you to forgive both of us."

"What am I supposed to do?" Kat looked Heavenward.

"You're supposed to deal with your own family. Love those kids when they're snots and act like you're nothing but a pain in the ass. Love that little girl, Amber, for being in your life. Love your husband, faults and all. But most of all, love yourself. Love yourself, first, because you are magnificent. You are a gift, Kat, and your family knows it. Whether they show it or not, they know it. I know it. You need to know it and believe it." He took her hand and squeezed. "You are truly a gift, my girl."

Damn! Irritating tears blurred her vision, and she quickly wiped them away and let out a small laugh. Mix wine and sentiment and there go the waterworks. She stood up and walked around the table, leaning over her dad. "Thank you, Daddy."

He stood and hugged her back. She spotted her mom at the hostess stand and then pulled away from her dad and shook her head. She walked toward her mom, who started to turn around. Kat grabbed her arm. Her mom turned back, looking surprised. "Why don't you come have a glass of wine with me and Dad?"

Her mom smiled and nodded.

***

The next morning, Kat woke to soft knocking on her bedroom door. Christian lifted his head. Amber stirred next to them. "Who the . . . ?" Kat whispered, her heart racing at the thought of an intruder. Jer had spent the night at a buddy's house, and Brian was at the Sperm Donor's. Intruders didn't typically announce their presence. Maybe Jeremy had been dropped off early for some reason. To their surprise, Kat's mother walked in, breakfast tray in hand. "Mom?"

"I know we're still on shaky ground, Kitty, and I know you're going to think I am overstepping my bounds here, but I love you so much, and I love Christian and this family, and the two of you need to be happy together."

Kat sat up. "What are you talking about?"

"It's all self explanatory," her mom said. "Take your time. Amber, you ready? Remember what Nanny V told you last night? That today was going to be our day? Why don't you wake on up now, and we can get going."

"Okay, Nanny V," the sleepy little girl said, giving Kat and her dad a hug. "Bye."

"Bye?" Kat asked.

"Yes, bye-bye. Amber and I are going for a nature walk and then Pop-Pop is going to pick us up and take us to lunch and the movies. Didn't you say Jeremy was staying at a friend's last night and Brian is at his dad's?"

"Yes," Kat replied.

"Good. Have fun." She winked at them, set the tray down, and closed the door. She opened it a minute later. "Sorry. Almost forgot the most important items." She set down a large gift box on their dresser.

"What in God's name has she gone and done now?" Christian asked.

"Who knows? I'm kind of afraid."

Christian clambered out of bed and walked over to where Venus had put the tray and box on the dresser. Kat got up and grabbed the box. She pointed to the tray. "Is that oysters on the half shell?"

"Sure is."

"Champagne, too?"

"Yes, and lookie here," he said. "Chocolate covered strawberries."

"I think there is a theme."

"What's in the box?"

They took the food and box back to the bed, where they opened the box. "Only my mom." Kat took out a book. "*Tantric Sex for Beginners.*"

"Let me see that." He took it from her and flipped through the pages. "How do they do that?" He showed her a page with two people facing each other, appearing to be in each others laps seated Indian-style. Kat turned the pages from side to side.

"Impossible." She turned to the back page to see the author photo. The man had long white hair and a braided beard set against his creviced face. "Come on. This guy? Who would even have sex with this guy, much less Indian-style, funky sex? I wonder if he can even have sex. He looks older than God."

"What else is in there?" Christian asked pointing to the box.

Kat pulled out a blindfold, some honey nectar dusting powder with a feather duster, chocolate sauce, and a vibrator thingamajig called *The Tongue.*

"I am so embarrassed."

"Have I told you lately how much I love your mother?" Christian poured her a glass of champagne.

"I'm going to kill her."

"Come on, Kat. Let's have some fun." He tickled her leg with his free hand.

"All right, let me see that book. Maybe I could learn something."

After two more glasses of champagne and some of the driest reading ever, Kat tossed the book aside and faced Christian. "Know what, honey, I don't need a book or aphrodisiacs, or dusting powder.

I need you and that's it."

He kissed the tip of her nose. "What do you say we play a game of spin the bottle?"

"Now we're talking."

CHAPTER THIRTY-SEVEN

Danielle

*D*anielle knelt down at the pews, the sleeping baby boy in his detachable car seat at her side. A month had passed, and there was no sign that her daughter would ever wake up.

She didn't hear Mark come in, but she knew when he knelt beside her who it was. It had become their ritual together. He would join her at lunchtime when he could. She breathed a sigh of relief at his company. Why they did this, she wasn't sure. She'd started coming in here a week after the baby's birth. Maybe it had something to do with Jamie's insistence on having faith. Danielle resigned herself that it was better to try to have faith than to not try at all. But she still didn't know if their vigil would change a thing.

"Hi." She glanced over at Mark.

"Hi." He touched her shoulder and squeezed.

"How's the little man?"

"Sleeping."

"He needed to." Mark peered into the baby seat.

Through all the pain and angst she'd suffered these past weeks, Mark had been right there for her. He'd taken to staying in the guest room at the house and getting up in the nights to help take care of the baby.

Two weeks after the baby was born, they all agreed he needed a name. Danielle asked Cassie if she had any ideas. She said Shane, after his mother. It was perfect.

Mark and Danielle hadn't become intimate; they hadn't even been out on a date since Shane's birth. But they'd grown closer to each other than either had ever been with anyone else before.

"Why do we do this?" Danielle asked him, sitting back into the pew.

"What?"

"Come here everyday? Waiting, hoping."

"There is nothing else we can do," he said. He scooted in closer to her. "I know you're angry and directing it at God because that seems easy. But you come here because there is nothing else to do. Medically, we cannot do anything more for Shannon. So you need to be here. We have to wait and see."

"I know. But for how long?"

He shrugged. "I don't know. I can't decide that."

"How did you do it with your son? How did you move on?"

He motioned with his hand inside the small room, set up with an altar and a cross. "I told you before that I prayed. Before we lost Kevin, I wasn't much into prayer. I accepted that there was a God but I didn't know how, who, or what that meant. It just *was* for me. And then we lost Kevin, and I grew angry and wanted to stop believing. But once you know something in your heart, you can't change it. With Kevin gone, I started praying daily for an answer. The thing is, when you lose someone you love, particularly a child, there will never be a good answer. No matter what. It's all in the questions. You can't ask yourself why did this happen to my child, but rather, how do I honor their memory? How do I live my life again? How do I find joy and peace again? When I saw you sitting in my office three months ago, I knew I'd found some of the answers to those questions. And, there will be a reason for all of this. I believe that."

The baby whimpered.

"You really think so?" she asked.

"Yes I do. He's waking up. I bet he needs to be changed," Mark said. "Want me to change him? Then we can take him down to see his mom?"

"Okay. Thank you. I think I'll stay here for awhile longer though, if that's okay with you," she replied.

"Of course." He kissed her." I love you. You know that?"

She nodded. "I know and I love you, too."

Mark picked up the baby and walked out of the chapel, leaving Danielle to wonder about God's answers.

After some time of sitting and doing her best to pray, Danielle got up and lit a candle for her daughter and for her grandson. "I don't know why, but I trust You have a reason." She made the sign of the cross, and heard Mark behind her.

"Honey, you need to come now. It's Shannon."

CHAPTER THIRTY-EIGHT

Jamie

Jamie rushed through the hospital doors, sprinting past patients and hospital employees to Shannon's room. She opened the door and saw Danielle and Mark standing over Shannon's bed. Shannon was wide awake and holding her son. Jamie couldn't believe her eyes.

"Hi, Jamie," Shannon said.

"Hi. How are you?"

"A little tired, but good. I think." She handed the baby to her mom. Even though she was under fluorescent lights and hooked up to monitors and IV's, there was something so beautiful and luminescent about Shannon at that moment, Jamie couldn't help thinking that the young woman looked like an angel. "I'm so glad you came. Mom told you?"

"Yes. She called me and said that you had to see me. That it was important."

"It is. Mom? Mark? Can you let me talk to Jamie alone?"

They left the room with the baby. Danielle shrugged as she walked past Jamie.

"It's a miracle," Jamie said. "Your mom and Mark have been here every day, and your sister. This is wonderful. When your mom called me, I couldn't believe it."

"I saw Nathan," Shannon blurted.

Jamie took a step back. "What did you say?"

"Your husband. I saw him."

"I don't understand, Shannon." She had to be talking nonsense. Maybe the coma had affected her brain somehow. "What do you mean you saw him? I met your mom after he passed away so you never knew him. I think you're tired, honey."

"I died. I died for eight minutes. They told me, but they didn't have to because I remember dying."

Jamie sat on the edge of Shannon's bed.

"It's exactly what you hear it's like, with the bright light. There were people I knew there, like my grandma and my uncle, and even a friend I had in seventh grade who moved away. I didn't know she'd died. And there were all these other people there that I didn't know and they were all sending me love. And Nathan, your husband, was there and he told me to give you a message."

Jamie choked. Shannon couldn't be telling her this. This wasn't possible. "What?"

"He's happy you liked the rainbow, and he said that it's time to love again. That's what he wants you to know. He's okay with everything. Then this beautiful white horse came over to him, knelt down next to him, and he got on the horse and they rode away."

"Oh, my God," Jamie said.

There was no way. No way that Shannon would have known any of this. Not about the rainbow that she'd seen after leaving David and Susan's house, or what Tyler had told her about loving again and certainly not about the horse that Maddie had imagined her father with. No way.

After a minute she smiled at Shannon and knew there was no processing this. All she could do was accept it, on faith.

"Thank you," she said. "Thank you so much."

"I'm just the messenger." Shannon took Jamie's hand and held it for a second. "That's all."

Jamie laughed through her tears and walked out of the hospital room on a mission.

***

Jamie ran through the front door of Tyler's house. She'd dropped Dorothy at his place on her way to the hospital. Maddie was out with the horses. Dorothy sat in the family room off the kitchen, watching none other than a John Wayne western. Jamie dashed past her. "Tyler?" she yelled out.

"In here," he replied. "What's wrong?" He walked out of the kitchen. "Everything okay?"

"It couldn't be better." She took his face in her hands and kissed him hard.

"What in the world?" he asked, pulling away.

"You. Me." Tears streamed down her face.

"What's wrong? What is it?" he asked.

"Nothing. Nothing at all." She laughed. "I'm ready. I love you. I am so ready to love you. I look at you and I can't think straight. I smell you and my god, I go crazy. I kiss you and I can't think of a better feeling in the world. And you make me laugh, and you're such a good man, and I love you. I really do love you."

"I love you, too, Jamie." He kissed her back.

Dorothy started clapping. They pulled away from one another and saw that she'd gotten off the couch and stood a few feet away, smiling and clapping. "That's much better than the movie, John," she said.

Laughing, Tyler picked Jamie up off her feet and swung her around, kissing her and telling her over and over that he loved her too . . . he loved her too.

CHAPTER THIRTY-NINE

Alyssa

*A*lyssa hugged Ian and Charlie goodbye. She'd be back in a few weeks and knew she would miss them so much that it ached. Ian was doing extremely well for only being out of the hospital three weeks. He had been in isolation for two weeks in the hospital after the donation, and he would need monitoring on a regular basis for up to a year. For now, though, his future looked bright. The admissions office at UCLA had agreed to let him begin his classes again in January. This would give him time to get stronger. In the meantime, he planned to help his dad and Darren out in their business.

Alyssa needed to get back to her business and art classes. She could breathe easier knowing that her son was on the road to recovery. One thing was still uncertain though—Darren. They'd grown so close during this time and spent much of it together. They'd been to lunches, dinners with the family, even a movie to help take their minds off of the heavy situation they found themselves in. There was something there between them, and that something had gotten bigger each day. Alyssa didn't know if she could give it up, or if she had to, and she didn't know what Darren wanted. There were so many questions that had gone unanswered. The focus had been all on Ian, as it should have been. But now that she felt she could relax some, she had no answers where Darren was concerned.

He insisted on driving her to the airport. But first he wanted to take her to lunch at their favorite fish taco place in Malibu—an offer she couldn't pass up.

They sat at the picnic table out front eating the delicacy and avoiding the real topic they both really wanted to talk about. After lunch, Darren took her hand and they walked down to the beach. This had become something they did together whenever she was in town.

"I want you to stay," he said.

"I have to get back. I have my gallery and my classes."

"I know. But I want you to stay." He paused. "For good. You won't have to get rid of your place or the gallery even. My job gives me freedom to travel, and we could spend weekends, holidays, and summers in Napa. I love it up there. But I want you here with me. With the family. You're family now, too."

Alyssa brought her hand up to her chest. "I don't know what to say."

"Will you think about it?"

"I . . . I, are you asking me to move in with you?" she said.

Darren got down on his knee. He took her hand as she sucked in a deep pocket of air. "I'm asking you to marry me. I know we haven't known each other long, and I know circumstances have been difficult, but I know that I have never felt this way about anyone before. I love you, Alyssa. I am in love with you, and I want you to be my wife." He took something from his pocket—a jewelry box— and opened it. There was a square cut, two-carat diamond encased in platinum.

"You're serious?"

He looked at the ring and his hands were shaking. "I'd say so."

She fell to her knees. "I did not expect this. No, I did not, but you . . . oh, boy, you. Yes. Yes. I will marry you."

Darren took the ring out of the box and placed it on Alyssa's finger. He held her face in his hands, drawing her into him; he kissed her with a sweetness that warmed her entire body. She pulled away just enough to look into his eyes and said, "Take me home."

***

Darren took Alyssa to his house. It was on the smaller side, like her cottage in Napa, but it had a view of the Pacific out several huge glass windows. She loved it—stark white walls with navy blue chenille sofas and butter suede chairs, platinum accents, and an open kitchen. The only real decoration was the deep, dark ocean itself stretched out beneath them.

"This place is beautiful," she said.

"This is our place now."

She smiled. "Where's your bedroom?"

"Our bedroom."

"Our bedroom. Where is it?"

He took her hand and led the way down a short hallway. The room was painted in a soft jade color, the velvet duvet was a darker teal, and again the view couldn't be missed. "Boy, you have taste," she said.

"No. I had a really expensive decorator."

"I love it."

"Good."

Alyssa stepped closer to him, breathing him in, taking this moment in. She unbuttoned his shirt and slid it off his shoulders. Darren started to undress her, but she shook her head.

"Are you okay?" he asked alarmed.

"Better than okay." She pushed him down onto the bed.

He laughed. "I see."

Alyssa undressed slowly in front of the man she'd just pledged her life to. When she'd been with Terrell, he'd healed her from the past. She'd been able to make love and temporarily forget what James had done. But she'd also given Terrell her power. She'd needed a leader. With Darren, she'd found a partner. What James had stolen had been given back to her, and Darren had been the one to help her on the journey.

He reached for her hand and she undid his belt and took off his pants. Naked, they laid in each others arms, their warm bodies fit together. She rolled him onto his back and kissed his neck, his lips and then slid her mouth down his body. "Oh baby," Darren said. "Come here," he insisted.

And she did. He laid her down next to him and now kissed her, taking her breasts in his hands and tracing them with his tongue.

Alyssa cried out. Love, power, security, it was all there between them as Darren entered Alyssa and together they moved slowly as the tide rolled in as rhythmically outside the window. With intensity, she urged him on and their rhythm grew faster, more passionate with Alyssa letting go of years of anxiety, pain and fear and Darren's love flowed through her.

He yelled out first and she soon after followed, their orgasms in sync, their hearts pounding hard against their bodies--their commitment to love one another cemented in that moment forever.

***

A few days later in Napa Valley, Alyssa sat in front of her easel, the photo of Louise and Ian pinned up in front of her, she went to work, finally finishing her oil, *Protected*. It had taken hours, but at least she now knew how to complete the painting. The little boy still reached for the wine, the mother's hand gently pushing it away. From the right top of the painting, a smiling face looked down upon the boy, casting light on the mother's hand. The illuminated face looking down on the scene was the face of Louise—one of Ian's mothers guiding the other.

CHAPTER FORTY

The Goddesses

*D*anielle stood over Shannon, who still had on her dress from the baptism. The poor girl was totally exhausted. Danielle pulled the covers up around her daughter and went to baby Shane. His bottom lip puckered into a pout and soft whimpers escaped from him. She sat down in the rocking chair and whispered to him. "It's okay, Shane, DeDe is here. Shh, baby boy, shh." The new nickname for Danielle had come from Shannon. When she'd woken up, she'd looked at her mom and announced, "DeDe. That's what he'll call you."

Danielle kissed the top of Shane's peach-fuzzed head and rocked him into a sound sleep. After a few minutes, she laid him back in his crib and covered him up. She checked on Shannon one more time, and then leaned over and kissed her on the cheek.

She headed back downstairs to where her friends were cleaning up for her. Mark, Tyler, Christian, and Darren were out back drinking good wine and smoking Cubans—a total male-bonding thing. Maddie and Amber were watching a movie in Danielle's room, likely sacked out by now. Brian, Jeremy, Cassie, and Ian were shooting a game of pool in the game room. It was nice to have all of them together tonight, and to finally meet Darren and Ian, too. With Alyssa moving to Los Angeles, it would change things. But that was life, wasn't it? Always changing. Never the same.

Danielle stopped and leaned against the wall, watching her friends for a minute. How lucky were they to have each other? She couldn't have handled the whirlwind of the last few months without them. She didn't think she could handle the rest of her life without them—her best friends. "Okay ladies, that's enough. No more cleaning up. I have something special I want to share with you."

Jamie closed the dishwasher and Kat turned off the disposal. Alyssa set aside the wine glasses that she'd been drying. "What?"

Jamie asked.

"Come with me," Danielle said and headed out the front door.

They reached the golf cart. Her friends looked at each other. "Get in."

"I think we better listen to her," Alyssa said. "She's a grandma now, and you don't want to mess with a grandma."

"Shut up, Alyssa. I'm a DeDe."

Danielle drove them down to the tasting room, a full moon illuminating the pathway. She flipped on the light in the room and walked behind the bar. She pulled out a bottle of wine and handed it to Jamie, then gave one to Kat and one to Alyssa.

They looked at the wines. "What's this?" Alyssa asked.

"Look at the labels."

Their jaws dropped. "Danielle," Jamie cried. "These are . . ."

Danielle nodded. "They are all three separate vintages. Each vintage and label represents you three. Alyssa, yours is the Goddess of Light." On the label was a woman who looked like Alyssa, her arms open and reaching upward, light coming from her hands and surrounding her.

"It's a gorgeous Chardonnay that will fit your taste buds perfectly. Bold, buttery, aged in French oak, and as Californian as they come. To me, you represent the Goddess of Light, because you deal with everything with grace and light. You are a true artist, whether you're at your easel or hanging out with us. And now look at you, with what you've been through with Ian. You've come out of this with your son and the man of your future." Alyssa smiled at Danielle's words.

"I don't know what to say. This is amazing, Danielle. Thank you." She wiped away the tears that formed in her eyes and glanced at Kat. "All three of you have helped me through such a difficult time and to have this . . ." She held up her bottle of wine, "To show what I, what we've come through is so thoughtful and gracious." She shook her head. "Thank you."

Danielle smiled and turned to Kat. "And you represent the

Goddess of Love." On the label was an etching in gold, purple, and red of Kat's face inside a pink-rimmed heart.

"This I have to hear," Kat said.

"You do. I've never known anyone to love their family and friends as ferociously as you do. Sometimes you love us so much you even get pissed off with us." They all laughed. "I watch you with Christian and your sons, and now with Amber. And your friends. I've seen you forgive people for things that some of us here might not be able to forgive, but you don't stop loving, Kat. No matter what, when it comes down to it, you love all of us."

"Ah hell. I do love you all. Sometimes I don't know why." She laughed, trying to make light of it.

"We know." Jamie leaned her head on Kat's shoulder.

"And you, Jamie. You represent the Goddess of Life." The label showed Jamie seated under a willow tree with flowers surrounding her. "I'm pretty sure that you wanted to die right along with Nate. But you didn't. You found the courage to go on living. You found in yourself the woman who needed to live, not just for Maddie, but for herself. You've dealt with something we all hope we never have to deal with—losing your soul mate. But you're living again, loving again, and, if I'm right, I think you're having a fantastic time doing it."

Jamie nodded. "You know that I would have never thought I could be happy again. I didn't think so. It's different. I mean there will always be a part of me that hangs on to Nate and feels empty without him, but through you three, and Maddie, and Dorothy, and of course Tyler, I've realized that I can be happy and I can love again. This means so much. Thank you. But what about you?"

"The Goddess of Faith." Danielle held up her bottle of wine. "I've learned through all of this that the only things you can really count on are friends, family, and faith."

They all nodded and laughed in agreement, wondering what the next season would bring. Would there be more trauma, more drama? Probably. Or, maybe not. Maybe the four friends would find a lull, some respite from the ups and downs life had tossed their way over the long, hot summer.

They could hope so.

The trade winds coming off of the Pacific shifted slightly, the soft whispers of fall beginning to maneuver between the lush grape vines. Maybe like the change of the seasons, their lives would soon reflect fall's ease.

Danielle uncorked a bottle of her wine and poured them each a glass. They raised their glasses together.

"A toast," Jamie said.

Holding them high in the air, Danielle said, "To the Wine Goddesses."

"To the Wine Goddesses," they repeated in unison, clinking their glasses together.

Recipes and Wine Pairings

Danielle's Mexican Style Quiche

Pastry dough
1 large garlic clove
3/4 tsp salt
1 lb poblano chiles (about 4 large), roasted and peeled
6 large eggs
1 c whole milk
1/2 c Mexican crema or heavy cream
2 Tbsp finely grated white onion (using small teardrop holes of a box grater)
1/2 tsp black pepper
1/2 lb Monterey Jack cheese, coarsely grated (2 ½ to 3 cups)

Special equipment: 9-inch (2-inch deep) round fluted tart pan with removable bottom; pie weights or raw rice

Put oven rack in middle position and preheat oven to 375°F.
Roll out dough into a 13-inch round on a lightly floured surface with a floured rolling pin. Fit dough into tart pan, without stretching, letting excess dough hang over edge. Fold overhang inward and press against side of pan to reinforce edge. Prick bottom all over with fork. Chill until firm, about 30 minutes.
Line shell with foil or parchment paper and fill with pie weights. Bake until pastry is set and pale golden along rim, 20 to 25 minutes.
Carefully remove foil and weights and bake shell until deep golden all over, 15 to 20 minutes more. Put tart pan in a shallow baking pan. Leave oven on.
Mince garlic and mash to a paste with salt using side of a large knife.
Discard seeds, ribs, and stems from chiles, then pat dry if necessary and cut into 1/3-inch-wide strips.
Whisk together eggs, milk, crema, onion, garlic paste, and pepper in a large bowl until just combined, then pour into baked tart shell.
Sprinkle cheese and chiles over custard and bake until custard is just set, 50 to 60 minutes. (Center will jiggle slightly; filling will continue to set as it cools.)
Transfer quiche in pan to a rack to cool at least 20 minutes before serving.

To remove side of tart pan, center a large can under pan and let side of pan drop. Serve warm or at room temperature.

Serve with Champagne or margaritas, if preferred.

Kat's Fettuccine, Goat Cheese, and Pancetta

1 c dry white wine
1 Tbsp minced shallots
5 oz goat cheese, at room temperature, cut up or crumbled
Salt and freshly ground black pepper
Pinch of crushed red chile flakes
1/2 lb dried fettuccine
1/2 c chopped pancetta or bacon (you can also use chicken or shrimp)
2 Tbsp chopped fresh basil

In a medium saucepan, combine the white wine and shallots. Over high heat, reduce the liquid by half, about 5 minutes. Whisk in the goat cheese until the mixture is smooth. Season with 1/2 tsp salt, 1/4 tsp pepper, and the red chile flakes. Set aside.
Bring large pot of salted water to a boil over high heat. Add the pasta and cook until just cooked, 9 to 11 minutes. Reserve 1/2 cup of the pasta water, drain the pasta, and set aside.
Heat 1 Tbsp of the olive oil in a sauté pan over medium-high heat and brown pancetta or bacon (if bacon, do not use olive oil until you add spinach). Add remaining olive oil and the spinach, and sauté until wilted, about 2 minutes.
In a large bowl, combine the pasta with goat cheese sauce; add the spinach and pancetta. Season with salt and pepper and serve in warm bowls, topped with basil.

This recipe would pair nicely with a pinot noir or lighter syrah. If you prefer, a white wine chardonnay would work well also.

Alyssa's Shrimp Salad

3 fresh pears
Salad greens
1 lb cooked shrimp – medium size
1 c chopped celery

1/3 c chopped green bell pepper
1/4 c chopped green onion
1/3 c mayonnaise
1/2 tsp chipotle or some type of red pepper powder, to taste
1/2 tsp chopped garlic
1/2 c feta cheese
1/2 tsp grated lemon peel
1 tsp lemon juice
1/4 tsp salt

Core pears; cut into narrow wedges. Arrange on lettuce-lined salad plates.
Combine shrimp, celery, green pepper, cheese and green onions.
Blend mayonnaise, garlic, pepper powder, lemon juice, lemon peel and salt. Toss with shrimp. Top the pears with the mixture.

Serve with a crisp sauvignon blanc.

Jamie's Salmon in Miso

1 c mirin (sweet Japanese rice wine)
4 Tbsp light yellow miso (fermented soybean paste*)
6 Tbsp sugar
4 salmon filets (about 5 or 6 ounces each)
1 ½ c snow peas

Add the mirin, miso, and sugar in a small, nonstick saucepan and bring to a boil. Reduce heat to medium and continue to boil for three minutes, whisking as it boils to create a smooth miso marinade.
Reserve 1/3 cup of the miso marinade and set aside. Pour the remaining miso marinade over the salmon filets in a gallon zip-lock bag or shallow dish. Let salmon marinate in refrigerator for at least an hour (or up to 12 hours). Grill the salmon filets skin-side down about 5 inches from the coals or heat for about 14 minutes or until salmon is cooked throughout. You can lightly brown the top of the salmon filets by broiling briefly in your kitchen oven or by gently flipping the salmon filets over and grilling them, flesh-side down, for a couple of minutes.

Meanwhile to make a miso sauce for the table, add the 1/3 cup of the reserved miso marinade to a small nonstick saucepan and stir in 3 tablespoons fat-free half-and-half and a teaspoon of flour. Bring to a gentle boil, stirring constantly, until the sauce has reached your desired thickness. Also, add snow peas to a small microwave-safe dish with 1/4 cup water, cover and cook on high until snow peas are just tender (about three minutes).

Serve each serving of broiled salmon over a scoop of steamed white or brown rice (if desired) and top with a drizzle of the miso sauce and fan some snow peas on top for garnish.

Serve with Viognier.

Book Club Discussion Questions

1. Do the characters in Happy Hour seem real and believable? Can you relate to what they experience?
2. What do you think was the main theme/idea the author was trying to convey?
3. Which character do you most relate to and why?
4. What was your favorite part of the book? What part did you not like?
5. How did each of the characters change/grow over the course of the novel?
6. Would you have handled Jamie's situation with her brother-in-law differently? How?
7. Why do you think Jamie's grief over her husband was so closely tied to her sense of guilt?
8. What role does Alyssa's art play in her healing process?
9. Had Ian not needed a transfusion, do you think Alyssa would have ever told anyone about her past?
10. Why does Kat feel such a great need to be in control?
11. What situations have you been in where, like Kat, something you assumed to be black and white was much more complex than you realized?
12. In what ways is Danielle's success as a winemaker tied to her divorce?
13. Danielle goes through a lot of heartache at the end of the book. Why do you think the author had her experience so much hardship?
14. Would you read a sequel to Happy Hour? If so, what would you like to see happen in the characters' lives? Where do you see these characters five or ten years from now?

About Michele Scott

Michele Scott is the author of the popular Wine Lover's Mystery Series. Michele grew up just outside of San Diego where she fell in love with writing and horseback riding. After graduating from the University of Southern California, she worked in the equestrian industry and began raising a family. Now a full-time writer with more than a dozen novels to her credit, Michele Scott is widely recognized as one of the most celebrated authors of her genre.

Visit Michele Scott at www.michelescott.com

ZOVA BOOKS
LOS ANGELES
zovabooks.com
zovabooks.blogspot.com
facebook.com/ZOVABooks
twitter.com/ZOVABooks